Romantic Times honors

Kathryn Kramer

WINNER
1986 and 1988
Romantic Times Reviewers' Choice Award
for
Best Historical Romance

Praise by *Romantic Times* for the novels of Kathryn Kramer

Destiny and Desire
"A POWERFUL PORTRAIT . . . FASCINATING
DESCRIPTIONS AND FABULOUS HISTORICAL
DETAILS . . . A BEAUTIFUL ROMANCE."

Under Gypsy Skies
"Portrays the vivid world of gypsy lore and customs
with a captivating hand. Shattered dreams and
illusions highlight this exciting adventure that
readers won't want to miss."

Flame From the Sea
"Kathryn Kramer has added a mystic aura to her
powerful and exciting story . . .
Readers will be captivated!"

Highland Bride

KATHRYN KRAMER

JOVE BOOKS, NEW YORK

HIGHLAND BRIDE

A Jove Book / published by arrangement with
the author

PRINTING HISTORY

Jove edition / February 1991

ISBN: 0-515-10510-4

Jove Books are published by The Berkley Publishing Group,
200 Madison Avenue, New York, New York 10016.
The name "JOVE" and the "J" logo
are trademarks belonging to Jove Publications, Inc.

PRINTED IN THE UNITED STATES OF AMERICA

10 9 8 7 6 5 4 3 2 1

To my grandmother, Helen Yahne Passmore. Though we haven't been close in distance throughout the years, Grandma, you have been in my thoughts, prayers and heart. This story is for you with special love.

A special thank you to my editor, Mercer Warriner, whose interest in Mary Queen of Scots inspired this story. Thank you for all your help. Your expertise and guiding hand has been an inspiration.

And most importantly a special thank you to my readers who are so supportive and without whom there would be no stories.

For ever it was, and ever it shall befall,
That Love is he that all thing may bind.
CHAUCER, *Troilus and Criseyde*, I

AUTHOR'S NOTE

MARY, QUEEN OF SCOTS, the great rival of Elizabeth I, Queen of England, was one of the most colorful personalities of the sixteenth century, as well as one of the most tragic queens in history. To this day, she allures poets. Historians still quarrel bitterly over whether she was a murderess or a martyr, victim or beguiler, saint or wanton. The extent of her guilt is continually being reexamined and scrutinized.

Mary Stuart's life began in turmoil. Her father, James V of Scotland, died close to her birth, and she was crowned Queen of Scotland at less than a week old. Because of Henry VIII's insistence that the infant Queen marry his son and heir, Edward, and because of his attacks against Scotland (termed by some as the "rough wooing"), she was sent to France to be raised at the court of Henry II.

In 1558 Mary married the dauphin, who upon his father's death was crowned Francis II, King of France. For nearly two years, Mary claimed to be Queen of France, as well as Scotland, and also laid claim as the rightful heir to the throne of England, a declaration that immediately made her the enemy of Elizabeth I—who had ascended the throne of England upon the death of her half-sister, Mary. (Elizabeth's father, Henry VIII, had broken all rules with his matrimonial adventures, illegitimately siring his daughter by Anne Boleyn. Thus, Elizabeth was an unacceptable monarch in the eyes of Catholics; to them, the rightful Queen of England was Mary Stuart.)

Upon the death of her royal French husband, Mary found that her sphere of influence had greatly diminished. No longer

Queen of France and at odds with the dowager Queen, Mary returned to Scotland to reign there. Because of her upbringing in a foreign court, her ways differed greatly from those of her Scottish subjects, and she found the country a difficult one to rule. To add to the tension, Mary was a Catholic in a now-Protestant country—thus, the reunion with the people of her native land was a stormy one. The fires of resentment were further fueled by John Knox, an ardent Calvinist who labored to extend his power. The Reformation had taken firm root in Scottish soil.

Mary faced the danger of her position with poise and charm. Her first three years of rule were successful in everything but religion. Knox speculated that some of the Scottish lords were bewitched, and condemned her efforts to bring culture to Scotland through dances and masques. Certain lairds and clan chieftains, however, actively plotted the overthrow of their Catholic, foreign-bred queen. They aspired to the wealth and power that the dissolution of the monasteries and acquisition of Church holdings in the Highlands could bring.

Mary's fatal mistake was to allow passion to ruin her diplomacy and become her guide. In 1565 she married her kinsman Lord Darnley (Henry Stuart), who also laid claim to the English throne. Though at first the handsome young nobleman plied her with adoration, he proved to be an unsuitable consort—even involving himself in a plot which resulted in the murder of one of Mary's councilors, and nearly in her own death. After the birth of their son James (who would later reign over England and Scotland as King James I), the union ended when Lord Darnley was murdered and the house in which he was staying destroyed. To the indignation of her people, Mary married the Earl of Bothwell, the very man accused of the deed. The angry Scots drove Bothwell from the country and imprisoned Mary. She escaped and fled to England, where she asked for the protection of her cousin, Queen Elizabeth, who instead kept her confined under house arrest.

In a tangled web of plot and counterplot, the two women waged a silent war. Elizabeth had secretly supported and aided the Scottish rebellion against Mary. Mary Stuart was forced to abdicate in favor of her infant son James, who was protected by a series of Protestant regents and raised in an atmosphere openly hostile to his mother. Elizabeth would not sentence her cousin to death, but neither would she grant her freedom. At risk was the possibility of an invasion from either France or Spain on Mary's behalf. The threat of assassination, therefore, was an ever-present danger to Elizabeth and to the fate of the country.

Mary remained Elizabeth's prisoner for nineteen years. During her incarceration, she became infinitely more dangerous to the English queen than she might ever have been if allowed to be free. The romantic aura of the captive Queen touched the sympathy of many men and was at the heart of numerous plots against Elizabeth. Moreover, the English queen faced excommunication by a papal bull of 1570, an edict which made lawful the assassination of Elizabeth in the eyes of the Catholic church. Attempts on her life were actively encouraged by Pope Gregory XIII. Considerations of political security often prompted Elizabeth's severe treatment of her cousin. Although her personal feelings for Mary Stuart were tinged with jealousy and resentment, Elizabeth was a staunch supporter of a hereditary sovereign's right to rule. She hesitated to become a willing party to the shedding of royal blood, fearing that it might set a precedent and endanger her own person as well.

The Catholic powers of Europe used Mary as their trump card against Elizabeth. Spain's ambitions in the New World was an added barb, one that England secretly challenged with bold seafarers, adventurers and privateers backed by merchants hungry for access to trade routes. More than Mary's freedom was at stake in this game. Elizabeth walked a tightrope as she sought to maintain peace; nevertheless, she was the target of one conspiracy after another.

Mary, angry at her cousin's actions, supported several plots to place herself on the English throne she considered hers. However, in a cunning pursuit, Walsingham—Elizabeth's minister—plotted to seal the fate of the Scottish queen with her death. He conceived a treacherous plan that, if successful, would mean the Scottish queen's beheading and that of anyone who sought to give her aid.

It is against this background of deceit and intrigue that a young Scottish beauty and her brothers undertake a daring and dangerous mission to free the captive Queen and place her on England's throne—a deed that will place the young woman at odds with an ambitious sea captain sworn to be Queen Elizabeth's protector.

Highland Bride

Prologue, December 1585

THE MORNING LIGHT STREAMED through the mullioned windows as Elizabeth Tudor made her entrance into the large room. Pausing in the doorway, she gave the two men who awaited her—Lord Burghley (William Cecil) and Sir Francis Walsingham—a chance to admire her and conjure up the necessary compliments. Perhaps now, as she was growing old, she needed them more than ever, though she would never have made such an admission aloud. Instead of issuing flowery words, however, the two men moved forward silently, obviously anxious to state their business.

"Your Majesty!" they exclaimed in unison.

Lord Burghley's bow was stiff, a result of his gout, while Walsingham's was more pronounced. Burghley and Walsingham were the two men she trusted with her life. Yet even so, her demeanor always reminded them that she was in control. There could only be one ruler of England.

"What have you come to see me about?" she asked, her voice a bit shrill. "At such an ungodly hour it must surely be urgent."

The sun's muted rays cast flickering light against the chambers richly-hued tapestries and draperies, dancing upon the gold threads which swirled through the fabric of her white velvet dressing gown. A stiff, lacy ruff rose behind her head, framing her bright red hair and pale, painted face. A long rope of gold and pearls glistened against her bodice, emphasizing the long lines of the slim figure for which she was so famous.

"Well—?"

Her eyes traveled in curiosity from one of her ministers to the other. Walsingham, a dark-haired, swarthy-skinned man of lithe physique and stern countenance, reminded her of a crafty weasel. ''The Great Spymaster,'' he was aptly called. He lived for his work and enjoyed it fiercely. She had to admit that he had served her well. Integrity. Obsession. Dedication. Those were the three words that defined him. His intent was to protect the realm and to ensure its peace and prosperity. Indeed, he loved to work in secret, and had fabricated a web of espionage that stretched from Edinburgh to Constantinople. His dark eyes scrutinized her now, and she thought of how relieved she was that Walsingham was the captive Scottish queen's enemy, and not hers.

No one loved England more than Walsingham except she and Lord Burghley. If Walsingham reminded her of a weasel, her elderly adviser reminded her of a wise old owl. In truth, Burghley had counseled her well all these years, and his prudent yet relentless advice had been a factor in her success. Dear Burghley had grown old in her service, she thought now, assessing him. His once-red hair and beard were now so gray as to be almost white. Bundled in his robes of office, a dark fur-lined gown pulled close about the ruff at his throat, and the flaps of his black wool coif-cap pulled over his ears despite the morning's warmth, he was a comforting presence. Nonetheless, the interruption of her morning toilet had put her in a peevish mood.

''Speak up! Has the cat got your tongues?'' Her voice was steady as she met their eyes. The way they looked first at her, then at each other, and then back at her again, clearly told her that some plan was afoot.

It was Burghley who spoke first, secure as he was in the Queen's favor. Those who knew nothing of her obstinacy, pride, and determination wrongly supposed he had more power than he did. Yet, was it not true that she always granted him the courtesy of listening?

''We have come once again to converse with you upon the subject of the captive Scottish queen. Mary—''

''Mary.'' Elizabeth threw her hands up in the air. ''Mary! Mary! How I tire of hearing that name!'' Why was it that the very thought of *that woman* still had the power to upset her? ''I have her in a cage, isn't that enough?''

''As I have said not once, not twice, but hundreds of times—

no!" Burghley thrust his gout-gnarled hands into the furred sleeves of his gown, a habit of his she had grown accustomed to over the years. "Like a restless tiger, she has tried every possibility of escape, as you yourself well know. She has been the cause of countless intrigues. Must I name all the names?"

"If you will not, then I will," Walsingham hissed. He was outspoken and would not alter his opinions because they were unpopular, even if they were also frowned upon by *her*. "Ridolfi. Norfolk. Throckmorton, to name but a few. And who could forget that because of that 'bosom serpent,' the Spanish ambassador Mendoza was told to leave England?"

"Enough." Elizabeth's thin lips tightened; the wrinkles at her eyes and mouth seemed more pronounced beneath her heavy makeup. Her expression was grim as she seated herself carefully in the large, red, velvet-cushioned chair. She rested her lovely, long-fingered hands on the chair's arms, gripping them tightly as she tried to keep her composure. Oh, how she wished the Scottish queen would just disappear. Certainly her life would be much easier then.

"As long as she lives, she will be a constant threat, your Majesty." Though it was Walsingham who spoke, Burghley's expression clearly showed that he felt the same way.

Elizabeth's voice was carefully controlled, though she seethed on the inside. "I have no love for her, God knows, but she is still a kinswoman and an anointed queen. I do *not* seek her death. To do so could well lead to my own undoing. When blood is let, the hounds often seek for more." The rising sun highlighted her face and she shaded her eyes in irritation, a mood brought on by the matter of their talk. "Close the draperies, Francis!"

"Yes, your Majesty." He hurried to comply, pulling on the long, braided silk cord until the room was but dimly lit. It was only then that she smiled.

"That is much better." Leaning back, she made pretense of relaxing, when in truth every nerve, instinct, and fiber of her being was vibrantly awake and alert.

Though she had never met her cousin face-to-face, she had heard glowing accounts of her beauty—so many times, in fact, that it was infuriating. Mary had always had an undeniable sensual allure, even in her girlhood, that drew men to her.

They wanted to protect her, even some of Elizabeth's own courtiers. But now Mary was much older, and reportedly had not escaped the march of time.

There was a long silence before she spoke. Then, stretching like a sly cat, she said, "I've heard that she is no longer the beauty that she once was. Is that true?"

"Time has laid its mark upon her. She is wilting like a flower in the shade. I've heard that her hair has turned gray, though she hides it beneath a wig," Walsingham blurted without thinking.

"Indeed!" Elizabeth's body stiffened at the reminder, and she kept her own face in the shadows. The passing of time had touched her as well. It had been many years since her own hair had sufficed to frame her rouged and powdered face. Her once-luxurious tresses were now thin and threaded with silver. Wigs had long been her refuge from the ravages of age.

"Her body has begun to thicken, so that her appearance has taken on a matronly quality." Seeking to make amends for his lack of tact and to soothe her ruffled feathers, Walsingham added quickly, "She is not slim as are you, nor is she as lively. She indulges in little exercise of late."

Elizabeth's eyes looked towards Lord Burghley. "And what say you, Cecil?" Her mouth relaxed into the semblance of a smile. "I've heard she has mended her ways and stopped plotting against me, that she passes the hours with embroidery, reading and gardening, or at play with her pet spaniels."

"Only because Paulet keeps an unending watch over her. Whenever she goes out, she is accompanied by a guard. Every night, soldiers keep their stations within and without the house, and watch has been set in the villages nearby. Any stranger in the district is suspect, and no one is allowed to enter the house or speak to her. But if you have heard that she no longer has ideas of obtaining her freedom then you have heard amiss," Burghley snapped. His frown was fierce, his brows knit as he stroked his white-frosted beard. "She will never change."

Elizabeth shook her head, preferring to believe that she had at last subdued her rival. "But I have heard that if released, she has offered to withdraw all claim to the English crown, to never more communicate with conspirators, and to live anywhere in England according to *my* choice. Never to go more than ten miles from that residence, and to submit to surveillance by neighboring gentlemen—''

''Do not trust her,'' Walsingham and Burghley said simultaneously.

''Shrewsbury tells me that a melancholy has taken possession of her soul. If so, then I pity her.'' For just a moment, she truly did feel sorry that someone who once held such a lofty perch had now been brought down so low.

''Save your pity, Majesty. She openly speaks against you.'' Walsingham's words had the desired effect, for Elizabeth's sympathy quickly turned back to anger.

''She is tamed for the moment, but like a she-lion, she is waiting to pounce. Must I remind you again of the plots instigated in her name?'' Burghley grumbled.

Walsingham strode to the table and pulled a stack of papers from a satchel. ''By a variety of desperate devices, she has managed to correspond secretly with the French and Spanish ambassadors, with her supporters in Scotland, and with representatives of the Pope. Letters have been smuggled in and out, in the washing, in firewood, in wigs, in the linings of shoes.'' Striding back to Elizabeth, he held the missives out to her. ''This is a collection I have gathered during her long captivity.''

Elizabeth waved the papers away. ''I don't need to look.'' Throughout the years, many, even some of her jailers, had fallen under Mary's spells. What was this web of fascination that she wove? ''If you say it is so, it is so.''

''I have uncovered every plot in time, have I not? Even that messenger disguised as a dentist.'' His mouth contorted into a rare smile. ''I even have agents among the students and priests of the Jesuit College in Reims. They keep me informed. Every man has his price.''

''And every woman?'' Even those Elizabeth had once trusted now veered to the banner of the Queen of Scots. Plots, plots, plots—how tired Elizabeth was of them. Ridolfi—a Florentine banker active in London—had been the first, then Norfolk— a member of her own family. Less than two years ago, Francis Throckmorton, the Catholic nephew of her late ambassador to France, joined Mary's cause, and was caught and executed.

Walsingham cleared his throat before he continued. ''Were

it the Scottish harridan who had you within her grasp, dare you imagine that she would hesitate to sign your death warrant?''

Elizabeth shook her head. "Nay, I will not hear of it!"

Walsingham lifted his head sharply. "You must consent! It is the only way your safety and that of the realm can be guaranteed. Do not tie my hands behind my back, Majesty!"

"Remember, Majesty, the Bond of Association, which pledges the signers never to accept as your successor any person who has sanctioned an attempt on your life, and to prosecute to the death any person involved in such an enterprise. The Bond holds the force of law," Burghley added.

"But you have no solid proof. The matter of the Throckmorton plot happened too long ago to bring up now. And as you have said, Paulet has her guarded well."

"For now!" Burghley spread his hands in a gesture of helplessness. "Without your cooperation on this, we are helpless."

"Helpless? You?" Elizabeth laughed softly.

"A wolf without his teeth, a lion without his claws."

There was another long silence. Elizabeth sat unmoving, staring at the two men. Lowering her head, folding her hands in her lap, her demeanor held an air of resignation, as if she knew her advisors' proposal to be the only way. Even so, she did not say the words that would allow them to proceed with it.

"As long as the so-called Queen of Scots lives, your life will be in constant danger, as well as those of your loyal subjects. I repeat: do you think that if Mary Stuart were in your place, she would be as merciful?"

It had little to do with mercy, Elizabeth thought. She had long been jealous of the Scottish queen, though loath to admit it. She thought Mary cursed with beauty, unblessed with brains, clever but seldom wise. Certainly she had been easy to best in the matter of Lord Darnley. Elizabeth's thoughts swept back to that time she had sent the handsome young Roarke MacKinnon to Scotland with the mission of spying upon the Scottish queen. He had ended up falling under Mary's spell, though Elizabeth's plot had nonetheless worked out perfectly. Mary's own foolish heart led her first into a union with the foppish Lord Darnley, then with the manly Bothwell.

And now she is my prisoner, Elizabeth thought. A hollow source of gloating; Elizabeth knew all too well the danger Mary presented, and yet the idea of signing her cousin's death warrant was abhorrent. She, frightened of so few things, was strangely fearful of causing Mary's death. To do so might somehow imperil her own soul.

"I don't suppose she would be merciful," she whispered. She had relished the triumph of having Mary within her power—yet, somehow, her victory had soured. The romantic aura of the captive Queen touched the sympathy of many young Englishmen and aroused the ardor of Catholic youths. Following the murder of Darnley and her marriage to his murderer, Mary had been reviled, but had now become the symbol of gallantry. A poor, beautifully bewinged lark who could no longer fly freely. The notion of helping her escape had fired the hearts of many a young man. Elizabeth did not want to be the villain in this well-enacted masque.

"Allow me to ensnare her so tightly that she can never break free," Walsingham was saying.

"And then?"

"She is a witch! A Scottish witch!" Walsingham exclaimed. "I will get proof. And if I secure the necessary verification—beyond a doubt that she seeks your life—then may I have the signature on the document I so desperately counsel you to sign?"

"Secure your proof, and then we will see." She would make no promises yet. Slowly, Elizabeth rose, reaching for the bell to summon one of her ladies-in-waiting; this signaled the end of the interview. With a bow, the councilors swept from the room.

"The fewer who know, the better," Walsingham cautioned to Burghley. The two men's eyes passed a silent message, and then the old, black-garbed Burghley shuffled away.

"Proof!" Walsingham mumbled as he emerged from the Queen's private apartments. He walked down the corridor, his eyes fixed on the floor. He had to rid England of the woman he considered to be the country's enemy. It was imperative that she go to the scaffold. And yet, he knew his Queen. She was stubborn about not giving the signal for Mary's execution. Was the memory of her own mother's beheading such a painful memory? Perhaps. The country was like her child, however, and every mother fought for her offspring. That was the answer. He must make Elizabeth see that England's very future was in danger. But how? Passing by a lighted torch, he set afire the papers he was holding. In actuality, they were useless. He needed something that would condemn the deposed Queen of Scots beyond a doubt.

Walsingham's obsession was to prevent the return of Catholicism to England—as much for his own well-being as for Elizabeth's, if the truth were told. To protect himself and the country, he had agents all over Europe as well as in taverns, cottages, and houses throughout England. The Throckmorton plot had been only one of many that he had unearthed; it would not be the last. Even so, that Scottish heretic was clever about hiding her own involvement. He would have to outmaneuver her. After her many months of incarceration under Paulet—a strict man who had forbidden his prisoner correspondence, or even a walk in the fresh air—the Scottish queen would surely be hostile, ripe for intrigue. She must be desperate for escape.

Suddenly, he knew just how to bring the Queen of Scots to her doom. He would lure her into a trap. Gilbert Gifford, just recently made a priest, had been arrested upon landing in England. After questioning, it emerged that he had been sent by Mary's agents to try to reopen secret communications with her. The weak and unpleasant character had instead consented to play the spy for Walsingham—not the first nor the last of his kind to be drawn into the spymaster's network.

"He will be perfect." The priest's parentage—a good Staffordshire family living near where Mary was imprisoned—made him a wise choice. Walsingham would let Gifford forge ahead to create a way for Mary's letters to get out. They would be intercepted, however, and studied carefully. There was no simpler or surer method of discovering plots, nor any device more likely to bring Mary herself into danger. Let her have a free hand and thus ensnare herself. And who better than a priest to lead her into a daring plot?

And Captain Ryan Matthew Paxton. He would have need of that daring adventurer's services too, for what he had in mind. Ryan Paxton was a perfect choice, for he was ambitious. As the son of a London tavern maid and a privateer, his position at court was tenuous at best. He had often solicited Walsingham's influence with the Queen. How cheerfully Paxton would oblige were it to further his future. With that thought in mind, Walsingham sought the haven of his own chambers to plot and to plan.

PART ONE

THE CAPTIVE HEART

Scotland and England, 1586

Stone walls do not a prison make,
   Nor iron bars a cage;
Minds innocent and quiet take
   That for an hermitage.

LOVELACE,
      "To Althea, from Prison"

Chapter One

THE GRAY MISTS of a ghostly January fog hung low and thick over London. It was a chilly, eerie evening, the kind that prompted a man to seek the warmth of a fire. Ryan Paxton was no exception. Opening the creaking wooden door, he entered the Devil's Thumb, a half-timbered inn near the City Bridge that was popular with sailors and sea captains.

Noise emanated from within the Devil's Thumb—drunken laughter, chatter, singing, and boisterous carryings-on. It was a beehive of activity, crowded to the beams with patrons. Indeed, there hardly seemed enough elbow-room to lift a tankard. Even so, his entrance did not go unnoticed. Even in a crowded room, Ryan Paxton was a man to draw the eye. His body was lean and hard, his skin a swarthy olive from the Mediterranean sun, a striking contrast with his red-gold hair and short-clipped beard. Lithely built, he had the grace of a cat and the strength of a lion. Dressed in an emerald-green doublet, a sleeveless jerkin of dun-colored leather with a standing collar, thigh-high brown boots fastened by straps to the waist of his buff-colored trunk hose and underdoublet, he cut a dashing figure as he strode across the room.

It was musty and smoky inside. Firelight danced and sparked, candles illuminated the scarred wooden tables, the uneven plaster on the walls, and the bowed ceiling-beams that rattled their decay. Against the west wall was a stack of large barrels that wobbled and swayed precariously as he passed by. Sprinkled liberally with a mixture of rushes and sawdust, the plank floor was in desperate need of a good sweeping. It had once been a prosperous inn with a well-kept taproom and a garden facing the river. Now, however, the yard was empty of any greenery and held naught but a brewer's cart.

"The Devil's Thumb," Ryan whispered. It was the place of his birth, his boyhood home. Now he was back to claim his inheritance. How ironic that upon the death of his stepfather, a man who had showed him little kindness, the inn should be left to him. Certainly it would not have been Thomas Bentley's intent, had there been any other choice. But then, wasn't life full of surprises?

Even now, the tavern reminded him of his boyhood and the pleasant hours spent with his mother, as well as more turbulent times. He was assailed by so many memories. Indeed, the sight, sound, and very smell of the room brought it all back. He had helped his mother work in this taproom, listening to her soft voice recounting treasured moments. Fionna Paxton was a woman who always smiled, her thoughts soaring beyond the sordid surroundings of the inn. Ryan had sensed that she counted the days until the man she loved would return to claim her. Ryan had found himself sharing her dream, hoarding his fantasies as surely as a miser hoarded gold. But his father never came back from roving the seas, and a bitterness had welled up inside the boy like the poison of an ill-tended wound.

Ryan had spent many an early morning and late afternoon sparring with the other youths. In truth, he had received more than a few lumps, scratches, bruises, and black eyes in defending his mother's name from those who had taunted him that she was a harlot. He had been called a bastard more times than he could count, learning at an early age that strength was his only defense. Now he would not take an insult from any man.

Nor had his mother had an easy time of it. Though she spoke not a melancholy word and always soothed his spirits, he knew she hated the drunken customers and their ever-pawing hands. It had been the only way she could earn a living for herself and her son, however; thus, she had conjured up a world of contentment where troubles could not bother her.

Standing in front of the fireplace, Ryan waited for a free table. He thought about those long-ago days and how he had ached for a father. In an effort to find respectability, his mother had at last married the owner of the Devil's Thumb; her son was then ten years of age. But while Ryan had hoped to at last find a companion in the portly man, he instead received only scoldings and the severest discipline. Telling the boy that a child conceived in sin stood in mortal jeopardy of his soul, Ryan's stepfather had made the boy work unmercifully hard, cuffing him if he dared to complain. Ryan had toiled from early morning until long into the night.

At last the abuse to his spirit and pride had become unbearable. Though Ryan had loved his mother fiercely, he ran away to sea, and at last made a reputation for himself there. Ryan had promised his mother many times, by letter, that he would someday make his fortune and take her away. But the words came back to haunt him now. He would never have the chance to keep his promise.

At twenty-one years of age he returned to England, his arms piled high with gifts, only to find that his mother—at last worn out from her toil—had departed the world. The treasures he brought home would never belong to her. He had taken too long to return, and now it was too late. The bitter truth had hit him like a leather-gloved hand. It was the only time in his entire life that Ryan cried.

Now he was a man of consequence, a captain of his own ship, with hopes of gaining the Queen's attention. It was *not* an impossible dream. Hadn't Sir Walter Raleigh done the same? A New World existed beyond the western seas, a place of dazzling wealth. He had been there and seen for himself. Great treasure fleets sailed home from the Spanish Main, galleons filled with incredible, plundered riches. English captains such as he wanted only their fair share. It was time that Spain's unchallenged dominance was contested, and he was just the man to do so.

Privateer? That was what some might call him, but he preferred to call himself an adventurer. The white flag bearing the red cross of St. George flew proudly on the mainmast of his ship. That he was also well acquainted with Burghley and Walsingham, the Queen's councilors, seemed to be in his favor. A man needed all the friends that he could collect at court. With Elizabeth backing him monetarily, he would be invincible!

"Ryan?" A dark-haired man of enormous girth accosted him.

"Seamus, you old devil!" The shaggily black-bearded giant was a welcome sight, though another reminder of his childhood. The brewer had been one of the few who had granted Ryan any smiles. "So, you are still supplying the Devil's Thumb with your excellent Staffordshire ale?"

"I am. It delights me that you are now the owner of the place. Somehow, it seems fitting." Wiping his hands on his coarse white apron, Seamus gave Ryan's back a hearty pat.

"Perhaps, but I have no time to run it. My ship is all that I need, and yet somehow I can't even think to let the inn go. The memories attached to my mother, I suppose. Ah, well. 'Tis a thing I will give thought to later."

"Much later. Come—I will not have you stand." Seamus grinned. "The inn belongs to you. Gads, man, push someone else away."

Ryan shook his head. "No, I did not come to cause trouble, nor to boast about my ownership. I came to observe and to do some thinking."

"Join me at my table, then. I'm all alone, and would relish the company. You can tell me all about your travels." With a gap-toothed grin, the brewer led him to a table in the corner of the taproom. "Where have you come from?"

"I sailed to the West Indies and back again, stopping in France."

"Ahhhhh!" The brewer plopped down into his chair, motioning Ryan down as well. "Was it all that you had heard? Paradise?"

"More so." Ryan's descent to his seat was more stately. He sat directly across from Seamus, then filled him in on all the details of his last voyage. "It is a lush, rich place in parts. There were times I thought it Paradise, and other times I thought it hell. There are brown-skinned men who I fear are most uncivilized."

"Like my Scots?"

"Far worse."

"I must hear more." Seeing a young woman wearing a gray dress and white apron, he motioned her near. "A tankard of my very best ale for my friend!" Seamus thundered. "Step lively now," he scolded the tavern-maid when she hesitated. "This man now owns *everything* in sight."

"Ohhhhhhh!" The tavern-maid needed no such prodding. One look at the new proprietor's handsome face, broad shoulders, and slim build made her quite acquiescent to the brewer's demands. She had no sooner left than she was back again, serving up the ale with a wide smile. "Yer ale, Sir." Hopeful of Ryan's attentions, she lingered just a moment or two after setting down the tankard. Licking her lips, she offered up a silent invitation; she cooed and flirted. Ryan shook his head, though he did give her an extra tuppence.

"Pretty wench! I'm overly fond of bright red hair," Seamus exclaimed, watching the gentle sway of her overripe hips as she walked away. "Had she looked at me with such hunger, I would not have sent her away."

"I have made it a vow not to trifle with young women of her profession, no matter how pretty." From head to ankles, Ryan's body stiffened perceptibly. Tavern-maids always reminded him too much of his mother. Though he was most definitely a ladies' man, he had never dallied with those young women who served up potent beverages. "And most especially not *here*." His mother's ghost was too real a presence.

Seamus' face turned as red as a newly plucked beet. "Of course. I meant no offense."

"None taken."

"Your mother was a fine woman. Chaste, despite her circumstances. It was just that she fell in love with a sweet-talking rogue who offered her the world. Blackguard that he was, he left in his ship and never came back." Lifting his cup, Seamus gulped the contents down, then wiped his lips with the back of his hand. "Certainly you were her sun, moon and stars, Ryan."

"That I was," Ryan said softly. "Just as she was mine." There had been a special bond between mother and son that even death could not sunder. Ryan had always known it was because of him that his mother was put out of her home. A silversmith's daughter, Fionna Paxton was sent packing when her father discovered she was with child. She had walked all the way to London to seek the charity of her brother, only to be turned out again. Waiting tables at the tavern had been the only path open to her. In return for board and lodging, she had agreed to serve in the inn's taproom, little knowing that she would never leave.

"Forsooth, you even look like her."

Ryan studied his face in the liquid at the bottom of his tankard. The thick, sun-streaked red-gold hair, his brown eyes, and the full, sensual mouth all marked him as his mother's child. In truth he had inherited her gentle temperament as well, until the cruelty of others had forced him to be strong and domineering. For all its pretense of being civilized, London was much like living in the wild, as was a life at sea. It was survival of the fittest.

"How did she die, Seamus? Bentley would never tell me, or at least I always suspected there was more to the story than he told." Ryan's voice was carefully controlled, though his eyes betrayed the depth of his emotions.

"He worked her to the bone, more a workhorse than a wife. And . . . somehow, after you left, she just lost heart." Seamus choked on his words, never confessing his own love for the woman, which was nevertheless revealed by the gleam in his eye.

"I should have killed him. If he wasn't dead already, I'd have his head." When he came home and found her in her grave, he should have laid the blame squarely on his stepfather's head. Yet, like a fool, he had been charitable. Now his mother's husband had followed her in death.

"I wish I had killed him."

Seamus was pensive. "She never put up an argument. She tried to please him, wanted him to love her. I think she thought that if he did love her, if she could have made him show some speck of kindness towards *you*, you somehow might have been persuaded to return."

"Then it was *my* fault."

"No! You had a life to live. Your letters gave her a great deal of joy. She was so proud. So very, very proud. She would brag to me that you were just like your father."

"My *father*!" Ryan spat out the word as though it were an insult. "Whoever sired me is unworthy of the name."

"Agreed! And yet I've heard it rumored that the man your mother loved was one close to the Queen. An adventurer, a privateer. Don't judge too harshly, my boy. Things are not

always as they seem. Perhaps there was a reason why he did
not seek to claim you—'' Seamus suddenly grew quiet, watching as a young boy, bedecked in jerkin and hosen, threaded
his way through the inn on his way to their corner table. ''A
page. Do you know him, Rye?''

''No. The last time I was in London, he would barely have
been out of swaddling.'' Even so, Ryan acknowledged him
with an upraised hand. ''Are you perchance looking for me,
lad?''

''Are you the sea-captain whose ship, the *Red Mermaid*,
lies at anchor? Captain Ryan Matthew Paxton by name?''

''I am.''

The corners of the page's mouth curled up as he sighed in
relief. ''I have been looking everywhere for you, sir. At the
docks, aboard your ship. One of the sailors told me that you
owned this tavern. Thus, I thought to inquire within.''

''Well, you have found me.'' Ryan suspected that Lord
Burghley was overly anxious to get the crown's fair share of
the cargo aboard the ship. ''He will just have to wait!''

''But he is impatient, sir.''

Not in the least bit vexed, Ryan nodded towards a three-
legged stool. ''Pull up a chair, boy. Running errands for velvet-
garbed lords is work that conjures up a thirst. An ale should
quench your dry throat.''

The page shook his head, sending his dark brown curls
flying. ''No, I haven't the time. I must bring you back with
me. It is a matter of utmost urgency, Captain.'' Warily he
looked at Seamus, as though afraid to speak in his presence.

''He can be trusted. Speak.''

The boy's high, shrill voice lowered to a whisper. '' 'Tis, I
am told, a matter of great urgency.''

''Indeed?'' Ryan asked, glancing apprehensively at Seamus.
''Surely not so urgent that I have not time to finish my ale.''

''*He* wants to see you right away.'' Boldly, the page plucked
at Ryan's sleeve. ''You must come with me. Please. If you
do not, it will be my ruin. Sir Francis is ever a choleric man
who will box my ears if you don't comply.''

''Sir Francis Drake?''

''Sir Francis Walsingham.''

''So—'' The Queen's spymaster. Ryan leaned back in his

chair, not in the least anxious to be confronted by *him* again. Influence or no influence with the Queen, the man could be as bothersome as a gnat, always up to some plot or other. Ryan had humored him a number of times, in the hopes of earning the Queen's favor, but was really in no mood to spar with the devious little man tonight.

"Please—"

"Tell him I have business to attend to." As soon as the words were spoken, he knew that they would do no good. Walsingham was used to all men jumping at his command. He was a powerful force to be reckoned with, a man to be feared. There was no use in tempting fate. "By God, never mind! I'll tell him myself." Rising to his feet, Ryan followed after the page, hoping to have done with this business and return forthwith to his ale.

Chapter Two

THE ROOM WAS COLD despite the fire in the great stone fireplace. Or was it apprehension that chilled his bones, Ryan wondered. What was it about Sir Francis Walsingham that always bothered him? The ghoulish manner in which he went after his enemies. The man was cold, calculating. Deadly, if any man were on his wrong side. Ryan would make certain that they would never be adversaries.

Trying to make himself comfortable in the hard chair, he leaned back and stretched his legs as he waited for Sir Francis Walsingham to make his appearance. Whatever the Queen's Secretary of State wanted, it must have been important if he had summoned Ryan to his own residence. Why, then, was he keeping him waiting?

In vexation, Ryan at last stood and paced up and down the long corridor. He hoped that Walsingham was not going to make another plea for him to spy for England. He had said 'No' several times and would do so again; Ryan Paxton would be no one's puppet. He would give the Queen his loyalty and his life, but he would not barter his soul for any price. Not even for a fleet of ships.

Ryan's impatience goaded him on as he continued walking up and down the long hall in an effort to calm his ire. He had no intention of eavesdropping, yet the muffled voices were so distinct that he was intrigued and paused to listen as he passed a door.

"I have further work for you, *priest*, now that you have returned from Thomas Morgan's presence in France." Ryan recognized Walsingham's voice. So, he was undoubtedly conversing with one of his trained lapdogs. What devious plot was underfoot now? Curiosity got the better of him, though he knew it dangerous to be too inquisitive.

"I am always ready to obey my lord's commands," answered a raspy voice.

"Good, good. I knew you would not be so foolish as to tell me 'nay.'" A deep-throated chuckle from behind the door sounded ominous. "By the way, how is our traitorous Welshman enjoying his stay in the Bastille?"

"They treat him well, more guest than prisoner. The King of France does not wish to ill-treat the friends of the Queen of Scots. The only reason he has been imprisoned is to placate Elizabeth's request that he be sent back to England in chains."

"So much for the treacherous French!" There was a pause. "Is he still conspiring against Elizabeth?"

"Now more so than ever. He was completely receptive to the matter of the letters. Just as you supposed, he places the utmost trust in me because of my robes of the church."

Ryan didn't stay to listen further. The sound of shuffling footsteps alerted him that the interview was ending. He hurried back to his chair, sat down, folded his arms, and put all that he had heard out of his mind. It was none of his business. When at last the great spymaster emerged, he was so silent that Ryan was unaware of him at first.

"So, you have come, Paxton." The voice crackled with an icy tone, and Ryan felt the hairs on the nape of his neck rise. God help him if Walsingham suspected him of eavesdropping. "Much sooner than I had anticipated." The dark eyes scrutinized Ryan, but seemed satisfied that he had overheard nothing.

"I felt that a matter so urgent must be quickly tended to." Rising to his feet, Ryan affected a polite bow.

"Your obedience is appreciated." Walsingham had always troubled Ryan, for in the five or six times he had been in the man's company, he had never seen him smile. Even now, he stood as expressionless and still as a statue. Then, with a grim nod of his head, Walsingham motioned Ryan into a small, carpeted room. "I will get right to the point. I want you to sail your ship to Edinburgh to take a loving message from Elizabeth to James VI, her vassal king."

"An errand to Scotland?" Ryan's cheek twitched with irritation. He had no liking for being relegated to the position of courier. His time was valuable.

"A bribe, as it were. We have been quite successful in securing his loyalty by dangling in front of his nose the promise of his succeeding Elizabeth." Walsingham tossed a log into the room's small fireplace, then watched the sparks swirl up. The crackle and slow hiss of the flames as they devoured the wood seemed to fascinate him; his eyes were fixed and staring.

"Why me?" Ryan asked, in a tone he hoped did not reveal his annoyance.

"I need someone who can be trusted, someone who sees the advantage of earning Elizabeth's favor. You see, I have not forgotten your desire for ships." He walked slowly to a wooden desk, shuffling and reshuffling papers there. "That you have been staunch in your refusal to spy for me is interesting. Perhaps if you won't bend to me, then you won't be tempted into any sort of Catholic intrigue."

"Catholic intrigue!" That his stepfather had been a staunch Catholic only served to prejudice him against all those who bent their heads to the Pope. "I have no liking for papists." He would have been a fool to have any dealings with those who professed the Catholic faith. It was dangerous during these times.

"Nor do I. I have spent too many years fighting against their treason. There will never be a Catholic on the throne of England, that I promise. Mary of Scotland will never wear the crown." Looking down at his hands, he began to twist his gold ring, the one Elizabeth had given him, in order to calm his anger.

"But her son will?"

"He is a logical choice to succeed Elizabeth; he is the Queen's own cousin and as opposed to the Pope as are we. It is important that we forge a strong bond with him now that he has come of age and rules without regents. Thus your 'errand,' as you call it, is more important than you could possibly realize."

"I will leave with the first light of dawn."

"I thought you would be cooperative once you understood." Walsingham's eyes looked like twin coals as he handed Ryan the packet. "Also enclosed are two additional dispatches—

one addressed to James's Chancellor Maitland, and the other to an acquaintance of mine.''

One of his spies, Ryan thought sourly, again reminding himself that it was none of his business. If taking a few missives to Edinburgh would ingratiate him with Walsingham and the Queen, it was a small price to pay. It only made good sense to comply.

It was nearly dawn when he left Walsingham's house. The empty streets were completely silent as he hurried back to his ship. For the moment, he put the matter of the Devil's Thumb from his mind. Better to avoid the inn and any prying questions. He would catch a few winks aboard the *Red Mermaid* and set sail as soon as the fog lifted.

Chapter Three

THE WINTER RAINS had stopped, though a faint sea mist hung in the air. It was a dull and gloomy afternoon, Moira April MacKinnon thought as she looked out the chamber window of Holyrood Palace, trying to get a clear view of Edinburgh. This was the first time she had viewed the medieval seaside city nestled in the ridge between a gray stone castle and Holyrood House—the first time that she had ever been away from her parents' borderland estates. She had to admit that it was vibrantly exciting, as exhilarating as the madcap horseback ride that had brought her here. She wanted to see all that she could before being called back home again.

Moira had traveled all the way to Holyrood to meet her betrothed, Iain Gordon, a councilor of the King. She would most definitely not agree to marry a man she had never seen, as she had boldly told her mother. Better to be sent to a religious house in France than to marry a loathsome man. Surprisingly, her mother had agreed with her for once, and was most lenient on the matter, perhaps because of Kylynn MacKinnon's unhappy first marriage to a brutal Highland laird. The Christmas and New Year's festivities were just the excuse that was needed. With the help of her twin brothers, Donald and David, Moira had maneuvered an invitation from the King. Now she was here at the court of James VI.

Shifting from one foot to the other, pushing up against the sill, she thought about how her mother had once looked out from this very window, or so her brothers had told her. Kylynn MacKinnon had watched mournfully as the man she loved rode away at the Queen's command. From this same window she had also viewed his return. Holyrood House figured importantly in the story of her parents' love, a tale Moira never grew tired of hearing. Even so, a great tragedy had occurred here as well, one which haunted all who resided within Holyrood's walls. David Rizzio, a councilor and trusted friend of Mary Stuart, had been set upon and murdered at the top of the secret staircase far beyond Moira's room. His blood still stained the floor, a reminder of the brutality and turmoil which had all too often been Scotland's lot. The very thought made her shudder.

In over twenty years the country had not changed. Four regents had ruled Scotland in James's name before he gained maturity—his uncle Murray, his grandfather Lennox, and Mar and Morton; all but one had died violently. Early on in James's teen years, movements for and against Morton, the last regent, had prompted a series of coups and countercoups. Peace was all too rare. That James granted a wealth of titles to new families caused much dissent, or so her father said. Everyone thought one's own to be a better and greater clan than someone else's. Such opinions, coupled with the ill-will between Catholics and Protestants, instigated feuding. She knew her father was right in his opinion that court intrigue was better kept at arm's length. She had most certainly heard him repeatedly give that counsel to his sons.

Pressing her nose against the glass, Moira began to wonder if peace would ever come to Scotland. She thought not, for surely men seemed stubborn and driven to quarreling and fighting. Given the example of Queen Elizabeth, women rulers were oftentimes not much better. And yet, things might have been so very different had Mary Stuart ruled the land—Mary, who was still a prisoner of Elizabeth Tudor. Moira was named after the exiled and imprisoned Scots queen; though she had never seen her, Moira often fantasized about her. In her mind, Mary was the noblest of women. How appalling that in all these years, James had not tried to rescue his mother. But then, the ever-present promise of himself assuming the English crown upon Elizabeth's death was all too tempting.

"If you press your nose any harder against that pane, you'll not be able to pull it free!"

With a smile, she turned her head to look at her brother, who had come upon her as silently as a thief. "Oh, is that so, Davie?" The auburn-haired young man was identical to his brother, but though others could never tell the twins apart, Moira could; Davie always wore such a mischievous grin. Indeed, Davie was the daring brother, and Donald the studious one.

"It happened to me also when I first came to court." He rubbed the end of his nose as if remembering, then winked at her. "Ah, but it is a fine city. Remind me to take you riding tomorrow so that you can see every nook and cranny. We'll tour the Royal Mile and I'll show you the house where resided that old goat, John Knox."

"Tomorrow? Must we wait so long?" She couldn't hide her impatience and disappointment.

"There is plenty of time."

"Not as long as you suppose. I wish I had more days to spend," Moira sighed wistfully. "But Mother was most adamant in allowing me only a week. 'Tis your fault, you know, writing to her about some of the dreadful things that have happened here. Is it any wonder Jeanne MacGregor has been requisitioned to be such a fearsome chaperone? She hardly lets me out of her sight unless I am in my chambers."

"Do not fash yourself, we'll slip by her." Davie joined Moira at the window. "But you must promise to stay close by my side. What I have told Father and Mother is true. Why, I remember arising one morning to find that one of the earls had gained control of the palace and was brandishing a sword in the King's own anteroom. Once I came upon the Grahams and their enemies fighting on the slopes of Edinburgh near High Street, just outside the court where the King was trying to administer justice. Violence is not a monopoly of the Highlands or borderlands, you see. It happens here as well, just like in the days when Mother and Father were at court."

"I'll be careful. On that I give my word." She wasn't afraid, but she would humor him just to make certain he didn't send her home early. "I'll stay close to your elbow at all times." As though to assure him she would make good on her promise, she looped her arm through his.

Davie looked at his sister with an appraising eye. She possessed a beauty no man could resist, a beauty that mirrored their mother's. The finely chiseled nose, high cheekbones, full lips, and enormous, dark-lashed green eyes were beyond de-

scription. Moira was still dressed in her mannish riding
clothes—round hose, hosen and doublet—emphasizing the
slim waist and long legs that were the envy of all the women
at court. Davie hadn't missed the looks of jealousy the other
lassies had cast Moira's way upon her arrival, nor the looks
of longing in the men's faces. Iain Gordon was a lucky man.

"A girl as bonnie as you could cause a riot if you do not
behave," he teased, touching the end of her nose.

"Bonnie?"

David nodded. "Mmmm-hmmm."

Moira's hair was dark like their father's, but also had the
reddish gleam of their mother's tresses. People told her she
was pretty, but she didn't pay their idle compliments much
attention. In truth she didn't really know. There were few
women with whom she could measure herself—except her
mother, and in that instance she thought of how feebly she
compared to her. There was no woman as lovely as Kylynn
MacKinnon, or so Moira had always thought. Even now, in
the autumn of her years and after five children, she was a
beauty. Besides, Moira thought herself much too tall.

"Do you really think I'm fair?"

"You are fishing for a compliment, Moira," her brother
chided. "I told you once, and I won't tell you again."

"Do you think Iain Gordon will be pleased?" Pursing her
lips, she asked further, "And will *I* be pleased with him?"
She hadn't come all this way to be disappointed. "Has he a
long nose? A weak chin?" she asked with a laugh. "Is he fat?
Too thin?"

"No! He is a comely man. Too much so, if you ask me,"
he grumbled. "Tall, well-formed with yellow hair. But vain.
Very, very vain. He reminds me of a painting I once saw of
Darnley."

"Ohhh!" She hoped he did not have that one's faults. "Has
he a foul temper? Does he drink overmuch? Does he keep late
hours? Does he display good manners?"

"No, yes, yes, and no." Davie gently disengaged her arm.
"But hurry and get dressed for tonight's festivities, and you
will see him for yourself." Something in his blue eyes told
her he was troubled.

"What is it, Davie?"

"Nothing! I will not repeat court gossip that might be false."
He forced a smile. "Iain Gordon will be enchanted with you
and I think you will be taken with him. He is, as Father has
often said, a very good match."

"No better than you or Donnie. The lassies that win my
brother's eyes will be fortunate indeed." Just as he had appraised her, she scrutinzed him now. He was dressed in hosen,
a jerkin, and the MacKinnon red, black and white plaid, a long
garment that reached from shoulder to knee, fastened with a
large brooch at the breast and at the waist by a belt; the very
picture of a handsome Scottish gentleman. "Is there any lass
you've set your sights upon?"

A frown marred Davie's face. "I have taken a vow."

"Not the priesthood!" Moira's face paled. She did not want
to lose him to the Church. Too many in that vocation had met
a frightful end in these troubled times.

"No. 'Tis something far different than that. Donald and I
have pledged not to marry or even consider a bride until the
Queen of Scots is free."

"What?" She might have thought he was joking, had he
not had his father's daring. "Certainly you do not have plans
to aid her?" The very thought set her hands trembling. Elizabeth Tudor had lopped off many a head for such daring.
"Davie! Are you thus so anxious to get yourselves killed?"

"We will not be forsworn! When we can think of the proper
plot, we will put it into action. Remember, she is our godmother." Jutting out his chin, David looked defiant. "Certainly
James has forgotten all about her. It is disgraceful that he has
let her languish in the clutches of Elizabeth of England."

"Disgraceful, but understandable, I suppose. It is politically
wise, or so Father has said. And after all, she was taken from
him when he was naught but a babe." He had been surrounded
by his mother's enemies ere long, men who betrayed her and
spoke not one kind word in her favor. He had been brought
up by self-seeking lords and teachers hostile to Mary, Queen
of Scots. "Jamie believes that his mother encompassed his
father's death. It has been dinned in his ears."

"I think he fears she will return to Scotland and take his
crown. She refers to him not as Scotland's king, but as Prince
of Scotland. Even so, he should do something—" The

MacKinnons held a precarious position in the land because of such opinions. Roarke and Kylynn MacKinnon's friendship with the exiled Mary, and their practice of the Catholic faith, had not soon been forgotten.

"I know. Were it our mother who was held captive, we would all do everything in our power to free her. I would think he would at least have a longing to meet the woman who gave him birth." She walked over to her wooden trunk, opened the lid, and rummaged through her garments, holding a white satin gown up for his inspection. "Shall I wear this tonight?"

He was quick to answer. "No. That would be bonnie for your wedding perhaps, but for tonight you need something with more color. Something cheerful. Something that will tempt Iain's eye."

"This?" Moira held out a red velvet dress that had belonged to her mother.

"Nae! It is woefully out of style. We do not want it said that the MacKinnons are an impoverished country clan." James openly showed disdain for Highlanders and those of border stock, and thus the twins were always on the defensive. "Let me see—" David walked over to the trunk to see for himself what lay inside, and found the perfect gown: green velvet, with a saffron kirtle and yellow brocade underskirt. "Wear this! It is perfect for impressing a king."

"Will I impress him? Or will he even notice?" Moira had heard gossip—even in the borderlands—that James, just like his father, was often partial to men.

David blushed, knowing exactly what she meant. "James appreciates anything of beauty."

He and his brother, having been at court since they were ten years old, knew the young King well. While they had developed an eye for young ladies, James seemed drawn to those of his own sex, a flaw that had often caused distress at court when his favorites were shown reckless partiality. In the instance of the King's cousin Esmé Stuart, this had caused a tragedy four years ago, when a group of Protestant lords, supported by the Kirk, imprisoned James in Ruthven Castle for fear he might submit to the influence of the Catholic Stuart from France. James had been released, but only upon promising to defend Protestantism and sign an alliance with England.

"You will find favor with him. Have no fear of that."

"In truth, I do not really care. He is insufferably conceited and headstrong at times. You've said so yourself." Though every young woman of marriageable age had hopes of securing a match with the King, and thus viewed him favorably, Moira was repulsed at the thought. "Even if he is the King, I find him wanting."

Moira had only seen him once thus far, but that was enough to form an opinion. He was plump, with a slightly swollen paunch, weak legs, a knobby nose and pale blue eyes that were all too melancholy. Certainly he had not inherited either his mother's or father's comeliness. It was not his physical appearance, however, as much as his loud voice and erratic gait that troubled her.

"If given half a chance, I believe he'll be a good king." David was quick to defend him. "Not perfect by any means, but he has sworn to put an end to all the feuds that are tearing our kingdom apart." He laughed softly. "Certainly he is a studious devil. He's bragged to me that he intends to be the only king since Alfred who has written a book, and seems intent on fulfilling that promise."

"Oh? And I suppose you and Donnie will be the ones to aid him." At eight years of age, her brothers had been chosen to go to court because one of James's tutors had heard they were already translating French to Latin, thanks to their mother's teaching. Most of the other lairds' sons were woefully undisciplined and loath to be scholars. Because of a mutual bookishness, Davie and Donnie had found favor with the King.

Davie puffed out his chest with pride. "He has suggested as much. Donnie and I have the King's favor."

"Do you, now? Well, I am proud, but I do caution you not to be *too* much in his good graces," she teased, knowing he knew full well what she meant.

"Moira, watch your tongue!" David's face turned a deep shade of rose, for she had struck much too close to a subject that had troubled both brothers of late. James was paying a bit too much attention to them, making their friendship a bit uncomfortable.

Moira was immediately contrite. "I was but pestering you. Forgive me."

"I might and then again I might not—" As their eyes met, they both burst into laughter. "You are an imp, do you know that? I can't stay angry with you—as spunky now as you were when we used to wrestle in the stables."

"And I can still hold my own." As the only daughter amidst four sons, Moira had learned how to defend herself at an early age.

"I don't doubt it." Picking up her cap from a small wooden table, he plopped it on her head. "You want to see Edinburgh, do you now? Well, there are still several hours before tonight's festivities begin. Perhaps if we hurry, we can see a goodly portion before the sun sets. It will be a time when we can be together."

Taking her hand, he led her out the door, through the long picture gallery, down the stairs, and into the garden. At the stables they saddled two horses and rode out through Canongate with its high-storied houses. The Royal Mile comprised four successive streets running down from the castle.

Edinburgh was ringed by hills, built on crags, an area of broad plateaus, steep cliffs and deep canyons, an effect that was exaggerated by the height of the buildings that lined the streets. Crow-stepped gables loomed against the sky. Steep, winding streets looked down over rooftops and up to soaring spires and castle battlements. Flodden Wall shaped Edinburgh, for the citizens did not feel safe enough to build outside. Instead, they built upward.

"It is a beautiful city," Moira exclaimed, letting her eyes sweep the panorama presented to her from atop a hill. "To think that there are so many people within these walls."

"Not nearly as many as in London, but many, I would wager." They dismounted and walked along the streets.

It was noisy and crowded, with the loud cries of merchants hawking their wares from carts, buildings and stalls, some so bold as to accost all who walked by. Chattering goodwives with wicker baskets on their heads or balanced on their hips sought to make the best bargains. It was a hustle-bustle of people elbowing or shoving their way through the alley-like wynds.

"Gingerbread!"

"Sweetmeats!"

Moira and Davie gave in to the temptation of the ginger-bread, partaking of its sweetness as they walked along.

"Lace, bonnie, bonnie lace!"

"Ribbons!"

Two young boys were playing ball with a pig's bladder in the street, and Davie briefly joined in for a moment, with Moira cheering him on. All in all, Moira spent an enjoyable time with her brother. She loved the city, but much preferred the wide open spaces of her father's lands. She imagined one could well feel caged living behind walls for any length of time. Besides, for all its rustic splendor, Edinburgh was dirty. Residents emptied chamberpots from tenement windows with a cry of "Gardyloo!" Davie only narrowly saved Moira from a wetting.

" 'Gardyloo'?"

"A corrupt form of the French *gardez l'eau*—mind the water," he said with a laugh. "Let's seek out our horses again. 'Tis safer from upon the animals' backs. Besides, I have a special place to show you."

They rode beyond Edinburgh's borders to the port of Leith, a seafaring town built where the Water of Leith enters the Forth. The ocean was dotted with ships whose sails fluttered in the breeze, and rowboats whose occupants were busy casting their nets. One ship, flying an English flag, rode at anchor.

"I thought this might have special significance for you, Moira. It was here that Mother and Mary Queen of Scots landed twenty-five years ago on their return from France. They stayed with a merchant, Andrew Lamb, whose house is near here."

"Mother's first glimpse of her homeland after a childhood spent across the sea. I wonder how it felt coming home?" She breathed in the scent of the salt air, eyes closed as the wind whipped at her hair, and she listened to the soft roar of the waves striking the shore. A sense of peace swept over her; there was something strangely calming about the ocean.

"Colin. Look. A *Pape*." The shrill voice intruded on Moira's serenity.

"A *MacKinnon*," a huskier voice answered.

"Catholic offal by me faith," taunted a third.

"Wi'out his brother." There were four in all, who by their manner proved themselves bullies.

"The King's favorite lapdogs!"

"Spaniels!"

"Let's have our fun. We willna hae such good fortune to find him alone again!" With the self-assured strut of roosters preparing for a cockfight, they strode forward.

"Moira, get back." Davie stepped in front of his sister protectively. "Take to your heels and flee back to Holyrood."

"Nae!" She would have none of that. She would not leave her brother to fight these young thugs alone. "By God's blood, I'm no coward."

"Get you gone I said! Go!" Davie's command was as fierce as thunder, but even so, Moira did not obey. The gleam of malice in his accosters' eyes, the way they stalked him with their hands hovering by their sword-hilts, spoke of violence to come. She would not run away while these brutal roisterers harmed her brother. Two against four was far better odds than one against such a number. Moira's eyes darted from left to right, searching for a weapon as she prepared to defend her brother.

Chapter Four

THE WATER WAS FOAMY and glinted green as it caressed the shoreline. Hugging the waves, a ship gently dipped
and pitched as it strained against the anchor that held it in the
bay. The *Red Mermaid* was a three-masted galleon, slick and
swift, with a low forecastle and upper deck, a ship manned by
a crew of over thirty men. It was unadorned, except for the
figurehead of a mermaid gracing the bow, with a face uncoin-
cidentally similar to that of Ryan Paxton's mother. It was a
magnificent ship that belonged to a proud man.

Standing solemnly on the quarterdeck, Ryan cast a critical
eye as his men scrambled up the rigging and along the yard-
arms, where they efficiently and speedily took in the ship's
sails and secured them. The anchors and cables were tested,
and only when he was sure that the *Red Mermaid* was ade-
quately at rest did he give the order for a boat to be lowered
into these waters off Edinburgh. Leaving the others behind,
he set off for his meeting with the Scottish king. By all means,
Walsingham must be placated.

The steady pull of the oars made a thumping sound as the
boat pulled towards the land. The screech of seagulls swooping
overhead added to the din of a furious fight raging on the docks.
Swords clashed and clattered, and loud, angry shouts rent the
air. Ryan shielded his eyes against the glare of fading sun right
off the water. Four men in plaids were accosting two others.

"Traitor's spawn!"

"'Tis you and yours who are traitors, Cameron."

"Ye willna hae the chance to hurl such slander again."

"My family has served Scotland well—just as I will in
ridding Edinburgh of you." Despite the fact that he was out-

numbered, one youth did not cower. "I've always been more than a match for you."

Reacting to the warning of his senses, and swinging his sword arm forward, the youth proved his boast to be true, blocking each thrust with a grace that won Ryan's admiration. Even so, the fact that he was woefully surrounded looked to be his end.

Ryan watched with his mouth set in a grim line, but told himself over and over again that it was not his place to come to this young man's aid. Scotland was not his land, nor did he want to risk the King of Scotland's displeasure by entering the melée. He had no idea who was fighting or why. Besides, hadn't he always heard that England's northern neighbor was filled with men scarcely better than the heathens he had visited far across the seas? All Englishmen viewed the Scots as little better than savages, all fighting among one another. Certainly they had not shared the peace Elizabeth Tudor had brought. Was it any wonder the English queen was loath to make James her heir?

"I will not let you harm my brother!" a woman's voice cried out, pleasant despite its anger. Ryan was amazed to see that the other young fighter was a woman. Certainly the waist-length dark hair and gentle curves beneath her garments gave her sex away. Even from a distance, he could see that she was quite comely.

I will not interfere! Ryan tried to hold to that admonition as he watched the confrontation. What happened on Scottish shores was none of his concern. He was a messenger and nothing more—not a peacekeeper. The young Scotsman and hosen-clad girl were nonetheless a sight to behold.

Sword upraised, the youth collided with his attackers in a battle-dance that would have made any experienced swordsman proud. Nor was he without aid. With her long, dark hair swirling out behind her like a cloak, the woman came upon her attackers with a fearsome fury, picking up anything in sight to hurl at their heads: rocks, shells, and even her riding boots, all the while shouting epithets. At last, she picked up a large piece of driftwood and used it as a club, unleashing her fury.

"Ye *glassatig*!" two men called out in fury. "Ye are a demon from hell. But I will see ye pay." In fury the Scotsmen turned their attention from her companion to the girl.

Not liking to see anyone outnumbered in a fight—much less a woman, whatever the circumstances—Ryan soon broke his vow. All too fresh in his mind were the times that he had fought so desperately against such odds. As one of the youth's opponents came at the girl from behind, Ryan threw himself into the fray.

"If you want a fight, I'll give you one!" he exclaimed. With his blade clanging powerfully against the largest Scotsman's sword, he met him thrust for thrust, driving the wild-eyed youth backward. There was a sheer fury in his attack. "So, when you cannot come upon someone from behind, you are not quite so brave," he taunted.

"An Englishman. I hae no quarrel with you." As if to prove that point, Ryan's opponent moved back.

"Well, *I* do," cried another of the attackers. "I willna let some *sassanach* interrupt me pleasure." Grabbing his sword with two hands, the second Scotsman rushed forward. Ryan ducked, circling, and then lunged. In the end, the man's clumsy, oafish strength was outmaneuvered by his English adversary's quick wit and feline agility. Proving himself lacking in bravado when in danger of being bested, the young man quickly initiated a retreat, as did the others.

"We willna forget this, *sassanach*," one threatened. "Ye dunna ken the harm ye hae done."

"Ye didna get yer due this time, MacKinnon, but ye will. That I promise, on my oath as a Cameron." With a nod of his head, the leader of the pack led the others away.

The fight over, Moira turned to face their unexpected ally. She had been so busy defending her brother that she had not really noticed the man in detail before. His hair was the first thing that caught her eye. It was a tawny shade of red, streaked gold by the sun, a lion's mane, yet the reckless ferocity with which he had fought reminded her of her father's wolfhounds. Her flashing green eyes met the Englishman's clear-eyed gaze as she smiled. What she saw pleased her.

His eyes, thickly lashed yet masculine, intrigued her. Indeed, the set of his jaw, the strength of his face, his stance, his muscular grace were most definitely male. "My thanks," she whispered.

"My pleasure to come to the rescue of one who herself fought so gallantly."

There were crinkles around his eyes as he returned her smile, a mark of exposure to the sun-brightened ocean, she thought. Even if she had not seen him come from the direction of the ship, she would have known him to be a seafaring man—hardly an impoverished one, however, for his hosen were richly fashioned, and his boots, gloves and sword-belt were of the finest leather. Attached to the belt at his left side, his sword was an integral part of his attire. How relieved she was that he had come ashore armed.

Davie came forward to give his own heartfelt thanks. "I doubt if my sister and I could have lasted much longer had you not come along." In a gesture of friendship, he offered his hand, which was accepted in a strong grasp. "My name is David, David MacKinnon. And this is my sister, Moira."

Ryan bowed. "Ryan Paxton." His brows furled in puzzlement. "If you are a Scotsman, you most assuredly do not talk like one."

"I have not the burr of some of my countrymen. My mother was raised in France, and my father is half-English, raised north of the border." Davie looked out towards the sea. "You are a sailor?"

"Ship's captain. The *Red Mermaid*; the largest ship laying at anchor in your tumultuous bay belongs to me." Ryan could not keep his gaze from wandering to the young man's sister as he spoke. She was lovely. During the fighting she had shown strength and courage, but she seemed all softness and femininity now. A green-eyed, dark-haired sea siren who could ensnare even the most guarded heart. Once again he smiled at her.

Davie witnessed the heated look that passed his sister's way, and suddenly felt protective. "Well, it is growing late. We must go."

"It's not so very late, Davie. There is still enough sunlight on the horizon." Moira didn't want to leave, not yet. This man's power and avid stare were mesmerizing. She wanted to be in his company for just a while longer. "We do not want to be lacking in our manners. Captain Paxton—''

"Ah, but it is late. We must not dally any longer." He whispered in her ear, "You would not want to anger the King."

"Fie on the King," she whispered back beneath her breath. If only she had been granted a little more time, she might well have finagled an invitation to go aboard the sea-captain's vessel. At the moment, that desire far outweighed her fear of James. Besides, she doubted the King would even notice if they arrived late. Donald had told her how much James drank. By the time they arrived, he would probably be in his cups.

"*Moira!*" A sharp nudge to her ribs made her wince. Certainly Davie could be infuriating at times, ordering her about as if she were a child. And yet, unfortunately, he was right. They had tarried much too long already. Regretfully, she abandoned any protestations she might have made.

"We thank you again, Captain Ryan, and I wish a safe journey back home for you and your crew," she said instead.

Moira doubted she would ever see the English sea-captain after today. They came from two different worlds that had little chance of merging. Even so, that did not keep her from turning back to look at him—not once, but again and again—as she followed her brother homeward.

Chapter Five

EDINBURGH LIES on a series of hills on the southern shore of the Firth of Forth, surrounded by lofty hills on all sides except to the north, where the ground slopes gently downward. Ryan Paxton took in the view as he rode the so-called "Royal Mile" to the gates of Holyrood House. The dun-colored castle walls loomed in the distance against the steadily darkening gray sky. The walls looked strangely foreboding. He was anxious to greet King James cordially, deliver his missives, and then be on his way. The skirmish with the three Scottish ruffians on the shore reminded him that this land was not a place for the unwary. Because his mission was to be kept secret, he had left his crew behind—which made him regrettably vulnerable, a fact that he did not like in the least.

The hoofs of his horse clattered loudly against the pavestones as he rode forth. He had procured the black mare from a stable outside Edinburgh for a hefty price, but had wanted to arrive in style. If he were to be the Queen's messenger, he would at least make a great show of it. Good first impressions, he had found, were always beneficial. As an opportunist, Ryan was not averse to furthering his own goals. At the back of his mind was the thought of perhaps securing James's patronage for one of his voyages, were Elizabeth not responsive to his request. It was a thought that took an even deeper hold in his mind as he approached the gates of Holyrood.

The courtyard was full of horses, doves, fowl, and ricks of hay and straw. The waiting hounds yawned, not even deigning to bark as Ryan rode up. Dismounting, he gave his horse up to the hands of a groom, then knocked upon the thick wooden portal of the King's palace. At first, his arrival was greeted with suspicion and a hint of hostility, until he mentioned that he had been sent from Elizabeth. Upon that disclosure, he was immediately ushered up the dark, winding staircase to the presence chamber, a wood-paneled room hung with tapestries. His eyes swept over the room, hoping to find some clue to James's personality. The room was not opulent by Elizabeth's standards, but was tastefully furnished, filled with bright colors and objects of art. But it was more like a woman's room than a man's, Ryan noted. It was missing the show of arms, the swords, shields, dirks, and battle-axes that he might have expected a male ruler to display. But then James was quite young, little more than a boy, really. Perhaps he had just not yet fully developed to manhood.

"Ach, so we do hae a visitor!" The voice was high-pitched and loud, jarringly so. Ryan turned toward the door at the sound of the voice and found himself face-to-face with James.

"Your Majesty." In show of proper respect he bowed, his gaze traveling from the toes of the young King's boots to the crown of his head. What kind of man was this ruler of Scotland? That he would undoubtedly one day be King of England made Ryan all the more curious. For a brief moment, he appraised the King man-to-man. James had light brown hair, ruddy cheeks, and a nose that was perilously close to being a bulbous one. His blue eyes might have been a redeeming feature were it not for the distrustful gleam within them. Even so, he greeted Ryan Paxton enthusiastically.

"Rise! Rise! And take a chair." As he spoke, he plucked at the lace on his sleeve.

He was elaborately dressed in doublet, hosen, and tight-fitting knee breeches in shades of beige and honey. The large peascod belly hanging well over his belt made it difficult to judge his physique. Still, he did not seem to be a very virile youth. "Ach, it always thrills me so to hear from my cousin Elizabeth!"

Jarred into remembering his mission, Ryan held forth the missive. "The Queen sends her deep affection, and this."

James snapped it up. "Yea. Yea." He wasted no time in breaking the seal on the letter. Hastily his eyes scanned what was written there. "Four thousand pounds! *Four* thousand pounds? 'Tis a puny offering." He muttered a string of foul words that were better suited to a sailor than a king. Then, remembering himself, he forced a smile. "Ye will thank the Queen for me, eh? 'Tis just that I had been led to expect that I would be receivin' five thousand pounds." He read on further, jabbing at the parchment with his finger. "No' a sign of recognition that I am her heir, or to my acquisition of my father's lands in England." The King drew himself up stiffly. "I am no poor relative, I am the King of Scotland!"

Ryan thought quickly, trying to mollify the irate James. "Undoubtedly, this is but a preliminary to other negotiations." Walsingham had spoken of the need for keeping James content.

"Perhaps." The blue eyes darted back and forth in agitation, settling on Ryan's face for an unnervingly long time. Suddenly the King smiled as if he found favor with what he saw. "But I hae been a boorish host at best. I hae no' e'en offered ye up some ale."

Clapping his hands, he soon had a servant in attendance. The cherubic-faced boy left the room, but soon returned with two brimming cups, one for Ryan and one for the King. James hurriedly quaffed his mug, then ordered more, taking a seat on the intricately carved wooden chair that was his throne.

"I fear ye'll be thinkin' we Scots lack in manners. I didna e'en ask yer name."

"Ryan Paxton. Captain Ryan Paxton." Ryan was slower in his appreciation of the ale, savoring it.

James's arched eyebrows shot up questioningly. "A seacaptain?"

"Aye."

James was notably impressed. "Och, how I hae always had a longing to ride upon the sea. To be a mon who seeks adventure. It must be a fine life."

Ryan shrugged. "There are times when it is very fulfilling, but there are also times fraught with frustration. I have had a fine chance to travel all over the world, however."

"Hae ye been to China?"

"Aye."

The King's blue eyes were open wide. "To Spain?"

"Several times." Seeing a chance to further his ambitions, he added quickly, "And the New World. There is no lack of riches to be had there. A golden opportunity."

"The New World." The King giggled, forgetting his dignity for a moment and revealing his boyishness. "Oh, that I could dress myself as a cabin boy and sail wi' ye just once." The intrusion of two breacan-clad men caused James to stiffen. Squaring his shoulders, he lifted his chin haughtily. "Cameron. MacAulay."

"Yer guests are arriving, your Majesty. There is clamoring for yer presence in the hall."

James nodded. "Aye!" Turning his back on Ryan, the King followed the two men toward the door. The audience was over.

Ryan regretted the entrance of the two men. He had been on the brink of asking the King to visit his ship with the thought of a mutual venture in mind. Now he realized the chance was lost. Rising to his feet, he finished his ale, handed his empty mug to the serving boy, and walked slowly across the room.

"Captain!" Just when Ryan thought he had been forgotten, James turned around. "I would like to hear more aboot yer travels; I am giving a banquet tonight. Be there!" It was a command, not an invitation. Ryan knew it would be a dastardly insult to refuse.

"I am honored." His ship would not be able to set sail until the morning hours anyway. Perhaps it was better that he didn't have time to approach the King about sponsoring a voyage. He would have more time to prepare himself now.

"One of the servants will show you to a room where you can wash yer face and hands. Of course ye will stay for the night."

"Of course." One didn't say "no" to a king. With that thought in mind, he accompanied the steward up the winding stone staircase to his chamber.

MOIRA SLIPPED INSIDE her room, closing the door tightly behind her. She would have to hurry if she wasn't going to be late for the King's banquet. She fumbled in her wooden trunk through the folded garments, then remembered that Davie had suggested she wear her green velvet gown. She gathered it up and draped it over the bed, wondering why her hands were trembling. That man. The sea-captain, she thought. For some reason she just couldn't get him out of her mind. When he had smiled at her, something warm and magical had happened.

"Oh fie, Davie." She couldn't help wondering what might have happened if only her brother hadn't interfered. A totally improper path of reasoning for a young woman come to meet her fiancé, she thought. Silently scolding herself, she put the handsome English seaman out of her mind and concentrated on getting dressed.

Standing before the polished silver mirror, clad only in her chemise, Moira appraised her body. Too slim in the hips and much too tall. Maybe Iain Gordon would be able to match her lofty height. Well, she would soon find out.

Moira pulled on her petticoats and knitted stockings, then drew the yellow brocade undergown over her head, followed by the saffron kirtle. She needed help, however, in fastening the corset. From the door, she called to one of the serving girls—who proved to be a chatterer, with all of the latest maid's gossip, but who had a deft hand at laces.

"Ye hae such a tiny, tiny waist," the girl sighed, regretfully stroking her own ample girth. "Ye'll hae all the laddies' hearts."

"I'm only interested in pleasing one. I'm here to meet the man I am to wed," Moira announced proudly. She motioned to her green overgown, requesting the girl's aid in donning the heavy velvet garment. Moira wondered if it did not place too much emphasis on her bosom, for the bodice was full but snug against her breasts. Certainly her mother would never approve of such a wanton display. But her mother wasn't here, she reminded herself.

The young woman appraised Moira's appearance. "Yer future husband is a very lucky mon—" Using a brush, she stroked Moira's shining dark brown tresses, then wove them into a braid at the back, leaving loose the shorter, wavy front hairs to curl around her face. "Such bonnie hair, hinny." The braid was pinned atop Moira's head, and a small velvet cap balanced on the crown. Curiosity seemed to get the best of the girl. "But just who is the lucky laddie ye be dressin' up to meet?"

"Iain Gordon!" Moira announced proudly.

"Iain Gordon?" The serving girl's lips tugged down in a

frown. It was apparent from her expression of disgust that he was a man she did not admire.

"What is it?" Such a reaction to her fiancé's name startled Moira, but though she tried to find out the cause, the girl was loath to say a word. It seemed that there was at least one thing about which she would not gossip. Moira didn't press her, perhaps because she wasn't really certain she wanted to know what the girl had to say. A strange feeling gnawed at her insides, but she ignored it, telling herself that it was possible that the girl was just jealous. Perhaps she coveted Moira's future husband. Was Iain Gordon the kind of man who dallied with the chambermaids?

Moira opened the door and moved quickly down the winding staircase, so immersed in her thoughts that she ran headlong into the lithe frame of a man going the opposite way. "Omph!" In her desperation to gain her balance, Moira reached out, touching the man's firm, muscled arm. The man grasped her around the waist to help her keep her balance. She looked up and was stunned to find herself face-to-face with the very man who had come to her rescue at the quay—the sea-captain. "You!" she cried.

"Well, by my faith, what a pleasant surprise," he said with a wide grin, eyeing her up and down appreciatively as he released his hold. He took a step back for a better view, and it was obvious that he liked what he saw.

A strange little quiver danced up and down her spine at the boldness of his appraisal. His gaze was a heated caress as his eyes touched on her bosom. "What are you doing here?" she somehow managed to say.

"Had I known that I would be blessed with your presence, I would have come here just for you," he whispered huskily. If he was to be a guest at the King's banquet, it would be all the more stimulating to have a pretty girl at his side. This one had fascinated him right from the first.

Moira's hand was taken in his long, hard fingers. A slightly roughened thumb rubbed over the back of her hand, relishing its softness. He was a man who knew women well, and was all the more dangerous for it. The thought that ran through Moira's mind was that this was the kind of charmer her mother had warned her about many, many times. Even so, she was

loath to pull her hand away, though she did lift her head with
all the dignity she possessed to look him in the eye.

"Fie, sir. Such honeyed words are as false as a miller's
weights, I would wager."

He laughed softly at her show of spunk, then quieted. He
squeezed her hand warmly, entwining his fingers in hers as if
their hands were making love. "I came to speak with your
King," he said, after a long, silent moment. "He has done
me a great favor by asking me to stay, for now I have been
reunited with you." His well-arched brow traveled upward.
"I hope that there are no ruffians pursuing you here."

"None, sir." She was almost dazed when she realized that
she was looking directly at the firm strength of his lips, wondering if his mouth would be firm or soft. Such thoughts would
lead to no good. Apprehensively, she jerked her hand away
from his grasp. "We should join the others, lest all the seats
be taken." She started to walk away, but he followed her,
taking her hand again and placing it on his arm.

"I will walk with you," he said, his voice a deep rumble.
"Perhaps fate has destined that our paths should 'twine."

They entered the great hall and were met by the sound of
boisterous laughter and mumbled voices of those talking politics, business and war. The King's voice was loudest of all
as he told one of his many stories. The large room was bathed
in firelight and candle glow, which cast large shadows of the
revelers on the stone walls. Moira looked for her brothers'
familiar forms, but didn't see them. Undoubtedly, Davie was
having trouble getting Donald away from his studying.

"You were right. The hall is already crowded to overflowing." Ryan touched her elbow to lead her to a seat, a place
above the salt, as befitted her station. Though there was not a
seat next to her, he managed to sit nearby, with only a glow-
ering, stout Scotsman in between them.

The air in the hall, lightly misted with the smoke of coal
fires, stung the eyes. Ryan looked around him, curious as to
the Scottish ways. By Scottish custom, men and women ate
with their heads covered; only servants went hatless. Flemish
linen was spread over the long trestle table, upon which was
placed a great saltcellar, an evidence of wealth and the division
of rank. Young boys brought metal finger basins to the King's

guests. In truth, there was a crude elegance here that amused Ryan. He suspected James of making a bit of a show for his benefit.

The aroma of roasting meat in the air made Ryan aware of how famished he was. Turning, he could see servants carefully tending huge spits near the hearths, basting the browning meat with succulent spiced juices that dripped into the pans beneath. Ryan had oftentimes heard about the strict frugality of the Scottish court, but in matters of food, James did not seem to be miserly. Even so, as he looked in the direction of the dark-haired Scottish girl, he was hungry for far more than food. She was beautiful, more so with her lovely features illuminated by the light of the blazing wall sconces, flawless as an angel. Ryan had always been partial to women with dark hair, women of spirit. Ah yes, perhaps tonight would prove to be far more beneficial than he had first anticipated.

Chapter Six

THE GREAT HALL RANG with raucous laughter, yet the revelry had not yet reached its peak. James's guests had not had the chance to drink themselves into a stupor, Moira thought dryly. Donald had warned her about what to expect. For the moment, at least, it was somewhat tranquil in the hall. She hoped that it would stay that way tonight. In truth, she didn't want the Englishman to think of her Scots as drunken barbarians, as some of their visitors had been wont to say.

Oh, the Englishman! Though she knew she should ignore him out of deference to Iain Gordon, it was difficult. He was a charmer, making use of every chance he could to secure her attention. Leaning behind or in front of the stout man at her side, he engaged her in tidbits of conversation. He had even, when the man seated between them had momentarily left his place, squeezed her hand affectionately under the table, and Moira had once more succumbed to the dancing butterflies inside of her that his touch seemed to bring forth.

A procession of servants bearing food came out from the kitchen, the pantler with the bread and butter, the butler with the wine, beer and ale. Moira's eyes met the English sea-captain's over the rim of her chalice as she sipped her wine. Something in his gaze deeply stirred her, though she knew instinctively that she should have looked away. Perhaps it was because while everyone else in her family—and even those at James's court—treated her like a child, he was reacting to her as a woman. How could that not be exciting?

"Moira!" She was so intent on the Englishman that she didn't even notice her brothers' arrival until Davie tapped her on the shoulder.

Looking up, Moira saw a tall, lithe, curly-haired blond gentleman standing in between her two siblings. He was attractive, with wide blue eyes, long eyelashes and a cleft in his chin. Instinctively, she knew the man was Iain Gordon. He bowed stiffly. "I should hae waited until a later hour to make proper introductions, but I was of a curiosity, lassie," he said. "I was anxious to see ye up close." His eyes raked over her, but instead of the same tingling heat that the Englishman's assessing glance had brought on, this man's stare caused her to grow cold, perhaps because there was little warmth or friendliness in his eyes.

"As I told you, my sister is bonnie!" Donald said boastfully.

"And she is always sweet of temper," Davie lied.

"Aye!" Iain Gordon's eyes continued their roving, running from the curve of her neck to her shoulders, then lower, in much the same manner as though he were buying a new horse, Moira thought indignantly. "She is, as you say, very bonnie. She'll do." Strangely even his compliment sounded less than sincere, nor was his smile genuine. In fact, his manner sorely wounded Moira's pride. He didn't act as though he truly liked her. This was hardly the meeting she had expected, far from it.

I'm being unfair, she scolded herself silently. He was being polite, and she could not fault him there. It was an awkward moment, meeting him this way; she could hardly expect him to show gallantry or passion when they were being watched by a tableful of people. Once they would be alone, she had no doubt but that he would show her a much different greeting. Perhaps he was shy, like Donnie, inhibited by so many eyes. She had to give him a chance and not jump to unfair conclusions.

Sensing the tension, Davie tried to rescue the moment, maneuvering it so that Iain Gordon could sit beside his sister. Those whom he pushed aside glowered in anger, but he ignored them as he cunningly bribed one of the servants to arrange it so that Moira and Iain shared a trencher. Winking mischievously in her direction, he patted Donnie on the shoulder and led him away.

Moira sought for something to say to the man at her side. " 'Tis my first visit to Edinburgh," she said at last. He mumbled an answer, concentrating on a piece of beef as though he were a man half-starved. "Perhaps you might give me a tour of the city." It would give them time to be alone.

"I willna hae time."

Moira felt a blush stain her cheeks. "Oh, but I will be here for such a short while."

"My duties to James take up a great many 'oors."

"I see." Moira tried again. "Holyrood House is much larger than I thought it would be. My mother told me that it was once a guesthouse of the nearby abbey. Certainly a great deal has happened here."

"A great deal, lassie." He seemed to be a man of few words.

"It must be very exciting being one of James's councilors."

"Mmmmm."

Though she had certainly never been timid, he was a difficult man to carry on a conversation with. "My brother tells me that later, there will be dancing. I've tried to keep up on the latest steps, but perhaps you can teach me those which I have missed."

"I dunna dance!" he said sharply, putting an end to the matter. "The Church frowns upon such behavior, though James still allows it on occasion."

"I see!" Moira could not help but be offended by his manner. He acted as though her talking to him were annoying, nor did he even deign to ask her one question about herself. Fearing her temper might well get the better of her, and that she might make some glib comment which she would regret, she hastily turned away.

"He seems to be a surly brute. I fear you won't get much talk from him." The sea-captain's look was sympathetic. "Better to have conversation with a man who appreciates a woman of beauty." His white teeth gleamed, and his cheeks dimpled in a youthful fashion that tugged at Moira's heart.

"You are a bold one!" She laughed, staring into those deep brown eyes that regarded her so intently.

"I'm a man who knows what he wants and reacts accordingly."

"Oh—!" Nervously she tugged at the neckline of her gown, suddenly fearing that it was much too low. Certainly, he was looking at her as if she wasn't wearing a stitch. His heated appraisal seemed to strip her bare, yet after Iain Gordon's neglect, she found herself receptive to the Englishman's attentions. Perhaps Iain Gordon was just a bit too sure of her; betrothals sometimes did that to a man. Well, it might do him good to know that someone else found her pretty. With that thought in mind, she capitulated to the sea-captain's attentions. What harm could there be in just flirting?

Picking up an apple, she offered it to him, allowing her fingers to linger on it as he took the fruit from her. His were a man's hands, rough and callused, but somehow that made his touch all the more stirring. Oh, that he were her intended and not the man sitting at her side! Iain Gordon was dull, but the Englishman made a most stimulating companion. With an impish smile, she wondered what her mother and father would do were she to give her heart to an Englishman. After all, her father was half English, which meant she had English blood. Was the sea-captain a marrying kind of man? Looking into his eyes, she somehow doubted it.

The Englishman leaned around the hefty Scotsman and grinned at her. Moira smiled back. "I like your mouth curved up. A woman like you should always be smiling. It makes you look very pretty."

Moira dimpled. "Then by all means, I must keep of a cheery mood."

All sorts of dishes were placed before her. The trestle table sagged with large platters of venison, mutton, and beef. There were pastries of every kind—plum, cherry, apple pies, tarts and cakes. Even so, Moira hardly touched a bite, though she did drink a bit too much wine. All she could do was look at the broad-shouldered Englishman. Cups, flagons, and tankards were filled again and again as the feast went on for hours, but there was no reality for Moira except the sweet magic that was being stirred between the sea-captain and herself. Her pulse raced as she stole covert glances at the handsome man.

It's not too late, she thought with a smile. Her parents had given her the privilege of saying aye or nay to her upcoming nuptials; she could break it off. Perhaps she should refuse Iain Gordon. Certainly, he deserved it after the way he was ignoring her. Besides, her heart had been stolen, pirated tonight by a pair of dark brown eyes and a roguish smile. It wasn't possible,

was it? Such things didn't really happen, did they? Ah, yes.
Her head was spinning, though not entirely from the wine. She
felt hot and flushed, as though Cupid's arrow had suddenly
pierced her heart. She wondered what the Englishman would
think of that! Had he felt it too?

Lovely little minx, Ryan thought. It had been a long time
since he had felt such strong attraction to a woman. He wished
the others in the room would just disappear, for his hands
longed to caress the ripe firmness of her body, to strip away
the green gown and touch her velvet flesh. He immersed himself in her smile, hardly tasting what he ate despite his hunger,
nor really hearing the conversation around him.

When at last the dishes were cleared away, the long trestle
tables dismantled and set aside, he saw his chance. Putting his
hand on her waist, he drew the Scottish girl aside to stand with
him in the circle of the crowd as a troupe of tumblers in green
and gold spilled through the doorway into the hall. They came
leaping and jumping, performing wondrous tricks, juggling,
turning somersaults.

"Upon one of my voyages, I transported a troupe much like
this one across the sea to Venice."

"Venice! Oh, how I would love to go there one day."

"It is a most exciting place. Perhaps one day you will see
it." He tightened his arm around her, unaware of the narrow
gaze of Gordon, who watched them closely.

Four pipers appeared. A skirl of bagpipes announced the
music as the room was cleared for dancing. Suddenly remembering her betrothed, Moira looked in Iain's direction, but he
was involved in a discussion with the King. He certainly
seemed to care more about James than about showing her any
attention. Besides, he had coldly informed her that he didn't
dance. Well, so be it; little did she care. She was in a mood
to dance. Recklessly, Moira turned her attention to the Englishman, then suddenly she was in his arms.

He was tall, much more so than she, making her feel feminine and somehow fragile. His chin just touched the top of
her head; he was even taller than Iain Gordon. "I've always
relished dancing," he said. He simply held her as the music
first began weaving its spell, then slowly his strength moved
her across the dance floor. Moira felt his hand on her lower

back as his fingers exerted a gentle pressure. She found herself closer to him, her breasts lightly brushing against his hard chest. The heat from his body enveloped her, making it difficult to think clearly. Oh, what was happening to her?

"This is the newest dance in England." His voice was soft as velvet, stirring a chord within her as deftly as a harpist's touch. She felt his breath ruffle her hair as he whispered in her ear. The sensation tickled the whole length of her spine. She could feel her heart beating so loudly that she was certain everyone in the room could hear.

Suddenly, the music changed to a livelier pace. The lutes, viols, brasses, and woodwinds of the court musicians sounded the strains of a familiar dance. The Englishman led her in a round dance, twisting and whirling through the intricate maze of steps until they were out of breath and dizzy. When that was finished, he claimed her for a stately pavan that brought her back-to-back with the Englishman, then face-to-face again. Taking her hands in his as the dance finished, he kissed them, letting his lips brush her fingers as lightly as the wings of a butterfly.

Ryan wanted this woman, with a hot passion that threatened his self-control. He longed to make love to her, to claim her. Perhaps when he left on the morrow, he would take her away with him. She said she wanted to see Venice; maybe he would take her there. It was a thought that played on his mind.

"Take a walk with me. Now!" Her hair was coming loose from its braid. He reached out and brushed a few stray strands from her eyes. He liked the feel of her skin against his hand, she was so soft.

"A walk?" She was very tempted, but knew that if she were to leave, her brothers would be at her heels in an instant. "No... I... I—"

"When I leave tomorrow—" he began, only to be silenced as a man's blaring, angry voice cut through the air.

"Ye seem to think ye can make free wi' another man's woman, Englishman!"

"What?" Ryan turned around in surprise to find the blond Scotsman standing at his elbow, his arms akimbo. He was radiating hostility, his eyes burning coals of malice.

"I said, ye make free wi' another man's woman."

Ryan looked incredulously at Moira, then back at the Scotsman. "What are you saying?" What was this woman to him? Certainly, he had not seemed to make any claim when they were all seated at the table.

"This woman is to be my wife!"

"Your wife?" Ryan was stunned and angered. The silly little chit! Why hadn't she told him? Had she uttered even one word about it, he most certainly wouldn't have been so bold with her. "I didn't know—" His eyes blazed fire as he looked at the dark-haired Scots beauty.

"Well, ye do now, I would wager!" The blue eyes flashed a warning that was heeded. Although Ryan was certain he could best the slim young man, he remembered the warning he had been given about the Scots, that they were very conscious of loyalty to friends and clan. Were he to pick a fight he might very well end up in the ocean, with a knife in his back. Besides, if the man already held claim to the girl, he would not tarry here. There were too many unclaimed women in England.

The room was silent, and everyone stared. Moira could hear the sound of her breathing. Foolish girl, what had she done? Davie would be angry, Donnie would be shocked, her parents would lock her in her room when she returned for creating such a scandal. Worst of all, she could tell by his reaction that she had angered the sea-captain. With the hope of soothing his ruffled feathers, she sought him out with pleading eyes—only to have him turn his back on her. With an air of finality, he stalked away, leaving her to face her chastisement alone.

"Ye will no' dance or e'en cast yer eyes at other men, Moira MacKinnon." Iain Gordon's voice was shrill in his scolding. "I will no' allow it! No wife o' mine will be so shamelessly bold."

"I am *not* your wife yet, Iain Gordon!" Though Moira knew she should be contrite, she just couldn't keep her silence. Wrong she might have been in dancing so boldly with the sea-captain, but she felt that Iain Gordon was just as wrong to upbraid her before the King's guests, like a child about to be spanked. She just couldn't abide it.

"And well ye might no' be if ye don't learn to keep a bridle on yer tongue!" With an outraged snort, Iain Gordon stomped out of the hall, leaving Moira behind to sort out her feelings about the coming marriage.

Chapter Seven

THE NIGHT BREEZE PLAYED upon the trees like a harp, ruffling Moira's hair and caressing her face as she stood outside. She had sought the quiet of the garden to soothe her frazzled nerves. How dare Iain Gordon bluster about so! Her face was hot with outrage and stung pride as she recalled the scene in the great hall a few moments ago. All she had done was dance! Now his anger had marked her as a target of scorn.

"Moira!" It was Davie, come no doubt to heap his own accusations upon her head.

"I did nothing wrong!" she said defensively, turning her back.

"It was not what you did, but for what might have come about that Iain was angry." Gently, he laid a hand on her shoulder, turning her around to face him. "That Englishman was looking at you as though he was a cat and you a bowl of cream."

"I can't help how he looked at me!"

"Aye, but you could." Davie folded his hands across his chest. "I watched the way you stole glances at him at the table. You led him on."

She had and she knew it, but even so, she would not admit it. "I merely indulged in conversation and dared a dance or two."

"Moira!" His tone of voice was the same as when they were children and she had been caught at some mischievous deed or other. "This is me, Davie, you are talking to! You and I both know that you were charmed by that Englishman from the very moment you saw him."

Moira blushed. "I was, I'll admit it. But I wouldn't have

given him even a minute of my time if Iain Gordon had tried to show me at least a measure of courtesy. The truth is, he didn't act as if he favored me at all!''

''That is just his way. He wouldn't have reacted in anger had he found you wanting. Give him a chance, Moira.'' He sighed in a long, drawn-out breath. ''You're a headstrong lassie. Father's fault, and mine and Donnie's. You've held our hearts and so we've given you your way. But now it's time you learned what the real world is like.''

''And what is that?'' It sounded as if her brother was about to give her a lecture.

''Grim. Sometimes cruel.'' He took a step closer. ''A person, man or woman, has certain obligations to fulfill.''

''Obligations?''

''Yours is to marry; Donnie and I are to fulfill another vow.'' Cupping her chin with his hand, he tilted her face to look up at him. ''Life isn't a game, Moira. It's serious, perhaps more than you can know.'' His voice lowered to a whisper, as though talking more to himself than to her. ''Dangerous at times. The rules are not always ours.''

''Oh, Davie!'' She threw her arms around him, hugging him tightly, suddenly fearful of what he might be planning. Suddenly, she regretted what had happened in the hall, admitting to herself that it was mainly her fault. As Davie said, she always had been overly spirited. Perhaps she owed it to Iain Gordon to give him another chance. ''I'm sorry that I acted unseemly.''

''Your attentions to the Englishman wounded Iain's fierce Scots pride.''

''I'll go apologize to Iain if you think I should.''

''That's my lassie.'' Davie kissed her cheek, then gave her a playful swat on the rump. ''Go on, now.''

''And fie on the Englishman!'' In probability, the sea-captain would leave on the morrow, and she would never see him again. It was foolish to throw away her future, her family's honor, and her chance for a brilliant marriage because of a pair of dark, piercing eyes and a roguish smile. With that thought in mind, Moira went in search of her yellow-haired suitor. It was not too late to make amends. Besides, his very reaction had shown her that he was jealous. If he had succumbed to that emotion, then he must have felt some attraction to her, or so she reasoned.

Hurrying back through the pathways of the garden, Moira opened the side door to Holyrood House and slipped back inside. Upon seeing that Iain was not in the hall, she sought him out, wending her way through the corridors, going in the direction she had seen him take when he had exited so abruptly. Strange—the hallway was darker than usual. Perhaps James was carrying his frugality a bit too far. Stumbling on a loose stone, she put her feelings into words, and uttered an oath; then, seeing that one of the chamber doors stood ajar, she walked in that direction.

The night sea-breeze had played havoc with her already tousled appearance. Moira paused to straighten her hair and smooth her dress, wishing there were a mirror somewhere in sight. She didn't want Iain Gordon to be reminded of her lascivious behavior in the hall. Using a window to make an assessment of her looks, she paused momentarily, peering at the darkened glass. It was then she heard the laughter. Giggles to be exact.

"Oh, Iain!" she heard a voice say. "Ye are wondrous fair. A bonnie, bonnie mon!"

What was this? A cold feeling gripped Moira as she crept closer, approaching the door that stood partially open. Though she usually made it a practice not to snoop, she peeked inside nonetheless. James stood inside the room, leaning on the shoulder of the man who, by the attentions being granted him, was the new court favorite. The King's well-manicured hand was stroking Iain's blond curls in a gesture of the deepest affection; then, unaware that they were being watched, he leaned forward and kissed the young man on the lips as if they were lovers.

"God's blood!" Moira gasped, using an oath that was her father's favorite. She had sought Iain Gordon out to make amends, only to find him in the arms of the King. The very idea sickened her. Such things were forbidden by God's laws. So much for Davie's view on obligation. It had been gossiped that James preferred men; now she knew for certain that Iain indulged in a like vice. Turning her back in disgust, Moira vowed she would never marry the fop. Let him have the King— she wanted no part of Iain Gordon. She would tell it to Davie, her parents, Iain Gordon and even James himself if need be. She would never be Iain Gordon's bride.

RYAN PAXTON STRODE the gardens trying to calm his foul mood. That foolish Scottish girl had ruined all his well-laid plans. He was being shunned by all those within the hall as if he had the dreaded pox! They couldn't have damned him with their eyes any more if he had abducted the young woman. There were even a few in their cups who had tried to incite him to tussle. Only by his wits had he escaped a fight. Well, it would be the last time he made a show of being attracted to a woman before ascertaining if she had a husband, betrothed, or lover hovering about.

She should have told him; that was the thought that played over and over in his mind. Had she but mentioned the fact that she was soon to be wed, he would have sent nary a glance her way.

"Marry that ever-frowning Scotsman will she," he breathed. "Ha!" It served her right. They made a perfect pair. He told himself that he didn't care a whit, and yet knew deep down that it was a lie. There was something about that damned Scotsman that troubled him, made him loath to think of *her* snuggled in that one's arms. Yet it was none of his business. "I wish them every happiness," he said aloud. Besides, by tomorrow morning at high tide, he would be far away from here. He would never see the little dark-haired beauty again. Why did that thought not please him?

Ryan tried to refocus on the plan uppermost in his mind. His ship! James had shown interest in his voyages, enough to make him hope that the King might be persuaded to invest in such a venture. It was even possible that if the King were to take such an initiative, it might prod Elizabeth into making a like offer. The Queen was ever of a mind to make a profit; the competition would do her good. There was only one problem. Though Ryan had looked for him, James had seemingly disappeared, an occurrence for which he blamed the young Scottish woman. When that surly blond Scot sauntered off, James had followed, no doubt intent on calming the laird.

Ryan Paxton stalked about the garden like a man chased by the very devil. God's very bones, but she was still on his mind.

She haunted him like a sea siren. The image of her lying in his arms came to his mind and did not go away, no matter how he chided himself. She had been all softness and smiles in his arms. How could he forget?

He paced about, trying to calm his disquiet. Suddenly, as if she had materialized out of his dreams, he saw her standing a few steps away from him.

"You again!" With a swish of her skirts, she stood before him, pouting petulantly. "Captain Paxton!" Moira wanted to make amends, to explain to him the truth of the situation. Perhaps Iain Gordon had been her betrothed before, but not now! She had to make the Englishman understand. Perhaps there was still a chance that they could part friends, if nothing else. "Please hear me out."

Her voice was soft and soothing, and he longed to listen, but his heart was hardened by the thought that she belonged to someone else. "Haven't you done enough harm?"

"Captain—"

"Leave me," he said between gritted teeth.

A streak of stubborn pride caused her to hold her ground; he *would* listen. "I will not go until I have a chance to explain to you about tonight." Reaching out, she grasped his arm in supplication. "Let me tell you—"

A rustle in the undergrowth gave evidence that they were not alone. Like a rampaging wild boar, Iain Gordon plunged through the foliage. "Ye must be daft, or else ye long for a fight," he said. "I told ye before all assembled that this woman is mine. Did ye no' hear me?"

"Damn!" Ryan whirled around, braced for a fight, just as the golden-haired man took a step forward, a sword clenched in his hand.

"No!" Moira was horrified. "Iain Gordon, lay down your arms. There is nothing amiss here. I was just trying to talk to the captain." Besides, after what she had seen, what right did Iain Gordon have to criticize her behavior?

"Talk. Bah!" Iain Gordon brandished his weapon with deadly intent, but gave Ryan the chance to draw forth his own sword. "I've always wondered what it would be like to spill English blood. Now I will find out."

Fearing the outcome of such a battle, Moira stepped in front of the Englishman, only to be pushed aside. "I will not hide behind a woman's skirts." Ryan had just enough time to block the Scotsman's blow. "So, I see you will not talk reason."

"Nae!" Iain Gordon struck out again. The blow was parried just in time. The Scotsman lunged again with a cry of anger. Once again, the thrust was parried.

The sound of sword on sword rent the air as the two fought a furious battle, a test of strength and skill. Though Moira had at first worried about the sea-captain's fate, she had to admit that he was making a good show of his prowess. Reacting to the warning of his senses, his sword arm swung forward again and again as she watched, fascinated—the two men were fighting over her, which was exciting. She hoped that the sea-captain would win.

"Halt!" James's shrill voice pierced the air. "I willna hae fighting here." It looked as though the battle would not progress long enough to determine the victor, for James, horrified of weapons, quickly came forward to stop the scuffle.

"He didna heed my warnin'!" Iain Gordon glowered, but put down his sword.

"Ach, I will hae no bloodlettin' nonetheless. I dunna want the Queen of England to hear word that we are uncivilized." James did, however, give in to Gordon's urgings that the Englishman be locked in one of the tower chambers for the night on the pretext of waiting until tempers cooled.

"Locked up? By God!" Ryan Paxton was enraged, such that his blood felt very close to the boiling point. He'd come to England on Walsingham's errand, only to be coerced into a quarrel because of a woman's scheming. She'd used him to make her young swain jealous, he thought, growing more irate. His pride was sorely pricked. As he was led away, he vowed to get even with the little wench at the very first opportunity.

Chapter Eight

THE SOFT RAYS of the full moon filtered through the leaves of the trees, casting eerie shadows on the stone wall that unnerved the young man as he waited for his brother. At last, the soft cry of greeting confirmed that his wait had not been in vain. "Donnie!"

"I thought you weren't going to come, Davie. I was of a mind to leave." Donald was still a bit puzzled as to why his brother had insisted they meet by the ruins of the old abbey instead of in the quiet of their room. But that was soon explained; it was imperative that they not be overheard. The walls of Holyrood had ears. Here, only the ghosts would be able to listen.

"Iain Gordon created quite a stir. He picked a fight with the Englishman over Moira. You know how squeamish Jamie is, how he dislikes a show of weapons. Our plans might all be put to ruin if James decides to keep him locked up."

"A fight?" The less daring of the two twins was intrigued. "Swords or fists?"

"Swords."

"How exciting!"

"Dastardly is the word, if the sea-captain is detained, Donnie! Then there will be no hope of our getting passage to England." David's voice was a hush. "We'll have to wait until another English ship comes in, and that will mean delay in coming to Mary's aid."

"By God!"

"I ought to have Moira's head. All would have gone well if she hadn't set her cap for the Englishman. You know how possessive Iain is of anything he considers his—even if he doesn't really want it.''

"I know. He nearly thrashed me once when I rode his horse to go hunting." Donald made a face. "I don't like him at all. Too filled with himself to be a good husband to our Moira. I wish Father would reconsider.''

Davie shrugged. "If he doesn't, I have the feeling that Moira will. Upon thinking the matter over, I believe Iain and our sister are ill-matched. Iain has a short temper and Moira can goad a saint to fury. I gave her sound advice but I think now I was wrong." He contemplated the matter, then directed his thoughts elsewhere. "But about our journey—it's fate that we go, Donnie. I know it is. When I first laid eyes on the ship and the captain came to my aid, I knew it.''

"We must not be hasty—"

"Oh yes, we must." Davie flipped the end of his breacan jauntily over his shoulder. "One of James's councilors received a message from Walsingham requesting that two Scotsmen be sent to the English court. What better men than we, who have English blood? I have hope of convincing James to send *us* back to the English court. It will fit in with our plans. And quicker by sea than riding, as we had first proposed.''

"A sea voyage. How I would love to skim the ocean, but . . . but, Davie—" Donnie's timidity showed through his bravado.

"Leave it all up to me, little brother. I'll make certain you come to no harm." Though they were twins, Davie always made great show of having been born first.

"But what if James won't let us go?" Donnie was of a more practical nature. "He needs us here, you know." He knew them to be among the few the young King could trust, and he almost hated to turn against him, even for this venture. "He might say no.''

Davie laughed, with a show of boldness. "You know that James can be twisted hither and thither by almost anybody he comes in contact with. I've always been able to handle him. I'll make Jamie see that sending us to England is good diplomacy. Elizabeth is said to have an eye for daring young men. With us, there will be two.''

"Elizabeth!" Donnie made a face. It had always been a sore

point with him that James seemed to adore the sworn enemy of his own mother, Mary, Queen of Scots. He often offered praise to the English queen as a mentor due extreme respect. "Fie on her."

"In this, the English queen will be of help to us. Little will she know that we've come to free her most illustrious prisoner."

"And just what are we to do when we get there?" Donnie was wary of his brother's schemes. Ever since they were boys, Davie had gotten Donnie in the stew with his plots and plans.

"There is a priest there—John Ballard, who we must contact. He is staunchly in favor of freeing Mary, or so my sources tell me."

"John Ballard," Donnie repeated, knowing well that it would be he who must make mental note of the name. His memory was better than his brother's.

"And there are others there. Hundreds and hundreds of Englishmen in northern counties who favor Mary Stuart over that bastard-born Elizabeth."

" 'Tis treason of which you speak."

"I prefer to call it a rescue mission." Davie grasped his brother by the shoulders.

"We'll end up on a gibbet!"

"We've taken a vow. We must do it." Davie appealed to his brother's sense of fairness. "It is not seemly that Mary remain Elizabeth's prisoner. Mary came to Elizabeth for aid, but her own cousin betrayed her. It is time the Queen of Scots was freed! The northern Catholics feel the same. They'll help us."

"And maybe we can get Spain and France behind us." Donnie was caught up in the mood.

"And the Low Countries."

"Elizabeth will rue the day she put a Scotswoman in a cage."

"Aye!"

"Aye!"

"The moment I saw that English ship, I had a plan. It's as if God sent that sea-captain here, Donnie. It's a sign, I tell you. We must move now, or forever damn ourselves as cowards."

They initiated the boyhood gesture they always used when sealing a bargain. Spitting on their palms, they slapped each other's hands, right hand against left, then left against right. "We'll free Mary from her prison, or our name is not MacKinnon." Thus agreed, they returned to the castle to seek out James.

Chapter Nine

IT WAS DARK in the windowless room, except for the flickering light of one lone taper. Ryan Paxton lay rigidly on his side in the large canopy bed, his mouth tightened in anger as he watched the glow of the candleflame. He was a prisoner, by God. A *prisoner*. Though he wasn't in a dungeon, the thick, locked wooden door was nonetheless a reminder of the barrier between him and his freedom. So much for James's hospitality.

"And so much for any chance I might have had to win the Scottish king's patronage," he grumbled. Lost because a pert young woman wanted to make her future husband jealous. He'd been used. He'd fallen under the spell of a laughing mouth and wide green eyes. Oh, how that thought rankled. Hearing laughter outside his door, he thought that the drunken chuckles might as well be directed at him. He, and not the King's buffoon, was the greatest fool.

Ryan turned over on his back and closed his eyes. Sleep. That's what he wanted, what he needed. There was nothing he could do tonight. He would rest, and then in the morning come to a decision as to what to do. Surely even James would not dare keep an Englishman confined for long. That, at least, was a comforting thought.

It was hot and stifling in the confines of the bedchamber. Tossing and turning upon the feather bed, he found that slumber was as elusive as escape. Over and over again, he relived the swordfight in his mind. He would have won, of that he was assured. Oh, how he wished the King had not interfered! The Scotsman had needed his comeuppance, and he would have been the one to grant it. Perhaps, then, the bold young swaggerer would have been less prone to picking fights. At the back of his mind was the wish that he could have proved himself the better man before the pretty Scotswoman's eyes.

Lying on his back, arms folded and head resting on his hands, he gave vent to such fantasies, amusing himself with different endings to the tale. He envisioned the girl pleading for her betrothed, throwing herself on Ryan's mercy. Another time, he imagined himself carrying the girl away. To the victor should go the spoils of any battle. Strange how he always ended each version of the night's happenings by claiming the girl himself. The more fool he!

"Damn her. Damn her, I say!" he muttered. Her face haunted him, and he could not get her out of his mind. It was a very dangerous sign, a reminder that he was taken with the girl.

In frustration, he sprang from the bed to pace the confines of the small room. Back and forth, back and forth, monotonous and tiring. And all the while the candle burned down to a nub, at last leaving Ryan in total darkness. Hoping exhaustion would aid him in securing his slumber, he returned to bed, but couldn't sleep no matter how hard he tried.

"A curse on Walsingham and his silly errand." Now it was the Queen's spymaster who came under his wrath. If he hadn't come to Scotland in the first place, he never would have met the girl, never would have sparred with her betrothed. He'd be sitting in his tavern enjoying a mug of ale, and not lying here behind locked doors. Walsingham! Well, that one had gotten his wish. The missives had been delivered, one to the King and the others to the appropriate fellows. Ryan supposed that some plot or other was afoot, but at the moment didn't really care what was planned. Far better to mind one's own business than to interfere, else he might be facing a far more harrowing fate.

Ryan didn't really know how much time had gone by, but suddenly noted that Holyrood House stood in total silence, the revelers at last abed. He saw a light beneath his door. Sunlight, or a reflection of lighted torches? Could it possibly be morning already? A rattle of metal sounded outside his room, then the scratch of a key in the lock. Bolting to a sitting position, he awaited his visitor. Perhaps it was one of James's guards come to set him free. He was surprised to find it was the King himself.

James entered, shutting the door firmly behind him. At first he said nothing, simply stood with his back against the door, leaning on it as though he were either weak or inebriated. Remembering the drunken laughter, Ryan assumed it to be the latter.

"I am sorry to hae locked ye up," the King said at last. "But 'twas for yer own protection."

Ryan looked at him sourly. "My protection. Strange, but I seem to remember myself doing quite well against your Scots."

"Aye, but had ye won, it might hae caused a tussle." He rolled his eyes, his head moving restlessly from side to side. A nervous tick, Ryan supposed. "Iain Gordon has many friends here at Holyrood. I wouldna hae wanted to send my condolences to Elizabeth upon yer death."

"I wouldn't have lost to any man," Ryan responded indignantly.

"But ye might hae lost out if there were several. We Scots are clannish in all matters. Already, there is the taint of blood at Holyrood. I wouldna want yer blood to be spilled as well."

"Rizzio?" Ryan asked, remembering the gruesome tale of Queen Mary's Italian minister, who had been set upon and murdered.

"Aye." James shuddered as though the very thought unnerved him. Perhaps he remembered that he had been in his mother's womb and might very well have been killed along with her that night. "I had ye put in here to guard ye, no' for any punishment." He attempted a smile in obvious hope of being pleasant. "Am I forgiven?"

"Yes. No harm done, your Majesty." What else could Ryan say? Besides, perhaps it had been for the best after all. Had the swordfight continued, and Ryan won as he supposed he would have, Elizabeth would have been furious when she heard. Brawling was one thing strictly forbidden by the English queen. And if by some chance of fate that he had lost. . . .

"Ye will be free to leave this morning." James thrust a piece of parchment in Ryan's hand, one affixed with the King of Scotland's seal. "Ye can take this back to Elizabeth if ye will."

Ryan nodded. "It will be done. Whatever I can do to accommodate you, you have only to ask." Ryan saw an opening for a business venture. "My ships are ever at your disposal."

"Indeed? How very kind of you." James put his hand on Ryan's shoulder in easy familiarity. "Then I won't feel I'm being overly forward in asking a favor of you."

"A favor?" Ryan backed away, ill at ease suddenly.

James's brows drew together. "I want to send two of my young Scotsmen wi' ye."

The King must surely be drunk to make such a suggestion, Ryan thought wryly. "What?" A pair of wild, brawling, and ever-fighting Scots was all he needed.

"I hae two bold young laddies who I feel will do me well as emissaries to my cousin Elizabeth's court." James was perfectly aware of what he was saying, not in his cups at all. Ryan noted that it was the restless movement of his head, his weak legs and rolling eyes that made him appear so, but the man was cold sober. "I would like to hae them sail wi' ye when ye go."

"Oh, no!" Ryan shook his head. "No." He didn't like the sound of it. "I never carry human cargo."

James was taken aback. "Ach, but yer own Walsingham suggested it in one of the missives ye brought wi' ye."

"Walsingham?" It figured. If only that sly bastard had let Ryan in on what was planned.

"He proposed an exchange of sorts." James gesticulated with his hand, putting up two fingers. "I send two Scotsmen and he in return sends two Englishmen to live at my court. Perhaps it will bring our two countries into a closer understanding of each other."

"It would be my hope." Ryan knew that he was cornered. He couldn't refuse, lest he appear to be uncooperative in the matter. "Two young Scots. I hope the man I sparred with will not be one of them."

James threw back his head and laughed. "Nae, though it might prove to be interestin' to see who arrived in England in one piece."

Ryan's answering smile was forced. Oh, how he hated to be forced into any action—most of all by Walsingham. "Then, by all means, I offer the hospitality of my ship and my crew for their comfort."

"In anticipation of yer agreeing, I hae already made arrangements to send them to yer ship. They are packing up their trunks at this very moment.'' He patted Ryan on the back. ''Ye will like them well. They are good laddies. Donald and David MacKinnon are their names. Twins.''

''Twins.'' Twice as much trouble as he had bargained for. ''Then so be it. I won't sail until they're safely aboard.'' He bowed low. ''Your Majesty.'' He had been anxious to leave these ever-feuding Scots behind when he returned to England. But now he'd be bringing trouble with him.

Chapter Ten

FAINT STREAKS OF SUNLIGHT broke through the heavy clouds, enough to radiate light, but not enough to give off any heat. The air was heavy and damp with the moist sea air. Clutching her cloak tightly around her shoulders, Moira tried desperately to keep warm as she looked out at the broad expanse of shimmering blue water lapping at the shore. The changing shades and colors—turquoise, sapphire, and indigo—of the vast sea—reminded her of an artist's palette. The ocean was beautiful and serene, except for the splashes of foam that curled around the rocks.

Moira had come to the shore to say farewell to her brothers, knowing that it would be a poignant farewell. London. How far away it sounded! The immense bulk of the English ship riding at anchor loomed ahead, reminding her that her brothers would be sailing away very soon. Davie had successfully cajoled James into letting the brothers go to England. Last night, her brother had come to her room and, in a burst of boastful pride, told her of his plans. Before a fortnight was over, the captive Scottish queen would be free, or so he had promised.

There had been no dissuading her brothers, though she had tried. Davie was adamant in his determination, and as usual Donnie followed his brother's lead. "We'll make of ourselves great heroes," Donnie was saying now.

"Or find yourselves minus your heads!" Moira countered, her face etched with concern.

"We'll be careful." Davie was cocksure of himself, a dangerous sign.

"Elizabeth is a crafty one. You are no match for her," Moira scolded, taking on a motherly tone. Though older than she, her brothers looked vulnerably young standing there—but caught, their youth would not aid them. The headsman's axe fell on all those deemed traitors, be they old or young.

"We won't be alone," Davie assured her. "There are hundreds and hundreds of English Catholics just waiting to rise up in Mary's defense if but called upon. 'Tis Elizabeth who should be wary." He kissed her on the cheek. "And what of you, sweet sister? Are you going to marry Iain Gordon?"

"No!" She didn't want to elaborate. Donnie and Davie had enough on their minds. Besides, there was something humiliating about telling them what she had witnessed between the King and her betrothed. "I'll not have a brawler. I guess you might say I've not met the right man yet, and until I do, I'll stay a single maid."

"And what of the English sea-captain?" Davie teased. "Shall I try to convince him on the voyage that he needs a Scottish bride?"

Moira's face flamed. "Davie!" She was not in the mood to be badgered, even in jest. Not after last night. The look on the Englishman's face proved all too clearly the loathing he felt for her. He hadn't understood Iain's blundering, and blamed her for what had happened.

Davie threw his hands up with a shrug. "Just trying to be helpful! But if you don't like him—"

"I don't!" she lied. She quickly steered the conversation to other matters. "Mother and Father will be furious that you didn't consult with them before sailing off to London. How unfair of you to leave to me the matter of telling them."

"Father will take the news much kinder from you than from me. You always were his favorite." Seeing her shiver, Davie reached for the clasp of his cloak, but Moira denied his noble gesture.

"I'll be all right. 'Tis you who will need it for your journey." A soft sob tore at her throat at the thought of her brothers going so far away, but she bit her lower lip to stem the tide of her misery. She had never cried in all her life and would not begin now. She'd prove to the twins that she was every bit as brave as they. "Have you forgotten anything?" she asked quickly.

"I don't think so." Donnie took her hand and squeezed it

tightly. "I have my crucifix and my clothing. I even have my books so I can keep occupied while Davie is being bold." Moira could hear the rumble of the carts bringing the trunks and barrels to the dock. If one were to judge from the baggage her brothers were taking with them, they planned on a long visit.

"You will take care of yourself?" Succumbing to her emotions, Moira clutched at Donnie, burying her face in his shoulder.

"I will!"

Moira hugged one brother, then the other, and with a last embrace, they took their leave of her. She watched in sadness as her brothers settled themselves in the small boat that would take them to the *Red Mermaid*, the Englishman's ship. Soon he would only be a memory to haunt her dreams as she strode the corridors of her father's hall. The thought made her sigh. How strange that things had turned out so differently than she had expected when she had first come to Edinburgh.

Wistfully, she began her walk back to the town of Leith, from whence she would return to Edinburgh, and paused only when overcome with thirst. The salt air, she supposed. Usually she would have drunk water but, seeing the wooden sign of a small tavern in the distance, she decided on a more fearsome spirit. Ale was what she wanted; it had been an emotional morning. Men partook of strong drink to drown their sorrows— why not she? Putting up the hood of her cloak, she reached for the door handle, wondering what her brothers would think if they saw her now. Decent young women didn't go to taverns, much less alone. Perhaps that was what made it all the more adventurous.

At the sound of the creaking door, the tavern keeper, a rotund man with flaming red hair, looked up but seemed not to care that she was a woman. Opening the door wide, he motioned for Moira to follow him, and led her to a seat at a corner table. Lowering her voice, Moira ordered a drink, then sat back in the shadows.

"Davie and Donald are lucky to be males," she whispered to herself. Indeed, they were doing exactly what she wanted to do. London—how she had dreamed of seeing it one day! Ah, a woman's lot in life was tiresome, always at the mercy of some man or other, she thought, feeling a bit sorry for herself. First the father, then the husband, and last of all, the son, with nary a chance to be free. Even her mother's life had revolved around her men.

Moira leaned forward as she took a gulp of her ale, imagining what a scandal it would cause if she were to return to Holyrood half-tipsy. What would Iain Gordon think then? The question made her smile. In truth, it would serve him right. A sudden burst of drunken laughter from across the tavern seemed to acknowledge her thoughts.

Suddenly she stiffened, squinting against the dim light of the room. Was she imagining it, or did she see one of the young thugs who had accosted her brother yesterday at the shore? Curiosity won out over caution as she stood up and moved closer. It was that ruffian and one of his companions.

"They're on the ship. I saw them wi' me very eyes," the young Scot was saying.

Ship, Moira thought, tuning her ears to the conversation. What were they talking about? A flash of intuition told her she should listen.

"Aye, I'll be lookin' forward to seein' David MacKinnon fall. He'll be swingin' from a gibbet before a month is up, I would wager." Throwing back his head, the young ruffian laughed heartily, evilly.

Moira listened, horrified, as the drunken revelers outlined the plot that had been hatched. Her brothers had been set up as scapegoats by James, who knew well of their loyalty to Mary Stuart. He had encouraged them to sail to London, knowing they had it in their minds to initiate an attempt to free his mother; James felt certain that the plot would fail. It was his way of vindicating himself for allowing his mother to have languished in captivity for so long. James had it in mind to adamantly deny having any part in the matter for Elizabeth's benefit, while convincing those diplomats of France and Spain that he *did* initiate the plan. It was a tricky game of intrigue, one which he felt he could not lose.

No, Moira thought, it would be her brothers who would be the losers here. The gamble they made was with their lives. Dear God! Moira realized that her brothers were about to be caught in a trap. That James himself was involved made it doubly lethal. She had to warn them, before the ship sailed. Donnie and David had to be told of the plan that was afoot.

Thrusting her ale mug into the hands of a startled tavern-maid, Moira raced out of the place and took to her heels, running all the way to the shore. The English ship still anchored in the harbor was the most welcome sight in all her life. It was not too late after all. A mist of tears stung her eyes as she whispered a prayer of gratitude. But how was she going to get aboard before it sailed away? It was a question that bedeviled her as she stared out at the unfurling sails of the *Red Mermaid*. She hadn't much time.

Her attention was centered on the ship that was so close and yet so far away from her. In desperation, she thought of swimming the distance, but knew the water was much too cold. Hiding in a trunk or barrel? No, she might suffocate. If she died, there would be no one to warn her brothers. As though in answer to her prayers, a small group of fishermen seemed to offer the answer. A boat—she'd pay one of the men to row her to the English ship. She'd warn Donnie and Davie and then return to shore. It seemed amazingly simple.

Chapter Eleven

A CLOUD PASSED in front of the sun as the young fisherman, silver weighing heavily in his pouch, rowed out to sea. The boat rocked up and down, and back and forth, causing Moira to reconsider her daring deed. She watched the waves warily. The ocean was rough, but she had to bolster up her sagging courage. Just the thought of her brothers coming to injury goaded her to carry on. She had to warn them! There was no other choice.

Moira clung to the side of the tiny vessel, hoping against hope that they could make it on time. Already, the anchor had been hoisted and the *Red Mermaid* was preparing to sail. She could see the sailors swarming across the deck and climbing the rigging as they made ready to leave the Scottish waters.

"Hurry! Faster!" she pleaded. Picking up another set of oars, she aided in the quest, pushing and pulling until she thought her arms would fall out of their sockets.

At last, the rowboat pulled alongside the mammoth vessel, just close enough so as not to cause undue attention. Moira had heard about a foolish sailor's custom that it was unlucky to have a woman on board. God's whiskers, what a silly superstition. And yet it made keeping out of sight a necessity, lest this journey be all in vain.

Taking off her cloak, Moira cursed her garments, wishing that she had gone to see her brothers off in hosen and breeches. Slipping over the side of the fishing boat, she found that her skirt and farthingale severely hindered her and threatened to drag her down. Uttering an oath that was far from maidenly, she stripped off her linen-and-wire undergarments and cast them adrift in the ocean. Swinging her body toward the ship's curving hull, she grasped for a rope dangling from the stern where the cargo had been loaded and pulled herself up to the carved balustrade, part of the gilded ornamentation decorating the stern. Climbing over the railing, she kept to the shadows as she searched for her brothers.

They were as difficult to find as a needle in a pile of straw! It was much like a game of hide-and-seek. The search was made more delicate by the fact that she couldn't take a chance on being seen. A woman's presence would cause a stir. Another confrontation with Captain Paxton was to be avoided at all cost, for she was certain that, in his mood, he would order her off his ship immediately.

Moira ducked into the shadows and hid behind a large pile of rope as the object of her thoughts walked by, issuing his orders. Dressed in a plain leather jerkin that emphasized the width of his shoulders, coarse sailcloth trousers which hugged his muscular thighs, and with his shirt-sleeves rolled high above the elbows to expose his strong arms, Ryan Paxton looked very formidable. Balancing himself against the rocking and swaying of the deck, he shouted at his men to set sail for London. Heart pounding, every nerve in her body vibrantly alive, Moira watched and waited for him to move away. Only then did she come out of hiding.

Glancing around her, Moira tried to get her bearings. She'd never been on a ship before, but that didn't daunt her; she had to find Donnie and Davie! Two rough-looking seamen loitered near the cargo hold, and Moira bit her lip to keep from calling out for their help in finding her brothers. No, she had to do it alone. She couldn't trust anyone. But having come this far, how was she to proceed without being detected? Time was running out. Soon the ship would be skimming the waters, and she had to succeed in her errand before that.

It was a difficult mission she had embarked upon. There were so many sailors, too many eyes that might spot her. Moira despaired of ever finding her brothers as she darted in and out of hiding places. Just as she was about to give up, she spotted them standing on the poop deck, scanning the shoreline. Summoning her courage, Moira bolted from her cover and ran across the deck to where they stood.

"Moira!" Davie couldn't have been more surprised had she

dropped down from Heaven. "What are you doing on the ship? Go back, little sister."

"I've come to warn you." Hurriedly, she pulled them behind one of the large masts. "James is not the friend you think him to be." The story came out in a gasp. "I saw the three men who accosted us, Davie. They were talking in a tavern about how James allowed you to go to London knowing full well what you intend." Fearing they might be overheard, she didn't fully explain, but knew Davie would know what she was inferring. "He wants you to fail for devious reasons which include his hope of keeping diplomatic ties with she who wears the crown."

"James would let us walk right into a trap?"

"Precisely! You must be careful! Be doubly cautious in your dealings lest you be betrayed." The warning given, Moira kissed and hugged her brothers one last time. "Be careful!"

"We will. Now be off with you!" Davie gave her a playful pat on her backside, his favorite way of teasing.

"There's a fishing boat waiting below to take me back." She laughed. "I've had my adventure for the day, but now I can rest easily, knowing that you have both been forewarned." With a jaunty wave, she strode across the deck and out of their sight, caring little if she was seen now. Her bravado proved to be a costly mistake.

"A woman!" Three sailors gave chase. Not knowing their intentions, Moira ran. The pounding of booted feet told her she was being pursued, but running as though she were being chased by the devil, she sprinted far out of their reach.

She had to get away, more out of a sense of pride than a feeling of real danger. The sailors were only going to force her to abandon ship, which she intended to do anyway, but the idea of being caught up like a ragged thief was humiliating. One punishment she just couldn't face was to suffer the Englishman's scorn again. He would undoubtedly think she was trying to stow away. Knowing him, he would not even let her explain.

In desperation, she took refuge in the only available hiding place, a large, empty barrel. Replacing the lid and securing it tightly, she suppressed a laugh as she heard the sound of footsteps pass by, then stop in obvious confusion.

"Where did she go?" she heard a deep voice ask.

"Over the side, if she knows what's good for her."

"She just vanished."

"Your ugly face frightened her away, Gabriel."

"Shall we look for her?" The grating sound of boxes and barrels colliding and being pushed aside told Moira that they were still searching for her.

"Not a trace. I think she must have been an illusion. We've been too long at sea, Stephen."

"Shall we tell the captain?"

"No, he'll think we're bait for Bedlam. Besides, there's work to do. You know what the captain said. He wants all this cargo down below."

It was stuffy and cramped inside the barrel, but Moira felt smugly victorious and ignored her discomfort. This was a story to one day tell her grandchildren. She waited a few moments until silence reigned once more, then slowly reached up to touch the lid of the barrel. I had best get out and back to the boat, she thought. It was then that her world was suddenly upended. "God's nightgown!" she breathed.

"This barrel goes below!" The quiet exploded with noises of various magnitude.

Her stomach threatened her with nausea as the barrel was swung up in the air. Through the slits in the wood, she could see a rope being tied around the small barrel; then she was suddenly swaying to and fro. Only with the greatest effort did she suppress a scream. Ignoring her lurching stomach, she forced herself to remain calm. Hysteria would only add to her troubles.

The barrel was set down with a thud a few moments later. Moira heard the sound of retreating footsteps, and there was silence again. After counting to twenty, Moira slowly raised the lid. Casting her eyes over the cases, boxes, barrels, bales, and trunks that surrounded her, she realized that she was in the hold of the *Red Mermaid*. Scrambling out, she felt panic come over her as she stumbled towards the door. Reaching the thick portal, she beat her fists against it in an effort to alert the crew that she was down below. But though she pounded the door until her hands hurt, no one came to investigate. A wave of helplessness washed over her. For the first time in her life, her daring had gotten her into serious trouble from which it appeared there was no escape.

Looking out of the tiny porthole, Moira watched as the shore disappeared from sight. In shock, she sat down on a sack of grain, trying as best she could to make herself comfortable. She was on her way to London, and there was nothing she could do.

Chapter Twelve

THE AFTERNOON SUN cast its reflection on the waves. With the coast of Scotland far astern, the *Red Mermaid* headed southward, white sails flapping in the wind, speeding the ship towards its destination. Ryan Paxton stood at the rail, looking out to sea. Freedom—ultimate freedom, he thought, brushing a hand through his wind-ruffled hair. It was so much more gratifying to stride the deck of a ship than to walk the stifled hallways of Greenwich. It felt good to be unencompassed by walls or the strict discipline of society.

Balancing himself against the rocking and swaying of the deck beneath his feet, he laughed as a wave sent salt spray into his face. I even relish the taste of the ocean, he thought, licking the water from his lips. This was where he wanted to be.

"I envy you, Captain. Someday, I too would like to sail the ocean."

Ryan turned around and smiled when he saw the dark-haired Scots youth come to stand at his elbow. Dressed in hosen, trunk hose, and doublet, the young man might have looked English were it not for the long swath of plaid he so proudly wore. The garment flapped snappishly in the breeze.

"It is a life far different from any other, that I will admit," Ryan said. "But it is only for those strong in mind and body."

"I am both!"

Oh, he was cocksure, Ryan thought. Just as he had been at that age. He couldn't suppress a grin. "Even so, it is not as easy as you would suppose. No man starts out a life at sea as captain. There is much to learn. Being a sailor is hard work."

"That is true of anything a man undertakes." A fiery glow

came into his eyes. "But somehow, as I gaze out at the ocean, it seems to me that there couldn't be a better life than this."

The other dark-haired youth voiced quite a different viewpoint as he came up to stand at Ryan's other side. "I am anxious to reach this London of yours; I have no great liking for the sea." His words were a reminder of this morning's wild storm, a gale that had brought forth Donald MacKinnon's fear. "Too turbulent."

"The ocean doesn't bother me." David MacKinnon gripped the railing, letting the wind whip at his face. "I think it's exciting."

"Dangerous," Donald interjected, looking down in awe at the tumultuous waves. "I'd much rather let others follow such a calling."

Ryan smiled at both young men. Far from being wild Scots, the two youths had proved themselves to be interesting young men, as different as night and day, despite the identity of their personages. One young man was all boldness and daring, the other caution and thoughtfulness. He'd enjoyed the voyage, short though it was. He nearly hated to see it end.

"How much longer before we're there?" the quieter twin asked.

"We've made good time. A few more hours." Ryan had an idea. "How would you like to take a turn at the tiller?"

"Tiller?"

" 'Tis a device, a lever used to turn the rudder of the ship from side to side. Steering a ship can be quite stimulating."

"Me? Steer the ship?" David MacKinnon's enthusiasm was contagious. As he led the young man to where the tiller stood, Ryan found himself remembering the first time he'd been granted the privilege of steering a ship. Keeping careful watch over David MacKinnon's efforts, he was nonetheless surprised. The young Scotsman seemed to have an aptitude for sailing.

"Oh, if only Moira could see me!"

Ryan Paxton stiffened at mention of the young man's sister. Undoubtedly, she was strolling the gardens at this very moment with the man she was to marry, secure in his affections after having tested the surly Scot's jealousy. Well, I wish the man joy of her, he thought sourly. Clenching his hands into fists, he vowed for the seventeenth time to put her far from his mind.

* * *

MOIRA WOKE to the creak and sway of the ship riding the swelling tide. It was dark within, and she had lost all track of time. Was it day or night? In truth, she really didn't care. The cargo hold was a dark, gloomy place from which she wondered if she would ever escape. No amount of shouting, kicking or hammering at the door had done a bit of good. Little by little, she was growing used to the distressingly murky confinement, making herself as comfortable as she could on a makeshift bed of rags.

It had been a trying journey, hardly the pleasant experience she had imagined when she had envied her brothers their so-called adventure. The ship's never-ending motion and the ocean's constant roar had made her deathly ill. Perhaps it was just as well that she had no food, as her stomach rebelled at the very thought of eating.

Luckily for Moira, there was a supply of water; several waterbarrels graced the ship's cargo hold. She blessed the captain for keeping a large amount, even if she didn't bless him for anything else. At least she would not die of thirst.

"Captain Ryan Paxton," she snapped. Had it not been for her fear of seeing him again, she wouldn't have hidden herself and be in this predicament. Well, she would demand that he take her back to Scotland as soon as she was found—*when* she was found. Dear God, that wouldn't be soon enough. The hold was hot and practically airless. Worst of all, it smelled of mold and decay. Oh, how she wanted to get out! With that thought in mind, she tried to rise, but the pitch of the ship sent her sprawling.

Moira felt dizzy and weak. Still, she forced herself to thrust her shoulders back and rise to her feet. Her mouth was set in determination as she shakily made her way to the heavy door and beat upon it once more. For a moment, she thought she heard voices on the other side and pounded on the door all the more furiously, but no one came to free her.

"Just the sea. The infernal ocean!" she grumbled. By now she should have been used to the ocean's murmurs as it pressed against the hull of the ship. With a sigh, she sank down on her haunches, trying to gather up all her strength. When were they going to reach land? This journey seemed to be endless.

Worst of all, there was nothing she could do to ease her hunger, her misery, or her fears. Leaning against a large bale, her head resting on her hands, Moira admitted defeat for the first time in her life.

Chapter Thirteen

LONDON WAS A SEETHING MASS of noise and motion as the *Red Mermaid* entered the estuary and sailed up the Thames. A great commercial huddle that hugged the river, the city cut a wide swath of buildings and people. The Thames was everyone's thoroughfare. There was commerce on the river as well as gilded pleasure barges, sometimes carrying royalty or dignitaries.

The docks of London were crowded with ships of every size and variety, from fishing boats to large merchant vessels resting at anchor. The docks were bustling with early-morning activity—sailors dressed in white, their sunburned faces matching the red of their jaunty caps, young women bidding tearful goodbyes to the men they feared they might not see again, warbling merchants hawking their wares, a throng of visitors coming to or leaving English waters.

The port itself was a forest of masts, flags, and banners. Three four-masted galleons were riding at anchor, their cargoes of tobacco, olives, sugar, cacao, and other New World luxuries having been unloaded. For a moment, Ryan Paxton assessed them with a gleam in his eye. They were a reminder to him of his fondest dream, an expedition to the new lands to the west. One day it would be his ship just returning, he vowed.

"There it is, Davie—London. What do you think?" Ryan Paxton asked, his eyes on the young man's face to see his reaction as he gazed for the first time upon the vast, bustling city sprawled along the Thames.

"It's big. Much larger than Edinburgh."

"Aye, much larger. And more boisterous, I would wager."

It was a city of loud noises—the yells of traders, the brawling of apprentices, the sound of horses' hoofs on the cobblestones. Even normal conversation sounded loud, for those talking competed with other noises. It was a cacophonous confusion; the air reverberated with the sounds of various languages. Donnie MacKinnon listened with interest to the chatter. "I've never seen so many people gathered all together like this before," he said.

"Much like a stew, you might say," Ryan answered. "I've been all around the world and there is nothing to compare to London. It's even outspreading the walls."

"Walls?"

"Long ago, London was contained within the confines of the old Roman walls, with gates to let people in and out. It is now outgrowing its enclosure." He pointed to the farmsteads and cottages just beyond the stone walls of the city. They could see the steeply-pitched roofs of three-storied, gabled houses, church spires, turreted towers, and chimneys that belched smoke over the hazy skies of the city. "That is Greenwich," he said, pointing to an imposing brick and timber building. "That's where you'll find the Queen."

"And is that London Bridge?" Donnie asked, pointing to a structure over the Thames, upon which were built two- and three-story buildings that leaned towards each other on each side.

"The same." He pointed to some other points of interest. "In that direction is Westminster. Over there is Whitehall Palace." A more gruesome sight were the severed heads on Temple Bar and on London Bridge itself, a warning to any who would challenge the English crown. The sight of them made Davie shudder.

"And the tower!" Donnie exclaimed, having read about the people who had been confined within. Warily, his eyes met his brother's.

"In that direction"—Ryan pointed west—"are the inns, taverns, and cookshops." He grinned. "On land you will be on your own, so try to remember." Striding to the quarterdeck, he cast a sharp eye upon his crew as they took in the ship's sails and secured them. Its anchors and cables proved, the ship laid to rest.

Davie and Donnie watched as their trunks were hoisted up

on ropes and lowered to a boat which would take them to their destination. "I've enjoyed the journey, Captain," Davie said, and extended his hand in a gentlemanly gesture.

"So have I," Donnie added, mimicking his brother's stance.

"It has been my pleasure to have you both on board." Ryan looked at David MacKinnon and smiled. "If you ever decide you would like to be a sailor, just let me know. I can be reached at the Devil's Thumb Tavern if you have need of me."

"I'll remember." Cheerfully, the twins took their leave of the captain, briefly looking back as the small rowboat took them towards the dock. Ryan watched until they had touched the wooden planks, laughing softly as he watched them try to get their sea legs. Soon they had vanished among the crowds, winding their way up the cobbled streets towards Elizabeth's palace. Ryan wished them well.

"All right, lads, I know you are anxious to visit the taverns. So am I. Let's get this ship unloaded and then we'll draw straws to see who goes ashore." A rousing cheer met Ryan's words, and each and every sailor set himself to work. Soon the ship was swarming with sailors, from the foremast to the rigging, and yard-arms to the deck.

Suddenly, a startled oath rent the air. "By God, a woman. Captain! Captain! There's a woman on board."

"What?" Ryan crossed the deck in three long strides. Other members of the crew followed. It was a woman. A very pretty one, curled up between two bales. "God's blood!" Ryan swore.

Moira squinted against the light and was unnerved by the sea of faces staring down at her from the open hatch. Her heart thudded wildly in her breast. Seeing the stern countenance of Captain Ryan Paxton, she knew the moment of reckoning was near. It was inevitable that she face him, but she wasn't looking forward to it. Something in his eyes told her he would be furious. Even so, she straightened her slim shoulders, stood up and faced him, eye-to-eye.

"Hello, Captain!"

He couldn't have been any more astounded had the ship's figurehead spoken to him. "You! What in heaven's name are you doing on my ship?"

A hesitant smile curved her lips; perhaps their reunion

wouldn't be as heated as she had supposed. "I was locked in," she said truthfully.

"A likely story. You were stowing away!" Ryan shouted.

"No!" Moira wanted to tell him the truth, that she had come to warn her brothers, but she choked on her words. How could she reveal to him the reason she had been on the ship without incriminating her brothers? She couldn't tell him the truth. "I . . . I came aboard to say a final goodbye to my brothers, that is all. I wandered about the ship and got lost in this dismal prison."

"She hid, Captain; I remember seeing her. I chased her across the deck. It appeared she was up to no good," a stout sailor insisted.

"So what if I did run? I got locked in just the same." Moira was indignant.

Ryan didn't know quite what to think. He was both appalled and pleased to see her, but didn't want any of the crew to sense his fondness for the girl. Thus, he reacted like a bear, an exasperated expression on his handsome face. "You thought to have an adventure, so you came aboard my ship and hid. It was a silly thing to do." There was a murmur of assent from the men watching.

"I did *not* stow away, if that is what you are saying!" She knew he would be stubborn about the matter. "Besides, it makes little difference how I came to be here. I must be taken back to Edinburgh at once. My family will not know what happened to me."

Ryan snapped his fingers. "Taken back. Just like that."

She nodded. "Yes." It seemed a simple matter, really.

Like a roar of thunder, the answer welled up from Ryan's throat. "No!"

"What?" She could not see that he had any other choice. No matter how she had gotten on his ship, she did need to return to Scotland.

Ryan tried to control his temper. This girl certainly never ceased to complicate his life. From what he could tell of her, she needed to be taught a lesson. He was the one to do just that. "I will not take you back. You came here without invitation from me, and By God, madam, how you get back is therefore *your* problem."

And a serious problem it was. Moira found herself in a harrowing predicament. She had no money with her, not even a few coins to purchase passage on another ship. For just a moment, a spasm of fear crossed her face. "You cannot mean that you would be such a rogue as to leave me here?"

"I can, and I do mean just that." A slight, sarcastic smile flitted across his face.

"Then I call you a loathsome bastard to your face!" Moira spat. Spinning on her heels, she started to march away, but the emotions of the moment, the fact that she hadn't eaten for days, the sway of the ship, and the time she had spent confined in the musty cargo hold all acted against her. Black dots danced before her eyes. Though she was not prone to fainting, she winced as the deck seemed to rise up to meet her. The last thing she remembered was her own whispered oath, and then she knew no more.

Chapter Fourteen

RYAN PAXTON STRODE frantically towards the crumpled figure lying on the deck. Her eyes were closed. She was frighteningly still. All his anger vanished quickly as he bent over her unconscious form. God's blood, but her face looked ashen. And why not? She had had no food, and had been locked in that terribly crowded cargo hold. The constant swaying of the ship had undoubtedly also been a factor making her unsteady on her feet.

"Moira!"

"I think she hit her head on the deck when she fell, sir," offered a sailor.

Ryan gently probed the injured area. She *had* bumped her head. There was a lump just above her right temple. Ryan motioned to the man. "Get some water. Quickly!"

"Aye, aye, sir." The sailor left for just a moment, returning with a full dipper. After putting his fingers in the water, Ryan touched her face. It didn't seem to do any good, for her eyes remained as closed as the petals of a frozen rose.

Carefully, he picked her up in his arms, cradling her head against his chest. He stared down for a long moment, mesmerized by how vulnerable she appeared. An all-consuming sense of protectiveness surged through him, an emotion he'd never felt for a woman before, except for his mother, but that was of a far different nature. Ah yes, Moira MacKinnon stirred him deeply. He felt the urge to safeguard, to shield her.

"She'll be all right, Captain. Some women take to vapors. Excitement from the voyage, I would wager," the first mate exclaimed. "Doesn't look to me to be a serious injury. Get her by a fire with the smell of bubbling porridge wafting to her nostrils, and she'll open up her eyes.''

Ryan Paxton took the man's suggestion. Holding his precious cargo in his arms, he requisitioned a small boat, took her ashore, and headed for the Devil's Thumb. His bed there was soft, with the warm coverlets his mother had made him when he was a child. He'd give her haven there.

Ignoring the stares of the patrons, Ryan kicked open the door of the Devil's Thumb and carried Moira up the stairs, calling over his shoulder for Seamus to prepare some porridge. Upon reaching his room, he made his way to the corner and gently placed her upon the bed, covering her with a thick, down-filled quilt. Oh, how he longed for her to open her eyes, to speak to him. Damn! If only he'd known she was aboard; he would have made certain that she was comfortable and well taken care of. Though he was not a man of fortune, he did know how to care for a gently bred woman.

It was chilly in the room. Ryan threw a log in the fireplace and stoked a fire. Standing over Moira, he studied her in the glow of the hearth. His breath was trapped in his heart as he stared at the loveliness before him. She looked so fragile, so young, so desirable. He tried to ignore the passion that stirred within him, recalling to mind that she was already betrothed, but faced with the sight of her curved form, he was lost.

''Moira! Moira!'' he called, over and over again. His fingers probed gently at the bump on her head—just a small one, but even a tiny lump could be bothersome. He'd had experience in tending to all sorts of lumps and bruises aboard ship when there was no physician available. Thus, he knew a cold damp cloth would bring some relief. Moistening a small piece of linen in the waterbasin by his bed, he let the coldness work its magic.

Ryan let his eyes feast on her beauty. She was so lovely, from the tip of her toes to the top of her dark-haired head. He let his eyes move tenderly over her, lingering on the rise and fall of her breasts. He was entranced by the way the sunlight came through the windows, playing across the curves of her body beneath the coverlet to create tantalizing shadows. For just a moment, he gave in to temptation and kissed her soft warm mouth. A parting kiss, he thought, in token of what might have been. She was the kind of woman he had been searching for, but a woman with a prior claim upon her.

"That damnable Scotsman!" he thought. "The arrogant young pup! A whelp with golden curls!" The thoughts rambling through his head caused all common sense and reason to fly out the window. He would be accused of all sorts of villainy if he gave in to his urge to keep the girl here. And yet—

Ryan Paxton had proved himself in the past to be his own man, doing just as he pleased, and now would be no exception. Though a gentleman would return the young Scottish lady to her home, he decided at that moment that the title "rogue" would be his claim to fame. Moira MacKinnon had made her choice the moment she set foot upon his deck. She had put herself in his power. The Scottish woman was not going back to Edinburgh.

Chapter Fifteen

THE TAPROOM of the Devil's Thumb was thick with smoke. Firelight danced and sparked, illuminating the faces of the tavern's patrons as if through a fog. It was crowded to overflowing, a typical Saturday evening with an uproariously boisterous throng. The laughter and chatter was deafening, such that Moira could barely concentrate on her own thoughts. It was just the kind of evening she detested, for she knew what was to follow. The assemblage of louts would grope, fondle, and stare, and she would have to resort to soundly slapping their wandering hands—a tedious and annoying situation.

A tavern-maid! Even after a week, the thought still stung her. Damn Ryan Paxton to hell for humiliating her so! *She*, the daughter of Roarke MacKinnon. To be brought so low was nearly more than she could bear. Yet she was in a precarious position, stranded in a strange land without money, as the English captain delighted in reminding her. With mocking gallantry, he had offered her room and board in exchange for her time. He proposed that she serve drinks in his taproom and help to keep the tavern clean, an offer she had adamantly refused at first—until she realized the severity of her situation. She simply had no choice.

Leaning on an ale barrel, Moira recalled all that had happened since she landed on English shores. She remembered fainting, and the pain as she struck her head. Through a haze, she also remembered Captain Paxton picking her up in his arms, gently and protectively. He had seemed so concerned, had brought her to the tavern, fed her, and tended to her as if he had at least some gentility. For a moment, it had seemed as if the spark that had ignited between them that first time

had a chance to be rekindled. Moira had reached out to take
his hand and he had responded, squeezing her fingers affectionately.

"I've never fainted before. Usually I'm of a stronger mettle," Moira had said softly. She was all too aware that she
was devastatingly drawn to him. Even now, her heart beat like
a raven's wing. She had sensed his presence in every fiber of
her being, and could barely think or breathe when he was so
close to her.

"Locked in that hold without food, I'm not surprised that
you would swoon," was his reply, his husky voice sending
shivers dancing up her spine. "How does your head feel?"

"Sore, but my father always told me I was a strong lassie."
She smiled up at him. "My stomach is what is aching. I'm so
hungry."

She had been surprised when he was so quickly able to
provide food. As though wanting to be prepared for when she
came to, he had a pot of porridge bubbling over a small fire
in the bedroom fireplace. After ladling out a small bowl and
adding cream and honey, he had actually sat beside her on the
bed and helped her to eat. So there is a gentle side to his nature,
she thought. It pleased her that he had one. It was one thing
she dearly loved about her father—that though he was a strong
man, he also exhibited the greatest tenderness for those he
loved.

Moira ate not only one bowl of the porridge but two, being
too famished to make show of a delicate appetite. She watched
as Ryan Paxton stood up and walked across the room to put
the empty bowl on a small table near the door. He reminded
her of a graceful lion, the kind her father had told her lived in
the Tower of London. He had drawn her a picture of the regal
animal that she remembered at this moment. Like the lion,
Ryan Paxton was also a proud animal.

"The porridge was good. Thank you," she had said, wanting
to say so much more, but not knowing where to begin. "I
feared I would never be discovered in that terrible place."

Somehow it seemed the wrong thing to say, for he stiffened
perceptibly. "Luckily for you, it was not a long journey"—
he raised one brow as he gazed down at her—"else you might
not have been found for weeks." He emphasized this last word.

Moira found the idea horrifying, but maintained her poise. "Then I'm glad that Scotland and England are such near neighbors."

Ryan had reached out to touch her face to brush away the dark hair that tumbled into her eyes. "So am I."

Taking advantage of his solicitude, Moira had made but a simple request. "So near to each other in fact, that I should think it would be but little trouble to take me back." Oh, how exciting it would be to stand next to Captain Paxton on deck, with the wind ruffling her hair as they both looked out at the ocean. Romantic visions filled Moira's head.

"Take you back?" Pulling his hand away, Ryan had stiffened again. "I think not."

Moira had been stunned by his sudden change of attitude. From gentle to hostile in the time it took to blink. "You must!" What else was she to do? He had to take her back to Scotland without delay. Not so much to ask, really. It was a relatively short journey, as he had said. Why then did he take on the look and intonation of a grumbling bear?

"You took it upon yourself to come aboard my ship," he had blustered, "knowing full well where it was headed. I cannot, and will not take you back at your whim, Madam!"

Madam—how she hated to be addressed that way! It made her feel ancient. "Then I should think my father will suppose that I have been abducted!" she snapped. Her eyes had narrowed in anger as she said, "I would not be the least bit surprised should he punish you dearly for what you have done."

"Then so be it. I will take the chance."

"You will not return me to my homeland?"

"No! And if you ask me again and again, the answer will remain the same." She asked again and he was steadfastly stubborn on the matter.

"Then so be it! I will find my own way home," she had countered. Leaving the tavern, she slammed the door behind her and roamed the streets of London until her temper had cooled. She had gone to the docks and tried to book passage on a ship, with the promise of paying upon arrival in Edinburgh. Not one captain would agree. Each had, in fact, been nearly as rude about the matter as Captain Paxton. Moira had decided that there were most definitely no gentlemen in England. She had returned to the tavern resigned to suffer her fate, at least for the moment. But woe be to Ryan Paxton when her brothers would hear of what he had done. That moment would come none too soon, for when she acquainted herself with the streets of London, she would find them.

"Moira! Girl, don't just stand there gawking." Moira looked up to see the man named Seamus motioning to her, a stout fellow whose demeanor reminded her of a pirate. It was he who seemed to run the Devil's Thumb. "Our special wine for Lord Ashford and his guests," he barked, by way of command.

Moira took a deep breath and filled several glasses with the pungent-smelling red liquid, balancing them on a tray. She glanced apprehensively towards a table of thirsty, rowdy men as she passed their table, but managed to dodge their pinches and pats to arrive unmolested at Seamus's side.

"Here, sirs—" She recognized one of them at once, a short, scrawny man with bright red hair and a face to match. A face flushed from too much ale, Moira thought. At his side was a particularly loathsome man with beady eyes and a fat stomach who had given her a devil of a time when he and his companion had visited the tavern the night before. It seemed that the knowledge that she was from Scotland sparked a special interest in her, though she could not begin to guess why. Tonight he was watching her with more than his usual intensity, such that he made her quite uneasy.

"The Queen of Scots has been put exactly where she belongs," he was saying to a man across the table. His comment made Moira bristle. "Aye, Sir Amyas Paulet will put end to her scheming. He is, or so I have been told, a most harsh jailer. There will be no more smuggled letters now that she is under his surveillance."

"No more schemes and treachery," the red-haired man piped up.

"Ha! Believe that, and you are a fool," whispered another. "As long as Elizabeth holds the Scottish queen like a canary, there will be trouble. Young romantic fools will feel it their duty to free her."

Thinking of her brothers' plans, Moira loitered about, taking an inordinate amount of time to ration out the drinks. She strained her ears to what the men were saying.

"She has been put in an inescapable cage. Paulet watches her like a veritable hawk," the beady-eyed man was saying. "She will never be free."

"Don't say never," the man Seamus had referred to as Lord Ashford replied sharply. "The Catholics are a devious lot."

"Care to make a wager?" The beady-eyed man took out a money pouch and hefted it on the table. "I say that Mary of Scotland will die Elizabeth's captive."

"I agree with Howard. The great spymaster is a man no one can best," another man said, adding his coins to the wager.

The great spymaster. Moira had heard her father talk of that scheming man, a man as dangerous as the devil himself. Like a spider, he had woven a web that had once nearly entangled her father. Walsingham. He was, she knew, Mary of Scots' foremost enemy, and therefore her own as well.

Moira listened attentively, but no more was mentioned about the matter of Walsingham. Instead, the conversation moved to other court matters. The little of what she had heard planted a seed in her mind, however. A tavern might well be a perfect way of gaining information for her brothers. When men were in their cups, they were often indiscreet. If Walsingham had his spies, why then could she not act in that capacity for Mary? The idea made her smile; perhaps Captain Paxton had done her a favor. Whereas before she was determined to leave the Devil's Thumb at the first opportunity, now she was equally determined to stay, at least until she found out something that could help Donnie and Davie.

IT WAS SMOKY inside the tavern. Ryan Paxton sat with his feet propped up on a table, listening to the crackling of the fire. The roasting mutton sizzled on a spit over the open flame, giving forth a tantalizing aroma. It teased his nostrils, making him acutely aware that he was hungry. He hadn't eaten a thing all day, and his growling stomach only added to his agitation— agitation caused from being unable to keep his eyes off of *her*. From the safety of the shadows, he watched as she moved about the taproom.

"I should have taken her back to Scotland and been well rid of her," he muttered beneath his breath. Why hadn't he then? It was a question he didn't want to come to terms with, at least not now, for then he might well have to admit that he just hadn't wanted to let her go. Somehow, the idea of keeping her from that young Scotsman pleased him.

"Here you are, hiding in the shadows. Care for some company?" Before Ryan could answer, Seamus positioned his girth in a chair across the table. His eyes traveled to the object of Ryan's stare. "Who is she?"

"What?" Ryan pretended not to understand the question. "Her name is Moira. A Scottish lass."

"Aye, I know her name and where she is from, but I asked *who* she is." Putting his elbows on the table, he leaned towards Ryan and asked the question again. "It is obvious that she is not some Scottish country girl come to London to make her way, nor the daughter of a crofter's family. The girl has breeding and dignity that even a cap of unbleached linen and an apron can't disguise."

There was no reason to keep her identity a secret, especially from Seamus. "She is the daughter of a half-English, half-Scottish nobleman, Roarke MacKinnon by name."

Seamus's thick dark brows shot up in surprise. "I've heard of him. He angered Elizabeth when he sided with Mary Stuart in some matter or other. Married the widow of a fierce Highland laird."

"So she has told me often enough," Ryan said dryly. "I am well aware of her nobility. She has also said that this Roarke MacKinnon will have my head."

Seamus threw back his head and laughed. "And well he might when he realizes what is on your mind."

"On my mind?" Ryan feigned innocence.

"It is clearly written on your face each time you look her way. You long to bed the girl." He patted Ryan on the back. "And why not? She is one of the prettiest wenches I've seen in quite a while."

"I hadn't noticed," Ryan answered sourly. What a lie that was. He had noticed it every moment of the hours in the day. Moira MacKinnon was any man's dream. But her parentage put her as out of reach as a star. She was a nobleman's daughter, and he a man with no real claim to a name.

"Hadn't noticed? Bah! I saw the tender look on your face

for the woman when you carried her in your arms into this very tavern. You sat by her side, holding her hand until her eyelids opened. You care for her. Admit it.''

"Nay!'' His protestation came much too quickly.

"Then why do you keep her here?''

"She stowed away, and because of that she must be taught a lesson.'' Ryan balled his hands into fists. He didn't want to feel the way he did, but somehow he couldn't help it.

"Punishment. Is that what you are saying?'' Seamus shook his head. '' 'Tis not the reason. You want her here because she fascinates you. But keeping her here like a trapped bird will do no good.''

Ryan clenched his hands. "I will only do so until I come to a decision as to what to do with her.''

"What to do with her?'' Seamus laughed. "You've never been befuddled over what to do with a woman before, Rye. As I recall, you have tumbled quite a few.''

"Lusty wenches all. This one is different.'' There was a dignity in the way she walked and talked, even dressed as a tavern wench. The truth was that Ryan had never come across a woman exactly like Moira MacKinnon before, and he didn't quite know what to make of her. That, and not his anger, kept him an arm's length away.

"Aye, different she may be, but a woman just the same. If you want my advice, I'd be telling you that she'll be getting you into some kind of trouble. They all do, you see.'' Seamus was half-jesting and half-serious, anxious to keep an eye on his friend so that the Scotswoman didn't get him into any unreconcilable difficulties.

Chapter Sixteen

MOIRA PUSHED at the rickety back door of the Devil's Thumb with the handle of her broom. Ryan Paxton was a stern taskmaster, of that there was no doubt. He had truly shown her little sympathy these past few days, adding to her work the drudgery of keeping the tavern clean, no less! She was expected to see that the inn was spotless from top to bottom, to make all the beds, wash the mugs, cups, tankards and plates, and do all the sweeping, mopping and dusting—as if she was naught but some scullery maid. Oh, how she had longed to tell him to go to the very devil! Were it not for her hope of finding out some information for her brothers among the tavern's patrons, she would have allowed herself the pleasure of doing just that, but caution had held her tongue.

"He's trying to wound my pride," she said to herself, thinking the matter out. It was the only answer that made any sense at all. He was not punishing her for stealing aboard his ship— oh, no! He was disciplining her for giving him her smiles when she was betrothed to another man. His manly pride was still smarting over the fact that he had openly shown interest in her, only to be upbraided by Iain Gordon. As if that were her fault.

Venting her frustration, she whacked her broom against a support post as if that poor object was Ryan Paxton's proxy. Shivering against the chill, she watched as the dust formed a cloud in the cold winter air. Well, it was time Ryan Paxton learned that he had met his match. She'd been on her best behavior of late, returning his sullen stares with smiles, fearful that a show of rebellion might cause him to cast her out. But no more—the next time he tried to bully her, she would show him quite different behavior.

Moira took pride in the fact that in just a few short weeks, she had made herself indispensable. When she had first come to this place, the tavern was in a shambles, and there was little or no discipline among those who worked in the taproom. She had taken it upon herself to change all that, reasoning that if she must content herself with working here, it might as well be in moderately pleasant surroundings. With that thought in mind, she had made several needed repairs on the interior of the tavern. The leak in the roof had been patched, the fireplace unclogged, several benches and stools with broken legs were put to mend, a loose floorboard nailed down. She had even made curtains for the inn's three windows. Most importantly, the tavern had been completely cleaned.

The tavern employed another serving-maid, a pot boy, and a usually tipsy old man whose job it was to pour ale and wine into the various tankards, cups, and glasses stacked on a wall shelf. They were lazy workers all, doing only what they absolutely had to in order to get by, working diligently only when Seamus was visiting or when the sea-captain was overseeing his premises. Moira had changed that quickly, delegating herself as the overseer when Ryan was absent, which was often.

He's a strange man, Moira thought about Ryan now, as she ducked back inside the tavern to enjoy the warmth of the fire. It was as if he were avoiding spending much time at the Devil's Thumb; he was seldom within. When he was on the premises, he always kept himself apart from all, except Seamus, whom he seemed to trust. Even with his sailors he was a master, never a friend. He seemed like a man with a great deal on his mind; quiet and reserved. There seemed to be a touch of loneliness about him that frequently tempered her anger with him. When he smiled or laughed, even at a ribald joke, the mood of the moment didn't seem to reach his eyes.

Leaning on the handle of her broom, Moira couldn't help wondering just what this Ryan Paxton was all about. Had he grown up knowing the warmth and security of a loving family? Somehow she didn't think so. What had made him decide on a life at sea? Had he run away, or followed in his father's footsteps? There were times when he seemed haunted by some secret memory, and that sparked her curiosity. He seemed to be as complex a man as he was a very handsome one.

Moira shrugged and went on about her morning routine. After the chill of the fresh morning air, the odor of the taproom was all the more noticeable. It smelled of smoke, grease, stale wine, and beer, and she was intent on airing it out. With that thought in mind, she opened all the doors and windows, then set about with her dust rag, skimming it over the scarred wooden tables.

"It won't do any good, you know!" Moira turned around to find the buxom, red-haired Gwen standing behind her. "What won't do any good?" Moira inquired, noting the dark circles beneath the girl's eyes, a telltale sign of another late night. It seemed to be a recurring pattern that Gwen would play up to one patron or other and slip away with him before the evening's work was finished, leaving Moira to serve the drunken patrons. She slept late those mornings, hoping to leave the greater portion of the work to Moira. Cunningly, however, Moira made certain she shared the necessary chores.

"Cleaning this stinking tavern! It will look and smell just the same tomorrow morning after those pigs quaff their ale at the trough," Gwen snorted in disdain.

"Nevertheless, we *will* clean it this morning, and tomorrow morning, and the next, and the next!" Moira shot back. She filled a bucket with water and soap and handed Gwen a mop. The girl took it with a grumble, but did set about the task of mopping the taproom floor. Moira continued with her dusting, humming a tune her mother had taught her as she worked.

"I don't know what you are so happy about. Merry-go-up!" Moira's cheerful mood seemed to irritate the red-haired young woman. "God knows *he* won't even notice what we do, if that is what you are hoping."

"He?" Moira pretended not to know who Gwen had on her mind.

"Captain Paxton, as if you didn't know just who I meant. I've seen you looking at him. I know what's on your mind. But it won't do you any good." Pausing in her work, she put one hand upon her well-rounded hip. "He won't have anything to do with tavern-maids. I know. I've tried."

That was an interesting revelation. Moira was secretly

pleased to think that Ryan Paxton had been one man who was able to withstand Gwen's charms. "What a shame," she said with a grin.

"Oh, you needn't smile like the tabby who ate the sparrow. You won't have any better chance with him than I." Her voice hushed to a whisper. "It's because his mother was a tavern-maid, or so I've heard it said."

"His mother?" Moira stopped her dusting, quite interested in learning anything she could about the captain.

"She worked at this very tavern until the day she died." For just a moment, Gwen paused to look around her as if fearing that that good woman's ghost might be listening. "There are some who say her spirit still roams about, watching."

"Her ghost? That's foolish." Though her brothers believed in such things, Moira wasn't really certain if she did. Still, it was unsettling to think that there might be a spirit roaming about.

"Believe it or not as you will." Turning her back with a sniff, Gwen returned to her mopping. "Ryan Paxton avoids tavern-maids as if they had the pox."

As though the mention of his name conjured him up, Moira saw him walk through the door of the Devil's Thumb. Moira stiffened, trying to relax the muscles of her stomach. They were suddenly knotted with tension as she awaited their encounter. Would he be his usually-aloof self? Though she would never have admitted just why she did so, she smoothed the wrinkles from her white linen apron, hastily checking her appearance in a small mirror behind the taproom's counter. There was a smudge of dirt on her nose, which she hastily wiped away. Her hair was coming undone from the confines of her hairpins, and she quickly set to secure the dark strands.

"Good morning, Captain Paxton," she called out as he entered the room.

"Good morning," he answered in his deep, husky voice.

Instantly, his eyes turned in her direction, though Gwen fluttered about and did everything she could to be the focus of his gaze. Moira met his eyes, stare for stare. Oh, he was such a handsome man, she thought, but hard and strong and fierce. And unrelenting when he gave in to his stubborn streak. Even so, whenever he was near, she was perilously close to losing her heart; there was always a potent charge that hovered in the air whenever he was close. She looked into the deep brown eyes that regarded her so intently, wishing she could read his mind.

"As you can see, there have been a few changes made since you were here last," she said softly. She faced him squarely, determined to earn his respect.

"Changes?" His eyes left hers for just a moment as he quickly scanned the room. "So I see." He folded his arms across his chest, and she thought he was going to express his dislike with what had been done. "At whose instigation?" he asked.

Moira held her head up proudly. "Mine!"

One well-arched brow shot up in surprise. "Yours?"

"Seamus is en route to Staffordshire to refill his empty barrels, and you—you are so seldom here that I took it upon myself to see that it was done." Moira braced herself for an argument, but none came. Instead, she was favored with a rare and disarming smile.

"You!" His eyes fixed upon her again, but this time they held a soft glow. Under the tutelage of her hand, the tavern had virtually blossomed to life, the once-dreary inn taking on a new warmth. He was surprised that she had the fortitude to take on such a project. So, he thought, at least on one matter I was wrong. Moira MacKinnon was not afraid of hard work, was not the pampered lass he had first supposed. "You!" he said again.

"Don't act so surprised." Moira basked in the warmth of his gaze for just a moment, then said, "I've often aided my father in overseeing his estates. I know what must be done."

"Estates." The word struck him like a fist, emphasizing to him what he had forgotten momentarily. She was a nobleman's daughter, not some village girl. At the thought, his smile vanished, and was replaced by cold resolve. "Ah, yes. I had forgotten." Though he enjoyed watching the Scottish girl and having her within his grasp, he was determined to keep an arm's length from her. As if dismissing her, he turned his back upon her and set himself in Gwen's direction. "You have mopped that same place for quite a while now, girl," he said to the red-haired miss. "Is something wrong?"

Knowing that she had been caught eavesdropping on his conversation with Moira, she flushed. "A spot. It won't come out."

He made his way to where she stood. "Let me see." Just as he had suspected, she was telling a fib. "Well, if I were you, I'd let the spot go. It's a big floor. If you took that much time with every stain, you'd be here all day."

"Yes, Captain." With a whisk of the mop, Gwen moved across the floor.

Moira might have laughed at such a scene, had it not been for her puzzlement. Why had Ryan so quickly turned his back upon her? Surely he changed as often as the tide. He had said the word "estates" as if it were a curse. Was he jealous of her father and all that he possessed? Did he dislike all Scotsmen? Or was there another reason for his sudden departure? She was determined to find out just what devils possessed the captain, for only knowing that could she find a way to tame him. That was her desire, to have that lion of a captain eating out of her hand.

Chapter Seventeen

THE TAPROOM WAS BATHED in firelight and candle glow, from the planked floor to the low-beamed ceiling. Flames in the vast hearth danced about, spewing tongues of red and yellow that illuminated the faces of the men seated around the tavern's tables. On a Friday evening the taproom was always thronged with sailors, dockworkers, apprentices, and the like. Boisterous laughter and mumbled voices filled the air, but all such rowdiness stilled as the crowd caught sight of *her*. Moira artfully made her entrance, slowly walking the length of the vast room, her head held high. All eyes turned her way, but she only longed for one pair to look upon her with favor, and they did. Raising his head from his tankard, Ryan watched with unbridled interest as she entered the taproom.

They are all taken with her, Ryan thought, looking around at the expression of the tavern's patrons. And why not? She was enchanting. Beautiful even in the drab garments of white and brown he'd insisted she wear. His eyes swept over her, taking in the breasts that strained against the tight bodice; he thought them to be just the right size. Her waist was small; he could span it with his hands. Of her hips he knew naught because of the full skirt of her dress, but had the feeling they were complementary to the rest of her.

"By God, she's a fine addition to the Devil's Thumb!" A patron Ryan recognized passed by, stopping to give Ryan an enthusiastic pat on the shoulder. "Is she taken?"

"Yes!" Without even stopping to think, Ryan thundered the word, nor did he mean that foolish youth awaiting her in Scotland. Ryan meant himself. Somehow, from the first moment he laid eyes on her, he had thus claimed her.

"She is?" The look on the rotund little man's face was nearly comical, but Ryan wasn't in a jovial mood.

"If you want what I think you want, you'll be going elsewhere!" Ryan said curtly. "The bawdy-houses are to the north of here." As if to emphasize his intent to protect the girl, he stood up to give the man full view of his height. It was all that was needed, for the fat little man quickly retreated into the shadows, seeking out a table in a corner far away from Ryan's own.

Sitting back down, Ryan watched over Moira, just in case another overbold buffoon might be inclined to take liberties with the Scottish girl. He soon found out, much to his amusement, that his intervention was entirely unwarranted. Moira MacKinnon soon made it obvious that she was a young woman who could take care of herself. She adroitly dodged the questing pinches and pats with a skill that was admirable, not once losing her poise except when one brash young sailor's groping hand searched out the fullness of her breast. For just an instant, Moira's smile faltered, but when it returned there was an air of mischievousness to her upturned lips. Without blinking an eye, she pretended to stumble and spilled the contents of a full mug of ale in the sailor's lap.

"Oh, excuse me, sir," Ryan heard her say as she pirouetted to escape the man's grasp. "I'll get you another."

With head held high, she walked over to the ale barrel. Her arm brushed against Ryan's sleeve as she passed his table. It was just the briefest touch, yet it stirred him deeply. Though he was loath to admit it, he wanted exactly what every other man here wanted—to make love to Moira MacKinnon. He wanted to possess her so masterfully, so passionately, that she would never forget him, even when she was with that insipid Scotsman of hers.

"Aye, that is what I want," he said to himself, regretting for the moment the harshness that had passed between them. At first he had sought to break her spirit, but now he found himself admiring it. That she had a passionate nature made her doubly interesting. In truth, it was she who drew him back to the inn time after time despite his vow to keep his distance from the Devil's Thumb, but he never would have let her guess that this was true. Perhaps that was why he turned his head whenever she looked his way.

It proved to be a riotous evening. Cups, mugs, and glasses were filled and refilled again and again with wine, whiskey, and ale. As usual, the taproom's patrons kept both tavern-maids amply busy. Ryan watched as Moira carried the trays and mugs back and forth. It proved to be a pleasant pastime which garnered him one or two of her smiles when he wasn't quick enough to look away.

When half the evening had at last passed, the taproom was in a shambles of spilled liquor and food. Patrons warbled lewd songs, sprawled upon the benches, or snored as they cradled their heads in their hands. The flames which had engulfed the huge logs in the hearth sputtered and burned low. One by one, the smoking candles and torches that had brightened the tap-room flickered, hissed, and died out. Darkness gathered quickly under the tavern's low-beamed ceiling, and shadows hovered in the corners like evil spirits waiting to pounce.

The hour was growing late. Fewer and fewer patrons lingered at the tables. Why, then, did he? Ryan wondered. He knew the answer to that question as soon as it came to his mind. He wanted to talk with her, find her alone. There were things that needed to be said, apologies to be made. Though she had done very well at her job here, his conscience had at last gotten the better of him. It just wasn't right for a woman of Moira MacKinnon's upbringing to be working in a place like this, to be pawed and leered at. He had been brutish and stubborn to ever have instigated it. It was time to make amends. With that thought in mind, he looked around the room for her, puzzled as to her whereabouts when he didn't see her shapely form in the taproom.

Quickly, Ryan went in search of her and found her near the wine cellar. His temper was fully unleashed when he saw that she was being menaced by three drunken sailors—an unfair ratio, to be certain.

"You're a real little beauty, aren't you?" one brash boat-swain was saying. "Much too haughty, though. It wouldn't be of harm for you to be a little more friendly, would it, mates?" As he spoke, he locked his arm about her waist, sending her tray of empty mugs clattering to the floor.

"Let me go!" Her eyes flashing, Moira struggled angrily to wrest out of his confining embrace.

"Let you go? By God, I don't think I will. Would you, lads?" His hand reached up to fumble with the strings of her bodice as the other sailors laughed, offering appropriate suggestions for what he should do to tame the wench.

"If I were you, I would let her go!" Ryan's voice boomed like ominous thunder. "Turn her loose, or you will rue the day you were born!"

"Captain!" Moira gasped as Ryan's warning sliced through the darkness. His voice was a welcome sound. She felt a flush of relief.

"I'll count to three. One. Two—" There was no mistaking the tone of fury in his voice.

The sailor hearkened to the warning and loosened his hold on Moira, but made the mistake of putting up his fists instead of running away. Lunging out, he connected with Ryan's chest, but the blow seemingly harmed him more than it did Ryan. He rubbed his fingers with a wheeze of pain, a sound that grew much louder as Ryan lashed out with a blow to the chin. Instantly, the sailor's other companions joined in the fracas.

"It looks as if you need a little help, Captain." Moira picked up an empty wine keg and, hefting it with both hands, smashed it as hard as she could against the thick head of one of the sailors. Shock glazed his eyes as he stared speechlessly at her, then toppled to the floor with a resounding thud.

"Well done, girl!" Ryan said in praise. He concentrated his efforts on the burliest of the three men, striking out first with his right hand, then with his left. Both blows connected with the man's nose, sending forth a spurt of blood.

"That is just a sample of what I'll give you if you ever bother this young woman again. Do you understand?" The frightened nod proved that he did. "Then take your friends and get out of my tavern." To help him along, Ryan aimed the toe of his well-polished boot at the man's backside. When the three men had gone, he turned to Moira, who was securing the laces on her bodice. "Did he hurt you?"

"No"—her eyes glowed with her appreciation—"thanks to you."

"I've watched you all evening. You know how to handle

yourself around the men, but three is a dangerous number."
Without even thinking, he gathered her into a protective embrace. Moira snuggled against him. He felt so warm and strong
that for a moment she reacted instinctively and put her arm
around his neck, laying her head against his broad chest.
"Cowards they were to corner you like they did."

"Cowards," she agreed. "But we fended them off."

"Aye. *We*." He laughed softly as he remembered her well-aimed blow with the keg. "You are a remarkable woman. I
thought that the first time I saw you fighting by your brother's
side, and I say so again. You are quite a woman." Ryan's
right hand tightened on her shoulder, as if he were afraid she
might move away.

"And you are quite a man, Captain." Moira had no intention
of pulling away; she had him right where she wanted him. Her
heart hammered in her breast as their eyes caught and held in
a heated gaze. Then slowly, he bent his head and claimed her
mouth in a kiss. And what a kiss it was! Fierce, hungry, a kiss
that devastated her senses. The attraction they had first felt for
each other was instantly rekindled.

Moira closed her eyes, pressing close to him. Her lips trembled beneath the firm, hard mouth that was plundering hers.
This man knew exactly what he was doing. The gentle caress
of his lips moved against hers in a way that made her very
soul sing. Clinging to him, she relished his strength, letting
his mouth and tongue explore hers.

Ryan's arms went around her waist, pulling her even tighter
against him. He too was lost in their kiss, but even so, kissing
didn't satisfy the blazing hunger that raged through him. He
was intoxicated by her sweetness, could think of nothing except
the hot pounding in his ears, the fire burning in his veins. Her
mouth was every bit as soft as he had imagined, her body just
as perfect a fit to his own. He fought to gain control of his
desire. Even so, he couldn't hide the moan that escaped from
his throat as his body blended with the curves and angles of
her form.

"Moira—" He mumbled her name in a breathless whisper
as he drew his mouth away. "I'm not sorry I kissed you." He
expected recriminations, but saw only her smile.

"Neither am I." His kiss gave promise that he had tender

feelings for her, and that pleased her. Raising her fingers to touch her lips, she found herself wishing he would kiss her again, but he did not.

"Your betrothal—"

So that was what had been bothering him, she thought. "Has not been officially proclaimed, nor will it be. Not now." She reached up and touched his cheek. Now was the time for explanations. "I came to Edinburgh to meet the man my father had chosen for me. I had never set eyes on Iain Gordon before—"

"Nevertheless you belong to him."

"No! I don't." Her mouth tightened stubbornly. "I will never marry him."

Tipping her chin up with his finger, he sighed. "Such things are not for a woman to decide, no matter how spirited a wench she might be."

Moira threw back her head, sending her dark hair tumbling all the way down to her waist. "Mayhap most women cannot so decide, but such a decision was granted to *me*. My father and mother granted me the last word on whether I said yea or nay to Iain Gordon." Briefly, she explained about her mother's unhappy first marriage, and her vow that her daughter would never suffer a like fate. "My mother married for love, and so will I."

Her determination intrigued him. "Oh you will, will you?"

"Yes, I will." And the man that I will marry will be you, Captain Ryan Paxton, she thought. The moment his mouth had touched hers she knew, even if he did not. It was only a matter of time.

Ryan succumbed to dangerous thoughts. Marriage had never crossed his mind before, but he suddenly found himself wondering what it would be like to wake up beside this dark-haired young beauty. At that moment, all his reservations about Moira MacKinnon were pushed away. He made his decision. He would woo the Scottish girl in the days to come, would do all that he could to make her fall in love with him.

Chapter Eighteen

SITTING BEFORE THE FIRE, clad only in her chemise, with a blanket pulled close around her to ward off the night's chill, Moira sat in a chair near the bed, watching the leaping fire tickle the hearthstones. She shivered, but not from the cold. Instead, another emotion rocked her body as she remembered what had taken place between Ryan and herself tonight. Touching her fingers to her lips, she remembered his kiss and gently licked her lips, as if to taste of it again.

She was in love, there could be no doubt of that. Ryan Paxton had shown her a side of his nature she had sensed existed, but had given up hope of seeing again—his passionate and romantic side. Every look, every smile tonight showed her that he was beginning to care for her. Was it any wonder, then, that she felt so happy and carefree?

Strange how she had those three loutish sailors to thank for her happiness. Had they not cornered her as they had, she might never have been so gallantly rescued. As it was, Ryan Paxton had flown to her defense like a knight in shining armor. She smiled as she remembered how he had fought for her, then comforted her. The kiss between them was inevitable, and might have happened sooner if not for the circumstances under which they had first met.

Iain Gordon had been the wall that stood between them. The thought that she was to marry another man had either brought out Ryan's nobility, or his jealousy and hurt pride. Which? Did it matter? Now she had told him the truth, that she was not going to marry the Scotsman. It seemed that it was because of her admission that the wall had crumbled.

He kissed me, she thought again. Moira knew in her heart

that both their feelings would soon soar to full flight. It was a
heady sensation. The Devil's Thumb was suddenly the most
important place on earth. It was where she wanted to stay, for
different reasons now than she had expressed to her parents in
a recent letter. It was not Davie and Donnie's scheming that
held her here, but a man who was becoming more and more
dear to her by the day. She wanted Ryan Paxton, and after
tonight, she could sense that he wanted her too.

I will not return home, she thought stubbornly, fully suspecting that when her father learned of her whereabouts, that
would be his adamant demand. She was no longer a child to
be ordered about and sent to her room when she disobeyed—
no. Instead, Moira was determined to follow her heart, which
at every beat led her in the captain's direction. Leaning back
in the chair and wrapping her arms around her knees, Moira
curled up in a ball and closed her eyes to envision his face
again.

"So, this is how my mother felt when my father stole her
heart," she whispered. Even though she had heard the story
over and over again, she had not really been prepared for the
potency of this feeling called love. It was so sudden, this desire
to follow this man to the ends of the earth if need be, to walk
in his footsteps, share in his dreams. If he asked her to, she
knew she would run away with him. Now, tonight, if that was
his wish.

Somehow, she had to make her father understand that she
had found the man she wanted to marry. Oh, he would object
to Ryan Paxton at once, this she knew. A wandering man. A
sea-captain! An *Englishman*! Roarke MacKinnon had envisioned a Scottish marriage for his daughter, an advantageous
union that would nonetheless be of her choosing. Though he
himself was half-English, people from south of the border—
sassenachs—had ever been a thorn in her father's side. What
would be his reaction when he learned that his daughter wanted
to marry such a man?

Moira's eyes snapped open. Her father would be as belligerent as a baited bear on the subject; he would roar and he
would threaten. Only her mother would be able to soothe him
back to reason. God bless her mother—she could be counted
on to make him understand the workings of the female heart

and mind. Kylynn MacKinnon was of a mind that a woman should be allowed to follow her heart.

"Dear Mother—" Moira whispered, sighing with relief to know that she would at least be on her side in the matter. But what about the captain? Would he be easy to convince in this matter of marriage? There was too little time for her to be overly coy. Her days left in England were numbered. Moira knew herself to be very eligible, knew that Ryan Paxton had strong feelings for her, yet she would have to be at least a little patient in the matter.

Moira rose to her feet. Patience! Up until now, she had seldom hearkened to the word. Could she now? She must. She had enough feminine wiles to know that in the matter of marriage, it would be far better if the captain thought a match between them was his own idea.

Padding on bare feet to the window to look out upon the night, she thought the matter over. She had to find a way to be alone with the captain, had to entice him into kissing her again. Then, perhaps, one thing would lead to another.

Closing the shutter, she smiled. The strategy of love was surely as intricate a matter as planning a war! But she did so want him. Walking back to the fire, she leaned her head back, trying to quench the flame in her blood that the very thought of him aroused. The memory of his hot, soft, exploring mouth and husky voice tormented her with yearning. She imagined his strong arms holding her, caressing her.

After snuffing out the candle on the bedside table, she slowly removed her chemise and undergarments, then hung them up on the horizontal pole above the head of her bed. Standing beside the soft feather mattress, she let her hair swirl about her shoulders, the long tresses tickling her back as she swayed from side to side. It was a sensuous, enticing feeling, that sparked a yearning to have the captain beside her loving her— unvirtuous thoughts.

The tolling of the night bell startled her out of her reverie. The midnight bell. The spell was broken for a moment, and Moira suddenly felt the chill of the room. Getting under the covers, she pulled them up to her chin. The quilt was thick, but even so, it was the thought of Ryan Paxton that warmed her. Oh, to have him beside her, holding her tightly against him. Was it any wonder that every living creature sought a mate? Closing her eyes, she smiled at the thought, drifting off in a deep, contented sleep.

MOIRA MIGHT NOT have been as easy of mind had she known that at that very moment, two pair of eyes were focused on her tiny bedroom window.

"The letter we intercepted was given to the messenger by the tavern-maid whose window you are looking at right now. A Scotswoman, I might add. Catholic, or so I would imagine."

"What did the missive contain?"

"It was short. Written to her parents to tell them that she had mistakenly been locked in the hold of a ship and thereby taken to London. That she was safe."

"Seemingly innocent enough. Why then did you call me here?" The tone did not hide the irritation.

"It seems the young woman has two brothers living at Elizabeth's court. Our young tavern-maid wrote in her letter that she intended to stay in our fair English city so that she could make certain her brothers' plans did not go awry. She wrote of a captive bird soon being set free."

"The captive bird?" Now the man's companion was interested. "Walsingham must be told at once. No doubt he will want that young woman watched every moment."

"Watched? I had plans of snaring the Scottish dove, or perhaps putting her to the rack to make her sing out about just what her brothers were planning."

"No!" The word was spoken with firm authority. "It is sometimes best to let a bird fly free so that it leads the hawks back to its nest. If you were of more noble stock, had your ancestors been involved in the delicate matter of falconry, you would know that, Selby."

"Are you telling me to leave the girl be?" Disappointment ran in every word.

"Yes. Unless Walsingham decides otherwise, that is exactly what I am telling you. But keep your eyes peeled upon her, taking note of every step she takes, every wave of her hand, every wink, and every sneeze."

Chapter Nineteen

THE NEXT FEW DAYS PASSED much too swiftly for
Moira, for she was young and in love, with the promise of
happiness shining like a beckoning star before her. Since the
night he had kissed her, the captain had effected certain changes
around the Devil's Thumb. First and foremost, Moira was no
longer a tavern-maid, but had been designated to run the es-
tablishment in Ryan's absence, to keep his ledgers, pay his
bills, and oversee the tavern's workers. It was Moira's duty
to greet the patrons when they entered the tavern, but she no
longer had to serve them wine and ale. To emphasize her
change in status, Ryan gifted her with a dress he had brought
all the way from Spain. He had also purchased the cloth to
make two new gowns, one of damask and one of velvet, and
a pair of black leather shoes.

Standing before the mirror, she appraised herself as she tried
on the Spanish gown, a somber creation made of black cloth
but rendered decorative with braiding and multicolored embroidery. It had been a bit overlarge for her, and needed a tuck
here and there, but now it looked quite fine, she thought,
plucking at the lacing of the sleeve. She liked the style. It had
a full, stiffened skirt of red and black, covered by a black
overskirt parted and open at the front to show the underdress,
which was worn over a Spanish farthingale. The bodice was
trimmed with three rows of red beads, and the oversleeves
were likewise trimmed and slit to show the puffed under-
sleeves. Unlike English garments, the gown had no ruff and
Moira's long neck was exposed to view, a neck of which she
was very proud.

To accent the red, Moira wore jet drop-earrings and a necklace of silver links set with red stones. Her hair was brushed back and rolled over a small pad that surrounded the forehead and temples. At the back, her dark tresses were arranged in a coil. Atop her head, she placed a narrow-brimmed black hat with a pleated crown. Ryan had promised to show her about London. This afternoon he was taking her to a London theater, so she wanted to look very fashionable.

The theater, she thought with a smile. How shocked would those pompous ministers that formed the great majority of the Scottish clergy be if they knew where she was going—they who were shocked by the license of the English stage, and who sought to prohibit such performances in Scotland, claiming that it was evil for boys to dress up as women and strut about upon a raised platform, that the brethren should be in church, not joining in lascivious gawking. Somehow knowing that such men—who had thwarted the Catholics at every turn—would disapprove made the thought of attending such an exhibition all the more exciting. Was that why her heart fairly jumped when she heard a knock at the door—or was it the thought of seeing the captain?

The soft orange-yellow glow of the hall's flickering torchlight illuminated his manly form as she opened the door. He was dressed in a doublet of purple velvet, the buttons and piping of a dull gold that matched his hosen, purple velvet breeches paned in bronze satin with decorations of purple velvet appliqué. An unpleated standing collar emphasized his regal bearing. No one would ever have guessed that he wasn't a nobleman. He was tall and muscular, his garments hugging his powerful shoulders with the right precision to proclaim the expense of the tailoring. He most certainly was not the kind of man anyone would ever forget.

"You are ready!" he exclaimed in surprise.

"Of course." Moira smiled at his amazement.

"Most women preen intolerably long, but then, perhaps, one of such natural beauty as yours has no such need," he answered huskily. Moira was vibrantly aware of the male intent that gleamed in the depths of his brown eyes. Her appearance obviously met his approval.

"My mother has always taught me the necessity of being prompt in everything one does," she exclaimed.

"Timeliness. A most valuable virtue." He extended his hand, gripping hers in his long, hard fingers, and placed her hand on his arm as he led her towards the door.

It was unseasonably warm outside for a winter's day; even so, both Ryan and Moira wore their cloaks. When the sun went down it would grow cold, the dampness in the air making it even more noticeably so.

"I'll give you a brief tour of that part of London where we will be going," Ryan offered as they walked along the slick cobblestones. "I fear it is long overdue." He turned his head to look at her as they made their way. "I'm sorry if I have treated you like a prisoner, Moira, but I will make up for it."

She had been confined to the Devil's Thumb, but by as much her own choice as by his restrictions. "A prisoner? I have not felt like one." Her voice dropped to a whisper. "In truth, I am beginning to feel as if the tavern is my home. I am most content there."

"Content?" He squeezed her arm affectionately. "I would hope to make you feel even more so in the future." His eyes raked over her, smoldering like embers, causing shivers to ripple through her. Instinct told her that he was thinking the same thing she was, that somehow it seemed as if she belonged there with him.

As Moira walked along, her thoughts were not on the city but on the man beside her. Still, she couldn't help but take in a glimpse or two of London Town, comparing it to Edinburgh. There was the same contrast between rich and poor, and splendor and squalor. Hundreds of beggars roamed the streets. There was the same competition among those who hawked their wares, though the markets were bigger, sprawled around the town in haphazard fashion. They were busier and rowdier than any Moira had seen so far. People in London seemed a bit more boisterous, more vocal in their likes and dislikes. But then, London was infinitely more crowded than Edinburgh could ever be.

"A bit like an overactive beehive, no?" Ryan Paxton exclaimed, making a sweeping gesture with his hand towards the noisy throng. He told her that it was feared that all the open spaces around the City would soon disappear, and that the increase in the population could not but increase the dangers of plague and riot, beggary and crime, even of famine and rebellion. "Far too many strangers, from other parts of England and abroad, are coming to settle in London's suburbs. The foreign population alone has doubled. Many of the newcomers are living in the most squalid of conditions."

"The same is true in Edinburgh, or so my brothers told me."

"Pestilence is rife in the seaports, and will be in London too unless the increase in people is checked. Is it any wonder I choose a life at sea?"

"Your ship is very important to you, isn't it?" As she asked the question, Moira couldn't help wondering if he had ever thought of settling down to a life without the feel of a deck beneath his feet, to have a home and little ones running all about. That was what she wanted, and yet, if he wanted to be a captain forever, she would accept that and settle for the times when he was near.

"The freedom I feel on the ocean is important to me, yes." He nodded towards the grinning heads displayed on London Bridge. "It keeps me out of the kind of political intrigue that can cost a man his head."

"I see." Moira turned pale as she viewed the gruesome, severed heads of those deemed traitors. Her thoughts immediately turned to her brothers. Love-besotted girl, she had forgotten all about them these past few days. That would have to be rectified immediately. She had to find them, speak with them before they got themselves in a kettle of hot water. This weighed heavily on her mind as they neared the area of Southwark, where the theaters and bear-baiting arenas were nestled. "The Curtain," a sign read.

The Londoners were summoned to the theater by the loud blasts of trumpets and the waving of flags. The theater was a cacophony of sound as women and men of every shape and size and children of assorted ages poured into the roofless, octagonal theater. Money for the seats was collected inside the door and placed in a box which was locked and then placed in an office. Ryan added his coins to the collection. Moira felt the strength of his hand on her lower back as he guided her to a chair.

The air was filled with clouds of tobacco smoke, which

caused Moira to sneeze. Men and women selling pies, pamphlets, fruit, and herbal cures struggled with their trays and baskets through the narrow aisles.

"Ale! Wine! If you've a thirst, I can quench it!" cried out a man selling liquid refreshment, holding up a bottle of ale. Ryan gave the man six pennies in exchange for a cup of wine for himself and Moira.

"Oranges, apples, nuts!" cried out another voice. "This way, this way! Get them in time for the performance." To shouts of encouragement from the noisy spectators, who sat on tiered seats all around the stage or on stools upon it, the play began.

"I pity the poor actors," Ryan confided, casting his glance in the vendors' direction. "If the audience does not like an actor or a play, they will soon make it evident by hurling that man's goods at the stage."

"Throwing the fruit at the actors?" Moira thought it an uncouth thing to do. Even so, the world of the theater was a world unto its own, and it fascinated her. It was a colorful sphere of make-believe, a world of pretense where, for a while, reality was put at bay in favor of the fantasies the actors created. She tried to make sense of the comedy, and found that it was a story making light of those whose profession was pirating.

"Well, what do you think?" Ryan gently touched her hand as he asked the question.

"That you are much safer being a captain than an actor," she said with a laugh, as one of those on stage was struck with an apple.

"So I can see," he answered with a chuckle. "My men would not dare to abuse me thus." He grinned, his brown eyes gleaming with merriment. Indeed, he had been in a most amiable mood all afternoon. "Nor, I hope, would you. I would not want to be an object of your anger."

She was reminded that twice he had seen her hit a man over the head, and blushed. "Only if you misbehave, sir."

Interrupted by cries of indignation, rebuttal, abuse, or satisfaction, the actors managed to work their way through to the end of the act. Then dancers, acrobats and jugglers took over the stage. Moira stood up to stretch, and in that moment noticed that a dark-haired, dark-eyed man was staring avidly in their direction.

"Ryan, do you know him?" she asked, nodding her head in the man's direction. "He is staring a hole right through either you or me."

Ryan turned his head, frowning in irritation as he recognized the man she was talking about—Walsingham. He was certainly one man he would have wished to avoid at all costs. He was in no hurry to be sent on some errand again, though he had to agree that, because of his meeting with Moira MacKinnon, the last journey had proved a profitable one.

"Who is he?"

Ryan wanted to confide in her, but hesitated; better for her not to be involved in any dealings with the Queen's minister. "I know him not," he lied.

"Then perhaps he thinks one of us to be someone else," Moira said, turning her back on those penetrating dark eyes. The man looked like some sort of devil, so much so that she shuddered. There was something sinister, dangerous, in a man such as that. She knew she would never forget his face.

"Yes, undoubtedly that is it. He thinks us to be someone else." It seemed to be the end of the matter, at least where Moira was concerned, and she put the matter out of her mind. Still, once or twice she dared a look at the man when she felt his piercing eyes on her back once again.

Chapter Twenty

THE DARK SILENT NIGHT was broken only by a soft shaft of moonlight that touched the waters of the Thames as the barge slowly drifted downriver. Ryan leaned back against the fancy cushions, drawing Moira to him, snuggling close against her to guard her from the chill.

"I've enjoyed tonight," he whispered, his voice a low rasp that touched every nerve in her body. As he spoke, his arm tightened to pull her even closer, marveling at how right it felt to hold her in his arms. How could he have ever been so stubborn as to hold himself away from this enchanting girl?

"So have I, Captain," she answered, fitting her head in the curve of his arm.

Seeing that the two young lovers needed their privacy, the bargemaster discreetly turned his head away, making no conversation on the short journey. Even the oarsmen allowed them their privacy, concentrating all their attention on the push and pull of their oars.

The night mist lent an air of enchantment as London lay before them in a sparkling panorama of lights. Lanterns glowed with a kaleidoscope of soft flickering flames. The babbling waters echoed with song, as sweet music drifted in the night breeze. It seemed a perfect night for love, and Moira was caught up in its hypnotic, magical spell.

The cushion was soft beneath them. For a long moment, Ryan stared down at her. She is so lovely, he thought, his eyes moving tenderly over her thick dark lashes, the finely wrought shape of her nose, the curve of her mouth. "You look like a vision conjured up by my dreams," Ryan whispered in her ear. "A dark-haired angel. Are you real?"

"Very real, and very happy at the moment." Moira waited breathlessly as he lowered his face towards hers. His mouth captured hers in a kiss that spoke of his longing. She gave herself up to him, her lips opening ardently under his to taste the sweetness of his kiss. Her arms crept up around his neck, her fingers tangling in his thick, tawny hair. She felt light-headed, happy. Everything was so perfect, so beautiful, with her sea-captain beside her. Love seemed to beckon, promising a whole new world.

Ryan was swept up in the moment as well. She was beside him, and it was a mesmerizing experience. God, how he wanted to make love to her. His gaze traveled slowly over her slim body, lingering on the rise and fall of her breasts, the long length of her legs. With a groan, he reached for the soft swell of her breast, caressing it with gently exploring fingers.

"I've wanted to touch you like this for so long. Since first I saw you," he said softly.

Moira shivered with pleasure. "And I to have you touch me."

They lay together quietly, contented to just be together for a long, luxurious moment. His fingers parted the neck of her gown and he reached inside her bodice to feel the warmth of her, stroking and teasing the peaks of her breasts until she moaned low and whispered his name. She yielded to his hands, those hands that searched the curves of her body.

Ryan was on fire for her. He wanted her to be naked against him, wanted to feel the warmth of her skin. He kissed her again, fiercely this time, allowing all the hungry desire that was clamoring for release to sweep through his body. He clung to her, wanting more than a kiss, so much more. Compulsively, tantalizingly, he slid his mouth over her throat, wanting her to desire him as much as he yearned to possess her.

"Were we only alone," he breathed. As if in answer to his wish, the gabled roof of the Devil's Thumb came into view, along with the trees that stretched down to the river's edge. The bargemaster skillfully brought his boat up against the dock, and the forward oarsman leaped out to secure the mooring ropes. Taking Moira's hand, Ryan helped her from the barge, eager to be within the confines of his bedchamber, where they could have privacy. With that thought in mind, he led her up the winding path to the tavern.

Inside, it was noisy and clamorous as always. Ryan clutched tightly to Moira's fingers as they "ran the gauntlet," as he called it. Ignoring the loud guffaws and questions from a few of the regular patrons, he led her up the stairs, turning not to the left, to her own room, but right.

Moira knew where he was going, and felt a delicious thrill of excitement as they neared his door. The very air pulsated with expectancy, each of the lovers achingly aware of the other. Ryan's fingers closed around hers. Bending his head, he pressed his mouth against the palm of her hand as their eyes met. "Moira—"

Such raw emotion was revealed in his expression that Moira was lost. All her resolutions about not trusting this man disappeared in the air like the smoke from a flickering candle. Ryan dropped her hand. Taking her by the shoulders, he pulled her into his arms, his mouth capturing hers in a kiss that left her breathless. She returned his passion, tangling her fingers in the thick red-gold bristle of his hair.

All Ryan could think about was the pounding of his heart as he relished the warmth of her body. She'd haunted his dreams no matter how fiercely he tried to put her from his mind. And now she was in his arms. He wanted her, was tempted beyond all endurance. Even the specter of his mother's ghost couldn't dampen his desire. Slowly, ever so slowly, he picked Moira up in his arms, kicked open the door, and carried her into his bedroom.

A hot ache coiled within Moira. Fear warred with excitement in her veins. Fighting against her own desire was more difficult than she could ever have anticipated. How could she push him away? How could she ignore the heated insistence in her blood? There was a weakening in her resistance, a deep longing that prompted her to move closer to him. She relished the warmth of his hands as he traced the swell of her breasts. She craved his kisses, his touch, wanted to be in his arms forever. Her senses were filled with a languid heat that made her head spin. She closed her eyes, giving herself up to the dream of his nearness.

Ryan Paxton carried his precious bundle to the bed and gently set Moira down. He traced a path from her jaw to her ear, to the slim line of her throat. He tugged at the fabric of her bodice, and his lips found her breasts, touching their rosy peaks. Dear God, she tasted so sweet. He was mesmerized by her, captivated by how right it felt to hold her in his arms. The longing to make furious love to her overpowered him. Kissing her was not enough to satisfy the blazing hunger that raged through him. She was too tempting.

"Moira—" He knew her to be a woman unused to intimacies with a man, and his gentlemanly side took hold. "I want to make love to you. Do you want me to?"

She did. Her body craved the maleness of him, but her logical resolve screamed at her to tell him no. What went on between a man and a woman was much more intimate than kissing and caressing. Embarrassingly more intimate. Her body warred with her mind. Through the haze of her pleasure, she felt his hands roaming more intimately. What was she doing? The question replayed itself over and over again. She wanted him, with a wantonness that stunned her. Even so, reason won the battle that was raging between her heart and mind. She had to tell him no. It was far more than bedding the captain that she had in mind. She had often heard the women in her father's employ twitter about the subject of marriage. A man was loath to marry a woman who gave her favors too freely. Well, she would not be as licentious as to besmirch her family's good name.

"I want to make love to you, Moira," Ryan Paxton repeated. He waited in anticipation.

Moira heard a soft voice saying "no," and knew it to be her own. Though she had worked as a tavern-maid, she would not lower herself to act like one despite her desires.

Ryan heard her words and recognized her undertone of determination. So, that which a man so wanted was not always so easily obtained. It only made the quest all the more challenging. Still, he would have been lying, had he not admitted to his disappointment. With an agonizing effort, he brought himself back to reality, breathing deeply in an effort to control his potent desire.

"As you say, so shall it be." He had taken things much too fast! His tone was a bit sharp and he tried to nullify the effect by forcing a smile. A lackluster grimace. "Your choice, Moira." It wasn't right. Not now, not like this. Moira MacKinnon was the marrying kind, not some wench to be taken in a moment of passion.

Taking a deep breath, he forced his breathing to a normal rhythm, and willed his heart to stop thumping so erratically. "But by God!" he swore, sitting back on his heels. "You cause quite a blaze, my sweeting."

Remembering all that had passed between them, Moira blushed. Fumbling with the cloth of her bodice, she held it over her breasts as she sat up. Ryan Paxton was a man of honor, that much she must credit him for. Other men would more than likely have taken her without asking.

"Ryan—" She wanted to tell him what was in her heart, how very special he was to her, but the intrusion of a young messenger boy silenced her. Boldly, the curly-haired youth pushed open the door, striding up to Ryan Paxton like a rooster.

"You must come with me. 'Tis urgent."

"Oh?" Ryan Paxton did not even try to hide his annoyance. "Come with you? God's blood, boy, the hour is late. A man should not be accosted at his own bedroom door! For God's sake, lad, don't you know the meaning of the word privacy? Doors exist for a reason."

The youth offered no apology. "*He* has sent for you. You are to come at once."

"He?"

"Walsingham!" the boy breathed. Though the name was barely whispered, it carried to Moira's ears.

Walsingham? What had he to do with Captain Paxton? Walsingham was the great spymaster, Elizabeth's creature! And yet how could she have forgotten, even for a moment, that Ryan Paxton was an Englishman, a man who might very well have ties to the Queen's councilor. She was devastated by the very notion. The thought struck her that this man she held so dear might very well be one of those involved with Elizabeth's minister. The captain, a spy?

No. She told herself that she had no reason to believe that. There could be a very good reason why Walsingham wanted to see a ship's captain. Hadn't Ryan Paxton been on a diplomatic mission when he had come to Edinburgh? Spy? Ha! She tried to brush the very thought from her mind and might have, except for the angry gleam in the captain's eye, the manner in which he had chastised the messenger for speaking the name. Ah yes, he had very quickly silenced the lad with a threatening glower.

Perhaps, then, he *was* one of those loathsome men who acted in a clandestine manner to obtain information that was none of his business. Such a man was beyond contempt! And yet, her father had once gone on such a mission. That thought calmed her ire a bit. Roarke MacKinnon had been a spy for Elizabeth when circumstances had led him to Moira's mother. A *spy*.

"Captain, I repeat: You must come with me at once!" The messenger was not so easily intimidated, not even by a man as tall and strong as Ryan.

Ryan Paxton muttered beneath his breath. Damn the cheeky brat! He had the audacity of a dockside pimp. Reaching in his money pouch, he handed the messenger a few coins, anxious to have him on his way. "Tell him I will be there, boy." He turned to Moira regretfully. They had a great deal to talk about. "I have been called away on some . . . some business," he said, lowering his eyes.

"Business?" She tried to act as though she hadn't heard the name the messenger had bandied about.

"The—the ship. I'm needed there." He was an unskilled liar. The fact that he was telling an untruth showed all over his face in a stain of red.

"Then by all means, you must go." Moira tried to maintain a calm tone in her voice, but all the while her heart was thumping like a drum. Walsingham was awaiting Ryan Paxton. Why? It was a question that even Ryan Paxton's parting kiss couldn't dismiss. She had to find the answer and quickly, before her brothers found themselves cornered by the Queen's bloodhound, Walsingham.

Chapter Twenty-one

IT WAS THAT TIME of night when thieves and other miscreants prowl, dark and dangerous. Was it any wonder that Ryan Paxton swore beneath his breath as he walked along? Trying to blend with the shadows, he made his way towards Walsingham's manor. Damn that man! His timing had been atrocious, at best. Here he had been seductively closeted with Moira MacKinnon in his bedroom and who should beckon him but the Queen's ghoul. What made him angry was that he was now padding after his master like a puppy being trained to heel. The more fool he.

"Well," he mumbled, "this had best be something of importance, or I will have the man's head. I don't care who he may be."

A sudden wind chilled his body—or was it a sense of foreboding? Ryan tugged his cloak more firmly around him, remembering how warm and contented he had felt a short while ago cradled in Moira MacKinnon's arms. Oh, how he wished for her softness now. Instead, he was walking alone, going to meet a man he detested for a reason he had been told nothing about. What made it even more unnerving was that he had the sense that he was being followed. A small, dark figure tagged along several paces behind him, walking when he walked, stopping when he stopped.

Ryan was cautious. Footpads roamed the streets, keeping a close watch on simple countrymen and unsuspecting foreigners. Was he being followed with theft in mind? Well, he would soon send the fellow on a merry chase. With that intent, he wove an intricate pathway of escape, up one narrow twisting roadway, down another. Pausing, he listened for any sound of footsteps, and was satisfied that whoever had been following now seemed left behind. With a pleased smile he continued on his way, coming at last to Walsingham's door.

Ryan knocked. He was anxious to get this matter over with as quickly as possible so that he could return to the tavern and Moira MacKinnon's waiting arms.

The door opened slowly. "Yes?" The voice was far from friendly.

"Captain Ryan Paxton of the *Red Mermaid* heeding your master's summons," Ryan answered, more than a bit peevishly.

"Very well, sir. You may enter." Ryan passed through the portal. The door closed behind him with a sense of finality that urged him to caution. He would not have doubted that there were men who had entered through that doorway only to find themselves the spymaster's prisoner. He thanked God that he had done nothing wrong.

Ryan was ushered to a different room from the last for this interview. It was a smaller, darker room. As he entered, Walsingham looked up with a grimace that Ryan supposed was a smile. "How good to see you again, Captain Paxton. I must say that your last mission went just the way it should have. Congratulations." Why was it that his words chilled Ryan to the very bone? It was as though there were a hidden meaning behind the compliment.

"There is little for which I should be congratulated. There were missives to be delivered, and I delivered them."

"And an additional boon as well." Walsingham's eyes narrowed.

"I do not know what you mean." Every muscle in Ryan's body stiffened.

"The two Scottish boys!" Walsingham answered, forcing another smile. "Queen Elizabeth is most pleased. Most pleased indeed." He lifted one thick eyebrow. "You know how she favors handsome men. She is amused that this time she has two who are identical."

Ryan relaxed. So that was all that Walsingham was talking about. "They are fine young men. James himself requested that I give them passage to London."

"Yes. Yes, I know all about it." Walsingham's look was

smug, as if he knew that there was more to the tale.

Ryan decided it best to tell the minister about the MacKinnon twins' sister. Undoubtedly, the great spymaster already knew that she too had come aboard his ship. "Their young sister was also given passage. It was an unfortunate matter. Somehow she was locked in the cargo hold after telling her brothers goodbye."

"So I was told." Walsingham leaned back in his chair, remaining silent for a moment, then asked, "Why has she not been returned to her family?"

"Because I have a fancy for her!" It was the truth, the real reason why Ryan had kept her at the tavern. Always, when in the presence of the great spymaster, it was a good idea to be sincere. "She is young and she is beautiful."

"And she is a danger to the Queen!" Walsingham's words were venomous.

"What?" Ryan was startled.

"Moira MacKinnon is a Catholic, and as such is suspected of being in sympathy with the captive Scottish queen." There were several papers on Walsingham's desk. He picked up one and crumpled it viciously. "Mary of Scots. Mary of Scots. How I loathe that woman and all who seek to give her solace."

"As do I. But Moira MacKinnon is not one of them!" Ryan came staunchly to her defense. "Catholic she may be, but she is no intriguer. She has been under my watchful eye and never once given me cause to suspect anything amiss."

"Oh, is that so?" Walsingham's eyes were piercing as he stroked his dark beard.

"Yes, by God!" Ryan was angry, so much so that he could not hide it any longer. "And I suggest that if she and your suspicions of her are why you called me out so late tonight, then you had best change your ways. I do not like being so disturbed."

"You do not like—?" Walsingham's expression hardened dangerously for just a moment, but then he shrugged. "I suppose it was a bit inconvenient. I saw you at the theater tonight with the young Scottish woman. I interrupted something, I imagine, and thus your irritation." He spread out the fingers of one hand, examining them one by one in a gesture that Ryan found doubly irritating. "But I assure you, she is not the reason I called you here tonight."

"Then what is?" Ryan was much too annoyed to think of being mannerly. He wanted this interview to be over.

"There is a young priest, Gilbert Gifford by name. He is going to Staffordshire. I want you to give him passage to Cheshire, on the western coast."

Ryan bristled. "My ship is for cargo. It is not for transporting passengers, sir." He should have known that bringing the MacKinnon twins to London would set a dangerous precedent.

"Your ship is for anything the Queen says it is for." There was an ominous warning in Walsingham's tone of voice. "This matter is of the utmost importance. I suppose you might speak of it as a 'life and death' matter."

Ryan wondered whose death. It seemed that something very sinister was afoot, and he hated like the very devil to become involved. But he was hardly in a position to say no. As Walsingham said, it was the Queen's right to instruct him on what to do with the *Red Mermaid*. If she wanted him to transport one of her spaniels, then he would be expected to say yes.

"Then, since you put it so strongly, there is nothing I can do but agree. I will take this priest of yours around the coast." And hope that if all went well, Elizabeth would be most grateful.

Chapter Twenty-two

MOIRA LAY IN BED mulling over a dozen things in her mind. She was chilled to the bone, tired, and confused. She had tried to follow Ryan Paxton tonight, only to lose him when he had used trickery to confuse his pursuer. Even so, she knew very well where he had gone. To see the great spymaster, Walsingham. Walsingham, who had done little to hide his hatred for Mary Stuart, who posed a danger to any woman or man who thought to free the noble Queen. Walsingham was Mary's enemy, and thereby hers and Donnie's and Davie's. Therefore, by his association with such a man, Ryan Paxton was also her enemy. It was a devastating blow. The man she loved posed a danger to everything she held so dear.

She shuddered as she remembered seeing those heads on the London Bridge. That very well could be the fate of her brothers, perhaps even herself, if she was not careful. She had given Ryan Paxton her trust, but she must use caution now that she knew what he was about.

Marry Ryan Paxton—how could she have been such a fool as to allow herself the luxury of that dream? Propping herself up on one elbow, she grew angry with herself. She had been such a fool! A silly dreamer. She and the captain came from two different worlds, had different loyalties that now looked to be perilously in conflict. She had thought life and love could be very simple, but now she realized how complicated, how dangerous it could all be.

She lay on her side, her head resting on one outflung arm, her dark hair tumbling across her face and spilling like a dark tide onto the pillow. She closed her eyes. Though she counted and recounted sheep, she couldn't relax enough to sleep, and was therefore fully aware when someone entered her room. Feigning slumber, she nonetheless opened her eyes just enough to catch sight of the intruder. It was Ryan Paxton. Entering quietly, he lit a candle on a table by the door and stood watching her.

Ryan's eyes moved over her tenderly. "Moira." Huddled up as she was, she looked almost childlike, and he was mesmerized by how truly lovely she was. The long sweep of her lashes against the curve of her cheek made her look vulnerable, and he vowed to protect her. Damn Walsingham. "Moira—"

Despite her resolve, his whisper stirred her deeply. She wished so many things. If only he weren't Walsingham's man, if only she hadn't heard the messenger whisper that name. What might have passed between them then? As it was, she couldn't help but be wary. The spontaneity of her affection for him had been swept away by the night's revelations. Now suspicion hovered in the very air.

"Moira, wake up. Please, we have to talk." He had to find a way of warning her without saying too much. Walsingham was like a huge spider, and Ryan wanted to make certain Moira would not in some way be caught in his web.

Moira sat up. There was no use in pretending to be fast asleep. Besides, she was curious as to what he had to say. "Ryan—?"

The sight of her lying there, the rise and fall of her breathing, stirring against the thin quilt, acted like an aphrodisiac. He remembered the way her breasts felt beneath his hands. For a moment, he couldn't think of what to say. Breathing a heavy sigh, he bent down and touched her dark hair in a loving gesture.

"I enjoyed our time together tonight," he somehow managed to say.

"Did you come here to tell me that?" she asked softly.

"No." Walsingham's warning had put things in an entirely different perspective; it made him realize how precarious life could be at times, how dangerous the world was. He wanted more than anything in the world to protect her, yet at the same time he had to use caution in his words.

"Then why are you here, Ryan?"

He knelt beside her bed, feeling again that treacherous warmth of attraction he'd felt from the first time he had seen her. Mere lust? No, it was a much different feeling than he had felt for any other woman. "I am sailing away at dawn. While I'm gone, I want you to be very careful."

"You are leaving?" That knowledge stung her. Oh, how she would miss him!

"I've been called away on a short journey."

By Walsingham, she thought. It had to be. "A sea voyage."

"While I am gone, I want you to be very careful, Moira. In what you do and who you see." He knew it a certainty that Walsingham would be watching her like a hawk.

"Be careful?" It sounded like a warning. Why would he feel the need to warn her? What did he know?

"London can be dangerous. There can be misunderstandings if one does not keep suitable company." How could he hope to make her understand without telling her things that by her knowledge would put her in danger of Walsingham's wrath?

"Suitable company?" She jerked upright, drawing the covers tightly over her breasts, all too aware of the thinness of her night shift. "Fie, sir, I see no one except those who frequent or work inside this very tavern." She tilted her nose up proudly.

She was right, he knew. What, then, had Walsingham been alluding to? Damn the man for causing trouble. "You are Catholic, Moira, and Scottish. That in itself might make you a target for trouble. All I am asking of you is to be careful."

"Then I will heed your words of caution," she said stiffly. But not in the way that he was intending. Something was going on, Walsingham was plotting something. Far from obeying Ryan Paxton's warning, she felt it important that she discuss the matter with her brothers at once.

"You are very precious to me. I wouldn't want anything to happen—"

"I will take care. I pray that you will do the same. 'Tis a turbulent time to be sailing, or so I would fear."

"I would just as soon stay in port, but sailing is how I make my living." There was something cold in her demeanor, a far cry from the passion she displayed only a few hours before. Her change of mood perplexed him. "It seems we have a great deal of talking to do when I return, decisions to be made."

While he was gone, he would decide what to do with Moira MacKinnon. Brave her father's wrath and marry the young Scottish woman? It was an interesting idea.

"Yes, I am certain we will have much to talk about," Moira whispered.

Bending down, Ryan kissed her on the cheek. "Remember my warning. Be careful while I'm away." He smiled, brushing back a tendril of hair that had fallen into her eyes. "I'll hurry back as soon as I can." He walked quickly to the door as if fearful of tempting himself further, but turned as he opened it. "You are very dear to me, Moira. Very dear. Please remember that."

After he had gone, Moira slid down in the soft bed. She had seen the soft glow of love in his eyes; how, then, could she doubt him? But what would happen if one day their loyalties were at odds? Would he still love her then? Could he be persuaded to change his loyalty from Elizabeth to Mary, as her father had been persuaded to do? The questions perplexed her as she closed her eyes and drifted off into a deeply troubled slumber.

Chapter Twenty-three

IT WAS NOISY on the waterfront as the reawakening sun spread its light upon the city. From the busy London dock, Moira watched as the *Red Mermaid* sailed out of the harbor and out to sea, straining her eyes until the last glimpse of sail was out of view. Strange, this lump in her throat at the thought of the captain's leaving. He'd promised he would be back in but a few days' time. Why, then, did she have this strange melancholy feeling? She tried to shake it off as she walked along the uneven boardwalk.

Moira weaved in and out among the crowd. There were merchants' wives who had come to stroll the docks and take quick inventory of their husbands' goods, warehouse workers with their ropes, hammers, and grappling-hooks flung over their shoulders and around their waists, and sailors hurrying back to their ships after spending the night ashore. Two inebriated sailors wound their way up the docks, and the air rang with their drunken laughter. It only emphasized to Moira how unhappy she felt today.

For a long time, she wandered about the docks, thinking about so many things. Last night Ryan Paxton had proved to her that he was a gentleman, that his affection for her was true, and yet Moira was uneasy. Wrapped in his arms, she felt content. But away from him, the old doubts and suspicions nagged at her mind. One thing she knew for certain: while the captain was away, she must contact her brothers. She had to warn them to be on their guard against Walsingham and his spies. First, however, she had to find them.

The common folk, not noblemen, frequented the docks, hardly people who would know the whereabouts of the Queen's current court. Nevertheless, Moira was fortunate enough to come across a bargeman who had taken noble members of the royal personage's court to their new lodgings.

"The Queen is at Greenwich," he told her, eyeing her up and down quizzically, as if to ask why one dressed as simply as she would inquire about Elizabeth's living quarters. Remembering Ryan Paxton's warning about being cautious, Moira was wary of telling the boatman too much, lest she cause undue suspicion.

"My brothers are with the Queen," she said. "I am paying them a surprise visit."

The boatman's curiosity did not seem to be appeased. "Your brothers? And you do not know where they are? It seems a bit strange to me."

Moira thought quickly, crossing her fingers as she told a blatant lie. "I fear, sir, that my brothers quarreled with my father and thus left in quite a huff. Alas, 'tis not a happy visit I envision, for I must give them some disquieting news about the family." She sighed deeply. "We have fallen on hard times. I come to plead their help."

The thick-girthed man was sympathetic. "Step in my barge and I will give you a ride up the river free of charge." It was an offer Moira couldn't refuse.

As the barge pulled slowly away from the shore, Moira shaded her eyes against the early-morning sun to watch several young boys shouting and laughing in enthusiasm as they sailed toy wooden boats in the river. There were people dipping jugs and barrels in the Thames as well. The bargeman explained that, for centuries, most of London's water had been drawn from the river, carted up to the streets in water-wagons, and sold from house to house in buckets by the water carriers. The river-water was augmented by numerous wells and pools in and around the city.

As the boat floated up the river, Moira had an excellent view of London, of its turreted towers, church spires, and steeply pitched roofs rising through the chimney smoke. The gray-white mist billowed about like thick clouds. London was a crammed commercial huddle that smelled of the river, a huge town swarming with people. Even the river itself was crowded, with the city's citizens crossing by boat-taxis, boats, barges and wherries all trafficking up and down the river. Moira heard the boatmen calling "Eastward-ho" and "Westward-ho."

The barge sailed past buildings of all shapes and sizes, past a rambling brick and timber building, a river palace just below London. "Greenwich," the bargeman called out.

Moira stepped out of the boat and made her way to the palace. As she crested the hill, she saw the magnificent walls and grounds which even in the approaching winter season was impressive. The outer walls seemed to rise up to the sky, and rather resembled an old castle. Sumptuous gardens, their leaves now at rest, surrounded the towering structure. The garden was filled with sculpted yews and fruit trees, and the hedges around the gardens were carefully trimmed. There were several ponds filled with ducks, geese, and swans. Moira rightfully supposed that she would never forget the sights and sounds which awaited her.

Taking a deep breath to still her nervousness, Moira knocked at the door. A scarlet-liveried yeoman of the guard stepped aside to open the portal, and Moira found herself looking into the midst of an opulent splendor which made the Scottish court pale by comparision.

"Who are you?" the yeoman asked, looking at her garments dubiously. To her regret, Moira realized she was wearing her damask gown but had forgotten to take off her apron. Undoubtedly, the guard viewed her as some sort of menial.

"I am Moira MacKinnon," she said proudly, holding her head at an angle that gave proof of her pride. "My brothers are David and Donald MacKinnon. They reside here with the Queen. I would like you to tell them that I am here." Apparently her show of pride worked, for with a nod the yeoman disappeared.

Stepping inside the crowded anteroom, Moira looked about her, impressed by the luxuries that she knew her brothers would be enjoying. The walls were of dark wood paneling covered with murals and richly-worked tapestries. At either end of the room were tall windows draped with lustrous brocade curtains. Raising her eyes to the ceiling, she could see the swirls and ornately carved designs of the pictures painted there. How many months, she wondered, had it taken the artist to work this magic?

Walking into the banquet-hall, she could see the rows and rows of royal portraits which adorned the walls. King Henry VIII, Jane Seymour, the poor ill-fated Edward VI, Mary Tudor, and the Queen herself. Grouped around the fireplace were chairs and stools covered in the finest brocade. A long table of solid mahogany, carved with designs along the edge, spanned nearly the entire length of the marble floor, which shone with such a bright polish that she could see her image reflected there. Moira paused to brush back a few stray strands of her hair.

"Moira! Moira?" She turned around at the squeaked shout of her name. "It really is you?"

"Yes, Donnie." She hastened to him, throwing herself into his arms, hugging him tightly as he stroked her hair.

"But what in the world are you doing here?" He looked around as if fully expecting her to have been accompanied by someone else. "I thought you were in Scotland—"

"No." She knew she was in for a scolding, but had to tell her brother everything nonetheless. With that thought in mind she found a secluded corner where they could talk privately. "After I came aboard the Englishman's ship, I mistakenly got locked in the cargo hold. The ship sailed and I with it. And here I am—"

"By God! Well, you are going right back home now, if *I* have anything to say about it." Donnie exhibited a rare show of bravado. "You never should have come aboard in the first place."

Moira took a step back, folding her arms across her chest. "Had I not, you would not have been forewarned of James's treachery," she countered.

"No, I suppose not—" For a moment his line of reasoning faltered. "But even so, you should have been more careful of where you wandered into."

"I was trying to escape the captain's notice. How was I to know I would get locked in?"

Donnie had to admit it was a mistake that he himself might very well have made. "But now you must go home."

"Back to Scotland, while you and Davie plot and plan." She shook her head violently.

"What's this? Moira?" Davie quickly joined them. If Donnie's attitude was critical, Davie's was scathing, as she told of her being locked in and her rough sea journey.

"You might have gotten yourself killed! Sailors are an unsavory sort." He clucked his tongue. "And to think, while we were on that ship you were—" He raised his brows. "Just where were you, really?"

"I told you. In the cargo hold. They didn't let me out until the ship had landed, and by then it was too late to seek you out." Taking Davie's right arm and Donnie's left, she led them into the garden, where they might have a bit more privacy. There were things she had to tell them that were not for others' ears.

"So you have been in England all this time." Davie looked her over from head to toe, shaking his head. "And just how have you survived? Where are you living now?" he asked, his eyes narrowing worriedly. "Someone must have taken you in."

"I'm living at a tavern, the Devil's Thumb. The captain of the *Red Mermaid* owns it."

"A tavern!" Davie nearly choked on his indignation. "Our sister living in a tavern?"

Moira lapsed into a discourse on Ryan Paxton and his sense of honor. "At first, Captain Paxton was angry with me for having, as he believed, stowed away on his ship. But lately he has been most kind to me."

"Not *too* kind, I hope!" Donald put a protective arm about her shoulder, no doubt remembering the turmoil created by the man who had sparked Iain Gordon's anger.

Moira couldn't hide her blush. "You might as well know— I want to marry him."

"Marry him?" Donnie and Davie exchanged worried glances. They seemed to be on the verge of a serious discussion concerning the captain, and Moira hurriedly changed the topic of conversation.

"That is not what I have come to talk about." Moira's voice lowered to a whisper. "Walsingham, the Queen's hound, is on the loose in London. If he even sniffs out a plot, and either of you are involved, you'll most likely lose your heads." She proposed an idea that would keep her brothers from sending her home. "At the tavern, I can mix among a variety of men and perhaps learn what is transpiring. Men talk freely when they are in their cups. I can help you both by transmitting any information I have learned.''

"No! Definitely not." The two brothers were united in their opposition.

"Yes!" She was equally determined.

"Donnie and I are taking you back home this very moment." Davie grabbed Moira by the hand, but she pulled violently away.

"Then you had best be prepared to take me there kicking and screaming, for I will not go voluntarily." In a stubborn clash of wills, Moira stared her brother down. "I mean that with all my heart, Davie. I am not a child. I will not be treated as one."

Brother and sister stared at each other for a long, long while. Then, suddenly, Davie threw his head back and broke into a laugh, recognizing in her a kindred spirit. "Whew! You are a stubborn lassie." He touched the tip of her nose. "If you are so determined, then I'll not be quarreling."

"I am determined."

His brows furled slightly as he issued a warning. "I will not be interfering as long as you don't get yourself in serious trouble. Do you understand?"

"Aye!"

"You are to listen for information only, not dare any dangerous doings on your own. Is it a promise?" Cupping her chin in his hand, he forced her to look him in the eye again. "A promise?"

Moira crossed her fingers behind her back. "Aye!" She smiled to herself. If her brothers thought that she was content to play a passive role in freeing the Scottish queen, then they were very, very wrong. Indeed, Moira was determined to do all that she could to aid Mary Stuart's escape. If she had her way, Walsingham would soon find that the butterfly had broken free of his web.

Chapter Twenty-four

IT WAS THE KIND OF NIGHT that prodded people to go inside—cold, wet, and miserable. The taproom was packed with a multitude of patrons fighting to get closer to the fire which burned brightly in the great hearth. Moira moved through the crowded room, greeting those she recognized, taking note of those she did not. Tonight, the tavern was a hive of activity, with friends and foes alike rubbing elbows as they sought to keep warm and at the same time quench their thirst.

As she moved along, Moira kept her eyes and ears alert to anything that might prove unusual, anything at all that might be useful to her brothers. She was sorely disappointed. Though there was a great deal of conversation, none of it seemed to concern Mary of the Scots or Walsingham. Nonetheless, Moira watched intently as the routine duties of the tavern were carried out, taking note that Ryan could very well use an additional tavern-maid or two. Gwen certainly moved like a snail, more interested in flirting with the patrons than in serving them in a timely manner. She would surely have to be taken to task for her sloth.

Wine and ale flowed freely as the night continued. It promised to be one of the most profitable nights the Devil's Thumb had seen since Moira's arrival. Several ships had put into the London port, which added to the tumult. The sound of their foreign tongues blended with those of their English-speaking counterparts, filling the tavern with chatter. Soon the noise was deafening, and Moira could only catch a word or two of several conversations going on at the tables.

"Lord, if you don't walk around here as though you were the Queen herself." Gwen moved out of the shadows, her ample hips swaying rhythmically beneath her gray skirts. Resentment oozed from her every pore. "Is that who you think you are?"

"I don't think of myself as anything other than the person the owner of this tavern has entrusted with a great deal of responsibility," Moira answered matter-of-factly.

"Which doesn't include serving the patrons, or so it seems. Even though there are more than I can handle." Gwen gave a huff of annoyance as she set down her tray, the mugs and cups clanking together.

"It seems to me that if you would stop disappearing from time to time, you would not have need of me," Moira answered, knowing very well what was going on. "I will do everything in my power to make certain all goes well, Gwen. Everything except being made a fool of."

"Including tattling, I suppose!" The tavern-maid's mouth took on the shape of a pout, yet her eyes flickered with worry. Gwen had her own way of earning extra money, which included bedding the tavern's patrons; such a thing was strictly against Ryan's rules. "Telling the captain about my—"

"No! I won't say a thing if only you take more care." Moira's jaw tensed. Gwen had a way of irritating her, but she hated to see the girl thrown out onto the cobbled streets. "But I remind you that you have certain duties, as do I."

"I know. I know." Gwen took a step closer, her resentment softening as she whispered conspiratorily, "But you won't tell?"

"I will forget what has happened up to now, but if you don't earn your keep, I will renege on that promise."

"There's no need for you to say a word. There are plenty of men about. More than enough for me to share." A slow smile spread over Gwen's face. "If you were smart, you'd do like I do." She patted that part of her bodice that held back her full breasts. A jingle gave proof of the coins nestled there. "You'd show a bit of friendliness to some of these gents."

"Friendliness? Is that what you call it?" Moira had another name for what Gwen was doing.

"Aye! Friendliness," Gwen defended.

"I've heard it called 'whoring'!"

Gwen's answer was an outraged shriek. Putting her hands

on her hips, she looked ready to start a fight. She might very
well have done just that had Seamus not entered the taproom
when he did, bringing a welcome supply of wine and ale.

"Mmmmm." He picked up an empty keg, tapping it with
his fingers to make certain it was completely dry. "Looks as
if I'm just in time, Moira me lass. Just in time to avoid a
catastrophe." The keg was immediately replaced by a full one.

"Just in time, Seamus." Feeling emboldened by his presence, Moira gave Gwen a push towards the barrel, reminding
her that there were still duties to be performed. Gwen was
never belligerent when the burly Seamus was around, but Moira
suspected that one of these days her ill-will would explode in
a full-blown quarrel. Well, if so, the blowsy beauty would find
that she had met her match, Moira vowed.

Seamus looked from one young woman to the other, sensing
immediately that he had interrupted a bit of a tussle. "Why is
it that I have the feeling I came between two spitting cats?"
Reaching out, he grasped Moira by the arm. "What's going
on, lass?"

"Nothing." Moira could see by the expression in his eyes
that he didn't believe her. Thus, she hastily explained. "While
you were gone, Ryan relieved me of my duties as tavern-maid,
giving me the responsibility of overseeing the work that needs
to be done in the taproom. Gwen resents that. She was merely
showing her frustration. That is all." Despite their argument,
Moira held to her promise not to tattle on Gwen.

Seamus grinned as if he could look straight into her heart.
"So. *Ryan* it is now. No longer 'captain'?"

Moira blushed. "*Captain* Paxton."

"So Captain Paxton has elevated you above yon red-haired
maid, and that has sparked her anger." He chuckled deep in
his throat. "As for you, I'm not surprised his gaze has fallen
upon you. Ah, Ryan and his women. He's always had an eye
for beauty."

"Oh?" Though it was a compliment, Moira frowned, re-
sentful of the reminder that there had been other women in
Ryan's life. She tilted up her nose at a haughty angle, much
to Seamus's amusement.

"Aye, and if you play the game right, you will soon have
him eating out of your hand." He winked at her. "Indeed, it

seems you already have him doing that. Imagine him agreeing to a woman overseeing the tavern when he's gone.''

Moira tossed her dark hair. "My new duties at the Devil's Thumb have nothing to do with any games. Captain Paxton is merely a man who has sense enough to realize a bargain when he sees it—even if it is a woman.'' Her eyes flashed fire at Seamus. "I am well worth my salt in many matters, as you will soon see.''

"Aye, lassie. Aye.'' Seamus knew when not to argue. Instead, he plopped his girth down upon a bench, patting the seat beside him. "Come, we'll drink to your new responsibilities. You can tell me all about what has been happening around the tavern while I've been gone, and I in turn will tell you a bit of the gossip I've been told.''

"Gossip?'' Moira was eager to listen, hopeful that the brawny man might have heard something of value to her brothers. Forgetting her stung pride, she poured a mug of ale for herself and Seamus, then hastily took a seat. "I've made a good start around the tavern. That which needed mending has been fixed. No man could have done better.''

Seamus looked around him, taking note that though it was raining, there wasn't a puddle on the floor from the hole in the roof. He noted the benches and stools whose legs had been repaired, the fact that the fireplace no longer spewed forth smoke into the room. He noted the bright curtains at the windows. More importantly, however, he noticed the respect that the other workers had for the tall Scottish girl. Damned if the tavern wasn't running as smoothly as a well-oiled wheel. He had to admit to a grudging respect for the young woman.

"You're right, lass. No man could have done better.'' Raising his mug, he toasted her, then drained his cup to the dregs.

Moira also raised her mug, but drank far more daintily. "How was your journey to Staffordshire this time, Seamus?'' she asked, trying to get him to loosen his tongue. "What are the latest tattlings?''

"There have been seven marriages, three birthings and two funerals since last I trod through the countryside. Most interesting of all, however, is the new resident there. A personage who will be of great interest to you.'' He savored the fact that he was teasing her curiosity. "She is keeping the women of the shire busy with their twitterings."

"A new resident. Who?" Moira knew very few people in England. Who could it be?

"Why, the woman who once ruled your fair land."

"Mary?"

"Aye, the captive Queen of the Scots. She has been moved from the strict confines of Tutbury to Chartley in Staffordshire, and is being allowed visitors for the first time in a long while. Of a certainty, it has the whole shire buzzing." Seamus cocked his head at a jaunty angle. "I've seen that lady with my own eyes."

"You've seen her?" Moira was enthralled. All her life, she had heard a great deal about the captive Queen from her mother, had fantasized about one day meeting Mary, of seeing the Queen of Scots set free at last. "You've seen Mary?"

Seamus nodded. "Aye, I've seen her. With me own eyes." Leaning back against the wall, he put his feet up on the table. "She even called me by name and granted me a smile." He recounted how he had been delivering ale and beer to the household at Chartley when Mary had swept into the room.

"Mary—" Moira tried to envision the scene, wondering what the Queen had been wearing, if she was still as beautiful and regal as Kylynn MacKinnon had always told her that she was. Though the Queen had been besmirched with rumors and slander all through the years, not one person had ever slighted her on her comeliness. Moira conjured up a vision of the regal Queen of Scots, imagining how she would have looked, a vision shattered by Seamus's next words.

"Poor, poor woman. She looked more ragamuffin than queen."

"What?" Moira was stunned. "What do you mean, Seamus? Mary is beautiful, poised and proud."

He clucked his tongue. "She was once, I suppose. Now she looks much like any other middle-aged woman who has not been able to escape the march of time. She is graying and getting a bit stout in the hips. The sparkle has gone from her eyes." An expression of sadness touched his usually cheerful face. "It is shame on Elizabeth for bringing her rival down so low. She shows more concern for London's beggars. Mary's gowns were practically threadbare. And yet, she still does have a certain royal bearing. I must give the woman that.''

Moira's heart ached for the once-pretty and charming Queen. She'd always disliked Elizabeth, but now that aversion was fueled into a feeling akin to hatred. Oh, that the English bitch would find her comeuppance! Mary had done naught to hurt Elizabeth, and yet she had been cruelly punished. It was unforgivable!

''Tattered garments or not, Mary Stuart is twice the woman, thrice the queen that Elizabeth the bastard shall ever be,'' she hissed.

Seamus quickly silenced Moira's tirade by putting his hand over her mouth. ''Silence, wench! Such words can make even one as young and pretty as you the companion of the rats in a dirty dungeon cell. Take heed!'' He waited until Moira's tense body relaxed, then moved his hand away.

''I don't regret my words, but I will pay attention to what you say, Seamus,'' Moira whispered. She cast a look over her shoulder to see if she might have been heard by the wrong ears. The buzzing of conversation in the taproom was too loud for her words to have been overheard.

''Be a good lass,'' Seamus warned softly. ''There are those who would seek monetary rewards by repeating an unwise word.'' He pointed towards a table where three velvet-cloaked gentlemen sat talking and drinking. ''The tall, skinny man with the thatch of black hair and nose like a bird's beak is one of Walsingham's spies, a vicious man. John Rothingham by name.''

Moira took due note, studying the man intently so that she would know him again if she ever saw him. She must remember to warn her brothers. John Rothingham, she repeated to herself.

''He thinks himself a clever man indeed, yet everyone knows him for what he is. A devil!'' He pointed to another man, shorter, fatter, and pockmarked. An unpleasant-looking character if there ever was one. ''That one is called Selby. He is Rothingham's creature. Deadly.''

A shiver traveled up Moira's spine as she remembered the times she had seen the man named Selby watching her. She was thankful that she hadn't done anything unseemly. Hoping to find out every detail, she refilled Seamus's mug. Every bit of information she gathered could be helpful to her brothers. Seamus revealed that John Rothingham had once been a friend of his, until the man's greed and brutality had turned Seamus away. He told her that Rothingham and his cronies often met at the Devil's Thumb to plot and plan.

"The men who sit at the table with Rothingham, and the two men disguised as sailors." He patted her hand. "Avoid their company as you would the rats that plague this city, for that is what they are."

Moira was determined to heed Seamus's words, remembering that Ryan had likewise warned her. But what of the captain? What was his part in all of this? Did these men frequent Ryan's tavern because he was one of them? Just what was Ryan's relationship to the men Seamus called "rats"? Did Seamus even know that Ryan kept company with Walsingham? Was he perhaps a spy? For that matter, could Seamus really be trusted?

Moira feigned a smile, uncertain as to Seamus's intent. "Thank you, Seamus, for taking such good care of me," she said softly, trying to effect an amiable tone to hide her suspicions. "I'd like to think that we could be friends."

"Friends?" Seamus's face was touched by a rare blush. "Aye, I'll settle for that. Though if I were but a few years younger, I'd be setting myself up as your young rogue's competitor." He took a long, drawn-out sip of ale, then sighed regretfully. "Ah, to be young again—" For a long moment there was silence as Seamus seemed to be caught up in his memories; then he turned his attention to Moira once again. "You're a good woman, lassie."

"If in that you mean that I try to be fair and do what is right, then I am that, Seamus."

Moira took a sip of her ale. And what was right was to see Mary free from Elizabeth's clutches once and for all. But how could Davie and Donnie help when duty kept them in Greenwich? She pondered the matter. Now that the vigilance over Mary had been relaxed, it seemed a pity that something could not be done to take advantage of the moment. Seamus offered an opportunity for at least corresponding with the Scottish queen, for he had access to her presence. Despite his warning her, however, Moira was wary of trusting him too much. Even though he was of Scottish descent, Seamus had lived in England his whole life, and had been brought up in the English faith. He swore unabiding allegiance to Elizabeth. She was therefore loath to trust him with any letters. No, if there were any communicating to be done, it had best be done another way. It was up to her to think of just what way that should be.

Chapter Twenty-five

A THICK GRAY FOG swirled over the Cheshire coast. A hazardous time to be sailing the western coastline, Ryan thought sourly, wishing again that he had never agreed to this voyage. He stared through the windspray at the wide expanse of shimmering water being slashed into waves by the ship's passing. The ocean was quiet, but it had been turbulent only a few hours before. He remembered battling the high winds and crushing waves on what had come to be a treacherous journey. Ryan had spent the majority of the hours on deck, busy shouting out orders that would keep the *Red Mermaid* from being conquered by the waves. "Never underestimate the power of the foaming sea" was his motto.

For just a moment, Ryan looked away from the path the ship was following to where his human cargo stood. No, he didn't like this voyage in the least. What was more, he didn't like this sniveling man Gilbert Gifford, this priest. There was something about the brown-haired man that bothered Ryan— a falseness in the smile, the blue eyes that never quite seemed to meet one's gaze, an insincerity in the voice. Ryan had tried to be amiable, but the truth of the matter was that he didn't like this man he was transporting. Not a jot, not a bit. Despite his vocation, the man seemed untrustworthy, shifty-eyed. He did, in fact, remind Ryan of a weasel.

Gifford, moreover, had made it clear right from the first that he expected special privileges on the voyage, and never ceased to remind Ryan that he came from an ancient Catholic family whose seat was at Chillington in Staffordshire. He possessed an honorable name, he had said quite haughtily, though Ryan thought to himself that this did not ensure the man's own integrity. Indeed, just the association with Walsingham was enough to make Ryan cringe. Something was afoot, but what? Who was to be the victim?

Ryan thought over all that he had been told about this passenger of his, trying to decide if the priest was, in truth, one of Walsingham's spies, or if he were himself meant to be the victim of intrigue. Was he masquerading as a man of the Church, perhaps? However, that seemed dubious, for Gifford had gone abroad to join the English college at Rome to train as a priest, was expelled, then roamed Europe before being received back into the fold. He seemed to have intimate knowledge of all that concerned the Church. His credentials appeared to be in order. Walsingham's pawn, then? Perhaps, though despite his faults, Gifford seemed to be highly intelligent, and was skilled in languages, or so he professed.

"Priest! Papist!" Ryan swore beneath his breath. His stepfather had put great stock in such dark-garbed men, always ranting and raving about the dangers of Purgatory and Hell. Was that why Ryan felt such an aversion to the man? He considered the notion, at last deciding that if the man were a tailor, tinker, merchant, or sailor, he would still find him sorely wanting.

"Captain!" The loud, raspy voice of the priest pierced through the sound of the waves, and through Ryan's musings. "Captain! How soon before we dock? The constant bouncing of the ship is upsetting. Besides, I must keep to a schedule, you know."

"A schedule?" Ryan raised a brow, his suspicions sparked anew. "You have an appointment to keep?" About what and with whom? he wondered.

Gifford hastily looked down at his hands. "No! No appointment," he said, all too quickly, as if fearing he had said the wrong thing. "It's just that I would like to arrive before dark, that is all. I still have far to go."

"We will." Ryan looked up at the sky. "Unless we're surprised by another severe storm, we will dock several hours before dusk. That should give you enough time to make whatever further arrangements you need for your journey."

"Good. Good." The priest forced a smile. "I'm going to Staffordshire, which is inland several miles," he said, as if needing to explain. "To see my father and visit my family home. A social call."

"I see." The manner in which the priest emphasized that fact made Ryan all the more certain that this priest was an integral part of Walsingham's net of spying. "I might offer the suggestion that you procure a large, sturdy horse in Chester. The roads between there and Staffordshire are deplorable. You'll need a strong mount."

"Thank you!" This time the smile was sincere. "Oh, how I do hate riding, but then, I suppose it is the only way."

"It is." Ryan looked at the priest askance, puzzling over why Walsingham would make use of such a man. He seemed to have very little to merit him for the calling of an agent. But then, that was none of his concern. He did, in fact, want to have very little to do with the matter. So thinking, he closed his eyes for a moment to rest them.

"I've been away for a long, long time; I've just come from France. I don't suppose that I will be recognized in my robes of the Church. Undoubtedly, my father and sister will not even recognize me. T'will be a surprise for them."

Something in the tone of the priest's voice made Ryan suddenly realize he'd heard his voice another time. Not here aboard ship, but before. He tried to remember. Ah yes, the first night that he was summoned by Walsingham. The spymaster had been cloistered in his office with another late-night visitor. He had been talking to a priest that night about returning from France. Now Ryan remembered.

"I'm certain that you are a man full of surprises," Ryan answered dryly. Let some poor soul beware, he thought. The ship skimmed the waves for what seemed a long time. "As you can see, we are approaching land."

The priest clutched at the railing, thrusting his head forward in an effort to see. "That tiny brown speck in the distance?"

"Aye." The foaming splash of the waves spread in a rolling line upon the rocky surface. "Land-ho!"

The captain's cry sent his sailors scurrying. Soon the foremast, deck, rigging, and yard-arms were swarming with men. They prepared to lower and furl the sails, and readied the cable to secure the anchor when they reached their destination.

"Careful, lads. Lower handsomely!" Ryan called out. He

watched as several of his seamen struggled to lower a sail, damning the wind aloud. "I'm not going to go all the way inshore. The coastline is too rocky and the waves too fierce. I'll have you rowed ashore in a smaller boat instead."

The priest looked over the side, shuddering at the sight of the swirling waters. "A smaller boat? No. It is far too dangerous."

"It is far too dangerous to do it any other way." Ryan's first and foremost concern was for the safety of his crew and the security of his ship. He would not endanger all that he held dear for the sake of one man, be he priest or king. He'd done as Walsingham had asked him.

"My safety will be on your head!" Gifford squinted his eyes in warning.

"So be it!"

Ryan watched as the boat was lowered, followed its progress as it made its way to shore. The waves lifted the small boat's prow high into the sea spray, but it did not capsize. At last it reached the shoreline, depositing the priest upon the dry, rocky beach. Just as Ryan had suspected, there was a small party of men to greet Gifford, which he sincerely doubted included the priest's sister or father. Even so, he was determined to mind his own business. He had other things on his mind, namely Moira MacKinnon. This journey had cleared his head and strengthened the ties she had on his heart.

Marriage. Perhaps because of his unhappy childhood, he had put such a serious commitment out of his mind, but now he realized that it was time he settled down. He wanted her, not just for a night, but for always. By God, even if he had to get down on one knee to ask her father for her hand, he was prepared to do so. He smiled at the thought. Love—it did strange things to a man, even those who thought of themselves as being quite logical about matters. Certainly he was bedeviled with a longing that only she could fulfill. He had therefore come to a decision. Just as soon as he reached London, he was going to ask Moira MacKinnon to take him, for better or for worse. He was going to tell her that he loved her, and then ask her to be his wife.

Chapter Twenty-six

THE COBBLED STREETS of London were dark and eerie. Moira held one of the tavern's lanterns before her to light her path as she moved along the winding road. She ought to go back; she shouldn't have been out so late at night. With each step, she scolded herself as heatedly as Ryan would have done had he been there. And yet she was so very anxious to tell her brothers what she had learned tonight from Seamus that she hadn't wanted to wait until morning. In truth, she couldn't wait. With the first light of the dawn, Seamus would be leaving again for Staffordshire, and an opportunity to communicate with Mary would be gone unless she and her brothers acted quickly.

The rooftops and towers of the city looked ominous at night, like sentinels keeping watch for any who would seek to betray England's queen. Above them all, the awesome Tower of London hovered with its ever-threatening promise of imprisonment. Moira could not help but shiver as she pulled the folds of her cloak around her body. For safety's sake, she had borrowed the potboy's garments, dressing like a boy for her late-night jaunt. It would at least give her a measure of anonymity as she walked along.

The Thames was dotted with boats and barges that looked like autumn leaves floating toward the shore. The water sparkled in the moonlight, looking deceptively inviting. Moira hired one of the boatmen to take her upriver, feeling relieved the moment she stepped into the boat. The water seemed a safer way to travel by far.

The Thames, with its system of docks, snaked eastward to elegant Greenwich. It was a slow journey, the heavy boat awkward against the current. To add to her discontent, Moira found the boatman a little too talkative and inquisitive for her liking. Thinking her to be on her way to a late-night rendez-vous, he plied her with questions. She answered with as few words as possible, fearing to give the truth of her womanhood away. She was doubly glad when the barge at last drew up at the dock that led to Greenwich. Handing him several coins, she stepped out of the boat and hurried down the pathway.

Though the hour was late, every window in Greenwich was lit. Elizabeth and her court were said to keep late hours. Moira took a deep breath and knocked upon the intricately carved wooden door. A young page in the Tudor livery of green and white answered. His eyes were scathing as he took in her appearance. He stepped in front of her to block her way when she tried to enter.

"If you are a minstrel, you had best be gone. We need no more musicians this night. We've harpists aplenty. Begone!" Beyond the door, a knot of ladies-in-waiting sat listening avidly to a singer espousing the wonders of love.

"I'm not a minstrel." Moira's voice was shrill in her annoyance, and she hastened to lower it. "I am a messenger, come with an important communication."

"A messenger?"

Head held high, shoulders back, she stared the young page down. "I have come to see Davie MacKinnon with a message from his sister. Lead me to him at once!"

The tone of command in her voice was effective, for the young lad did as he was told. Moira followed him through a maze of corridors that smelled of cloves and perfume. The page stopped before one of the doors, pointing out the room which housed the MacKinnon twins, then left her. As soon as he had vanished down the hallway, she rapped upon the door with the secret knock she and her brothers had used since childhood. One tap, then two, one tap again, then three. The door was flung open.

"Moira! What on earth are you doing here at this time of night?" Davie was more than irritated; he was angry. He looked at her, both eyebrows coming together in rebuke. "And dressed like some pauper, no less." Her garments, compared to his black velvet doublet trimmed in gold, looked all the more threadbare.

"Shhhh." Entering the room, she shut the door behind her. "I didn't want it known that I had come, so I dressed this way for safety's sake."

Donnie came to her defense. "I think she looks charming. So much so that she had best take care lest she catch Elizabeth's eye. The Queen is ever watchful for handsome young men." He tugged playfully at Moira's hair and unloosened the combs, sending the dark tresses tumbling down her back. He put several strands to her nose, forming a mustache. "Hmmmm, what do you think, Davie?"

Pushing his hand away, Moira was quick to give censure. "Fie on you! I have not come here for jest!"

"Why have you come?" Davie settled himself in a chair, stretching his long legs out in front of him. "You must have some astounding news to bring you out so late at night when I have strictly ordered you to have a care."

"I know of a way to communicate with Mary!" Moira savored her triumph as she saw Davie pale.

"Mary? Communicate with her? How?" When she did not answer at once, teasing him, he admonished her. "Moira!"

Her voice lowered to a hush. "I have made a friend at the tavern. A brewer from Staffordshire."

"Ha! A brewer. Of what use could such a fellow be?" Davie was quick to scoff.

"He delivers wine and ale to the Devil's Thumb from his brewery in Stafford. He also delivers his brew to Chartley, where our blessed Queen is a guest. He has come face-to-face with Mary."

Sensing the importance of his sister's information, Donnie walked over to the window, staring out at the night, keeping watch for any intruders or eavesdroppers.

"Can he be trusted, this brewer friend?"

"I don't know." Moira thought about the matter. "He is honest, good-natured and very kind, but loyalty to the English queen might make of him our enemy . . ." Moira paused.

"Well, go on—"

"We will have to think of a way to deliver missives to Mary other than to give them to him—at least until I'm certain that he would not give us away." She clasped her hands together so tightly that her knuckles turned white. "But we must do something! Mary is not being treated kindly. Her gowns are patched, the manor drafty. Seamus said he felt sorry for her." Moira told her brothers the story that Seamus had related.

"Hmmmm." Davie sat quietly for a moment, taking in all that Moira had said. "It seems strange that the man named Paulet, who has kept such a barbarous vigil, should suddenly have a change of heart. He who interrogated even the chambermaids suddenly lets a common brewer in to see the Scottish queen? It could be a trap."

"Or it could be that he has taken pity on she who has been so unfairly imprisoned." Donnie expressed his opinion. "Mother has always said that Mary could charm a bull out of his horns. Why not then this Puritan jailer?"

"It's possible, but we must be very careful." Davie tugged at Moira's hair as she walked by. "You did not reveal too much to this man Seamus, did you? You didn't mention us?"

"No. I only told him that I felt sorry for the Scottish queen, and that I admired her." Donnie left his post by the window to pace the floor. Moira followed quickly, keeping close to her brother's heels.

"That in itself is no sin. But if he guessed—"

"Seamus gave me warning. He pointed out several of Walsingham's agents who frequent the tavern." Moira paused before her brother's chair. "John Rothingham is one. A man named Selby another. I looked at them closely. I will never forget their faces."

"Good girl!" Davie was quick to scold, but just as swift to praise.

Moira gave her brothers a detailed description of the men she had seen. "All of them have the look of the devil, if you ask me. Like their master Walsingham."

"Aye, Walsingham is the devil. Don't ever underestimate him, Moira." Davie's expression was stern. "I've seen the man, heard rumors about what he has done. He has brought many men to the block."

"Be careful that you and Donnie are not two more," she admonished. "Oh Davie, mayhap we should all go back to Scotland where it is safe, and put an end to all of this—"

"No!" both brothers shouted aloud.

Moira threw up her hands in surrender. How then could she do less than resolve to help them? "Were it not for my duties at the tavern, I could go with Seamus tomorrow, but I promised Ryan Paxton that I would oversee the tavern in his absence." That seemed to be the end of that matter.

"Oh, that I could go! I would give everything I own to see Mary of Scots just once." Donnie closed his eyes for a moment, as if giving himself up to such a dream.

"Or I. But the truth is, we would be instantly suspected were we to leave court, even for a day." Davie was ever the realist.

"Then what about Moira?"

"No! We cannot involve her in such plotting. It is out of the question." David was adamant. "You and I have taken a vow, but Moira is just a girl. She doesn't understand these things."

"I do!" Moira was angered that her brother should speak of her as "just a girl." "I am just as loyal to Mary and the cause as are you."

"Let Moira go. Let her take a message. This Seamus, after all, is her friend. It seems logical." Donnie grinned at his sister.

"No! A hundred times no! Moira's head is much too pretty to be severed from her neck." To emphasize the danger, Davie ran his index finger across his throat. "Being beheaded is most unpleasant, or so I would imagine."

"As much so for you as for me," Moira answered. "Let me go." A few moments ago she would never have made such a request, as she was too caught up in her emotions for the captain to volunteer. Now, however, Davie's attitude piqued her.

"No! I tell you that again and again." Davie shook his head, but the frown faded from his face. He paced about in a circle as he thought the matter over, slowly coming to a decision. "And yet, as Donnie says, it would seem a most logical thing." He walked to the door, opened it, and looked out. Satisfied that no one lurked beyond, he closed it again. "Can you convince this Seamus to take you with him?"

Moira wasn't sure. "I'll have to try."

"Anything begun must be completed, or all is lost," Davie exclaimed. He took off his ring, a gold piece with a topaz stone and engraved with the MacKinnon seal. He held it for a moment, then placed it in Moira's hand. "Mary will recognize this. Father gave it to her to give to Mother a long, long time ago, with the admonition that she send it to him if she had need of him. Tell Mary that if she has need of Donnie or of me, we will answer her summons. We dare not risk writing anything until we are certain that we can trust your friend."

"I will be doing nothing treasonous if I journey to see my godmother. If I am caught with the ring, there will be nothing amiss. After all it is our family ring." Moira was already making plans in her head for what she would say to the brewer. "Perhaps it is a beginning, and will give Mary at least a ray of hope."

"Precisely!" Davie gave her a kiss on the cheek. "But be careful."

Donnie likewise showed his affection, taking her hand. "In these perilous times, no one can be trusted. No one!"

Moira knew in her heart that he meant Ryan Paxton as well as any others. "No one," she repeated. Above all, not a man who heeded Walsingham's call. And yet, it troubled her to have to leave the tavern. Ryan had entrusted her with the care of the Devil's Thumb. How was she going to explain leaving the premises? It seemed to be the only kink in the plan. She would have to think of some reasonable excuse.

Moira took her leave of her brothers, making her way out into the long hallway and down the stairs. She retraced her steps to the dock, procuring another boatman for the voyage home. All the while, her thoughts were on the impending journey. Would Seamus agree to take her with him? Would he think it strange that she wanted to go to Staffordshire? Could his suspicions be put to rest by her skillful explanation? Even if Seamus did suspect, would he keep silent on the matter? Could he be trusted?

Moira stepped out of the boat, paying the boatman an ample fare. Pulling her cloak tightly around her shoulders, she braced herself against the sudden, chill breeze that was wending its way through the city. Never would the fire in her bedroom be more welcome! Moira hurried along, but soon paused. Danger—she sensed it. It pulsated in the air like lightning before a storm. Someone was following her. She felt it in every nerve, every bone in her body. Moira was filled with a sudden compulsion to flee.

Darkness spread its cloak over London, broken only by the moonlight as Moira walked briskly down the slippery cobblestoned roadway, trying to outdistance her pursuer. She could hear the footsteps, and thus knew that someone was following her; it was not her imagination. She started to run, but whoever was behind her also broke into a run. She was terrified, yet the instinct for survival took hold of her. Up one rutted street and down the other she ran, only to hear the sound of tramping feet close behind her. Many twisting and turning alleyways were spread out like a spider's web, but she chose the third one she came to, frustrated that she didn't know the streets of London better.

She paused for just a moment, fearful and trembling, to catch her breath—but upon hearing the footsteps again, she quickened her pace. Who was following her? It was a question that plagued her. She fought to still her panic, forced herself to use logic and reason. Hide—it was the only answer. The dockyards loomed ahead, and beyond them lay the safety of the tavern.

Moira ran until she was winded and couldn't run any more. Not another step, not another pace. Ducking behind some old wooden crates, she took cover, anxiously peering through the gap between them. A dark shape loomed in the fading moonlight, a figure that crept closer and closer. Moira held her breath, fearing discovery, but her pursuer merely uttered a strangled curse and walked on. She stared intently at the face revealed by the soft rays of the moon.

It was the man named Selby, Walsingham's agent, the one Seamus had warned her about. He had been following her, and the very thought made her blood run cold. Did he know about her late-night visit to Greenwich? Did he suspect anything was amiss? He had to, or else why had he followed her?

Moira crouched behind the barrels for a long, long while, trying to sort things out. It wasn't the first time she had been followed, nor did she think it would be the last. Someone suspected her, knew where her loyalties lay. But how? Seamus. Had he feigned concern for her, only to betray her? Somehow she couldn't think so. Ryan? No—her heart refused to believe that he was responsible. Even so, London seemed to pose a danger for her, a peril that she was now all too aware of. Helping Mary was not a game, not now!

Squeezing her father's ring, Moira made a vow that she would do everything in her power to aid Mary—even if it meant forsaking her own happiness.

Chapter Twenty-seven

A LIGHT DRIZZLE FELL on the occupants of the wagon
as it lumbered along the muddy road, wheels churning slowly
through the mire. Clutching her cloak tightly about her shoulders, Moira reflected on her room back at the tavern and the
fire she might have been enjoying. Ah, well. The die had been
cast; there was no turning back now. She had begged Seamus
to take her with him and he had complied. Now she was well
on her way to Staffordshire and could have no regrets.

Moira had returned late to the tavern last night, thankful for
its haven, only to find an unpleasant surprise. Her room had
been torn apart, pillows, sheets, and quilts thrown about on
the floor. The latch of her wooden clothes-trunk had been split
open, and her garments scattered about. Had she not already
decided to go to Staffordshire, she would have made such a
decision at that moment. London was growing increasingly
dangerous for her.

Not really knowing who she could trust, Moira had kept a
watchful eye on any suspicious-looking persons roaming about.
She had not slept all night, and waited until Seamus was ready
to leave before approaching him.

"Seamus, take me with you," she had said.

"What?" He shook his head most fiercely. "I'll not be
bothered with a woman. It's a rough journey that takes several
days. I'll not be putting up with any complaints."

"I'm not the kind of woman to give you any grumbles."
She tossed her head. "In truth, you will hardly even know that
I am there."

"No! You've your duties right here to keep you more than
occupied."

She plucked at his sleeve. "Please! Mary of Scotland is my godmother, and yet I have never even met her. She was taken captive before I was even born. Can you deny me an opportunity to see her just this once? I might never get another chance, Seamus."

Though he growled his denial, it was obvious by his expression that he was weakening. "And what about Ryan? What will he think if I spirit you away from your duties here?" Seamus was not of a mind to ruffle the captain's feathers.

"Ryan Paxton does not own me." She was free to come and go. "I am not a prisoner. I earn the food I eat, and the bed that I sleep in. If I aid him in keeping his fine tavern working, it is my generosity to do so. I was the one who instigated such management." God knew he took little note of the tavern's workings.

"Aye, but he will miss *you.*" Seamus knew that to be certain.

"I must go, else I would not even consider it." Moira had told Seamus about being followed late at night, and her room being ransacked. "I think I might be in danger here, though I have done *nothing* to warrant any such treatment. You must believe me. If I do not leave London, I am certain that something will happen to me."

"Well—"

He had reminded her of a big, grumbly bear, but in the end he complied. Moira had kept her eye on him lest he get the idea of revealing her plans to someone who she would not want to know such details, but the brewer had not betrayed her nor given her reason to doubt that he could be trusted. Moira knew she would be forever grateful to the stout, smiling man. Now she was on her way to Staffordshire, leaving London and Ryan behind. A sad reality, lightened only by her determination that she would return to him once the matter of Mary was settled. She could only hope that he would understand why she had run away.

"Fool nags!" Seamus scolded the horses. "Move it along, move it along." The sky was dark gray; a downpour seemed imminent. Seamus was anxious to find shelter. "I told you it would be a rough journey, lass. Are you now sorry that you came along?"

"No! If you can survive this, then so can I." Somehow she would.

"That's the spirit." Seamus grinned as he looked over at her. He flicked at the reins, urging the horses on at a lively pace, at last taking shelter under a tree as the rain came down all around them. "A veritable flood, as if an ale barrel had sprung a leak." The clouds emptied themselves, furiously pelting the earth. Then, as if a tap had been turned off, the rain suddenly ceased. A short rain, yet even so it had done its damage. The roads were a quagmire. It would be, as Seamus said, a long and tedious journey.

Moira shivered convulsively as a chill wind penetrated the folds of her cloak. The rain-soaked cloth of her gown clung to her form like a second skin, the sodden skirt weighing on her legs. Her teeth chattered and her hands trembled. As she had promised, however, not one word of complaint passed from her lips.

The wagon lurched roughly over the ruts and potholes made worse by the rain. Moira turned to look back, watching as London grew smaller and distant behind her. She tried not to think, not to let thoughts of Ryan start a storm of tears. She had to think of Mary, of her brothers. It would do no good to either cry or think of what might have happened. Even so, she could not keep the captain from intruding on her thoughts— not once, but many times on her journey.

THE CHILL WINTER WIND BLEW FIERCELY, whipping Ryan Paxton's cloak about him wildly as he stood at the dock. The rain had soaked him to the core, yet never had it felt so good to be home. Home. Strange, he thought, how London and the tavern had never seemed like home before. Now it did, because he knew that Moira would be waiting for him.

Ryan felt more at peace than he had in a long while, secure in knowing what he wanted: to be united with the woman he loved. Breathing in the salt air, he felt invigorated, hopeful that he could find happiness. Somehow, that blessed emotion had always seemed to elude him until now. Now, for the first time, he had hope that the turmoil of the past could be redeemed. With that thought in mind, he strode down the planks of the dock towards the Devil's Thumb, his heart quickening as he spied the familiar landscape of the tavern's grounds.

Ryan pulled open the heavy door of the tavern. The usual melée of laughter and chatter met his ears as sailors, merchants, and dockmen all quenched their thirst. He might have joined them once, but today he had other things on his mind. Walking into the taproom, he scanned all those assembled for the familiar figure of his Scottish love. As she was nowhere in sight, he supposed her to be upstairs in her room.

I will surprise her, he thought, touching the ruby ring he wore on his little finger. He intended to give it to her this very night. I will take her into my arms and never again let her go. We belong together, she and I; I will make her realize that.

Ryan headed for the stairs, surprised when the red-haired Gwen blocked his way. "She isn't here!"

Ryan looked at her with mild annoyance. "What game are you playing, girl? Stand aside."

"She is not up there."

"Not upstairs?" His eyes sparked fire. "Then where is she?"

"She is gone!"

"What gibberish is this?" Ryan pushed the tavern-maid aside, hurrying up the stairs, taking them two at a time. At Moira's room, he flung open the door, but found Gwen's words to be true. Fearing the worst, he retraced his steps to Gwen and grasped her arm. "Where is she?" A hundred dark thoughts ran through his head.

"Back to Scotland, for all I care!" Gwen couldn't hide her dislike for her rival.

"What? Scotland?" The disappointment, the pain, was like a physical blow. "I don't believe you."

Gwen smiled, showing her dimples. "Aw, come now, sir. It's good riddance, I say. That haughty miss was out of place here."

"No, she was not. Moira MacKinnon gave this tavern dignity."

Not believing the tavern-maid's insistence that Moira was gone, Ryan looked all over for her, returning at last to her room. Taking stock, he could see that Moira's few possessions were gone: irrefutable evidence that Gwen was telling him the truth. Moira had left the premises, and he could only conclude that she had returned to her own land.

"Scotland! Damn the wench!" She couldn't wait until he returned before wandering away. "By ship or on horseback? How did she travel?" He thought about going after her.

"Ship, I suppose, but I wouldn't rightly know." Gwen gave him a small pout, then hastened away, turning her attention to a small group of sailors.

"Back to Scotland! By God." Ryan fought against his temper, but it reared its ugly head nonetheless. Damn! He felt betrayed, angry. He had been so certain that Moira liked it at the tavern, had thought she felt something for him. The more fool he. Balling his hands into fists, he was determined that somehow, someway, he would put Moira MacKinnon out of his heart and his mind.

PART TWO

A MATTER OF THE BARRELS

Staffordshire, England

The best-laid schemes o' mice an' men
    Gang aft agley,
An' lea'e us nought but grief and pain,
    For promised joy!

BURNS, "To a Mouse"

Chapter Twenty-eight

IT WAS AN EXHAUSTING and uncomfortable journey to Stafford over rough and rocky roads. Anxious to arrive as quickly as possible, Seamus kept a rigid and often harrowing schedule that left little time for comfort or relaxation. The wheels of the wagon seemed to be moving constantly, with stops made only at night or in times of a personal need. They traveled from London to Oxford to Coventry and beyond, staying at whatever inns were available, passing through village after village until Moira felt much like the gypsies her father had told her about.

The area consisted mainly of a broad belt of rich pastureland crossed by canals and gently-flowing rivers. To the south were several square miles of moorland and forest—once a hunting ground of the Plantagenet kings, or so Seamus told her. To the northeast were the oaks and hollies of the vast Needwood Forest. To the southwest was the River Trent, which meandered through the countryside, its banks touching on several towns. Stafford itself was a charming country town located on the River Sow. Standing around the village green were a church, with a fine chancel arch and nave arcades dating back to before the Norman conquest, a market square flanked by half-timbered cottages and shops, and one or two seemingly busy inns.

"It's still early. We'll bypass the inns and head directly for Chartley," Seamus announced, flicking the reins of the wagon. It was a decision he was to rue as they traveled along, for the weather quickly became most miserable.

A chill wind gusted. The skies were dark with clouds that threatened a storm as the brewer's wagon creaked over the hill, six miles from the town of Stafford. "There it is. Chartley

Hall,'' Seamus announced, making a grandiose sweep with his hand.

''Chartley—!'' Moira scanned the manor house and grounds with a close eye, the better to report to her brothers if the need arose. Situated on a hill rising from a fertile plain, the multi-windowed, gable-roofed manor house with a circular keep and towers was encircled by a large moat.

''I would suppose this place has been chosen to house the captive Queen because of that ditch,'' Seamus said, noticing the direction of her eyes. ''It is most suitable for security reasons, for I doubt it would be easy either for Mary to escape or for unwanted visitors to get beyond the walls.''

''No, I don't suppose it would be easy.'' How thankful Moira was that Seamus had given her the means to get inside Chartley.

Even so, when at last they arrived at the entranceway to the manor house, Moira was suddenly beset with nervousness. She had heard about Mary for so long, had idolized her so very much that she desperately wanted the Queen to like her, wanted to make a favorable impression. She was certain that she would not—the rigors of the journey had played havoc with her appearance. Her dress was wrinkled and dirty, her hair in need of a washing. She hardly looked like the daughter of a prominent Scottish laird. Stiffening her back and clenching her hands into fists, she was tense as Seamus made announcement of their arrival.

''Look, it's our old friend the brewer,'' announced a man at the gate to one of his companions.

''With more of his fine ale!'' exclaimed the other man.

Seamus was welcomed onto the manor grounds with congenial enthusiasm. His gift to the two men was a small cask of his finest brew. ''The better to stay in their good graces,'' he whispered to Moira.

While Seamus made his delivery, Moira made a tentative exploration of the outer rooms of the manor house, careful not to cause undue unrest. The house was roomy and well built. It was an imposing structure, nearly as grand as Greenwich, with a rustic splendor to it. Built of stone, it looked to be a sturdy fortress, albeit one that seemed comfortable inside. Was Mary happy here? From what Moira had heard, this was at least a less rigidly-guarded confinement than Mary had suffered at Tutbury. The question Moira asked herself was if she could take advantage of that fact. Would she be able to seek out the Scottish queen with impunity? She had to try.

Knowing well that it was always the servants who knew all that went on in any household, Moira sought out the kitchens. Striking up a conversation with one of the chatty young scullery-maids, she learned Mary's daily routine. By all calculations, the Queen would be in the library now. Thanking the young girl, Moira slipped into the shadows, working her way to that room. Surprisingly, the library door was unguarded. She quickly opened the door and went inside.

Moira found the large oblong room occupied by a chestnut-haired woman who sat by the window, reading. "Mary—?"

The woman responded to the name, immediately turning her head. Moira was stunned. This round-faced, plain woman couldn't possibly be Mary of the Scots. No, she couldn't be. This woman was not at all queenly. Though she had been warned by Seamus that Mary had changed, Moira found herself staring. This woman looked so old. No, this couldn't be her godmother. She was besieged with a certainty that this was some other person, and not the Queen of Scots at all. Another Mary, perhaps, one of the Queen's ladies-in-waiting.

Moira somehow found her voice. "Excuse me, but I am looking for Mary Stuart."

"Then you have found her," the woman answered, putting down her book.

She was dressed all in black, like one in mourning. It was a dress that was sadly out of fashion, its faded skirts puffed out by a Spanish farthingale, not the French hooped version that Moira had seen at Greenwich. The woman's face was overly pale, and lined at the mouth and eyes.

"But who are you, child? Why do you seek me out?" The voice was soft and soothing, with just a hint of a rasp. She eyed Moira up and down stoically, noting the dust from the road, and the snags and tears of the young woman's garments. Moira thought again that she must have looked much like a pauper. Even so, she was treated with the utmost courtesy. "Speak, child. I will do you no harm."

"I have come to Chartley from London. I wish to see Mary,

Queen of Scots. You tell me that you are Mary?'' Somehow, even now, Moira fully expected the woman to deny it. This woman with the unhappy face and matronly form could not be the legendary, beautiful Mary. No, some unfortunate jest was being perpetrated here.

''I am she!'' There was such pride in her tone of voice that any doubts Moira might have had were swept away. As Mary stood up, there was a regal bearing to her form, a pride that no amount of suffering could smother. All that remained as a reminder of what she once had been were the elegant height of her rapidly thickening form and her long-fingered hands, yet she conducted herself like a queen. Her head was held high as she swept forward. ''But tell me, who are you?''

Moira's voice lowered to a whisper, her eyes darting about the confines of the room to ascertain that no one might overhear. ''I am Moira April MacKinnon. Kylynn's daughter.''

''Moira? Moira MacKinnon?'' Mary stepped closer. ''Can it be true? Kylynn's youngest babe?''

''If you need proof that I am who I say I am, this should dispel any doubts.'' Taking off her father's ring, Moira gave it up to Mary. ''I have come in the hope that I can be of help to you.''

Mary's fingers trembled as she took the offering, and Moira noted that some of her joints were swollen. ''I remember this ring. I remember it very well.'' For a long, long time, she was silent, as if recalling a myriad of memories. At last, she said, ''Your coming here brings back so many memories. It is a good omen, child. I feel it in my heart.''

''I hope to make it so.'' Moira curtsied, showing proper respect.

''Kylynn's daughter—'' Mary's eyes sparkled with unshed tears. ''Let me look at you.'' Slowly, she circled Moira. ''Ah yes, I can see a great deal of Kylynn in you. You have her beauty, her grace. Your nose, high cheekbones, and large green eyes are replicas of Kylynn's. And I can see a touch of Roarke in you, too. The hair, the smile. You have his height.'' Gently, she touched Moira's shoulders. ''You are a stunning combination of the two people I hold most dear. I shall hold you to my heart as well.''

Moira was deeply touched. Forgetting all else, she put her

arms around Mary's neck, and the two embraced in mutual affection. Once again, Moira thought of the injustice that had been meted out to the Scottish queen. Oh, how her heart ached for Mary. She remembered that her captivity had lasted nineteen years, longer than Moira had been alive. She tried to understand the desperation Mary must have felt, her sense of grievous wrong. Even so, Mary had not steeped herself in self-pity, or turned into a whining, bitter and shrewish woman as some others might have. There was still a kindness in Mary that Moira could sense in her presence.

"There are many who would seek to free you," Moira said, when at last she pulled away. Her heart swelled with a righteous cause. "My brothers and myself are among them."

What might have happened to Mary if . . . ? It was a question that plagued Moira's mind. What if Darnley had been a proper husband? What if Mary had never fallen in love with Bothwell? What if Darnley had escaped the plot against his life? What if Mary had never ventured onto English soil, had never asked her cousin Elizabeth for sanctuary? But all those questions had come to pass. Now she was England's prisoner.

Poor, poor Mary, she thought. What was most tragic, moreover, was the perpetual look of sadness in the Queen's brown eyes. Even when she smiled at Moira, there was no flicker of happiness in her face. Though she knew it unfair to make comparisons, Moira could not help thinking how young her mother appeared, still beautiful in her middle years, and how old Mary seemed, even though she and Kylynn were near each other in age. Loving her father had kept her mother young and vital, Moira thought. It was as though Mary had lost interest in caring for herself. As though in regard to her beauty, she had given in to the passing years. Was that why Moira had noted so few mirrors about the rooms? Damn Elizabeth!

"Free me?" Mary shook her head sadly. "There have been attempts over the years, but they have all failed. I have at last willed myself to accept my cage."

"You must not." Moira took Mary's hand. "I have come here to help Donnie and Davie formulate a plan!" She emphasized her resolve with a heartfelt squeeze of Mary's fingers.

"No!" Mary reacted strongly, but not in the manner which Moira had expected. She pulled her hand from Moira's grasp.

Suddenly her voice was stern, as if speaking to a wayward child. "You are much too young. You must return at once from whence you have come." Mary's expression gave hint of her doubts and fears. Her hope of freedom had faded as the years had passed and the plots fallen into ruin. "I will not let you put yourself in any danger. There have been those who have attempted such daring and met with a tragic fate. I would not see you end up in the Tower, or worse—"

"In truth, I tell you I will not. Nor will my brothers." She flung her arms out, as if in supplication. "Please believe me. Davie and Donnie are ever an ingenious pair. Why, even now they have ensconced themselves in Elizabeth's court."

"With Elizabeth!" Mary paled. "Foolish young pups; Elizabeth is no simpleton to be so easily taken in. She will know of the ties your family had to me. She will have the lads watched, every minute of every day. If they but blink in the wrong direction, they will find themselves in serious trouble."

"I know," Moira conceded. "I had the same worry. That is why I knew I had to come to their aid."

"You? *You* are doubly vulnerable. Elizabeth adores handsome young men, but she is intensely jealous of any woman younger or prettier than she. Your punishment will be twice as harsh as your brothers'." Turning away, Mary walked to the window, staring through its panes. "You must go back at once. Forget about me."

"Forget?" Moira knew she could never do that, not now. Mary would forever be embedded in her mind.

"You will be safe in Scotland. Your father is a prominent man and will give you his protection." She looked over her shoulder. "Return there at once! Tell your brothers as well. They must leave England before something tragic happens."

Moira walked towards the Queen. "They are ever a stubborn lot. I know that Donnie and Davie will not even think of leaving. They have made a vow to free you, and will hold themselves to that until 'tis done. I am just as stubborn. A terrible injustice has been done and must be righted."

"And a greater injustice still will be meted out if you and your brothers do not listen to reason." Grasping Moira by the shoulders, Mary forced her to look at her. "I am past my youth, as you can see, but you have your whole life ahead of you. I cannot let you put yourself in danger. I have many enemies here in England who are ever on the watch.''

"Such as Walsingham."

Mary grimaced. "What do you know of him?"

"I know that he is vicious and dangerous. I know that he has spies crawling all over London like vermin. I myself have come to the attention of one of his rodents.''

"Mon Dieu!" Mary clasped her hands together and placed them at her heart. "Then think of yourself. You must leave without delay. Send for your father. He will come posthaste to take you home again, of that I am certain.''

"And end up with his own head on the block." Moira was determined. "It is more dangerous for my father to set foot in this hostile land. Elizabeth has never really forgiven him. No! I will not endanger him." Moira thrust back her shoulders and held up her chin, knowing beyond a doubt that her arrival in London had been no accident of fate. "The die has been cast. God has sent me to England for a purpose. I truly understand that now.''

Quickly, she told Mary about her intent to warn her brothers, her incarceration as a stowaway aboard the *Red Mermaid*, Captain Paxton's insistence that she work as a tavern-maid, of her determination to master the task while garnering necessary information. She spoke of the spies Seamus had pointed out to her in the Devil's Thumb taproom, and her journey to Greenwich to warn her brothers. Lastly, she told of coming back to the tavern and finding her room ransacked. She was too deeply involved to think of stopping now.

"There can be no turning back. I have committed myself to a most noble cause.''

"Freeing me?"

"Yes!"

"And just what do you hope to accomplish in coming here?'' Though Mary's tone was harsh, her eyes were gentle. "Do you not see that you have put yourself in even more danger? Seeking out the company of one considered Elizabeth's foe will only put you deeper in the stew. Whatever could you have hoped to accomplish by such a daring venture?''

"When Seamus told me he had seen you, and that he could get into Chartley, I knew that an opportunity I could not reject had been opened." Moira wanted to convince the Queen of her sincerity, her good intentions. "I wanted to talk with you, comfort you, and aid my brothers in any way that I could."

"And just what do you intend to do? How are you, a young woman in the first flower of her youth, going to save me when others have failed?"

"I don't have a definite plan—yet." It was a humiliating admission. "But I feel in my heart that somehow, some way, I can prove to be valuable. I can go with the brewer back and forth to London and be a liaison for my brothers. Thus, we can keep informed with what is happening in London, and they likewise will be able to contact you freely when they have plotted out their strategy."

"You think to move back and forth between here and London?"

"Yes!"

Mary was adamant. "I tell you that you cannot. Must not! Walsingham's agents are ever on the lookout for just such foolishness. When it is found out who you are, you will be watched as closely as a falling star. Were you to be caught with a missive upon your person, your fate would be sealed."

Moira wasn't so easily swayed to defeat. "I will keep the messages in my head." She tapped at her temple with her finger.

"If you think that that ensures your safety, then I tell you that you are wrong. Walsingham has ways of unloosening the firmest of tongues. One turn of the rack's wheel, and you would be babbling like a babe." Mary looked deep into Moira's eyes.

"I'm not afraid! Nor will I be caught." Moira knew that she was too smart to be cornered. "I am quick of wit and will use the utmost caution."

"Caution? It is of little use when you are constantly scrutinized, as am I." Mary put a hand to her mouth as if to stifle a sob. She seemed perilously close to the breaking point. "I cannot let you go through such an experience. Dear blessed Jesus! Kylynn would never forgive me if she lost her children because of my plight."

Moira bristled at being called a child. "It will not come to that! I promise you that I will be careful."

"Careful? Careful?" Mary threw her head back in vexation.

"You have already roused Walsingham's spies. How do you know that they are not watching you even now?"

"Because they do not even know that I am here." Moira hoped that to be the truth, though Seamus had told her that some of Walsingham's agents seemed to have eyes in the backs of their heads and ears that could hear everything. It would be dangerous, were her whereabouts known, dangerous not only to herself, but to her brothers. "I was doubly cautious. Only Seamus knows my destination."

"Seamus?"

"The brewer who brought me here in his wagon. He is Scottish, but raised under England's loyalties. Still, I have the feeling that I can trust him. He has proven himself to be trustworthy so far."

"And does he know what you plan?" Mary wrung her hands nervously.

"No, he only knows that you were friends with my mother, and that you are my godmother. He brought me here to visit a woman I hold most dear. For all his great bulk and menacing appearance, Seamus is all heart. On the journey, I came to see that I can trust him, and—"

"You can trust no one! *No one*," Mary repeated. The Queen was adamant. "Only those who have proven themselves loyal to me or to the cause. All those who swear allegiance to Elizabeth are enemies to me. It must be so."

Sadly, Moira concurred, knowing that Ryan Paxton would therefore be thought of as a foe. That she loved him would make him that much more dangerous. Even so, she yearned to see him again. She wanted to tell Mary about him, confide her feelings, but instead said, "Any enemy of yours is likewise mine."

"Were it up to me, you wouldn't have an enemy in the world," Mary sighed, shaking her head sadly. "Oh, Moira. Moira—how sweetly loyal you are, touchingly so. I should insist that you do as I say, that you leave this country—"

"No!" Moira put her hands together. "Please."

"Perhaps it would be no great wrong for you to stay here, at least for a while. Until you are made to see how cautious you must be."

"Stay here?" Moira was taken totally by surprise. She had

never foreseen an invitation to stay with the Queen, had in fact planned to return to London with Seamus.

"I am lonely, child. Your company would greatly please me. And perhaps I can keep you safe from Walsingham here. At least until I think of what must be done." She confirmed what Moira suspected, that Mary's change of heart was because she thought to protect her. Mary feared for her, intended to look after her and keep her out of mischief. What better way than to keep her within her line of vision? Whatever the reason, however, it would do for now.

"We will think this out carefully, my dear, and think of just what to say. It would be better if your real identity were unknown, that it was thought that you are an English girl. Your manner of speech is certainly precise enough for you to be successful in pretense."

"But Seamus knows who I am." The brewer could cause complications in Mary's plan.

"Then he must not know that you intend to stay here."

"I told him that I would return with him when he returned to London. What shall I say?"

Mary's brows arched up in surprise. "Why, that you have decided to return to your home in Scotland, my dear. What else? It is ever a woman's prerogative to change her mind." She took Moira by the hand. "I will have to think this out very carefully, but I do believe that if we are very, very clever, all will work out just the way it should." She thought a moment. "I have been nagging Sir Amyas Paulet unmercifully about the lack of sufficient servants about this place. Would you be offended if we passed you off as a lady's maid?"

Moira laughed softly. "Not after all the days I spent as a tavern-wench."

"Then I will speak to Paulet about it at once. Ah yes, the more I think of it, the more I favor such a notion."

Well, so be it, Moira thought. Hadn't it always been her dream to serve Mary? Wouldn't she feel great satisfaction when her brothers found out? She was here at Chartley with Mary, Queen of Scots. It was something even her brothers could not brag about. Indeed, her journey here seemed to be a most promising beginning. Why then was it so hard to smile? Perhaps because staying here with the Queen was also an ending to what might have been. If only Ryan Paxton were not a Protestant Englishman loyal to Elizabeth, and she a Catholic Scots, sworn to serve Mary.

Chapter Twenty-nine

THE DAY DAWNED CLEAR with just a snap of frost in the air. Winter was relatively mild in Stafford, or so it seemed thus far, Moira thought as she looked out the window at the rolling hills and pasturelands. From the windows of Chartley, she was afforded a magnificent view: acre after acre of snow-dusted ground, blue ribbons of icy water winding over the hills, leafless trees with upraised branches, as if in prayer. There was a serene beauty to the countryside that reminded her of her home in Scotland, and made her a bit homesick at times. But her longing to see her home again was nothing compared to how much she missed Ryan Paxton. How was it possible for a man to have become so very integral to her happiness? Without him, loneliness had taken on a new meaning.

"I must not forget him for the time being." she whispered, trying to put all selfish thoughts from her mind. It was easier said than done, for not one day passed that she didn't think of Ryan with a heavy heart. When she returned, would she ever be able to make him understand why she had left London? Would it be too late? He was a handsome man; would he find another love to take her place? She could only hope that he would not, that it would not be too late to tell him that she loved him and would make amends.

Moira tried to think of other things lest she give way to melancholy. She had taken on a new last name, "Mowbray," pretending to be related to two of the women already in Mary's employ. It was an identity that Paulet did not seem to doubt, though he did scold her from time to time with the admonition that she must earn her keep and make certain her hands were busy. In truth, there was always a great deal to keep her occupied, for she had been given the task as lady's maid to Mary. It was a request surprisingly granted by the stern-faced Paulet, who nonetheless kept a stern watch over Moira's every move.

Moira aided Mary in dressing, and attended the Queen at morning Mass. After religious services, she sat by Mary's side for breakfast, then kept her company at her sewing. Mary tried to while away the long hours of her confinement with embroidery, reading, gardening or at play with her pet spaniels—she who had once relished riding, hawking and hunting. Now Mary suffered from an inflammation in her joints and pain in her muscles, no doubt brought on by her lack of freedom, and thus the chance for proper exercise. Sometimes her legs were so swollen that she could not even walk. When her health and the weather allowed it, Mary should most certainly be given the privilege of seeking fresh air. Surely the frown-faced Paulet must have some compassion. Or did he? Moira wasn't so sure.

Paulet. Oh, how Moira loathed the man. He was a cold-blooded pinch-penny, a solemn, dull man who seemed to enjoy Mary's suffering. When the Queen complained of aching joints, he showed no sympathy and acted as if it were her due. He too had the same ailment and never complained, he would say. Nor did he try to hide the fact that he hated all things and persons Catholic; he openly condemned them for heresy. The "devil's spawn," he called those who obeyed Pope and priests. Moira often saw him looking at her as if he fully expected her to grow horns.

Sir Amyas Paulet had revealed his harsh character from the very first moment that Mary had been given over to his care. He had gone out of his way to prove that he was immune to Mary's charms, and nearly declared himself the Queen of Scots' mortal enemy. Mary told Moira that his first official act had been to take down from above her head and chair the royal cloth of state by which she set great store, since it constituted proof of her queenship. The fanatical man had cited the reason as being that the cloth of state had never been officially allowed, no matter how long Mary had displayed it. Though Mary had wept and protested vigorously, he had not changed his mind.

"A pox on that man and all his kind!" Moira muttered beneath her breath.

Paulet was certainly an obstacle to her hopes for a daring
rescue. He watched everyone in the household like a hawk,
especially the laundresses, whom he had caught more than
once in the merry trade of message-bearing. Mary's generous
habit of alms-giving had also been curtailed as a method in
which she might stir up the countryside in her favor. Little did
he know that Mary was already aware that there were several
families friendly to her cause living in the neighborhood. Moira
wished she could find a way to make use of them, but that
could have serious implications if she were caught—for herself
as well as Mary.

Mary's place of imprisonment had been repeatedly changed,
lest the sympathy felt for her in the surrounding area should
inspire new plots against Elizabeth. Mary was therefore uneasy. She had confided to Moira that as rigid as its confinement
was, Chartley was a pleasant change from Tutbury, where she
had been under constant surveillance. What had been worse
was that Mary had been completely deprived of the news she
wanted so much at Tutbury. Here at Chartley, Paulet had not
yet enacted such a stringent ban. Oftentimes, the servants'
gossip kept Mary more than amply supplied with tidbits of
goings-on.

"There has to be a way to get correspondence out of
here—"

The sound of a bell put an end to Moira's musing. It was
Mary's signal that she was up and ready to get dressed. Moira
poured water from a pitcher into a small china basin, hurriedly
washed her face and plaited her long dark hair, securing it in
coils on either side of her head. Hastening to put on a dark
green dress trimmed in gold—one of Mary's own—she went
to the Queen's chambers.

The routine was always the same. Up early to help the Queen
dress, aiding her in lacing up her corset, putting on her farthingale, fastening up her petticoat and gown, and slipping on
her neck and wrist ruffs. Moira then brushed the Queen's hair
and helped her don one of her wigs. Though at first Moira had
thought Mary's hair to be still chestnut with a few tendrils of
gray, in truth the Queen's hair had turned almost completely

white—she whose hair had once been her glory. Shock and grief had perhaps caused the change, Moira thought, once again touched by the Queen's plight.

"Take special care, Moira child. I am to be allowed a visitor today." Mary's tone was light, almost cheerful. Her mood startled Moira.

"A visitor?"

It struck her as odd, for Paulet was usually most strict on the matter. Upon Mary's request that Moira become her lady's maid, the frowning man had interrogated Moira so heatedly that she had been certain she would melt under the blazing heat of his stare. Still, she had somehow maintained her composure, not even blinking as she repeated the story Mary had told her to tell, that she was the daughter of a Worcester farmer of English Catholic heritage, and had come to Chartley to seek employment. Barbara and Gillis Mowbray had aided in the deception, welcoming their dear "cousin" with open arms. Even so, Moira had been prepared to be turned away. She was instead allowed to stay, though Paulet had been tightfisted about her earnings, saying that the Scottish queen and her servants would soon impoverish him. "This Queen's servants are always craving and have no pity at all on English purses," he had said angrily.

"A priest has arrived at Chartley. His uncle's residence is but a few miles away. Sir Amyas has agreed to let him visit me. I want you to be there," Mary explained.

Mary had Moira take much time with her person, as if she were a young woman again, and he a suitor. She wants to charm him, Moira thought, sensing that there was much more to this priest's attendance on the Scottish queen than whispering prayers or hearing her confession. Upon entering the solar and seeing the priest for herself, she was positive of it. There was something in his blue eyes that struck her, a certain look that she had seen in the eyes of Walsingham's spies. Perhaps those who intrigued always looked thus? She wondered if her own eyes held such a gleam, or perchance a glow of apprehension that someone would suspect.

"Gilbert Gifford is my name," the brown-haired priest said, in a voice that sounded as if he had a cold. He bowed low.

"It is a privilege and an honor to at last meet she who has held my heart for so many years."

Mary swept forward with a gait that ignored her aching legs. For just a moment, she seemed to be the young, ever-laughing Queen again, as she welcomed the priest with great warmth and affection. "And it is a joy to meet you, Father. I so seldom get the chance to converse with one of my own faith, particularly one as learned as you."

"I, learned?" He bowed his head in a show of feigned humility. "Fie, your Majesty—compared to your knowledge, I am but a child. That you are well-read is known all over Europe. I would say then that it was you who inspired me in my pious vocation."

"I am flattered." A flush stained Mary's cheeks.

"It is the truth. You have inspired me my entire life. I have but recently—" He looked at Moira as if to ask if she could be trusted.

"Anything you say to me can be spoken of in her presence. Moira is as dear to my heart as if she were my own child." For just a moment, a shadow flitted over Mary's face, as if remembering her own son's perfidy and lack of loyalty. "More so, for she would not seek to turn her back upon me for her own reward." James's betrayal and his friendship with Elizabeth still stung her.

The priest nodded. Walking to the two doors of the solar, he closed them tightly. "Then I will give her my trust as well." Putting his hands behind his back, he paced the room. "I am not just here for a visit," he said. "I have but recently come from France, where I went to see a man by the name of Thomas Morgan. A man most loyal to freeing you and putting you on the English throne where you belong."

Moira could see that Mary's hands were quivering. "I know of the man."

"He sends you this." The priest pulled a letter out of his sleeve and handed it to Mary.

Moira read the missive over Mary's shoulder. It said that the bearer, Gilbert Gifford, was a priest of the Roman Catholic Church, a man of skill and loyalty in whom she could place the utmost trust.

"So, I have not been forgotten after all." The expression in Mary's eyes softened as she smiled.

"I have a plan to thwart your jailer. Paulet? Ah yes, that is his name. Am I right in saying that he has cut off all your letters from the outside?"

"Yes!"

"Then perchance you need my help." His raspy voice dropped as he detailed a plan. Every week, a barrel of beer was sent from Burton to the Queen's apartments. One of the draymen had been taken into confidence, whereby the bung of the barrel was to be replaced with a corked tube in which letters could be concealed. "Messages to you will come into Chartley Manor with the full keg, and letters from you will be smuggled out in the empty barrel. And none will ever be the wiser."

It sounded like a foolproof plan. Moira regretted that she had not thought of it. Even so, Mary was overly cautious, perhaps because of the failed plots of previous years. "The letters will be discovered. Paulet has examined the laundry on its way to and from the wash, had soles of shoes inspected. He will find the letters. You will come to ruin. I do not want that on my conscience. Already, too many have died. The scaffold still drips with the blood of those who have been executed for coming to my aid."

"This plan will not fail." The priest looked upward as if for reassurance from a heavenly presence. "God is on our side."

"I think it has merit," Moira said, wondering if Seamus could not likewise have been of some help. Oh, how she had hated to lie to him and tell him she was going back to Scotland! It had somehow seemed as if she had betrayed his friendship by telling him a falsehood. But Mary would not have it any other way.

"The letter I just gave you was the test," Gifford answered. "It was brought here in such a barrel, right under Paulet's very nose. I retrieved it before our meeting."

"Then it did work." Mary clasped her hands over her heart. For a moment, Moira feared for her health, but the light trill of laughter from Mary's throat calmed any such fears. "So I can begin to live again—to hope again. The world with all its powers, its exhilarating possibilities, is mine again. I will no longer be cut off so cruelly from the world." Mary seemed intoxicated by the thought of renewed communications. "Then let us begin. This very day."

Nevertheless, some instinct warned the Queen to be cautious. In her reply to Morgan, she advised him, "Keep yourself from meddling with anything that might redound to your hurt, or increase the suspicion already conceived against you in these parts, being sure that you are able to clear yourself of all dealings for my service hithertill." She handed the missive to Gifford to put into the hands of this dear brewer, "the honest man," as she now called him, who would smuggle it out for her.

"And so we are closer this day to accomplishing our ends." The priest smiled at the two women. "Ah, yes. Let us hope that all goes exactly as it is supposed to."

"And all will be well," Moira breathed.

Two MEN STOOD by the front doorway, watching as Gilbert Gifford took his leave of Chartley. The priest reached up and pulled at the lobe of his ear, a signal that all had been successful.

"She took the bait, Selby." Even though he perceived victory, Rothingham kept his face impassive. There were still many things which could go wrong if one was distracted by conceit. "What Mary of Scots does not know is that it was one of Walsingham's spies who presented himself to Morgan and the French ambassador as Mary's confidential agent. Mary's supposedly secret correspondence will be fully supervised by her enemies."

"Taken out of the barrels?"

"You can be such an idiot at times, but yes! Every letter to or from Mary will be inspected by Gifford. The Scottish harridan thinks that she has contacted the outside world, but in fact she will merely signal her private thoughts and schemes to Paulet and Walsingham."

"And then we can hang all those she contacts. And the Scottish girl as well." Putting his fingers around his throat, Selby made jest, sticking out his tongue in the semblance of those who became gallows-bait. "Or chop off their heads."

"Fool! Buffoon. It will not suit Walsingham's purposes to

send a few noblemen and one Scottish girl to the block.''

"By God! Why not?"

"Think, you son of a dim-witted whore! What is the use of cutting off a few heads or hanging one or two men, if by morning someone else but takes their place? Think! The great spymaster has more ambitious thoughts in his head. His aim is to provide Elizabeth and England with sufficient evidence to prove beyond a doubt that it is too dangerous to keep Mary alive. To make an end to Mary Stuart once and for all!''

Chapter Thirty

IT WAS SMOKY AND MUSTY inside the Devil's Thumb. The smell of spilled wine, whiskey, and ale mixed with the odor of sweat and leather. The clank of tankards, mugs, and cups rang in the air. It was the last day of the week, and as usual the tavern was filled to overflowing. Ryan sat listening to the raucous laughter and boisterous chatter that reverberated in the room. It was noisy, yet not any more so than usual. Why, then, did the laughter annoy him so? Why did he sit here brooding? Because it bothered him that others could find frivolity when he was so miserable.

There seemed to be a chill in the taproom. The fire had burned down to ash. Ryan rose to his feet and threw another log onto the fire, watching as it flared up. His heart was heavy, his temper on edge. He missed her. By God, how he missed her. More so than he had ever thought it possible to miss another human being. He needed her. She was a balm to his soul. There was something about her that he craved, like a man hankered for strong drink. No, it was an even greater yearning than that. Something had been missing from his life until he looked into her enormous green eyes, until he had kissed her. She had given his life new meaning, and now she was gone.

"Moira! Moira!" The sound of her name to his lips brought both comfort and pain. He knew he should forget her, and yet he could not.

He could envision her now, sweeping into the room so haughty and proud, catching every man's eye. The tavern was a constant reminder of her. Why, then, did he torture himself by coming here so often? He answered the question at once.

He was the biggest of fools, hovering inside the Devil's Thumb, hoping by some miracle that she would walk through that door and come back to him.

"God's gray beard!" he mumbled darkly, rubbing his fingers across the stubble of his whiskers. "I'm in love with the chit! Totally, irrevocably besotted." He knew he couldn't deny it. The question was, what was he going to do about it? In truth, how could he do anything when he didn't even know where she had gone? Back to her family? It was the only thing that made sense. She had become homesick and returned to Scotland while he was away. Could he blame her for that? And yet, that she had left without even a word stung him.

Had she really been so very anxious to get away from the tavern and from him? Perhaps. He had been the worst kind of rogue to keep her here. Had he been Roarke MacKinnon and she his daughter, he would have scorned such a man as a blackguard.

"I should never have held her here so long." But he had. The truth was, he just couldn't bear to see her go. Thus he had selfishly and thoughtlessly kept her at the Devil's Thumb. He had hoped that the attraction he felt for her would be returned, that what sparked between them would turn to passion and love, but perhaps he had longed for too much. The moment he was out of sight, she had gone away.

Ryan stared into the fire for a long, long while. A decision needed to be made as to what his next action would be. Waiting docilely until the wench came to her senses and sought him out again was not his way of doing things. He was a man of action, a man who went after what he wanted. Had that not been so, he would not be a ship's captain with at least a touch of respectability.

I should take my ship, he thought, and sail to Edinburgh, procure a horse, and ride all the way to the MacKinnon lands to woo her and bring her back. Women liked a man to be decisive and strong, to carry them away. For the first time in a long while, Ryan smiled as the idea of throwing her over his shoulder and sweeping her from her father's hall flitted before his eyes. What would the MacKinnons think of that? No doubt it would be the talk of the Scottish countryside for quite a while.

His daring plotting was disturbed as the front door of the tavern was thrown open. Sleet gusted through the open portal, swirling about the cloaked figure that walked into the room. The man made his way into the taproom, immediately seeking out the warmth of the fire. As soon as he took off his wet outer garments, Ryan recognized him. The young gentleman of fashion was a frequent guest at the tavern, one whom the captain had no liking for at all. Anthony Babington was his name, a flamboyant and unusually handsome but foppish man. He was one who always demanded the best service, overstayed his welcome, but never paid his bill. There was always a haggle over every penny owed, as if the young man could not afford to pay. Ha!

Babington was a young country gentleman, the married and well-to-do scion of an ancient Northumberland family who had settled in Derbyshire. His family was Catholic, and his mother was a devout woman, or so the young man had said often enough. On his father's death some fifteen years before, Anthony—a boy of ten—became the ward of Lord Shrewsbury and was trained as a page. He had gone to London and been well-received at court, a fact that still rankled Ryan, for due to his lack of a wealthy family, he himself had been nudged aside in favor of the more prominent Babington.

Babington's lineage was always made evident. Even now, the young man was dressed in an elaborately decorated red velvet doublet, red trunk hose, and gold hosen. Ah yes, Babington was rich, his family having benefited from two marriages to heiresses. His income was fabulous, well over a thousand pounds a year, or so it was bandied about. He was in a position to entertain and act as host to innumerable friends and companions. Why, then, did he always frequent Ryan's tavern?

"As long as he pays." Ryan grumbled. The Devil's Thumb was not in the habit of granting annuities.

Babington was just one among many noblemen in the tavern this night. A peacock, to be certain, but then there were others. Few noticed the silent young nobleman as he moved towards a seat in the corner, but Ryan kept him in sight. The man was walking as stealthily as a midnight robber, looking over his shoulder, seeking out the shadows. He was soon joined by several other well-dressed gentlemen who immersed themselves in talk at the table. Babington's party had grown in size—noblemen all, and all Catholics. Ryan recognized each and every one of them. Something was afoot.

The noise in the tavern was deafening. Ryan strained to catch at least a word or two that the men were saying, but was unsuccessful. Whatever was being planned would remain unknown by him. Perhaps it was just as well. Sometimes knowing too much got a man in a great deal of trouble. Babington suddenly seemed to be aware that Ryan was staring at him, for he looked up and forced an innocent-looking smile. Ryan's lips tightened fractionally, but he couldn't quite manage a similar salutation. Intriguers—oh, how they annoyed him. Always causing trouble in the realm, plotting to the detriment of Elizabeth and England.

"By God, Paxton, you are beginning to sound like Walsingham," Ryan mumbled angrily beneath his breath. Whatever was being talked about was none of his business. He would do well to remember that and leave the spying to Walsingham's cronies.

Turning his back, he shrugged, putting the matter out of his mind. There were other things he needed to think about, like getting back Moira MacKinnon. He remembered the feel of her soft body pressed against his, the sweet fragrance of her hair. By God, but the haughty wench had gotten into his blood. He wanted her in his bed, wanted her mouth trembling and soft beneath his. She was an enchantress. Just the thought of her banished the image of any other woman from his mind. Indeed, though he had sought out other women, *she* had ever been on his mind.

Hailing the potboy, Ryan ordered the tavern's finest ale, Seamus's brew. Wrapping his fingers around the handle of his tankard, he took a long draught of ale, drawing solace from the brew. Nothing warmed a man quite as well on a cold night. Except for the arms of a beautiful woman, one you loved, he thought.

Seamus was right, Ryan thought. Seamus knew I'd end up being smitten with the haughty little Scottish miss. Mark one up for the brewer. As soon as he returned, Ryan would tell him that he had won his bet. And mark one up for Moira

MacKinnon as well. His heart was a pawn to her green eyes. Men thought they ruled the world but they were wrong. It was women.

"Women," he breathed, already feeling the warmth of the drink course through his body. One woman in particular was on his mind. "Moira—" Over and over again, her name kept whirling about in his head.

The hour was growing late. Soon, very few patrons lingered in the taproom. Why, then, did he? he wondered. Perhaps because he dreaded the solitude of his thoughts, he chose to remain in the huge room, moodily drinking tankard after tankard of ale. Soon his vision blurred, his head buzzed, but he continued raising the cup to his lips. As a general rule, he'd never let his drinking get out of hand, but then he'd never lost a woman before.

It was almost dawn when Ryan left the Devil's Thumb to return to his ship. He drew his cloak about his shoulders. He was no longer quite drunk, but near enough to have lessened his heartache. Not so much so that he wasn't capable of making a decision—to sail for Edinburgh upon the morrow.

Chapter Thirty-one

MOIRA SHIVERED AT THE COLD in the room. In just a month's time, winter had come to Stafford with a harshness that was startling. It was full upon the area, with freezing, long nights, and gloomy, dark-clouded days. The air inside Chartley was stuffy, and Moira found herself longing intently for spring. Oh, to be outside these dreary stone walls, to breathe in fresh air again, to hear the birds sing.

Damning Paulet beneath her breath for his miserly ways, she rested her needlework in her lap and pulled her chair closer to the fire. Despite the weather, Mary's "guardian"—as Paulet called himself—had been stubbornly strict in his rationing of wood. Only a third of the rooms in Chartley were allowed to have a fire, and even then, only one log at a time was to be meted out to feed the flames. Was it any wonder that it was damp and miserable inside the hall?

Moira looked down at the sewing she held in her hands and tried her best to concentrate once again upon her stitches. As if to taunt her, it was an intricate pattern abounding with flowers and birds. Breathing a sigh, she stuck her needle into the coarse cloth, then cried out in pain as she stuck her finger.

"By—God!" she swore, forgetting herself for a moment as she uttered one of Ryan Paxton's favorite oaths.

"Moira! Such an expression does not become you," Mary chided gently.

"I beg your pardon, your Majesty."

Moira looked at the Queen out of the corner of her eye. Mary's face was pale, and though she made no complaint, Moira knew the cold was affecting her. She rose from her seat, picked up a large log, and threw it on the fire, basking in the warmth and glow it gave as the flames consumed it. Let Paulet scold; she would not let the Queen suffer.

"Ah, that does feel better. But I would not want you to be denied your ration of wood, child. You know what Paulet said."

Moira did. If he found out it was she who had been wasteful with the wood, she would be denied her nightly share. "It doesn't matter. The quilt you made me keeps me warm enough." A strong bond was being formed between Moira and her godmother. It seemed that Mary, hungering for companionship, was becoming very attached to dear Kylynn's daughter.

Every day, Moira was coming to feel more and more affection for the Queen. If Mary's appearance had changed, her charitable nature had not. Kylynn MacKinnon had always told Moira how generous and charming Mary was. Now Moira could see for herself that this was true. Though her hands often ached from sewing, it was the Queen's greatest pleasure to make gifts for those who served her. Even now, she was stitching gloves for the drayman who brought ale to the household.

A barrel of beer was sent every week from Burton for the Queen's servants, and every week, the bung of the barrel was replaced with a corked tube in which letters were concealed. Communications were carried out with a regularity that lightened Mary's mood and gave her new hope for the future.

Week after week the "honest man," as Mary dubbed the drayman, brought the barrel of beer to Chartley. Once it was safely in the cellar, Mary's butler removed the corked tube which carried the incoming letter, while last week's empty barrel, in like manner, conveyed an outgoing letter. Being of generous nature, Mary paid the honest man well for his services.

Lately, Mary had reason to be so content. She was stimulated by a revival of hope, intoxicated by the pleasure of renewed communications with the outside world. The barrel post was working wonderfully, despite the weather. Somehow, even when the roads were covered with snow, the drayman got through with his cargo. Mary had been gifted with the letters once denied her, letters hidden in a water-tight box.

The barrel post was a new spring of life for Mary. It opened again the great, living world with its friendly powers, its secret combinations. Exhilarating possibilities were hers again, and all her dormant energies rose up, fully alive. It was as if she had miraculously been transformed before Moira's very eyes. She suddenly looked younger, more vital. Though she was still often plagued by pain, the hope that had been rekindled seemed to lessen its effects. What was more important was that Mary had taken to smiling again.

"I praise the day my dear priest came into my life," she would say again and again. She in fact praised Gifford in her conversation every day until he took on the semblance of a saint.

Mary showered rewards with a lavish hand on Gifford and on that "honest man," the drayman. It was thought better not to know his identity, lest the poor man suffer for his loyalty through an inadvertent slip of the tongue. The Queen was also generous in granting rewards of gifts and money on every subordinate messenger.

Ale also continued to come from Seamus, and when the brewer was near the premises, Moira's heart ached anew with the reminder of Ryan Paxton. She wanted to talk with Seamus, to inquire after the captain just to make certain he was well, yet she had been instructed most sternly that she must hide from the Staffordshire brewer lest her own safety be endangered; such a thought made her sigh.

It was silent in the room, as all the women were engrossed in their stitchery. There was always mending to be done, as well as embroidery. Moira cast an assessing eye over the room and Mary's women. Two were dressed all in dark gray, another in a bright blue dress; the other two wore gowns with as many colors as the rainbow.

A varying assortment of height and weight was represented, as well as stations in life. There were five in all sitting in the solar, including two laundresses and one young woman who had recently delivered a babe. Two others were noblewomen of prominent Catholic families. Mary never discriminated against those whose labor was menial, but gave them the same friendship as she did those of more noble birth. Her reward was an all-abiding loyalty. Not one of the women present would ever seek to betray the Queen. Even so, for their own protection, Mary had been selective in who had been told about the correspondence she was receiving. Of the women assembled, only Moira and the woman in the bright blue dress were aware of the barrel post.

Moira cocked her head to listen to the sounds outside the window. She could hear the faint sound of wheels hitting against the stones, the clop of hooves. "Listen." By now, she had familiarized herself with the sound of the drayman's wagon.

Mary paused in her sewing to listen. She exchanged a knowing look with Moira, then stood up slowly. Though she tried to hide her excitement, it was nonetheless obvious, at least to Moira's eyes. "Please excuse me—"

Moira followed Mary, sweeping from the room with a rustle of skirts. Their footsteps blended together on the stairs; Mary's heavy tread and Moira's lighter step. Moira could feel the blood rising in her cheeks. There was something exciting in all of this, though she knew that what the Queen was doing could also be considered dangerous.

"I wonder if I will receive another letter from France?" Mary said at last when they were safely sequestered in her chambers.

"We will soon see."

Though the Queen was anxious to read the missives arriving in the barrels, she held her poise, merely watching from her window as the barrels were unloaded and taken to the cellar. With Moira at her heels, she made her way to the library, awaiting her secretary's entrance. It seemed to take an inordinate amount of time, but soon Nau entered, securing the door behind him. Taking a packet from beneath the confines of his doublet, he held it forth.

"Another communication from France," Nau whispered, flourishing his plumed hat as he bowed gracefully. "As well as one from Mendoza."

For months, Mary's correspondence had been accumulating at the French embassy. By Gifford's contrivance, a large packet of letters had been brought in the arriving barrel.

Mary seemed much like an excited child as she spoke. "We have much to do."

Soon, she and her secretary Nau were vigorously at work,

weaving the old web of intrigue with Spain and Guise and the Catholic nobility of Scotland and England. Mary put herself at once in touch with Mendoza, informed him of her intention of transferring all her rights to his master, Philip of Spain, and begged that he would take her under his protection.

The Catholics in Scotland had formed themselves into a party, and she wrote to Lord Claude Hamilton, appointing him her lieutenant and planning a rising in Scotland to coincide with the Spanish invasion of England.

Moira watched as Nau took down the letters according to the Queen's dictation; with the help of his own notes, he put the Queen's writings into a code in case they were intercepted. Next, Nau wrapped the letters securely in a leather packet to be handed privately to the Chartley brewer. The packet would then be slipped through the corked tube in the bung of the cask. The "honest fellow" would drive away, his destination being London and the French embassy. From there, the letters would go to Paris in the French diplomatic pouch, and arrive in Thomas Morgan's hands in France as soon as possible. For the return letters, the process was merely reversed. Mary would receive her secret post via the drayman as before, in a small packet containing a cover note from Gifford, who had brought it down from London.

Mary Stuart congratulated herself. "I have outwitted Sir Amyas Paulet, that stiff Puritan who has been so very cruel to me." She smiled as she expressed what a rage her jailer would be in if he knew that despite all his sentries, and the locks and bars he had once condemned her to, she was exchanging weekly letters with Paris, Madrid, and Rome, and that her agents were working busily on her behalf.

"Armies and navies are making ready in support of your cause," Nau exclaimed. "Daggers are being sharpened to pierce the hearts of your enemies."

"It shall be so," Mary said, unable to hide her look of triumph.

Moira feared that sometimes the Queen showed her delight too plainly, thus giving herself away to Sir Amyas Paulet's watchful eyes. In those moments, Moira would make it a point to nudge the Queen as a signal to stifle her smiles.

"Excuse me, but may I write a letter too?" Moira was given

permission to make use of the barrel post by writing a letter to her father, telling him just what she was about, that she was with Mary, and that she was safe. Closing her eyes, she whispered a prayer that the Queen's friends would soon come to rescue Mary, and that she would be safely taken out of England. Only then could Moira even begin to think about her own happiness.

THE HIDDEN PASSAGEWAY WAS CHILLY, and a breeze through a crack in the wall's foundation caused the tapers to flicker, casting eerie shadows against the wall as five men—Selby, Rothingham, Gifford, Paulet, and a man named Phelippes—stood in the corner, staring down at the pieces of parchment lying there: Mary's missives. Unbeknownst to the Queen, her "secret" missives, only recently handed to the agreeable little drayman, were being looked over by Walsingham's men.

"Mary thinks she is so sly, but we have bested her," Paulet said, his mouth trembling in an unfamiliar smile. "Her private thoughts and schemes are just as I imagined."

"Ah, yes. It was a stroke of genius to put the drayman in our pay. But then, any man has his price." The "honest man" was being paid by the English authorities for his cooperation, a tidy profit.

The drayman had indeed driven away, but he had backtracked, placing the packet into Gifford's hands. Gifford had secretly brought the packet back to Chartley. Here, the messages were opened and deciphered by a man named Phelippes, who was skilled in breaking any code. The decipher was then sent forward to Walsingham in London. Every letter to and from Mary was likewise inspected by Gifford and Walsingham's men.

"Ah, though they have changed the code somewhat, it is an easy one to break. Not a particularly subtle one. Just a mixture of Greek letters, numbers and other symbols for letters of the alphabet." Bending his head to the task, Phelippes scrawled out the contents of the letters. "Here. Very easy." He handed the letters back to Gifford.

Once the deciphering had been achieved, the packet was

resealed, to be taken by Gifford to London and its original destination.

"She incriminates herself with these letters. Look! Dispatches to Paris, urging the invasion of England by Spanish troops. Her goose is as good as cooked." Selby's voice was shrill; he sensed victory.

"No, it is not! Fool." Rothingham nudged his companion roughly in the ribs. "These missives will be useful when the Scottish harridan is brought to trial. Unfortunately, however, she has not written that which Walsingham has so hoped. Namely, Mary has not sanctioned a plan for the assassination of Elizabeth Tudor. Without it there can be no public trial, and therefore we cannot see that she is put to death. We need definite proof of Mary Stuart's consent to the killing of the rightful Queen of England. It is the only way."

Chapter Thirty-two

THE RAW ICY WIND ruffled the sails as Ryan put into the port near Edinburgh. He pulled his cloak tighter, wondering what had possessed him to brave such a fearsome storm. In truth, the weather of the last two weeks would have forced even the most daring to turn back. Instead, he had braved the storm. And all for the sake of a dark-haired chit who had left him without a word.

"I must be the biggest of fools!" he swore, clutching at the railing to keep from being swept overboard. If that was what love and passion did to a man, he was better rid of it.

A veritable gale rattled the masts and sent waves at least twenty feet high sloshing over the deck. Even the most fearless of his men were ready to swear that the captain had lost his mind; Ryan wondered himself. And yet, what would a sane man do? Wait and take the chance that the most precious thing in his life might be lost to him?

"No, by—God!"

Ryan had been deeply troubled by Moira's sudden departure. Even when Seamus had returned to confirm that she had returned to her family in Scotland, he had been besieged with worry. What if she had run into bad weather? It was a rough journey to the lands across the border, more so in the dead of winter. What if she had been thrust into danger? He had heard about the ever-feuding Scots. There were reivers—brigands—at the border, and they were dangerous men. What if Moira had somehow fallen into their hands?

Hoping to allay his disquiet he had visited Moira's brothers at Greenwich, but instead of soothing his anxiety, the meeting had only added to it. Something in the MacKinnon twins' demeanor made Ryan all the more wary. It was as if they were hiding something from him. Certainly they had been uncomfortable in his presence. When he had asked about their sister's whereabouts, they had hemmed and hawed without really answering his question. For the life of him, Ryan could not understand why they would want to keep such a thing secret. In frustration he had taken on Donald, the more timid brother, asking him outright if Moira had gone back to Scotland. After a pause to seek out his brother's eye, the young man had at last reluctantly agreed. When Ryan had expressed his decision to go after her, both men had all too hurriedly tried to dissuade him. Their reaction had only spurred him on.

"In truth, Moira MacKinnon will have many questions to answer before I am satisfied," he grumbled now. It was obvious by her brothers' reaction to him that he was considered anything but trustworthy, a foe more than a friend, and he wanted to know why. Had she painted him to be an ogre? Or was it that they didn't think a mere ship's captain good enough for their sister? Would Roarke MacKinnon feel the same?

In an effort to make the best impression possible, Ryan had brought his best clothes for his arrival at the MacKinnon lands, a dark blue velvet doublet laced with silver, the garment cut to emphasize his broad shoulders and narrow waist. Dark blue hosen, silver trunk-hose, and high black leather boots completed the outfit.

"I'll prove to all concerned that an Englishman—bastard or not—is as good as a Scotsman any day," he swore. With that vow, he turned the *Red Mermaid*'s prow into the fierce, storm-driven waters of the North Sea.

It was a turbulent docking; the ship rocked precariously at anchor. Ryan was the only one who would dare brave the ocean in the small rowboat. Thus he rowed to shore all alone. Picking up the oars, he pushed and pulled with all his might, fighting against the waters. The small boat rocked from side to side as the ocean pounded viciously against its stern. The rumble of the sea was so loud, it caused the boat to vibrate. Even so, he maneuvered the rowboat skillfully. He knew well the danger of capsizing upon the jagged rocks.

Never had the shore felt so good under his feet. After procuring a horse, Ryan rode towards Edinburgh, there to seek directions to the lands Roarke MacKinnon claimed. Though James's court had moved to Stirling Castle to the north, one of the Scotsmen left behind was able to give him accurate directions. Thus, shouting out a heartfelt thanks, Ryan was on his way.

A strong north wind gusted, striking him in the face as he rode towards the west. Rain, sleet, and snow swept across the valley, blanketing the surrounding countryside in an endless white shroud. It was cold, and the dampness made it a miserable journey. The cold in Scotland certainly made the winters in England seem as warm as spring, he thought. Even so, he did not even think of turning back. Clutching his compass, he navigated on land as skillfully as he did on the sea. Determination led him on. He had to make certain that Moira was safe. He had to talk with her, tell her that he loved her. Even if she refused his proposal, he would at least have the satisfaction of knowing that she would be guarded from harm.

Ryan came across crofters' cottages as he traveled. He was warmed by their friendliness; they gave him shelter from the wind and rain and fed him various baked, boiled, and steamed fish dishes. When he neared the MacKinnon castle at last, he hoped with all his heart that he would be just as welcome.

The rough brown walls of the MacKinnon keep loomed in the distance against the gray mist of the fading day as Ryan rode forth. Inside the wall, the castle was bustling with activity. It seemed that everyone knew his job, and scurried to do it as best he could. It spoke well for the lord of the castle, Ryan thought.

The entrance to the great hall was welcoming as he stepped inside. "And just who might ye be?" A short, wizened old man with thinning white hair stepped forward, peering at Ryan with squinting eyes.

"Ryan Paxton. Captain Paxton, if you please."

"An Englishman! A ship's captain, to boot. Well, I wouldna hae believed it." Throwing back his head, the little man laughed in glee. "And just where is your ship, me laddie?"

"Docked in a small little seaport just outside Edinburgh."

"Ach, I see. So ye were no' jesting." Crossing his arms across his bony chest, the man stood evaluating Ryan. At last—as if he fully accepted Ryan, Englishman though he was—he stuck out his hand in a welcoming gesture that would have done any Englishman proud. "Kinny is me name." The old man said the name with as much pride as if he were royalty. "Once I was a tinker, but now I'm the honorary keeper o' this castle. Family, ye might say."

"Kinny," Ryan repeated. He liked the man at once; there was a warmth and a natural charm about him. Ryan's smile was genuine as he took off his cloak. Answering the curious look on the old man's face, he told Kinny that he had come to see Roarke MacKinnon. "For some man-to-man talk concerning his daughter," Ryan added.

"Ye dinna say?" Thick white brows shot up in surprise. Kinny tilted his head to one side, studying the younger man. He seemed to like what he saw. "Well then, 'tis best I lead ye to him." Motioning with his head, he led Ryan to the warmth of the hall's hearth.

Two figures stood there, framed by the carved posts of the inner doorway as if they had been painted upon a canvas. Roarke MacKinnon and his lady. Ryan knew at once that that was who they were. The man was tall, handsome and muscular, with a strength and grace that belied his age. Only the wings of gray at the temples of his dark hair told that he was a man of later years. His wife was eye-catchingly lovely. She was slim, her face flawless. There was not even one strand of silver in her thick auburn hair. Ryan thought them to be by far the handsomest couple he had seen in quite a while.

The sound of his footsteps roused the MacKinnons from their reverie. As he and Kinny approached, they both looked up to greet Ryan, but it was the woman who spoke. Kylynn— Ryan remembered her name. It suited her. An unusual name, just as she was unusually beautiful.

"Who have you here, Kinny?" Her voice was as soothing as an angel's, just as Moira's could be when she was calm.

"An Englishman, he be! Captain, so he says. Wants to see Master Roarke about an important matter." The elderly Scotsman grinned.

"Captain Paxton." Ryan bowed politely, though he could not take his eyes from her face. It was like looking at Moira. The reminder quickened his heart. She was here, within these walls, his lady love. Would she greet him happily, or had he come all this way for naught?

Kylynn MacKinnon's smile was warm. "Welcome, Captain Paxton." She held out her hands in greeting, allowing him to bestow a light kiss on each, as was the French custom. Ah yes, Ryan remembered now that Moira had said her mother had been raised in France. "But you must be chilled to the bone. Kinny, tell Gordie to fetch some hot spiced wine for our guest."

Kinny complied. The beverage was good and thawed Ryan's body throughout. He smiled his appreciation, looking from Kylynn's face to that of her husband. Roarke MacKinnon, unlike his wife, was not as welcoming.

"Captain Paxton!" He glowered as he said Ryan's name. "I remember. It was upon your ship that my daughter sailed to London against her will."

"She stowed away, as I remember," Ryan answered dryly. Obviously this meeting was not going to go at all smoothly. He wondered just what Moira had told her father.

"Inadvertently stowed away, perhaps." Roarke MacKinnon eyed the ship's captain up and down critically. "A gentleman would have brought her back."

Ryan did not want to argue. How could he, when he knew that he was in the wrong? "Circumstances were such that I regret that I could not. But I did give your daughter the warmth and security of my tavern to shield her from London's ills."

"Indeed!" A frown flickered across Roarke MacKinnon's face. " 'Twas no charity at all, sir. She earned her keep, as I recall from her letter."

"You were very kind. And for that we thank you, sir." Kylynn MacKinnon, sensing the tension between the two men, tried to soothe the ill-will. "I fear that Moira is a headstrong girl who at times creates her own troubles." She punctuated her words with a playful poke to her husband's ribs. "Just like her father."

"Perhaps Moira is daring, but in this instance she was without blame." Roarke hurried to his daughter's defense. He shrugged. "But that is all in the past. I am a reasonable man. I am willing to let bygones be bygones if my daughter is returned to me promptly, sir."

"Returned to you?" Ryan could do nothing but stare. What was the man saying? "Perhaps I should have been the one to escort her back to her home, but Moira took matters into her own hands by coming here. She left while I was at sea."

"Left?" Now it was Roarke MacKinnon's turn to be surprised. "What are you saying, man? The last time I heard from my daughter she was in London, staying in your godforsaken tavern. Against my wishes, I might add."

"She's not here?" Ryan paled. He was not certain if Moira's father was being truthful or playing some sort of game. "But of course she must be. Seamus told me so, her brothers verified it." Or had they? Hadn't he put words into their mouths because of his own opinion on the matter? "God's bones!"

Kylynn MacKinnon gasped. "Moira!"

"My daughter is not here!" Roarke MacKinnon's voice rose to a shout. For a moment, he looked as if he might come to blows with the younger man. "If you know what is good for you, you will be prepared to explain."

Ryan realized that Roarke MacKinnon's anger was sincere. "Then dear God, where is she? When I returned from my voyage, she was gone. Seamus told me—" Never before one to panic, Ryan did so now. Grabbing his cloak from Kinny's hand, he bolted for the door. "I've got to find her. God's blood, if anything has happened, I will never forgive myself." He had been so filled with hurt pride at Moira's disappearance that he had not thought that something sinister might have happened. Walsingham. It was a name that sent chills up and down his spine.

"Nor will I!" Roarke MacKinnon growled. He grabbed Ryan by the shoulder. "If something has happened to my daughter, I'll have your head."

Ryan's eyes glittered with self-condemnation. "If anything has happened, there is no punishment that you can mete out that could possibly be greater than that which I will inflict upon myself." As if the devil were on his heels, Ryan turned his back and strode towards the door. A blizzard was raging outside, but he didn't care. All he knew was that somehow, some way, he had to find Moira—even if he had to turn London—nay, all of England—upside down.

* * *

RYAN WAS DRIVEN to an incautious frenzy as he pulled himself aboard the *Red Mermaid*. All he could think of was Moira. God's blood, where was she? Where in God's merciful name could she have gone? Had her leaving been voluntary, or had she perchance fallen victim to some villainous scheme or other? He knew that he had to hurry back to London as soon as possible. He had to find out.

"If anyone has harmed a hair on her head—" Even Walsingham would not be immune from his fury.

Though it was the heart of winter, he ordered his sailors to turn the *Red Mermaid*'s prow into the fierce, storm-driven waters. "All hands to quarters!" The ship slammed into wave after wave. The wind howled treacherously in the rigging. Water hit the deck, causing the timbers to shudder.

"He's bloody crazy. He should wait out the storm! Bait for Bedlam, he is," said one sailor. Several of the others agreed. His crew shivered in disbelief. Some crossed themselves, others just whispered a prayer. Yet not a one had the courage to defy him. Crazy or not, there was no one who knew the ocean better.

Soon, the rugged coast of Scotland fell astern as the prevailing winds swelled the ship's sails. Working together, the crew held the ship steady on her course despite the interference of nature. Only then did Ryan allow his thoughts to return to his lost love.

"Her brothers! They must have known." Anger boiled within him. Had they but been honest with him, so much trouble and heartache could have been averted. "Damn them. Damn them, I say." Woe be to David and Donald MacKinnon when he caught up with them.

Chapter Thirty-three

FLICKERING TORCHES cast a soft glow upon the room, silhouetting the revelers. Silver-gilt cups and tankards clattered against each other as they were filled and refilled many times over with the finest red and white wines. The table stretched the entire length of the smoky room, and was strewn with platters that held the greatest delicacies, oysters and stuffed pigeon among them.

Davie MacKinnon glanced down the length of the long table, gauging the expense of the food, beverages, and the candles. Anthony Babington was an experienced host, one who by all appearances was very wealthy indeed. Certainly he had enough to entertain lavishly and act the host to his friends and those he welcomed into his circle. Most importantly to Davie, however, Babington knew the right people.

"What did I tell you, Donnie? Aren't you glad we came?" Davie nudged his brother in the ribs. He was impressed by Babington. The man had a charm and personality that attracted many young Catholic gentlemen of good standing. The kind of men needed for any kind of daring enterprise. Gallant men. Adventurous and daring, but also of good breeding. "Shall we join up with him?"

"It's too early to tell." Donnie, always cautious, was not so easily swayed.

"Too early? What more do we need to know?" David tested the pigeon cooling on his plate and found it just to his liking. Skillfully wielding his knife and fork, he captured a piece of meat and lifted it to his lips, savoring its flavor.

"There is a great deal to be found out. We know very little at all about the man, except that he is five years older than we, Catholic, and wealthy. That alone does not qualify a man to play hero, Davie.''

Both young men's eyes turned to look upon the young gallant. He was dressed in a doublet the color of the richest burgundy, the sleeves, embroidered with silver, slashed to show the fine Holland linen of his shirt underneath. His trunk hose and hosen were ornately embroidered in silk threads of various colors. His light brown hair was worn long, brushing the collar. As was the fashion, he wore a single gold earring in his left ear, a gesture to style that the twins had not yet dared, for fear of their father's rebuke.

''He studied to be a lawyer.''

''Ah, but he abandoned the bar for a fashionable life on the fringes of the court.''

Davie shrugged. ''He is well-read. He has read Plutarch's *Lives* just as we have.''

''Reading is not the same as doing.''

Davie put down his fork. ''No, perhaps not. But I, for one, recognize a man of leadership when I see him.'' He grinned. ''He and I are of the same mettle.''

Donnie laughed softly. ''Then woe be to him.'' For the time being, the matter was laid to rest as the two young men enjoyed the evening, eating their fill.

There was venison, roast swan, roast beef in a wine sauce. Stewed and pickled vegetables lent color to the table, though they were not as readily partaken of as the other foods. Fish caught fresh from the Channel and the River Thames was served broiled and smoked. The platters were emptied quickly, but not as quickly as the bottles and barrels of wine and ale.

''Another bottle, Davie?'' Babington asked. There was a general murmur of agreement from those at the table, though Davie knew well when he had had enough. He was here to discuss business, and that meant keeping a clear head.

Politics and business ventures were the topics of the evening. Only those of unquestionable loyalty to the Catholic cause were in attendance. Davie knew that his being Scottish had drawn the young gallant to him. Even so, it had taken several weeks before he and his brother had been invited to Babington's house in Barbican to dine; they had been invited only after Davie had spoken of his fondness for the Scottish queen. He and Babington had played a sort of cat-and-mouse game at first, fearful of incriminating themselves lest the other be untrustworthy. But ever so slowly, they had come to respect and trust each other.

Babington, he had soon learned, had formed a Catholic league, and intended to soon be in correspondence with Mary and her agents, a fact that inspired Davie's admiration anew. This man planned to do what he and his brother had only talked about. But now fate had taken a hand, giving David MacKinnon just the chance he had longed for. That his sister was already in attendance on the Queen at Chartley made Davie and Donnie integral to Babington's plan.

Davie leaned back in his chair as the maidservants cleared away the plates and platters. The glow of the candlelight worked a magic on the room, enriching the color of the tapestries and paintings which adorned the walls. He couldn't help but notice that Anthony Babington had added his own portrait to the collection. Vanity? Perhaps. And yet, if all worked out well, this man would be entitled to have his image revered, as the man who had saved Mary Stuart from the clutches of an evil harridan. The warm light in the room worked a sort of alchemy on all the faces assembled. It transformed even ordinary faces into ones with heroic features, Davie thought.

Babington well understood the spell cast by the wine and the candlelight. Slowly he rose to his feet, his cup raised high in his hand. "To she we hold most dear," he said softly. "To our Catholic princess held in an English Protestant tower. May we soon rescue her from the monstrous dragon who holds her captive."

"Aye! Aye!" One by one, each man rose to his feet in silent tribute. Donnie and Davie did the same. How could one not salute their Queen—the one they held most dear to their hearts?

While the assembly was standing, Babington made a short speech—witty, impassioned, inspired, and stirring. He swore that before the year was out, they would free Mary of Scots from her prison. He revealed his loyalty to the cause; even now he was supporting a secret society for the protection of Jesuit missionaries in England. That and his many travels abroad would be of help when the time came.

"I am a man with a destiny. Fate has chosen me. Serve me

and you will reach heights you have yet to dream of." He received a rousing cheer when he was finished. He was recruiting adherents from among his friends, and inducing various individuals of his own faith and station to join him.

Davie's eyes met those of his brother. "What do you say now? We must do it, Donnie. We have been waiting for a chance. I think this could well be it."

Donnie was jostled by a young man at his right and another elbowed his way to Babington's side, poking the young Scotsman in the ribs. "All talk with little substance if you ask me. I'm leery, Davie. Some of these so-called patriots seem to be little more than hotheads. I have yet to hear a definite plan." Always cautious, Donnie didn't want to hasten into anything. "Just one false move, and we could both lose our heads."

It was a subject they discussed heatedly on the long ride back to Greenwich. "Babington knows the right people already, Donnie, people we can only hope to meet. He is ready for any enterprise that might advance the cause. You want to see Mary freed, don't you?"

"Aye!"

"Then I say we do it."

Dismounting, they gave their horses up to the keeping of the groom and hurried into the palace. All argument stopped the moment they walked inside. In silence they made their way to their room. Davie paused outside the door, then turned the handle. The room was very dark, the shutters closed and barred against the cold night air, and the lamps and candles were all extinguished. Shutting the door behind them, Davie reached for a candle, intending to light it, but before he got the chance an angry voice broke through the silence.

"Where is she?"

"What?" Davie recognized the voice at once. That damned English captain. He had most certainly made a pain of himself on the subject of Moira, but Davie thought that he and his brother had put an end to that.

"I said, where is she? She is not in Scotland, for I have just returned from there. Your father has not seen her since before she stowed aboard my ship. I repeat, where is she?"

"I . . . I don't know," Donnie answered, with little conviction to his tone.

An angry oath rent the air. "Damn you for a liar! Your falsehood caused me a great deal of worry, as well as trouble." The scratching of flint against iron told the twins that the captain was lighting a lamp. Soon the room was aglow with the light from the oil lamp on the desk. Captain Paxton squinted angrily against the glare. "Tell me where she is, or by God, I'll shake the truth out of you." Like a lion, he moved slowly and stealthfully towards Donnie, as if to make good on his threat.

Davie stepped in front of his brother to protect him. "We don't know where she is, Captain." Davie sounded more convincing than his brother, but not enough to persuade Ryan. "Thus, your manhandling of us will do you little good. We can't tell you where Moira is if we don't know."

Ryan knew instinctively that the young man was lying. There was no alarm in his voice, no panic, as there would surely be if the lad thought his sister to be in peril. It seemed that he knew very well that she was safe and exactly where she was at the moment. He just refused to tell.

"Then if that is true, I intend to alert the Queen. I'll have her guards search every house, shop, and dwelling in London until Moira is found." He was certain that the threat would loosen the young man's tongue. "I will not take the chance that she is in any danger."

"You are a stubborn man!" In an unusual show of bravado, Donnie came forward. "Why can't you just leave us be?"

"Because I must find her! Now, I can either draw the Queen and her councilors into this," Ryan said by way of bluff, "or you can trust me and avert a very scandalous situation."

"She is safe. That is all I can tell you. Moira doesn't want to be found." Davie was incensed. The interfering rogue was going to ruin everything. Damn Moira and her flirtation with the overbold man!

"Nevertheless, I intend to find her." Ryan was relieved to be assured that the woman he loved had not come to any harm. Her brother admitted that she was safe. But where?

"If you have any care for my sister, you will leave her be."

"It's because I do care that I must find her." Ryan took a step towards David, frowning with concern. "There are those who might seek to harm your sister. I want to protect her." Though he had threatened physical assault, he couldn't really force the matter. A show of strength and anger would only alienate the young men. "Please."

Davie was resolved. There were too many risks in revealing Moira's whereabouts. The captain was English, and worse, a Protestant. The Queen's man. Even if his intentions were honorable, he might somehow give Moira's part in the blossoming conspiracy away.

"I cannot tell you, Captain Paxton, though I wish that I could. You can shake me until my teeth rattle, beat me, bruise me, and tie me up by my toes, but it will not do any good. My lips are as firmly sealed as the Queen's ledgers."

"Then so be it." Ryan Paxton knew it would do no good to tarry here. The lads were obviously involved in something that included their sister. If he pried too much, it might mean all their ruin. No, if he was going to find the girl, he would have to look elsewhere.

Chapter Thirty-four

THE STORMS OF JANUARY blew through February, and February's snows into March. Winter's stiff, cold fingers still gripped Staffordshire. Moira stood with her nose pressed against the window. Never had she longed as fervently for the days to pass. The terrain seemed to stretch out unendingly, as endlessly as the days, its hills and valleys rippling like waves. In the distance, the vast, windswept pastureland teased the eye with a promise of spring. Bushes and plants poked out from beneath the white mists, waiting for the sun's warmth to rekindle them to green. The sky gave promise of a deep azure blue above the gray. The days were growing longer and sunnier.

"Oh spring, blessed spring." She yearned for it.

Perhaps by then, Moira would not feel so cooped up, so much like a prisoner. The days had plodded by so unmercifully slowly that she had thought once or twice that she would go mad. Every day was the same—dull, boring. Even so, she had been loath to give Mary even a hint of her unhappiness. She didn't want to spoil the Queen's newfound contentment with worries about her own woes. Therefore, she had forced herself to smile.

It seemed that the only excitement around Chartley concerned the barrels. Jacques Nau seemed to enjoy being employed in his task of writing the notes. Just to vary his routine, he changed the code from time to time, just in case it came to the attention of unwanted eyes. He had fallen in love with Bess Pierrepoint, Bess of Hardwicke's granddaughter. Moira knew he was making use of the "honest fellow" as his own cupid to further his courtship, though he kept it secret from the Queen, for fear of her displeasure.

There were others who made use of the drayman as well. Every week, messages came in and went out. Moira was concerned that they were carrying on the barrel post much too long. Surely one of the letters was going to be intercepted someday, and that would mean trouble for them all. She therefore cautioned Mary against writing anything that might be overly incriminating. At first the Queen listened, but as time went on, she threw caution to the winds.

"A chance to see my hopes come to life has been granted me. I cannot be faint of heart now," she had said.

Mary took the matter of the secret correspondence very seriously, and lived for those days when she received her letters from the barrel post. Moira, however, yearned for other things. She was young and vibrant. She wanted to laugh, to dance, to sing. Instead, she spent her hours among women whose only talk was of cooking, sewing, and other womanly chores. Or with the Queen, whose talk always seemed to return to earlier days, before Moira was born.

Moira sighed slowly, deeply. That was not the real reason for her distress. Ah no, her pain went much farther. Boredom gave her time to think, and that led to thoughts of her English captain. Time did not heal the heart's wounds. If anything, it only deepened them. Missing Ryan Paxton had become a physical pain, a throbbing ache in her heart. She thought again of how he had kissed her that night in the tavern, how she had melted in his arms. Oh, how she wished they had made love! Now she would perhaps never know what happiness their joining could bring.

"If only I could see him, just for an hour, a day." It was an impossible dream. For fear of Walsingham's reprisal, Moira couldn't risk contacting Ryan. She loved the captain with all her heart, but at the same time she was afraid to give him her trust. Mary was much too vulnerable, especially now. Nor would her sense of honor allow her to leave the Queen, even for a moment.

Moira turned away from the window. There was no use in tormenting herself with thoughts of what might have been. She had made a choice and now had to live with it, even if it meant her own unhappiness.

"Moira?" A young woman named Alice peeked through Moira's chamber door. Alice was as short as Moira was tall, as blonde as she was dark—a stocky girl. The large-boned chambermaid was the daughter of a Staffordshire farmer. Being near the same age as Moira and likewise tired of the tedious routine at Chartley, she had given her friendship readily. "You left your embroidery in the solar." She held it out like an offering.

"Embroidery! Fie," Moira scoffed. "I could care less if I ever saw another needle."

"But your work is so lovely. Such little tiny stitches." Alice touched the threads with awe. "I would welcome the chance to work such magic, but my needle strokes, I fear, are too overbold and unwieldy. Comes from having large hands."

"Nonsense, I can teach you how to sew with stitches just as small as mine. It only takes practice." Moira thought to herself that it might be enjoyable doing something nice for the young woman. It seemed that Alice had few pleasures in her young life.

"Merry-go-up! You would do that?" Alice seemed most definitely pleased. "Your needlework is so beautiful." She giggled. "Why, there are times when I'm almost certain I can smell the flowers. And the birds—they seem almost ready to sing."

"My longing for spring shows in what I do."

"Aye, spring. I too am longing." Alice's face brightened. "Perhaps if we smile wide at that old codger Paulet, he'll even let us indulge in the Mayday celebrations." Alice rolled her eyes. "It's a time for lovemaking and tomfoolery the likes of which you have never seen."

Alice explained that before daybreak, the young people of the village—and some times their elders, including the clergy—joined in bringing in the month of May. They ventured into the woods to cut wildflowers, greenery, and hawthorn boughs, and oftentimes spent the night in the forest.

"We have such celebrations where I come from, too."

"Sleeping beside a man can be very pleasurable."

"So I would imagine." Moira couldn't help but imagine Ryan lying beside her on the soft grass.

"Ah yes, I will be glad when the season turns warmer." As if envisioning it, Alice started to hum a tune, dancing around the room. Her skirts floated around her as she spun about on her toes.

Alice's merriment was contagious. Soon Moira was caught up in the mood. One of Mary's spaniels had followed Alice into the room. The little dog nipped at their heels as they skipped about. They danced until they were exhausted, then Alice threw herself down on Moira's bed.

"The stable boy fancies himself in love with you," she said, rolling onto her stomach and resting her chin on her hands. "He told me so."

"No!" Moira didn't want that. He was a nice boy and she didn't want to hurt him.

"Yes!"

"I don't want him to be. My heart is already taken." It was the first time she had made that admission to anyone, even the Queen.

"You are in love?" Alice seemed fascinated. "Is he terribly handsome?"

"Terribly."

"And is he strong?"

"Of body and of mind." Moira smiled sadly. "I left him behind when I came to serve the Queen, but I will never forget him. Not if I live to be a hundred."

"Ohhhhh!" Alice showed her concern, patting Moira on the arm.

As if expressing his sympathy, Mary's spaniel jumped up beside Moira. Unable to resist him, Moira scratched him behind the ears. "But it is best not to talk about it, for it only brings me heartbreak."

"Then we will not discuss it." Alice wanted to lighten Mary's mood, so she changed the subject. "The mouser Paulet brought in was not a tomcat at all. Had you heard about it?"

"Paulet made a mistake?" Moira did laugh at that, for the old man thought he was always right.

"A mistake that he cannot argue. You see, the cat that we all called Mister Paws just had kittens."

"Kittens?" Moira remembered when the gray tabby at home had likewise given birth.

"So tiny that they have not even opened their eyes. All fluffy and soft." Taking Moira by the hand, Alice led her out of the room and down the stairs. "We'll go have a look at them before we must go to supper."

Putting on their heavy woolen cloaks, they went out the back way, through the kitchens to the courtyard. "Are they in the stables?"

"I made them a warm bed in the cellar. In an old ale barrel."

It amused Moira to think that the barrels were being put to yet another use. "I see." Moira was so engrossed in the matter of the kittens that she didn't see the wagon or recognize the driver until she was upon it. How could she have been so blind? It was Seamus. Her eyes met his for just a moment before she thought to hide her face in the folds of her hood.

"Dear God!" She wasn't certain that she had been seen, yet the chance that she might have been unnerved her. It was just such a mistake that could very well be the ruin of Mary's plans.

"Did you know that man?"

"No!"

"Then why did he stare?" Alice's brows flickered up questioningly.

"I suppose he might very well have thought that I was someone else." Moira whispered a prayer that Seamus would doubt his eyes, that he would think her a figment of his imagination. As they walked towards the wine cellars, she talked herself into the feeling that all would be well. Even so, the sight of Seamus had shaken her to the very core.

Chapter Thirty-five

AS IF IN JEST, the spirit of winter touched London with a devastating hand as it drew close to spring. The air was crisp, the ground frozen, so much so that it crackled beneath the horses' hoofs as the wagon weaved up and down the road. The noisy clatter announced Seamus's arrival. Watching from the window, Ryan wasted no time in scurrying out the door to meet his friend. By his reckoning, Seamus had a great many questions to answer.

"Seamus, you old dog! I was beginning to think you had decided to sell your ale elsewhere." Shivering against the cold, Ryan managed a broad smile, though his heart was as chilled as the weather. He couldn't help but wonder just how much Seamus really knew about Moira MacKinnon's disappearance.

"I've had my share of woes. Rats got into my cellars and ate some of the grain. I fear for my supply of brew for next year." Seamus flung his arms up in a gesture of vexation. "And to add to that, one of my brothers, the one who oversees my ale supply, eloped with a penniless dairymaid. Add that to the quagmire that the rain and sleet has made of the roads, and that will explain why I am more than a little late in coming this time." Seamus strode purposefully toward the back door of the tavern, only to be surprised when Ryan blocked his way.

"God's eyebrows! Would you deny a frozen, unhappy man the warmth of your fire? What kind of a show of friendship is that?"

"What kind of a show of friendship is it to keep secrets from one who has always trusted you?" Ryan shuddered, more in anger than from the chill early morning air.

"Secrets? I keep no secrets. All that I know, you are privy

to.'' Seamus motioned to a dutiful stableboy to see to the unharnessing of the wagon's horses.

''Are you certain?'' Deciding that he was punishing himself far more than Seamus, Ryan opened the door and, grasping Seamus by the arm, led him inside. Because of the early hour, the tavern was virtually deserted. The warm air of the room swept over them like a lover's caress. ''I'll share my fire, Seamus, but not a drop of drink until you tell me what you have been about.''

''About?'' Seamus was puzzled as to just what Ryan was alluding. ''Nothing out of the ordinary, if that is what you mean. I'm just a common man trying to make my way.''

''I'm talking about Moira MacKinnon.'' Ryan's eyes glowed like the coals of the fire. ''You told me she had gone to Scotland, old friend.''

''And so she has. She told me so herself!'' Seamus snorted in indignation. ''You're being grumbly, if you ask me. As if it is my fault you had a lovers' quarrel.''

''There was no quarrel!'' Ryan brought his fist down hard upon the top of a barrel. ''When I left to take my ship up the coast, we were as lovey as two people can be. Foolish lout that I be, I had even let my dreams soar. Then, as if in a puff of smoke, all my illusions about a contented life were gone, just as she was.''

''I'm sorry, Ryan. Truly I am.'' He was eager to make amends. ''If it were up to me, I'd see you with the girl.''

''She's not in Scotland, Seamus!''

Seamus looked at Ryan in surprise. ''How do you know?''

''Because, like a love-besotted fool, I went after her. I expected to find her in her father's hall, but he informed me that he had not laid eyes on his daughter since she left for Edinburgh.'' Ryan winced at the recollection. ''Her father nearly had my head. He blames me, and rightly so.'' Ryan looked into his friend's eyes, and his torment was revealed.

''She's a headstrong lassie with a mind all her own. Surely he can see that.'' Seamus shifted nervously from leg to leg. ''When she's had time to sort out her feelings, she'll come back. I know she will.''

''Come back from where?'' Ryan had thought to give his friend the benefit of the doubt, but now he could see that

Seamus knew something that he was keeping within his own mind. "Where is she, Seamus? That guilty look on your face gives you away. Tell me, or by God, our friendship is over this very minute."

Seamus twisted his hands behind his back. "I did think she went to Scotland, Ryan. You must believe me. That's where the lassie said she was going the day I left her at the manor."

"The manor?"

Seamus cleared his throat. "Chartley Manor."

"Chartley?" Ryan could not have been more thunderstruck had Seamus told him she was in China. "What in the name of God is she doing there?"

"I took her there." Seamus tried to make Ryan understand. "You should have seen her that morning. Though she wouldn't admit it, I think she was frightened out of her wits. That little tart of a tavern-maid told me that someone had torn up Moira's room looking for something. Walsingham's agents were eyeing her like two cats after a rotund mouse. I wanted to help her. It seemed for the best that she leave London."

"Why didn't you tell me?" Ryan was in an uncompromising mood. When Seamus reached for a cup with the hope of quenching his thirst, Ryan pushed it away.

"Because it was after the fact. I really did believe that she'd gone back to her home. I thought perhaps she'd be better off there, at least for a time." Seamus related all that he knew about the tale. He told of his conversation with Moira, his telling her about seeing Mary of Scotland, of her being at Chartley. "She wanted to see her godmother. It seemed a reasonable request, so I took her with me."

"And that is where she is? This is not just another story to keep me away from her?"

"I stopped at Chartley on my way here. I saw her. She tried to hide her face from me, but I recognized her nonetheless." A frown flickered across Seamus's brow. "I thought she trusted me, but it seems not. Poor lassie. I would not harm a hair on her head. But then, I suppose she can't be sure."

"Nor would I." Ryan held out his hands, feeling a strange sense of helplessness.

"Not even if Walsingham were to will it?" Seamus's hand trembled as he placed it on Ryan's firmly muscled arm.

"Not at Elizabeth's command. I love her!"

"I'd hoped so. She's not the kind of woman to love and leave. Moira MacKinnon is the marrying kind."

"I know." He looked at Seamus a long, long time, then said, "I want you to go with me. To Chartley."

"Go back there? But I just came from there." Clearly, Seamus thought he was mad.

"Then we'll think of an excuse to return so suddenly." Ryan worked the plan over in his mind. If Walsingham's spies were interested in Moira, they'd be searching Heaven and earth to find her. He didn't want to be the one to lead them to Chartley, yet he had to see her. "You took Moira out of London without anyone suspecting. Now I want you to do it again, only *I'll* be the one hiding in your wagon."

"You're going after the lass!" Seamus showed his obvious delight. "To woo her and win her." He reached for a tankard, and this time was not denied. Ryan filled it to the brim. "Then here is to love!" They both drank to that.

Chapter Thirty-six

NEVER HAD A JOURNEY seemed so endless, or a road so long. More than once, Ryan glanced impatiently at the wheels, which seemed to be churning so slowly and, it seemed, ineffectually through the thick mud. What he wouldn't have given to have the firm, muscled flesh of a fine stallion beneath him, to be able to touch his heels to its flanks and send the horse galloping at thrice the speed that this creaking monstrosity was going. Or to be in command of his ship, to feel the power of the waves as the prow sliced through them. As it was, they were guarded by caution and the need to arrive at Chartley without drawing undue attention.

Ryan's feet ached from the uncomfortable shoes he wore, stout foot coverings of thick leather made for wear, not style. He had to admit, however, that his own soft leather boots would not have survived the journey. There were times when the condition of the road meant stopping to help Seamus push and pull the wagon out of the mud, times when he walked instead of riding on a long stretch of road, just as he was doing now.

A steady drizzle mixed with sleet blew into his eyes, and Ryan wiped his face with his sleeve. "What miserable weather!" he grumbled, trudging along behind the wagon. "How far are we from Staffordshire, anyway?"

"We'll be there in a few hours." Seamus was whistling contentedly, flicking the reins now and again to keep the wagon trundling along at a steady if tedious pace. Well, he was used this kind of thing, Ryan reasoned.

"A few hours." Ryan shook his body, much in the manner a dog might do to rid itself of the unwanted rain. "It will seem an eternity, I am certain. By God, if I'd known what I was in for, I'd have found another way to get to Chartley, Walsingham or no Walsingham.''

''Stop your complaining,'' Seamus chided good-humoredly, ''or I'll make you walk the rest of the way.''

''Oh you will, will you? We'll see about that! I'm of a mind to trade places with you. No wonder you can chirp like a bird, perched as you are upon that seat of yours. You're well out of the rain, my friend.''

''Trade places? Ah no, laddie. I'm the captain on this voyage,'' Seamus teased, scratching his thick dark beard, ''and I won't abide any mutinies.''

''Alas, you can be an unrelenting man, Seamus.'' Despite his discomfort, Ryan smiled. ''But the tables will be turned when I get you on my ship one day. Then I'll be the one giving orders.''

Ryan looked down at his garments. He hardly resembled a captain now. He had dressed himself to resemble a drayman, in a tunic of russet wool buttoned down the front from the close, uncollared neckline to the low waist. The garment came to mid-thigh, brushing against his long breeches of light brown canvas. The coarse pants were tied at the ankles and bound with straps at a point just below the knees. A cloak of dark green wool was fastened at the neck by a rope. Seamus had told him that his red-gold hair would instantly give him away, so he wore a hat of brown felt with the brim turned down over a coif of unbleached linen. Walsingham himself would not have recognized him.

''Walsingham!'' He spat out the name. If not for that old, graying raven, all of this might not have happened. He would have been with Moira to protect her so that she wouldn't have felt the need to leave London. By God, without Walsingham there would be no spies, no threat at all to his darling Scottish girl. ''Seamus, do you think Moira is safe at Chartley? Walsingham has spies everywhere. Surely there are some in the Scottish queen's own household.''

''I wouldn't be a bit surprised. They are surely as thick as maggots on a corpse. We will have to use special care, lest by our actions we endanger the Scottish miss. But if I know

you—and I do—you'll be able to rescue her. True love is said
to always win the day.''

Ryan and Seamus journeyed the rest of the way in compar-
ative silence. It was uncompromisingly chilly and wet, and
they had much on their minds. Unselfishly, Ryan had decided
to take Moira back to Scotland, to her home. She would be
safe there, away from Walsingham's foolishness. Though he
had not gotten off on the right foot with Moira's father, he
knew him to be an admirable man, one who loved his daughter
very much. Under his protection, Moira would not come to
any harm. That, at the moment, was Ryan's utmost concern.

The pathway led through woods barren of any leaves, only
skeletal remains of once-green oak trees. Ice-crusted streams
meandered through the countryside like discarded blue ribbons.
Now and again, there was a patch of blue sky that allowed the
sun to shine through with its welcome warmth. Cresting a hill,
Ryan could see the tiny cottages of the shire, and sensed his
destination was not very far.

"Chartley is just up ahead," Seamus announced with a
wink. "That should set your heart beating at a merry rhythm.
Climb aboard; you'll need to be rested if you are going to make
the most of your reunion." Ryan needed no prodding to take
advantage of that comfort. Soon the towers and walls of Chartley rose before them.

"Here again, brewer?" Though he was greeted with
surprise, Seamus nonetheless had no trouble getting beyond
Chartley's walls. Others might have found it more difficult to
get inside, might have been searched, but the brewer was
regarded as a special friend. The gates were opened for his
admittance. Ryan noted at once that the guards all wore the
Tudor colors of white and green, which spoke beyond a doubt
that they were Elizabeth's men.

"I bring a special surprise this time," Seamus said. "I've
just come to London where I purchased some newly-arrived
Rhenish wine. I brought a small keg of it here as thanks to all
my patrons who have been so congenial during my visits."

"Wine?" One of the men beamed his gratitude.

"A rare pleasure. Sir Amyas is so stingy, we rarely get any
good wine," said another, nodding in the direction of a som-
berly dressed man with a tight, unsmiling mouth above his

pointed gray beard. A sourpuss if ever Ryan saw one.

"That which he calls wine is more aptly labeled vinegar." Grumbling behind his hand, the guard spoke scathingly of Paulet's miserly ways. "Your gift is therefore doubly appreciated, brewer."

Seamus took the time to chat with Chartley's guards and servants, giving Ryan a chance to guide the wagon through the gateway with no attention being focused on him. Remembering Seamus's description of the premises, Ryan followed them as accurately as if he was looking at a map, and ended up in the courtyard. It was as good a place as any to begin his search for Moira.

"Ah, there you are! It's about time, drayman. You're later than usual." A rotund man swathed in a dark cloak approached Ryan, obviously thinking him to be someone else. "Well, let's be about it." Not even waiting for Ryan to get down from the wagon, the man pushed aside the canvas covering and fumbled about with the barrels. "Which one is it?"

"Sir?" Ryan was anxious to maintain his anonymity, wanted to play along, but he didn't know what the devil the man meant. Just what was Seamus involved in?

"*She's* anxious for the letters." He looked up at Ryan with scathing regard. "Don't be dimwitted, man. I need your help. Get down from there."

Ryan did, towering over the man on the ground. In that moment, the man realized he had made a mistake. The tick in his jaw and the flash of fear in his eyes clearly revealed his apprehension about what he had said. Something strange was going on, but before Ryan had a chance to determine what it was, the man recovered his composure.

"The vinegar! For the cook. Which barrel is it?" Now that he realized Ryan wasn't the man he had been expecting, the dark-cloaked man kept a careful distance between himself and this new drayman.

"Vinegar? For the cook?" Seamus had not made mention of any such commodity. Ryan studied the man out of the corner of his eye. He was on edge, pacing back and forth nervously. He obviously knew that he had spoken carelessly. He had mentioned a letter. From and to whom? And what would a brewer or drayman be doing with such an item? Playing messenger? Ryan could only wonder, pondering the matter as he unloaded barrels of wine and ale, which the butler ordered down to the cellar.

I need to find a way to extend our stay at Chartley, he thought. Once the full barrels were unloaded and the empty barrels put on the wagon, Seamus would be expected to move on—unless he thought quickly. The answer came to him at once. If the wagon were inoperable, then there would be reason to stay while it was being repaired. A broken axle, a loose wheel, or perhaps a combination of the two might give him just the extension of time that he needed—until the morning. Moving the wagon into the shadows, Ryan cautiously set about his mischievous task.

Chapter Thirty-seven

RYAN LAY AWAKE in the darkness of the hayloft, shivering against the chill as he swaddled himself in the old woolen blanket. It was not quite the sleeping arrangement he had hoped would be offered. Indeed, the stern-faced Paulet was hardly what one might call a gracious host. He had fed Seamus and Ryan on table scraps and, despite the cold, had relegated them to the stables where the groom and stableboy spent their nights—making it very clear that come morn, he expected them to be gone. Food stocks at Chartley were low because of the winter, he had explained when Seamus had grumbled indignantly.

"So much for your brilliant plan of sabotaging my wagon," complained Seamus, who was lying a few feet away from him now. "All for naught, for neither one of us caught even a glimpse of Moira, nor even has the first idea of where her room might be."

"As soon as the household is asleep, I'll find her." Ryan was determined.

"And bring down old Pruneface's wrath?" Seamus chided. "You can't just go rampaging about, or you just might get yourself in more trouble than you are prepared for."

"I haven't come all this way just to leave without seeing her, Seamus. I've got to find a way."

"Mmmm, well, when you think of a plan, wake me. I'm bone-tired." The brewer's loud snores soon told Ryan that he would be of no help.

Lying awake in the darkness, Ryan listened to the noises of the animals in the stalls below and the wind rattling the loose boards of the stable walls. Seamus was right. Just how was he going to find Moira without bringing the household down on his head? For all the laxity in Mary's guards of late and the easing of security from previous days, it would still be out of the question to go meandering about, particularly when old Paulet had such disdain for anyone he relegated to a menial position. Yet he refused to leave without seeing Moira, without knowing for certain that she was safe. How did he know that she wasn't as much a prisoner here as the Scottish queen? He didn't. But somehow, he would find out.

Fearful of closing his eyes lest he fall asleep, Ryan concentrated his attention on a crack in the stable roof. A faint glimmer of moonlight floated through the space, giving promise that the skies were clearing. Even so, a cold draft wafted under his blanket, and Ryan hugged himself to try to find some comfort from the chill. Oh, how he longed to have Moira in his arms, her body pressed against his own, warming him. The very thought of her brought forth tantalizing memories, stoking the embers of his desire.

"Oh, Moira—" Where was she? If only by concentrating upon her could he sense her presence—but such was not to be; he was not one of those so gifted.

The stable was startlingly quiet. Even the animals at rest in their stalls had ceased their moving about. Placidly Ryan was just pondering whether now was the time to make a move when he heard the boards creak on the ladder down below him. Peering over the edge of the loft, he saw the silhouetted form of a young girl. Here in the stables for a midnight tryst? It appeared so.

"Johnnie! Johnnie!" She called out the name, then let out a squawk as she was answered by a rough embrace. Giggles and the rustle of two bodies rolling about in the hay told Ryan what was going on. It seemed the groom had found more to warm him than a tattered, woolen blanket. Groans and panting of love wafted in the air, sensual sounds that only served to remind Ryan of his own loneliness. There were more giggles, then silence pervaded again.

"Ohhhhhh, Alice!" A whisper down below him gave proof that the groom had been well pleased.

"I just didn't want to wait until spring—"

"I'm glad that you didn't." By the sounds coming from the

hay, it sounded as if the girl named Alice had renewed her amorous activities. The stable came alive with the soft sounds of lovemaking, a sound which fiercely stirred Ryan's own passion.

"I had best get back inside before I am missed. Paulet is a strict one. If it were found out that we . . . that we— Well, I might be thrown out."

"Don't go!"

"I must!"

"Then first a kiss!" It seemed the girl willingly obliged.

Ryan focused his hearing on the sounds in the stable. It sounded as if the woman were getting dressed. Before she could get the chance to go very far, Ryan would have a few questions to ask. Suddenly, it seemed to be the way to get the information he so longed for. He must intercept the woman named Alice before she had the chance to return to the manor. She was fearful of Paulet finding out about her dalliance with the groom. Perhaps if he threatened to reveal what he knew, if she was properly chastised, he might be able to strike a bargain with her: his silence in return for knowledge of where Moira MacKinnon's chamber was, and how to get to it without being seen. With that thought in mind, Ryan moved ever so quietly down the ladder and slipped out the stable door. Resting one hand upon the wall of the stable, he waited.

The moon gave him just enough light to see the woman's shape as she moved through the door. Like a cat on a mouse, he pounced. She opened her mouth to scream, but before she could make a sound, he clamped his hand over her mouth, blocking out any cry. As quietly as he could, he pulled her away from the stable's entrance, lest her lover come to her aid.

The woman struggled in the grasp of her captor. The silence of the night was shattered by her deep, throaty moans. "Mmmmmm."

"Be quiet, I mean you no harm," Ryan whispered in her ear. She ignored his words, struggling until exhausted. "By God, you are a lively one!" He held her even more firmly, swearing beneath his breath. She was short but big-boned, with a strength that, in a woman, amazed him. "Hold still, I won't harm you. I just want the answer to a question."

His words seemed to soothe her, for she stopped squirming. Taking a chance, Ryan pulled his hand from her mouth. "What—what do you want?" Her voice was like a shrill, frightened hiss.

"There is a woman named Moira MacKinnon within these walls. I want to know where she is," Ryan answered softly. The woman seemed to be regaining her calm, but he held her around the waist nevertheless.

"Moira MacKinnon? There is no one here with such a name."

"No one—" Her answer acted upon Ryan like a blow to his stomach. Fear crept up his spine. What if something had happened to her? "She has to be!"

"I know the name of every woman here, but there is not one MacKinnon." The woman tried to shrug off Ryan's hold. "Old Paulet would have apoplexy if there was anyone he didn't know lurking about. No Scotsmen, that is for certain."

"If there is no MacKinnon, perhaps there is a dark-haired girl confined on the premises. A girl with wide green eyes and a long neck. Tall. Graceful, if a bit haughty and stubborn from time to time."

"There is a Moira that fits such a description. Moira Mowbray is her name. A girl who is lady's maid to the Queen." The woman tilted her head to get a look at Ryan. "Mmmmm. You look to be the kind of man a woman would be pleased to have find her."

"Moira Mowbray?" It was possible that it was she. Were she afraid of Walsingham and his spies, it would be a logical thing for her to change her name.

"But if you have your heart set upon her, you had best think otherwise. She left a man behind when she came here, says she will never forget him, and that she will always love him." Alice looked at him again. "But if there was ever a man who could win a woman's heart, it would most likely be you."

"Then I will try," Ryan breathed huskily. He loosened his hold. "Tell me where she is, how I can find her." When the woman remained silent, he whispered, "Please!"

"Her room is in the servants' quarters. Second floor at the top of the stairs. Third room to the right. It's always kept unlocked. Paulet won't allow anyone to have the leisure of privacy.''

''Second floor, third room to the right. Thank you.'' Giving the woman a peck on the cheek, Ryan released her. He ran as fast as his legs would carry him towards the manor, towards Moira.

Chapter Thirty-eight

ALL WAS QUIET in the household. It was well after midnight, and thus everyone was abed. Paulet's strict rules were "early to bed and early to rise," and no dallying. Even so, Moira could not sleep. For more than an hour she had sat contemplating the fire as it burned brightly in the hearth of her quiet chamber. The reason for her disquiet was that Seamus had paid another visit. It was a break in his usual routine to return to Chartley so soon, and Moira could only suppose that he had seen her that day in the courtyard and came back to investigate. With that apprehension in mind, she had been doubly careful, keeping to the library until she was certain he was settled down for the night. She had even taken the evening meal in her room, pleading illness. If the jolly brewer's coming here was to find out if she was at Chartley, he would go back to London disappointed.

Moira's room seemed welcoming tonight, a haven of comfort and safety. It was the only place where she could be alone with her thoughts, where she did not have to force a smile. Her emotions were in a turmoil: she wanted to talk with Seamus, to ask him to take her back to London, yet knew that such a request would be totally out of the question. Selfish, foolhardy. The matter of the barrels seemed to be coming to a head. The Queen needed her more than ever.

Standing before the large circular mirror, Moira began to undress, and had proceeded as far as her underskirt and chemise when suddenly she thought she heard the sound of footsteps on the stairs. One of the servants snuffing the wall sconces in the hall, she thought. She did not give it another thought, and resumed dressing for bed, donning a white linen sleeping-gown.

Moira looked towards her bed. It was the one thing about the bedchamber she had loved at first sight. It was wide and piled high with quilts over the feather mattress stuffing. What delighted her, however, was the canopy and curtains that often made her feel as secure as a caterpillar inside its cocoon. Picking up the long-handled warming pan, she filled it with coals and positioned it to warm the bed. Yet when that was done, and she had tucked herself beneath the covers, she found she still couldn't sleep. Taking a coverlet from the bed, she returned to her seat by the fireplace.

The fire had burned down to glowing embers when Moira heard the footsteps outside her door. She gave them little heed. In truth, she was reluctant to leave the warmth of the hearth. Unable to sleep, she had curled up close to the fire. Yawning, she stretched out on the quilt, listening as the heavy trod came closer. Paulet or one of his men come to scold her for wasting the lamp oil and tell her to go to bed, she supposed.

The thought annoyed Moira. Surely Paulet ran the household as if he were the sovereign of an impoverished realm. And all the while, Chartley was as richly ornamented as a palace, with its high glass windows and paneled walls, stone fireplaces with great hearths, high-ceilinged rooms ornamented with tapestries and velvet hangings. Even so, Mary's expenditures had been cut to the bone, her joy of giving alms taken away. That thought sparked her annoyance when a soft tapping at her door disturbed the silence.

I'll ignore the sound and then they will go away, she thought. She was wrong. The knocking sounded, louder this time.

"Oh!" So much for her privacy.

Lighting a taper with one of the fire's embers, Moira made her way to the door, fully prepared to be chastised for not complying with Paulet's rules. "Yes?" In the flickering candlelight, Moira appraised her late-night visitor, her eyes flicking over his garments. Not a servant at all, but a drayman. A drayman? What did he want with her?

"Moira!" An all-too-familiar voice startled her into awareness of who it was.

"Dear God!" Startled, Moira jerked her head up, looking

•

the man full in the face, gasping as she recognized him.
"Ryan!"

They stared at each other for a long while, two quiet shadows
in the darkness. A knot squeezed the pit of her stomach. She
didn't know why, but her eyes misted as she took a step closer.
So—despite her best intentions, he had found her. There would
be no more hiding.

"You've sent me on quite a chase. I've gone to Scotland
and back trying to find you." Ryan pushed aside the door, and
kicked it shut behind him. For a long moment, he merely
looked at her, at the way her nightgown clung to the tantalizing
curves and planes of her body. His blood surged wildly through
his veins as he slowly and sensuously reached out and took
her by the shoulders. His fingers seemed to burn through the
thin cloth of her sleeping-gown, melting her flesh, stripping
her very soul bare.

"To Scotland?" How was she to know her lie would catch
up with her?

"I had it in mind to bring you back with me, to carry you
away, if need be." His eyes glittered as they swept over her.
"So beautiful. How was I to know that one woman could get
under my skin so, taunt my heart so?" He pulled her roughly
against him, anchoring her to him as he cupped her chin in his
right hand. "My sweet Scottish lass."

The excitement that raced along her spine was very much
like fear as she saw the male intent in his eyes. Pure, raw
desire. "Ryan—"

His mouth came down and muffled his name on her lips.
The fingers of one hand tangled in her hair as he kissed her
with a fierce, sweet fire. Moira gave in without protest. Her
hands slid up to lock around his neck, drawing him closer. It
had been so long since he had kissed her.

As if to familiarize himself with her again, Ryan slid his
hands down her back to cup the firm roundness of her buttocks,
lifting her even closer to him. The feel of him, so hard, so
strong, was all she wanted in the world. The heat of his body
warmed her, aroused her, turning her thoughts into chaos. His
hand swept up to close over her breast, his expertise making
them harden with desire. The sensations that tingled inside of
her made her body a dizzying maelstrom of need.

"I want you, so much so that I can hardly think of anything else," he whispered. "I should have made love to you, should have branded you as mine."

Moira's pulse quickened at the passion that burned in his eyes. "Should you?"

"Perhaps then you wouldn't have run away."

"I had to go, please believe me. But there hasn't been one day I haven't thought of you, longed for you." Perhaps this passion between us was inevitable from the first moment our hands touched, she thought. Certainly now that he was here, he was the center of her world. Being in his arms eclipsed any other thought, any other memory.

"Nor a day that I haven't dreamed of seeing you again. When Seamus told me that he had seen you here, I had to come. Oh, Moira!" he groaned, his mouth roaming freely, stopping briefly at the hollow of her throat, lingering there, then slowly moving downward to the skin of her bare shoulder. Ryan held her against him, his hands spanning her narrow waist. Murmuring her name again, he buried his face in the silky strands of her hair, inhaling the delicate fragrance of flowers in the luxurious softness. His fingers parted the fragile fabric of her gown to cup one firm, budding breast. His fingers brought forth a tingling pleasure.

She knew she should pull away, but she could not. She was lost in a flush of sensations. She felt wanton, aware of her body as she had never been before. Deep inside of her was the need to belong to him, to be his woman. At long last, Ryan was to be her lover. She knew it was going to happen and she was powerless to stop him, and in truth, didn't want to even think of pushing him away. What would follow, then? Would he betray her to Walsingham? Alas, she didn't even want to think of that, of anything past this moment.

It seemed that his hands were everywhere, touching her, setting her body afire with a pulsating flame of desire. Moira writhed beneath him, giving herself up to the glorious sensations he was igniting within her as he slipped the gown from her shoulders and let it slide slowly to the floor. When at last she was naked, her long, dark hair streaming down her back, he looked at her for a long while, his face flushed with passion, his breath a deep-throated rasp.

"You are so lovely!" he murmured, putting his thoughts into words. His hands moved along her back, sending forth shivers of pleasure, he by touching and she by being touched. Her waist was small, her breasts perfection, her legs long and shapely. As she stood bathed in candlelight, his eyes roamed over her body.

"Am I, Captain?" Moira made no effort to hide her curves from his piercing gaze. Gone was her maidenly modesty. This was her fate, her destiny to belong to this man, just as it had been her mother's to belong to Roarke MacKinnon. She felt that in every bone, every muscle, every sinew of her body. As he touched her, she gloried in the thought that her body pleased him, her pulse quickening at the passion that burned in his eyes.

"Moira—" He spoke her name softly, caressingly. Their kisses were tender at first, but the burning spark of their desire burst into flame. Desire flooded his mind, obliterating all reason. He had been a gentleman once, had left her untouched, but by God, he wouldn't be so noble again. Time was much too fleeting, happiness all too precarious a pleasure. He wanted her, and she wanted him; it was as simple a thing as that. Sweeping her up in his arms, he held her against his heart for a fleeting moment, then carried her to the bed.

Wrapped in each other's arms, they kissed, his mouth moving upon hers, pressing her lips apart, hers responding, gently exploring the sweet firmness of his. Shifting her weight, she rolled closer into his embrace. How could she deny what was in her heart? She was woman and he was man, it was as simple as that. God had made it so, had made woman to be cherished, and in turn, to love. Nothing else was as important as being here with him.

Oh, blessed Christ, Ryan thought. How could he have ever realized the full effect her nearness would kindle in him when he was with her again? She fit against him so perfectly, her gentle curves melting against his own hard body. It was as though Moira had been made for him. Perhaps she had been. At this moment, it certainly seemed so.

"I want no other woman. Only you can fill my heart," he whispered against her mouth. He kissed the corners of her lips, tracing them with his tongue. He parted her lips, seeking the sweetness he knew to be there. His hands moved over her body, stroking her lightly—her throat, her breasts, her belly, her thighs. With reverence, he moved his hands over her breasts, gently and slowly, until they swelled beneath his fingers. He outlined the rosy-peaked mound with his finger, watching as the velvet flesh hardened. Her responding moan excited him, but he wanted to be gentle. He wanted to make it beautiful for her, wanted to be the perfect lover. Nevertheless, it took all his self-control to keep his passion in check.

Ryan lingered over her, exploring her body with his hands and mouth, discovering the sweetness of it. His gentle exploration was like feathers everywhere upon her skin, arousing a deep, aching longing. Moira closed her eyes to the rapture. Without even looking at him, she could see his strong body and bold smile, and thought again what a handsome man he was. Yet it was something far stronger that drew her, the gentleness that merged with his strength. Even though she was new to this matter of passion, she knew instinctively that he was concerned with her pleasure.

Wanting to bring him the same sensations that she was feeling, Moira touched him, one hand sliding down over the muscles of his chest, sensuously stroking his flesh in exploration. She heard the audible intake of his breath giving her the courage to continue in her quest.

"Moira—!" He held her face in his hands, kissing her eyelids, the curve of her cheekbones, her mouth. "Moira. Moira," he repeated her name over and over, as if to taste of it on his lips.

"I am glad that I please you, for you please me too, so very much." Her fingertips roamed over his shoulders and neck and plunged into his thick hair as he kissed her once again, a fierce joining of mouths that spoke of his passion. Then, after a long pleasurable moment, he drew away, taking off his shoes, and then drawing the tunic over his head, stripping off his shirt and canvas pants. All the beauty of his masculinity towered over her. He was so very male, powerful and aggressive.

For a moment, Moira had second thoughts as she glimpsed his hardness, but knew that he would turn his strength into tenderness and love. When he was completely naked, he rolled over on his side and drew her down alongside him. ''I like the feel of your skin against mine,'' he breathed.

The candlelight flickered, illuminating the smooth skin on his chest. He was a muscular man, more so than she had thought. Although he was slim at the waist and hips, his chest was expansive. She found the thick chest hair soft as she reached out to him. Her hands caressed his chest, her large green eyes beckoning him, enticing him to enter the world of love she sensed was awaiting them both.

Moira was shattered by the all-consuming pleasure of lying naked beside him. Like a willing sacrifice, she entwined her arms around his muscled neck, writhing in a slow, delicate dance. Heat rose within her as she arched against him in sensual pleasure. Her breathing grew heavier, and a hunger for him that felt like a pleasant pain traveled from her breasts down to her loins, a pulsing, tingling sensation that became stronger as his hand ran down the smoothness of her belly to touch the softness nestled between her thighs.

Moira gave in to wild abandon, moaning intimately and joyously as her fingers likewise moved over his own body. She felt a strange sensation flood over her, and could not deny that before he left, she wanted their spirits to be joined together. She wanted him to fill her with excitement and pleasure. His strong arms were around her, his mouth covering her own. She shivered at the feeling that swept over her.

The light of one lone candle illuminated their bodies, hers as smooth as cream, his muscular form a darker hue. He knelt down beside her and kissed her breasts, running his tongue over their tips until she shuddered with delight. Whispering words of love, he slid his hands between her thighs to explore the soft inner flesh. At his touch, she felt a slow quivering deep inside that became a fierce fire as he moved his fingers against her.

Supporting himself on his forearms, he moved between her legs. Slowly, he caressed his pelvis against her thigh, letting her get accustomed to the feel of his maleness.

''Love me, Ryan,'' she breathed. Arching up, she was eager to drink fully of that which she had only briefly experienced.

''Aye. Oh, I will, my sweet, sweet love.'' His mouth closed over hers with a hard, fierce possession, his breath mingling with hers, probing her mouth with his tongue as he entered her with a slow but strong thrust. He pulled her more fully beneath him as he buried his length within her softness, allowing her to adjust to his invasion. She was so warm, so tight around him, that he closed his eyes with agonized pleasure.

"My God!" he muttered hoarsely. Closing his eyes, he wondered how he could ever have thought that anything meant more to him than this. At the moment, the only thing he wanted was to bring her pleasure, to give her his devotion.

As they moved together, spasms of sensation wove through Moira like the threads of an embroidery. She had never realized how incomplete she had felt until this moment. Now joined with him, she was a whole being. She clung to him feverishly, her breasts pressed against his chest. Their hearts beat in matching rhythm even as their mouths met, tongues entwined, bodies embraced in the slow, sensuous dance of love. Consumed by his warmth and his hardness, she tightened her thighs around his waist and she arched up to him, moving in time to his rhythm. He was slow and gentle, taking incredible care of her.

"Ryan—!" She clutched at him. It was as if he had touched the very core of her being. There was an explosion of rapture as their bodies blended into one, an ecstasy too beautiful for words. Love. Such a simple word, and yet in truth, it meant so much. She had never realized how unfulfilled she had been without him until this moment. She tried to tell him so, with her hands, her mouth, and the movement of her body, declaring her love with every motion.

Ryan groaned, giving himself up to the exquisite sensation of her flesh surrounding the entire length of him. Again and again he made her his own, wanting to blend his flesh with hers, to bring her the ultimate pleasure of love, and succeeding beyond his wildest expectations. With Moira MacKinnon he knew the shattering satisfaction of being whole, of being completely and unselfishly one with a woman. Though he had thought to make her his, he wondered if she hadn't already placed the mark of her possession upon his heart.

Languidly they came back to reality, lying together in the aftermath of passion, their hearts gradually resuming a normal rhythm. Time drifted past, yet they were reluctant to move and break the spell. Ryan gazed down upon her face, gently brushing back the tangled dark hair from her eyes. From this moment on, she was his. He would never share her with anyone.

"Sleep now," he whispered, still holding her close. With a sigh, she snuggled up against him, burying her face in the warmth of his chest. He caressed her, tracing his fingers along her spine until she drifted off.

Chapter Thirty-nine

THE DAY DAWNED CLOUDY, yet even so, the commotion of a few of the servants—early risers anxious to be about their tasks—awoke Moira. She stirred, stretching her arms and legs in slow, easy motions. There was something different about the morning. She sensed it, yet didn't recall what had happened until she noticed the unaccustomed warmth against her as she moved. Her eyes snapped open instantly as she remembered. So last night had not been a dream after all. Ryan Paxton was lying beside her, his breath rustling the strands of her hair.

All the details of the past night came flooding back to her, causing her to blush. By God, as Ryan was wont to say. She had behaved like a wanton last night, allowing herself to surrender completely to the man beside her. What on earth could have possessed her? How could she have so easily surrendered her virtue in a mindless moment of passion? She was stunned by her behavior—but to be truthful, she would not have traded one moment of the delightful ecstasy she had shared with the man at her side. It had been the most beautiful, most astounding moment of her life. Somehow, she sensed it had been the same for him.

"He loves me!" she breathed. He had not said so in words, but his lovemaking had surely proved it. He had even traveled all the way to Scotland just to find her, and after finding that journey to be a wild goose chase, had come straightaway here. Stretching languorously, Moira smiled. She loved him too. Oh, what a blessed emotion.

Cautiously, so as not to waken him, she turned over on her side and watched him as he slept. Somehow, she would win his loyalty over to Mary's cause, just as her mother had swayed her father. She would make him see the injustice with which Mary had been served, make him understand her need to see Mary free. Let Walsingham beware—she had the upper hand now. After last night, how could she ever think that Ryan would betray her?

Her eyes touched on his forehead, his nose, his lashes, and well-formed lips. She found herself looking at him as she had never done before, noting the line of his brows, the angle of his jaw, the way his wavy red-gold hair touched his neck and temples. With his eyes shut, he looked boyish, and almost innocent, but in truth, he was a passionate lover. He had learned every inch of her body with his hands and mouth, had seen her naked as the day she was born, and yet she felt no shame. What had passed between them last night was beautiful, incredibly so.

Over and over in her mind, she relived each look, each touch, remembered his husky cry of passion when he had whispered her name. "Moira!" Upon his lips, it had sounded so beautiful.

"Love," she whispered. Love had a way of bringing gentleness to the heart, radiating out to others like sunshine. Though her knowledge of courtship and lovemaking was limited to him, she still knew that Ryan Paxton had made love to her with the greatest of tenderness. He had known just how to touch her, how long to linger—not once, but several times, he had brought her to the brink of near-madness. Aye, she loved him, desired him. There could never be doubt of that henceforth. Even now, she could feel the world whirling and spinning around her when she imagined his hands upon her.

Ryan Paxton. Her own heart's desire. Her captain. Perhaps when the time came, Ryan's ship might aid in the escape of the Scottish queen. The idea appealed to her. Imagine whisking the Queen out from beneath Paulet's very nose and setting her out to sea.

Whispering his name, Moira stroked the expanse of his shoulders and chest exposed above the bedcovers, remembering the delights they had shared. His skin was just as she remembered, warm and smooth, roughened by a thatch of hair on his chest. Against her breasts, it had been more pleasurable than she might have ever imagined.

"Moira?" Ryan asked sleepily. Still only half-awake, he smiled. Their gazes locked. She couldn't look away. Then he was rolling her over, and pinned her beneath him. His hands moved over her back, sending a tingling sensation along her spine. "What a pleasant surprise to wake up and find you beside me." His voice was husky, his breath warm in her ear.

"I will be by your side as long as you want me there."

"That will be forever."

He caught her lips, gently nibbling them. His tongue touched hers and her mouth opened to allow him entrance.

They lay motionless until she could hardly bear it, then he slowly began the caressing motions that had so deeply stirred her last night. He touched her from the curve of her neck to the soft flesh behind her knees and up again, caressing the flat plain of her belly. Moving to her breast, he cupped it, squeezing gently. Her breast filled his palm as his fingers stroked and fondled. Lowering his head, he buried his face between the soft mounds.

"So smooth. 'Tis said there is nothing like a woman's softness."

"Nor a man's strength." She was not content to be only the recipient of pleasure, and felt a need to give pleasure as well. With that desire in mind, she moved her palms over the muscles and tight flesh of his body.

"Moira—!" A long shuddering sigh wracked through him. "Oh, how I love your hands upon me."

Moira was instilled with a newfound confidence, knowing that she could so deeply stir him. She continued her exploration, as if to learn every inch of him. In response, she felt his body tremble against hers.

"Ahhhh—" The sound came from deep in his throat.

Stretching her arms up, she entwined them around his neck, pulling his head down. Their lips met in a long kiss, sealing the promise of their newfound love. His mouth played seductively on hers, his tongue parting her lips at the same moment his maleness entered the softness between her thighs. She felt his hardness entering her, then moving slowly inside until she gasped with pleasure.

Slowly, he made love to her again, molding and shaping her. When he entered her, she felt her heart move. It was as if he were draining her soul, then pouring it back again, filling her to overflowing. Her joyous cries mingled with his as they joined together in a fiery union. For the moment, the world was held at bay.

This time their lovemaking was not quite as gentle, but satisfying nonetheless. Moira couldn't help marveling at how their bodies fit together as perfectly as if they had been made for one another. It was like falling off the edge of a high tower. Falling, and never quite hitting the ground. Her arms locked around him, and she arched up to him, joining Ryan in expressing their love.

Afterwards, she cuddled happily in his arms, her head against his chest, her legs entwined in his. Noticing that he was tense, she gazed into his face, disconcerted to see a frown there. How could he be even remotely unhappy after the bliss they had just shared? "Captain?" Such a formal greeting after what they had shared.

"Ever since I first saw you, I've been fighting against what we just experienced," he said softly. "You are the kind of woman a man takes to wife, Moira. I didn't intend for our passions to flare full flame."

"Nor did I, but I think that somehow we have both been fighting a losing battle, Ryan. What we feel for each other was meant to be."

He turned his head, staring into her eyes. "I felt that too, particularly last night. And yet, the feelings that we share may cause complications in our lives. Your father did not act in the least as if I were his favorite fellow. I think he blames me for all of your troubles."

"I think he might. He is overprotective at times, but lovable nonetheless. Once you get to know him, you will see what a fine man he is." She lay against him, soft and warm, her breasts pressed tightly to his chest. Her long, dark hair tickled his chest as it flowed between them. A wave of tenderness washed over him as he reached out to stroke the soft brown tresses, brushing it out of her eyes.

"Moira—" His thoughts were clearly written in his eyes.

"I don't want you to be hurt in any way." Leaning over, he kissed her gently.

"Hurt?" What on earth did he mean? With him beside her, all her hopes and dreams had been fulfilled.

Ryan came right to the point. "It is dangerous for you here. There are intrigues that you could not possibly be aware of. I do not want you entangled in the middle."

"Intrigues?" Moira tried to keep her poise. As if she didn't know that he himself was in the midst of such deviousness. "Why, whatever do you mean?"

Her coyness unsettled him for a moment. "Seamus told me why you left London. I don't have to tell you again that I warned you to have a care."

"You did!" She was piqued by the reminder. "And I was careful. There was little I could do, however, when certain odious men followed me. It was not at my plea that they searched through my belongings."

"Nor will it be your fault when you are accosted here. And you will be." He patted her well-rounded buttocks. "So up with you. It's all decided."

"Decided?" She didn't remember having any discussions about anything. "What is?"

"Seamus brought me up here so that I could give you safe escort back to Scotland." Looking towards the window, cursing the light of day, Ryan bounded from the bed. "It's growing late. We must hurry. Pack your belongings."

"Just like that?" His authoritative manner dismayed her.

"Aye. We have little time. I worked a bit of havoc on Seamus's wagon as an excuse to spend the night here, but that old man who has set himself up as keeper will undoubtedly be shooing us away at any moment."

"Paulet is his name."

"Aye, I remember." He dressed hurriedly, motioning for her to do the same. "Will he let you go freely, or shall we think of a way for you to hide inside the wagon for our jaunt out of here?"

"Let me out? What are you saying?" She had no intention of leaving.

"That I am taking you out of here. Surely you didn't think I just came for a visit, my love." It made him feel good to be her rescuer. "I repeat: can you leave of your own free will, or must you answer to that dried-up old weasel?"

"It doesn't matter!" He was so cocksure, so arrogant, that she thought it best to let him know at this very moment that she would not be so treated. "For I am *not* going anywhere."

Ryan tensed his jaw stubbornly. "Ah, but you are! For of a surety, I will not let you linger."

"You will not let? You will not let?" Moira laughed derisively. "You, sir, have not anything to say about it. I am in the Queen of Scotland's employ. I answer only to her."

"By God!" Ryan clenched his hands into fists. "You stubborn, ungrateful little chit. I rode and walked through almost knee-deep mud just to see that you were safe. You are going to Scotland, even if I have to carry you every step of the way."

"I am not!" She was defiant.

"You are!"

"I most definitely am not!" She would not allow him to treat her like some brainless child.

"Then I'll take you back to London where I can keep an eye on you." He'd marry her and put her under his protection. Perhaps Walsingham's spies would not be as likely to bother her if she were an Englishman's wife.

"For sooth, you do not understand me. I am staying here, with the Queen." Moira donned her chemise and a blue woolen gown. "She is lonely, and I can give her comfort and good company."

"And accompany her when they march her to the block," Ryan said scathingly beneath his breath.

"What did you say?" Moira looked up, her eyes angry slits.

Ryan's wrath evaporated. He tried valiantly to understand Moira's view of things. She seemed to have a misguided loyalty to Mary of Scots and that endangered her own person. But then, she was not the only one. The captive Queen did, as Walsingham always admitted, have a certain charm. The situation was dangerous for everyone.

"Please, Moira. Come to your senses. I do not want anything to happen to you." He came forward to kiss her, but Moira turned her head, and thus he caught only her cheek. "So, that is the way it is to be."

"I cannot leave." Moira immediately regretted her coldness

to him. She wanted his affection, not his anger. "Please understand. She needs me."

"As do I, Moira. As do I."

Never had her emotions been so torn apart. With all her heart, she wanted to go with him, yet her sense of honor dictated that she remain with the Queen, at least until spring. How could he think that she could just slip away?

"Ryan, please understand."

He was desperately trying to. What was the hold that Mary of Scots held over Moira? Indeed, over so many Catholics? By all reports, the woman was an adulteress, a murderer. She had been chased out of Scotland by her own countrymen after a blazing scandal. Why then had she suddenly taken on the semblance of a saint?

"You are suffering from a misguided sense of loyalty, Moira. The Queen of Scots is a star who, alas, lost her luster years ago. If you think to see her rise again, you are supporting a losing cause, one that will cost dearly. Being on her side will only make you an enemy of the Queen's councilor."

"Walsingham!" She spat his name out like a curse.

"Aye, Walsingham."

"Your master!"

"Mine?" He was taken aback. "No. I have no liking for men of his mettle."

"And yet you have served him." All too vivid in her mind was that time he had gone on a mysterious errand. "Deny that, if you can. You, sir, are a spy."

"I say that I am not, and I do not lie." He was anxious to set her mind at rest. "I have served Elizabeth, my sovereign queen, by making use of my ships upon occasion. Only that."

He spoke so earnestly that she believed him. "I'm glad, for I would not want to you to be my enemy, Captain."

"Never that, Moira." There were so many things he wanted to say, needed to say, but already the tumult in the hallway announced that the household was coming fully awake. He had to leave quickly while he might; were he seen leaving Moira's room, it would make for unsavory complications. Once more he pleaded to her. "Come with me. Let me take you to safety in Scotland. Your father will give you protection

until things quiet." Then they could plan for their future together.

"Ryan—" Oh, how she wanted to go, to spend the nights
cradled in the crook of his arm. If she left, Mary would understand. Hadn't the Queen likewise pleaded with her to seek
the safety of her father's lands?

"Gather up your possessions and meet me in the courtyard
as soon as you can." This time, when he came forward to kiss
her, she did not pull away. She was engulfed in the warmth
of his nearness. When his lips found hers, she arched against
him, returning his kiss hungrily, fiercely. "In the courtyard,"
he repeated. Then he was gone, slipping out her chamber door.

Chapter Forty

THE INNER COURTYARD RANG with the sound of dogs, horses, and men. The servants of Chartley were astir. Roused from their pallets in the attics and cellars, they lighted fires and prepared for the coming day. Ryan recognized the young woman named Alice, her cap askew, the laces of her bodice hastily done up. Through half-closed, puffy eyelids, she looked at him for a long time but did not approach him, or say even one word. She had kept her part of the bargain; Ryan would keep his as well.

Through the large windows, Ryan could see into Chartley. Most of the household was gathered around one of the long tables where a wheel of cheese, a basket of bread, and a platter of salt herring had been set out. It made him realize how hungry he was, but though he loitered about hoping for a show of generosity, it was not forthcoming. Apparently, Paulet was going to make good on his word to be stingy. With a gruff snort of annoyance, he moved toward the stables.

The stable was startlingly quiet. Most of the other wagons had their animals harnessed and were ready to be on their way. Ryan moved towards the ladder and paused, letting his eyes adjust to the dim light. Softly, he called to Seamus.

"Where the devil have you been?" Seamus's head appeared over the edge of the loft. He was disheveled, his leather jerkin only half-laced, his stockings sagging. "Well, it doesn't matter. After you left last night, I had a most pleasant visitor." He winked. "Old Paulet might be a prissy old soul, but his maidservants are most delectable." Hand over hand, he climbed down the ladder. "I assume that you found Moira."

"I did."

"And is she coming with us?"

Ryan grimaced. "I tried to convince her to, though at first she was reluctant. I can only hope that she will see the sense of it and act in her own best interests. She's to meet us in the courtyard. Let's move as slowly as we can to give her enough time."

Seamus nodded, following Ryan to the wagon. Bending down, they both examined the wheel, making pretense of tightening it, then turned their attention to the axle.

"So, your wagon gave out on you. Well, perhaps I can help." Much to Ryan's dismay, one of the guards stepped up to lend them a hand, to repay them for the generous gifts Seamus always brought.

"The axle is worse off than I had at first thought," Ryan exclaimed, his eyes fixed on the door. Was Moira coming? His heart lurched as the possibility that she might not crossed his mind. By God, last night had been nothing short of perfect. How then could she choose to serve Mary over leaving with him?

"You're right, the axle looks as if it just might fall off, but do not despair," the guard said. "The blacksmith here at Chartley can work wonders. I'll have him fashion a metal brace for you that will make this axle better than it was when new."

"Thank you." Ryan welcomed the extra time that the offer gave them. Even so, the blacksmith worked much faster than he would have liked. All too soon, the axle-brace was securely in place.

"Your wagon seems to be quite sturdy now." The guard grinned.

"I'll bring you something special for your trouble, next time I'm here," Seamus said pleasantly. "You have been a great boon to us, my friend."

Ryan judged by the position of the sun that approximately a half hour had passed. And still no sign of Moira. Where was she? He felt the urge to go after her, but held back. Should he make good on his threat, and carry her away? That would surely set some tongues wagging. No, it was her choice to make. His fierce, stubborn pride wouldn't let him ask her again.

Ryan sought out the young groom who had tended their horses, and found him sleeping on a pile of straw. Apparently, his tryst with the young woman named Alice had tired him. Shaking him gently by the shoulders, Ryan woke him up. Collecting the horses, Ryan and Seamus nonetheless allotted an inordinate amount of time for harnessing them to the wagon. Even so, there was no sign of Moira.

"She's not coming!" Ryan realized he was being overtly stubborn in not admitting that fact. Even the Queen of England herself wouldn't take so long to pack.

"No, it doesn't look as if she is. I'm sorry, Ryan. To have come all this way for naught must be very disappointing." Seamus patted his friend on the shoulder sympathetically.

"You'll never realize how much so," Ryan answered. Closing his eyes, he remembered the feel of her in his arms, the softness of her womanly form. He was tempted to stay, to seek out employment at Chartley just to be near her, but knew that there was no way. His ship and tavern were in London. And yet, as he climbed aboard the wagon, he knew his heart would be left here.

"It's going to be another miserable day," Seamus was saying, looking at the formation of the clouds. "Rain. It's waiting for us on the horizon." He shook his head sadly. "If we don't want to get right in the midst of the storm, we had best be on our way."

"Just a few more moments. Please—"

Seamus obeyed, counting to three-hundred-and-three as slowly as he could. Then, with a flick of his wrists, he sent the wagon on its way, moving towards the outer gates of Chartley.

Ryan looked back, not once but several times, hoping beyond hope to see Moira running after them. Alas, it was not to be. "I came to her," he said softly. "The next time she'll have to come after me." It was a vow he intended to keep. A man couldn't make a damned fool of himself time after time. He'd gone to Scotland and come all the way here. If Moira wanted him, she'd have to come to London; it was her turn.

"ALICE, what ails me? My hands are trembling so violently that I can scarce hold my brush!" Moira hurried to braid her hair for the long journey.

"It's called love," Alice answered, with a deep, husky laugh. "I feel the same for Tom."

"Tom?"

Alice blushed. "Aye, I've found myself a young man."

"I'm glad. Everyone needs someone to love." It had been a difficult decision to make, but in the end, Moira could make no other choice. She had to follow her heart. Hadn't Mary herself fallen desperately in love with Bothwell long ago? She would understand.

"Had I not met with Tom last night, you might not be smiling so prettily." Alice related the tale of the young drayman's search for his lady love. "He is a handsome one."

"Very handsome!" To her, he was the handsomest man in all the world. Her lover, the man she had chosen above all. "Oh, Alice, I love him so."

"And he loves you. I could tell right away last night." Alice gave Moira a tweak on the nose. "Now, hurry. Go to him. I'll give your letter to the Queen."

With her clothing tied up securely in a bundle, Moira made her way down the stairs. She was going with Ryan, but not to Scotland—her place was at his side. Whether that meant London or on his ship at sea, she didn't care a whit. All she knew was that she loved him. That was all that mattered.

Moira had hoped to have a chance to talk with Mary in person about her decision, but when she looked for her, the Queen was nowhere in sight; and so Moira continued on her way. Dressed in a plain blue woolen gown, a cloak thrown over her head and shoulders, she was well-prepared for the tumultuous journey. She did not foresee any problems with her leaving Chartley. Unlike Mary, she was not a prisoner and was free to come and go. She was therefore stunned to be approached at the door by Paulet himself.

"Miss Mowbray!" His cold, beady eyes assessed her garments. "Are you going somewhere?"

"Yes, I am. I have no liking for the cold here in Staffordshire. I've decided to go where it is warmer."

"Indeed?" When she tried to sidestep him, he positioned himself so as to block her way. "I'm sure if you but wait, you will see that spring in Staffordshire can be most beautiful."

"Unfortunately, I cannot wait that long." Again Moira tried

to walk away, but Paulet acted as a barricade. "Please, sir, someone is waiting for me outside. I would not want them to wait overlong."

"I fear they must—until eternity, if they are that patient. You see, Miss Mowbray, you are not going anywhere." His voice was gruff as he spoke to her, his tone holding a warning.

"Then I too am a prisoner." The very thought struck her hard. She had been so very smug in thinking that she had outsmarted this old goat by coming here. Now she realized that she was the one who had been tricked. But by whom? Paulet? Or a more sinister enemy?

Oh, God—Ryan! she thought. He would wait for her, of that she had no doubt, but when she did not come, he would be forced to leave without her. He would eventually think that she refused to come with him, that she wanted to stay at Chartley. He would somehow think that she hadn't loved him enough. That, more so than being a prisoner, was the most heartbreaking thought of all.

Chapter Forty-one

WALSINGHAM WAS ANXIOUS AND FIDGETY. His plan was a good one indeed; the Queen of Scots was passing letters back and forth with a frequency that suited him well. The missives were passed by the brewer into Gifford's hands, then promptly conveyed to the Queen of England's councilor in London. There they were opened most skillfully, with not even the most observant eye able to detect that the seal had been broken and resealed. Some of them contained genuine plotting, and others only harmless prattle. Not one word which passed between the Queen of Scots and her treasonous friends escaped him, thanks to Gifford and the workings of the decipherer Phelippes. But it was moving much too slowly.

It was a source of irritation to him that the Queen of Scots had not incriminated herself as he wished, though he had given her ample opportunity. She had not yet done enough to warrant her death, had not instigated nor consented to the murder of Elizabeth. If Mary Stuart was not fully cooperative in bringing about her own death, if she would not write the fatal words that would put her head atop the block, then he would help. With that thought in mind, he called Gifford into his presence.

"You have done well," he said, with a cold, calculating smile. It was always far better to begin such a conversation with praise, he had learned. Gifford was much more pliable when being lavished with compliments.

"Thank you, Sir Francis." Gifford bowed and bent on his knee.

"The little matter of the barrels is working smoothly. I do not believe even one letter has not passed my desk."

"Not a one, sir!" Gifford was quick to assure him.

"Selby and Rothingham have been a great help, have they not? I do not believe that Mary or any of her followers can sneeze without my knowing it," Walsingham said. Gifford nodded. "And though Mary's secretary has changed the code here and there, Phelippes has most aptly been able to decode the letters." Again Gifford agreed, smiling like a fat tabby. Walsingham went on. "But—we still have not fully succeeded. She is in the trap, but we cannot close the door. We do not have her!" He shut his mouth with a snap of teeth.

"Sir . . . Sir, I . . . I c-can not force the woman to say things she does not w-wish to say. I, I—" Gifford looked much like a large fish, his eyes bulging, mouth open. Obviously afraid that he might have displeased Walsingham in some way, he sank to his knees.

"Oh, do get up." Walsingham waved his hand. "Up, up. I am not finding fault with you. I am merely stating a fact."

Gifford stood up and cleared his throat. "I have had many conversations with Mary. She is really a gentle soul, more concerned with complaining about her treatment here to those across the Channel than in stirring up any real harm. For the years that Elizabeth has imprisoned her, I do not really think she wants to see her harmed."

Walsingham sprang to his feet. "The woman is a murderess! She brought about the death of her own husband." Leaning towards Gifford, he shook his finger in his face. "Do not tell me that she is a gentle soul."

"But . . . but, Sir, I . . . I, I only meant that perhaps the matter needs be handled in a different way."

"Precisely. That is what I want with you. You are to figure a way to fan the flames of this intrigue we have begun." Sir Walsingham smiled, though the smile was more sinister than reassuring. "Do you understand?"

"Yes." Gifford's eyes slowly widened. "And I know how we can do it. My—my brother knows a soldier, Savage by name, who has come to England purely with murderous intentions. He has bragged that he will kill Elizabeth, though either the opportunity has been lacking, or he has been too awed by the Queen's serene courage. He has not done the deed."

Indeed, Walsingham knew all about the man named John

Savage, an ardent Catholic who had joined the Duke of Parma to fight for Catholicism in the Low Countries. The man was a fanatic, one who by all reports had made the assassination of Elizabeth his life's goal. A man like that was just who Walsingham needed.

"He will never get close enough to harm one hair on the Queen's head! I will see to that. But in the meantime, make use of him!"

Then there was John Ballard, a Jesuit. A vainglorious priest, but a man fond of good company. Irresponsible and altogether extravagant—perfect for the plot. Walsingham suggested him, knowing well his enthusiastic zeal to free the captive Scottish queen.

And, of course, there was the well-dressed Anthony Babington. Both Walsingham and Gifford mentioned his name at the same time. Babington's conspiracy was innocent enough, at least for the moment. A group of young Catholic gentlemen who wanted to free the imprisoned Queen—misguided romanticism, Walsingham thought with scorn. They had far more money between them than brains. Well, if they lost their lives, perhaps it would teach others a valuable lesson.

There were two sets of conspirators, one under Babington and the other under Savage. "It will be your duty, Gifford, to bring the two together. One plot will be much easier to deal with than two, and make for more amusement, I would suppose." Gifford was set up by Walsingham to play the part of the agent provocateur.

The matter was referred to as the "Enterprise." Babington, Savage, and Ballard. Just like the perfect stew; if he put them together, he would come up with just what he wanted, Walsingham thought craftily. To secure this last turn of the screw, Walsingham decided to single-mindedly devote his energies to merging all the plots.

Chapter Forty-two

THE SUN ROSE in a cloudless blue sky, gilding the day in a golden hue. Fragrant red, pink, blue, and white blossoms walled the country lanes. The woods were carpeted with bright green grass. The trees proudly displayed their covering of newly-sprouted leaves. It was finally spring, a perfect day, with a warmth that was uncommon.

Moira unlatched the window in her bedchamber to let in a bit of fresh air. She had longed for spring, but now that it was here, it brought her little joy. Her world was empty. Having experienced love, only to be alone come spring—that time of love and frolic—was a mockery. Besides, now that Paulet had made it absolutely clear that she was a captive, how could she even pretend to be happy?

Birds trilled sweetly beyond the open, mullioned windows, but Moira couldn't enjoy their song. How could she, when even they were a painful reminder of her circumstances? Those birds were free, but she and Mary were caged.

Oh, if only I hadn't been so sure of myself, so certain that I could right the wrongs of the world, she thought. All her life, Moira had been stubborn, carefree, and much too daring. Now she was paying for it dearly. She had walked right into a trap, and it appeared that there was no way out, despite all of Mary's protestations and demands.

"Oh, Ryan. Ryan—" It seemed that even the breeze called out his name. Closing her eyes, she remembered their night together, her body tingling with the very thought of it. He had made her a woman, had made her body come alive. That memory was more precious to her than gold. Would she ever see him again? Dear God, how she wanted to.

Every time she saw a wagon approaching the gates, her heart lurched in her breast, hoping that it was him, that he had returned for her. Alas, each time she was disappointed. When Seamus came, he came alone. Though she tried to catch his eye, Moira was not allowed to approach the brewer, nor even had the slightest chance to speak with him. Thus, her predicament remained unknown and unresolved. Even so, what truly pained her was that Ryan would think that she hadn't loved him enough to go with him. Though she had written him a note of explanation through the barrel post, he had yet to reply.

In dejection, Moira sank down in the chair by the window. Wrapping her arms about her legs, she drew them against her chest, resting her chin on her knees. She had been such a fool, much too impulsive. She had swooped down on Chartley as if she were the Queen's angel, as if only she could set her free. And what had she accomplished? She was now incarcerated behind the very same walls as the Queen. Cloistered here, she could not even protect her brothers if the need arose. The rescuer was now in need of rescuing.

"Oh, Ryan," she thought, sighing deeply, "I do love you so." She hugged herself, pretending for a moment that her arms were his. Had she experienced love only to lose it? That was her greatest fear indeed.

"Moira. Moira, child, may I come in?" Moira looked up to see the Queen peering through the doorway. She had been so immersed in her own thoughts that she had not even heard her approach.

"Yes, please do. I need some company." At the very least, they could commiserate.

Mary pushed open the door. "I brought you a present." How like the Queen to try and bring joy to someone else in spite of her own unhappiness.

"A present?" Beneath Mary's long, full sleeves something was wiggling. "What is it?"

Mary pushed back the cloth to reveal her surprise, a tiny, plump ball of long, wavy fur and large, droopy ears. "One of my spaniels had pups. I thought you might like to have one. I know how very much you love animals, just as your mother did."

"A pup!" Moira stared wide-eyed at the tiny creature, feeling an instant warmth in her heart. "Mine?"

"Yours!" Closing the door behind her, Mary set the tiny dog down. As if knowing instinctively who its new owner was to be, the puppy ran straight to Moira, jumped up in the chair, and settled itself beside her. "It's a male, and thus not surprising that it is so very bold."

"As bold or even bolder than someone else I know," Moira laughed softly, scratching the little dog's ear. Its fur was the same red-gold color as Ryan's hair. How could she not love him? "I think I'll call him Cap, short for 'captain,' for there is a bold bit of a swagger in his gait, don't you think?"

"I do!" For a moment, a frown crossed Mary's brow. "You miss him, don't you? The real captain, I mean."

Moira didn't even try to hide her sadness. "Yes, I do. He is all things good in a man. Strong. Daring. Gentle." Moira had opened her heart to the Queen, telling her about Ryan Paxton and how they had met, about his visit to Chartley, and his determination to rescue her.

"You should have gone with him, without any second thoughts of loyalty to me. Had you but talked with me, I would have told you so." For just a moment, Mary's eyes glittered with memories. "I gave up much for Bothwell. Yet even so, were I to get the chance to relive those days, I would do so."

Moira's heart ached for the Queen, and for Bothwell. After their defeat at Carberry Hill so many years ago, Mary had agreed to surrender if Bothwell were permitted to escape. He had fled to the coast and made his way to Denmark, only to be imprisoned there. He had been passed from prison to prison, each worse than the last. He had been a pawn in European politics, until his value was exhausted. Eight years ago, he had died, a madman, chained to a wall. Moira shuddered at the thought.

"If only he would come for me again, I would most gladly go. But he hasn't and perhaps he won't."

"I think he will. There wasn't any obstacle that could keep your father away from Kylynn, not even a brutal Highlander husband!" Mary came to where Moira stood and stroked her long, dark hair. "Have faith. Some things are meant to be." Caught up in their own memories, Moira and the Queen were silent for a long while, but at last the puppy brought them out of their reverie. Full of energy and not content to be quiet for long, he scampered about, playing with the drapery cord or running up and down the length of the room, causing havoc. Moira could just imagine what Paulet would say were he here, for he abhorred cats and dogs, calling them "flea-bitten nuisances." She would have to carefully guard her little pup.

Thinking the same thing, Mary hastily straightened the draperies, glancing out the window as she did so. "Look, Moira. We are to have a visitor."

Moira hastened to the window, the puppy nipping at her heels. She thought she had given up all hope, but the sight of the wagon looming ahead rekindled her optimism. Let it be Seamus, and please let him have brought Ryan again! Opening the window wide, Moira leaned over as far as she dared, only to feel the sting of disappointment. It was only Mary's dear "honest man."

"Not your Captain Paxton at all. I'm sorry, child, for I know well what you were thinking." Mary took her by the arm. "But come, perhaps the barrel post will contain some reply from him. Hmmmm?"

Moira accompanied Mary to the library, anxiously awaiting the letters, only to be disappointed. There was nothing for her. It seemed to be the same old letters from the same foreign dignitaries. However, there was one new addition, a letter from Mary's former emissary, Nau's brother-in-law Fontenay. Mary's secretary read it aloud.

"He says that there is a dispatch for you from Scotland, which is now lodged at the house of Sir Anthony Babington in London."

"Babington? Babington?" Moira repeated the name. It struck a chord in her memory. "Sir Anthony Babington!" She remembered receiving a letter from Davie in which he mentioned the young man by name. Her brothers were involved with him. "Donnie and Davie have spoken of the man. Remember, Mary?" Excitement stirred in her blood. Perhaps, at last, this matter of the plot to free Mary was coming to a head. That would mean freedom—not only for Mary, but for her as well.

"And a missive from Morgan in Paris," Mary replied, scanning another letter. "He mentions Babington, officially approves of him as a contact." Mary repeated the name. "Babington. Babington. I seem to remember that name."

"He was a page when you were incarcerated at Sheffield Castle. Even then, he gave you his devotion, looked upon you as a veritable goddess," Nau said, jogging the Queen's memory.

"Ah, yes. A pretty boy. I remember that he composed a poem for me once." She laughed softly. "Well, I would be remiss if I did not write him a letter."

Moira listened while the Queen dictated to Nau. It was a short but very gracious letter. She acknowledged that she had received word that there were some letters from France and Scotland in his hands. She instructed him to deliver them unto the bearer of her communication to him, who would see them safely conveyed to her. As with the others, the letter was put into the beer keg with the incorrect address of "Master Anthony Babington, dwelling most in Derbyshire at a house of his own within two miles of Wingfield." Nau nonetheless assured her that it would be duly delivered.

Mary impulsively hugged Moira to her bosom. "Ah, I have been blessed many times over. In truth, it really is a wonderful world, Moira. It does my heart good to know that I have so many good friends, loyal friends. You, your parents, Gifford, Morgan, the honest man. This young man, Babington. And so many I have yet to meet. How, then, can I not have faith in the future?"

"Indeed, how can we not?" Moira felt her own spirits rising. Perhaps her own happiness was in Anthony Babington's hands. If so, then she doubly wished him well, and hoped with all her heart that whatever was transpiring would bring her safely into the arms of her lover.

Chapter Forty-three

THE AIR WAS CHILLY AND DAMP inside the hidden passageway as David and Donald MacKinnon made their way to the designated meeting-place. All through June, the plotters had met secretly, sometimes in taverns such as Ryan Paxton's Devil's Thumb, sometimes in Giles Field, and often in Babington's house in Barbican. There were now fourteen conspirators in all, counting a man newly accepted into their ranks, a man named Gifford.

"Who is this man Babington is so excited about?" Donnie asked, cautioning his brother to watch his step as they went down the rickety, winding stairs.

"A true admirer of Mary." Davie paused to knock at the dark, wide door, using a secret code, the same one they used with Moira. It was Donnie's idea. "Someone who is to be the key to the plan."

The door was opened, and the twins stepped into the dimly lighted room. Inside, standing as if in a ceremonial circle, were twelve men.

"Ah, the MacKinnons!" Sir Anthony Babington, dressed elegantly in gold velvet and satin, with a diamond studding his ear, stepped forward to greet them. "He is here—John Savage. I want you to meet him."

Donnie saw Babington as a dreamer, unrealistic in his aspirations. An empty-headed popinjay with his head in the clouds. To Donnie's way of thinking, it made him a dangerous man to become involved with. Even so, he grudgingly held out his hand to Babington, determined to see this through to the end, even if just to protect his brother.

"By all means, we are anxious to meet him," he said dryly.

Babington led them to the edge of the circle, where a bearded and balding, tawny-haired man stood talking to two others in the group. Donnie's appraisal was critical. Why, this man looked as out of place here as a duck among swans. His garments bordered on ragged, the dark green doublet worn in several places, the high, white neck-frill graying from lack of proper cleaning, the breeches snagged here and there. The buff-colored leather thigh-high boots and gloves the man wore also looked as if they had seen better days. A soldier of fortune if ever there was one.

"Donnie, Davie, may I introduce John Savage," Babington said graciously, giving them both a nudge towards his special guest. "These are the twins I was telling you about. Their sister is this minute with our dear Mary Stuart."

The man grunted, obviously more interested in his wine cup than in conversation. That is, until Elizabeth Tudor's name was mentioned. It was then that his eyes burned with a frightening light. "The bastard queen," he hissed. "Usurper." He smiled chillingly at the MacKinnons, his teeth gleaming yellow in the torchlight.

"Let me introduce you to my other colleagues." Davie went around the circle, moving clockwise. "Edward Abington, Edward Windsor, Thomas Salisbury, Robert Barnwell." He paused to take a breath. "John Traves, Henry Donn, Chidiock Tichbourne, Charles Tilney." The men inclined their heads as their names were said. "Edward Jones, and last but not least, Gilbert Gifford." Davie was particularly impressed by Gifford's zealous passion for freeing the Scottish queen.

"I know Gifford." John Savage grinned. " 'Twas at his suggestion that I was brought here."

It was a strange circle of conspirators, including a priest named Ballard, a few Donnie thought of as hotheads, and various young gentlemen much like Davie and his brother. Donnie whispered scathingly that a desperado such as Savage was aptly named.

Savage was, as Donnie said, a strange sort of duck. The twins learned through his conversation that he had already been intent on killing Elizabeth for the past eight months, and thus agreed readily to joining in with this plan—"the Enterprise," as Gifford called it.

Babington seemed anxious that the newcomers in their midst be made to feel comfortable among his group. He gave an impassioned speech, one which the twins had already heard several times, concluding with a brief summary of why he had gathered this particular band together.

Each one was valuable in his own way. John Ballard, a graying, middle-aged priest who was new to their ranks, was in contact with dignitaries on the Continent, men ready to support an armed uprising once Elizabeth was out of the way.

"There are sixty thousand foreign troops ready to aid the captive Scottish queen," he boasted. "I have but to give the word." He expressed his determination that he was not afraid to die for the cause, if need be.

"Die?" Donnie whispered, clutching his brother's arm. "Let us hope there is no call for that kind of sacrifice."

"Coward," Davie chided. "I would gladly give my life if I knew that by my death, Mary would be given her chance to rule here." They were brave words, uttered as he tried to still his trembling hands.

John Ballard was a good talker whose enthusiasm soon calmed the twins. He could not envision failure, he said, not when there were so many ready to support the cause of Mary Stuart. "There are allies inside and outside of England, noblemen as well as peasants. The entire Catholic nobility of England will not hesitate to support us, the King of Spain is at our beck and call, and the Pope himself is with us. I know— he told me so with his own voice." An audible gasp clearly said that the assembly was impressed.

"We will bring England back to the Catholic faith. It will be a great moment in this country's history," Babington added.

The meeting was just the first of several more. Each time, a new face was added to the group. Soon their ranks were swelled by more clear-headed and resolute persons. Donnie looked upon the assembly more and more favorably, hoping that those of a more daring nature would be calmed by the new intellectual influences.

The wheels of the conspiracy had begun to turn, but at a much more hazardous pace than the twins had first anticipated. Donnie realized the dangers involved—indeed, even Babington had had a second thought or two. Even so, by the end of spring, they had a complete scheme to submit to Mendoza, who, with hearty approbation, forwarded it to Philip. It was urged that the Spanish king support a work "so Christian, just, and advantageous to His Majesty."

It appeared that the plan would be successful. There was, however, one phase that sincerely troubled the MacKinnons, the part about Elizabeth's death. "To kill a queen, Davie. Even if she is one with whom we do not agree. Murder is murder. Think, brother, think!"

Davie didn't like it either. For all her faults, Elizabeth had been very kind to them. How then could they take part in planning her death? They had come to England to free Mary, not to commit regicide. For several agonizing weeks, he hesitated to give his assent, hovering just on the brink of the plot. When all was said and done, his reluctance paid off. Though he and Donnie were to take part in freeing Mary Stuart, six others had been chosen by Babington to do what Babington termed "the grisly deed."

Six gentlemen in close attendance on the English queen. Those with upstanding positions. Members of her household. Second generation. Sons of trusted men, the Under-Treasurer, the Master of the Wardrobe, a Gentleman Pensioner. All awaited Babington's signal to "dispatch" the Queen of England.

Meanwhile, Gifford was emphatic to Babington that now that Mary had shown confidence in him, he must respond by giving the captive Queen a full account of his plan. "A thing so dangerous as an attempt upon Elizabeth's life must not be undertaken without the express approval of the Queen of Scots," he said. "With the weekly visits of the honest man, there will be a safe way of conveying all necessary information and getting the royal instructions in return."

Donnie's prudence prompted him to argue. "It is best to keep Mary ignorant of the darker aspects of what we plan. Just in case we fail."

"Fail?" Gifford was scornful. "We must not even contemplate that."

It was obvious that Babington looked to Gifford as the brains of the Enterprise. Taking pen in hand, he ignored Donnie MacKinnon's advice and wrote a long missive addressed to his "trés chére souveraine," disclosing every detail of the plot.

"Why should the unhappy Queen not be consoled in her captivity by knowing what is afoot?" he asked peevishly. "Why should she not be informed that the hour of her liberation is at hand?"

"We will rue it, Davie. He has more courage than wit, he babbled on like a fool. God help us if that letter falls into unfriendly hands." Another thing troubled Donnie: Babington was much too smug, too sure of his success. Foreseeing immortality, he had even commissioned a painter to create portraits of himself and the rest of the band who were to put Mary on the throne of England. Davie and Donnie refused at first to have their portraits made, but upon Babington's espousal of the memorial of "so worthy an act," they at last agreed. Then Babington decided that only "the six" would be so honored.

By the last week in June, the portrait was finished, and so were the details of the Enterprise. The plot had three distinct phases. First, the old plan of a Catholic uprising was to synchronize with a Spanish invasion. Second, the prelude was to be a dash on Chartley to rescue the Queen, in which Donnie and Davie would take part, and free their sister as well. Third, Elizabeth would be assassinated.

"And give that old man Paulet a taste of our vengeance," Davie exclaimed. Having received a letter from Moira informing him that she was being held as a captive, he was irate.

"Aye, that old man will regret his harshness once Mary is on the throne." It seemed to be so close, an obtainable dream.

Simultaneous with the freeing of Mary Stuart was the bloodier task by far—the assassination of Elizabeth, involving the six gentlemen, of whom John Savage was one. As for Babington, he chose the most glorious role of the plan—to ride, with ten other gentlemen, at the head of the body of horsemen who were to deliver the Queen of Scots.

Chapter Forty-four

TORCHES AND TAPERS BLAZED BRIGHTLY, casting a magical glow on the brightly bedecked lords and ladies who moved gracefully about the mammoth room. It was a lively throng of giggling women and boisterous men. The great hall of Whitehall Palace echoed with the sounds of laughter, the buzzing of voices whispering the latest tattlings, and the chatter of politics, as well as grumblings of a more serious nature.

On a raised dais, in the far corner of the hall, musicians strummed, plucked, and tooted their instruments in accompaniment to the clamor and talk of courtiers and guests. A noisier crowd amused themselves by dancing, flirting, and playing at dice. Sitting in a highbacked chair, her head held high and shoulders back, Elizabeth Tudor assessed the crowd. Ah, but they always reminded her of birds. Cocks, geese, robins, brightly plumed peacocks, canaries, pigeons, and swans, as well as those who could well be birds of prey. Burghley, that wise old owl. And then there was Walsingham, dressed all in black as usual. He reminded her of a raven, that bird that lived high in the Tower of London and which was traditionally said to protect England from invasion.

As if sensing her eyes upon him, the object of her intent looked the Queen's way and nodded. Much to her dismay, he started walking in her direction. Though she had want of handsomer company, Elizabeth accepted him nonetheless.

"You see, Sir Francis, I can still bedazzle them, even after all this time." And indeed she did. In a room full of gilt and glitter, she shone like a star despite her age. Dressed in a white and gold gown, the sleeves and bodice of which were sprinkled with sequins and jewels, she looked every inch a queen, from the tip of her red, bewigged head to the hem of her voluminous skirt.

"Indeed you can, your Majesty."

Elizabeth demanded perennial adulation and savored it insatiably, surrounding herself with handsome men who vied with each other to be her favorite. Courtiers impoverished themselves just to entertain her, poets smothered her with sonnets expounding on her beauty, and musicians strummed songs to praise her. Even so, the position of Queen's favorite was often a tenuous one, for Elizabeth was quick to anger and glaringly surly when crossed. Now, however, she was in a smiling mood.

"A particularly handsome group, don't you agree, Sir Francis?" Her gaze swept over the assembled young men with the keen eye of a connoisseur. "James Howard is so delightfully tall. Roger Morgan as fair-haired as a Viking. And then there are the MacKinnon twins. How delightful to have two of a kind, and not just one; a pleasant change. And I do so favor dark hair." She pointed at another young man, dressed a bit more gaudily than the rest. "That one's name is Babington. What a pity that he is married. Had I seen him first, I certainly never would have given my consent. I like to keep them bachelors, you see. Makes it far more entertaining."

"Yes, yes!" Walsingham fidgeted with his ruff. "That's all very well. But come with me, your Majesty."

"Come with you and leave all the fun?" She wrinkled her nose, supposing he was planning some devastatingly boring meeting again. "Some other time." As Davie MacKinnon glanced her way, she reached up to straighten her diamond necklace, then waved her fan at him. If only for a little while, she could fulfill her dreams by sitting at the sides of handsome young men. It made her feel young again, and beautiful, to bask in the warmth of their adulation.

"Please, your Majesty. I have something of interest to show you," Walsingham said, "knowing well how you favor the great gift of art."

"Walsingham, I am enjoying myself," Elizabeth said, nevertheless rising from her chair. "Ah, well. Show me what it is, you tedious man." She picked up her skirts carefully, preparing to follow him. "Whatever it is you wish me to see had best be more amusing than dancing with yon red-velvet-bedecked young man.''

He smiled. "What I have to show you, I assure you, will pique your interest, your Majesty. I show you not one, but several handsome young men.''

"Ahhhhhh!" Elizabeth was clearly intrigued. "At last, Sir Francis, you know how to amuse me.'' Walsingham led her down the long corridor, stopping, as she suspected he would, at his own chambers. "Sir Francis!" Her voice held warning.

"Wait. Have patience.'' Taking a key from his pocket, for he always kept his chambers locked, Walsingham opened the door, standing aside to let the Queen enter first. Stepping around her, he hurriedly lighted the three oil lamps about the room, the largest on his desk. " 'Tis here.''

Elizabeth looked in the direction of his nod. A large, bulky object, covered with a canvas, rested on an easel. "What?''

Walsingham unveiled a portrait. "I paid a handsome bribe to see this before the young man who commissioned it. But it was well worth the money I paid. What do you think?''

Elizabeth squinted at the portrait, not wanting to admit that her eyesight was not what it once had been. Nevertheless, she could appreciate the artist's flair for color and the attractiveness of those whose images looked back at her. "A handsome gathering, to be assured. Or at least most of them.'' There was one with a bulbous nose, another lacking any hair on his head.

"Yes, I would say they are undoubtedly the best-looking assortment of traitors that ever have had the effrontery to so exhibit themselves.'' Walsingham's voice was kept to a whisper.

"Traitors?" Elizabeth sucked in her breath, obviously surprised. "But some of these men I recognize. Explain yourself, Sir Francis!''

He walked around the easel three times, as if performing a ritual, then paused. "Before you, your Majesty, is a portrait of a dastardly bunch of conspirators who have seen fit to have their faces emblazoned in oil for the sake of posterity. My sources say that they plan to hang this painting right here in Whitehall—*after* they dispose of you and put Mary in your place!''

"No! Never!" Elizabeth took a deep breath, her thin mouth

turning down in a frown. "She will never wear my crown."

"She will if they have their way." Walsingham pointed them out, one by one, his face—which might almost have shown amusement—impassive as usual. "You will recognize some of these. Others are, like rats, consigned to the shadows."

Elizabeth stepped even closer, determined to remember each and every face, lest she have need to defend herself from their treachery. Her expression was sadness personified as she named them one by one. "Even Sir Anthony Babington, he to whom I have given my smile again and again. A handsome angel of a man."

"More devil than angel, I fear."

He replaced the shroud over the painting. "Now I must see that this is delivered to young Sir Babington before it is missed. You understand."

"You are a cruel man, Sir Francis. Thank God you are on my side." Elizabeth shuddered. "You speak of devils. I am not at all certain at times that you are not one." She was silent for a long moment, and then asked, "Are you going to arrest them?"

"For what? Being vain? I do not have the proof I need of sufficient mischief, only the testimony of my spies. Men who have infiltrated Babington's snug little band."

"They should be brought to trial and hanged!"

Walsingham waved his hand impatiently. "No, no. It is another prey that I am after. The Queen of Scots herself."

"Mary? How is she tied in with this?" Elizabeth looked toward the painting, a faint smile upon her face. "I do not see her image there, lest it be in disguise."

"She is not there, but that does not mean she is not implicated, or will not be. She is corresponding with Babington. I have copies of her letters, if you need proof."

"And does she speak of killing me?" Elizabeth asked slowly, measuring her words.

"No, but—"

"Then?"

"She will. I feel that certainty in my gut!" He doubled over as the pain in his stomach attacked without warning, as it always did when he was agitated, either for good or ill. "She will."

Elizabeth raised a brow. "You seem so positive about it all." Her voice rose to a shrill rasp. "Enough so to let known conspirators roam about here freely."

"Not freely. They are constantly watched. Not one hair on your head will be harmed. I promise that, your Majesty."

Elizabeth's jaw ticked with suppressed anger. "See that you keep that promise, Sir Francis. If I am even frightened by these horrid men, it will be your head. Do I make myself clear?"

He nodded, going down on both knees. "Yes, your Majesty."

With a rustle of her skirts, she was gone, leaving him to grovel to no one. Putting his hands behind his back, Walsingham paced back and forth, deep in thought. He was determined. He would tighten the net. Before summer was out, he would have the Queen of Scots, the "bosom serpent," right where he wanted her, no matter what he had to do. Indeed, even if it meant he had to forge Mary Stuart's reply himself. He hoped that it would not come to that. If everything went according to plan, the foolish woman would incriminate herself. He would talk at once with Gifford and see that she did.

Chapter Forty-five

THE AFTERNOON SUN BEAT DOWN in fiery rays upon
the green fields and shone vibrantly through the windows.
Summer, such a lovely time of year. From the library window
Moira could see the gardens, and longed with all her heart to
be outside, smelling the flowers. Instead, she was cooped up
with Mary and Nau, deciphering some silly old letter. Sighing,
she shifted impatiently from one foot to the other as she gazed
out at Chartley's vast grounds. What if she were to attempt an
escape? Could she make it? She pushed the thought from her
mind. If she were successful, it might not go well for Mary.
Paulet was certainly acting strange lately. Touchy, always in
a bad mood, and impatient. But why?

"'Most highly and excellent Sovereign Lady and Queen
unto whom I owe all fidelity and obedience'. . . ." Mary was
reading. "Moira, come here, child."

With a bit of reluctance, Moira complied. "Yes, Mary?"

"A letter from Babington." Mary's face grew pale as she
scanned the letter. "Moira, Nau. Look down the hall. Make
certain no one is lingering about."

Moira's mood changed swiftly as she noted Mary's expression. Perhaps this letter was not so silly after all. Carefully
she saw to their safety, securing and bolting the door to ensure
valuable privacy. "What is it, Mary?"

Mary took a step closer to the window, holding the letter
up to it for better light. Taking a deep breath, and trying to
control her trembling hands, Mary read the missive aloud.
"With ten gentlemen and a hundred of followers, I will undertake the delivery of your royal person from the hands of
your enemies. For the dispatch of the usurper, from the obe-

dience of whom we are by the excommunication of her made free, there be six noble gentlemen, all my private friends, who for the zeal they bear to the Catholic cause and Your Majesty's service, will undertake that tragic execution." She read on, ending with, "Your Majesty's most faithful subject and sworn servant, Anthony Babington."

Moira had been listening intently, but she quickly came forward, deeply disturbed by what was contained within the letter. "If I understand what is written correctly, this Babington intends to assassinate Elizabeth. No! It must not be done." Her worry was for her brothers as well. Freeing Mary was one thing—Donnie and Davie had vowed to do that—but a party to murder! "That missive will send them all to the block."

Mary turned to Nau. "Well, Jacques, you have heard Moira's opinion on the matter. What say you?"

He clucked his tongue, shaking his head in agitation. "I bid you, do not answer it. Leave it unanswered, as you have done before with similar offers. Do not set down one word, for if anything goes amiss, it might well be used against you."

"Two against." Mary turned to Gifford. "What say you, my dear priest?"

"I say that to refuse an answer, to decline encouragement to those who are so chivalrously ready to devote themselves to your service, would be the cruelest injustice of all. They are taking great risk for your sake. How then can you break their hearts by keeping silent?"

"Indeed, how can I?"

Moira took a step forward. "Let me see it." Mary held it out to her, but like a huge snowflake it slipped from her hands and floated to the floor. Moira picked it up, clutching it tightly. The words danced before her eyes as she re-read the decoded words written on the parchment. Her own code, fashioned from Gaelic words—". . . will undertake the tragic execution. . . ." Moira warned her godmother against becoming actively involved in such a plot, as did Nau.

"I will think about it for a few days," Mary decided. She dismissed the others, but remained closeted in the room with Nau and another secretary, Curle. While she pondered, she merely acknowledged receipt of Babington's plan. Then, just as suddenly as she had dismissed Moira and Gifford, she summoned them again.

"Read the letter, Nau. I would hear it again, but this time from your lips." Nau did read the missive, which detailed the main points of a conspiracy even now being carefully plotted. First, there would be an invasion from abroad, of sufficient number to ensure success; secondly, the invaders were to be joined by English Catholics living in England; and thirdly, Mary was to be extracted from prison by Babington himself, with ten of his friends leading a hundred followers. Fourthly, Elizabeth was to be assassinated.

Once again, Moira tried to dissuade Mary. "Elizabeth has her faults, but she has never shown any sign that she wanted you dead. Think, Mary."

Mary gave the matter careful thought. "Why do I owe any loyalty, even a thimbleful of sympathy, to Elizabeth? Has she thought about me these last miserable years? Has she? She has claimed to be my protector, but all the while she is nothing but my jailer."

Moira had never seen this side of Mary. Gone was the gentle, sweet woman; in her place was one set on venting her anger upon another woman. "Elizabeth will have to atone for her own sins, but if you—"

"She has treated me heartlessly these past years. Perhaps this is God's justice."

"Murder?" Moira was horrified by the thought. "I hardly think He would act in such a way."

"Elizabeth has been excommunicated," Mary responded. "That makes a difference. The Pope himself has condoned her overthrow."

Gifford saw that she was more attuned with his view on the matter than with that of any of the others. He pressed his advantage. "Just think, Majesty. The crowns of England and Scotland can be yours again, if you can only get free."

"Freedom. What a sweet word that is—" Mary shook her head. "But I do not want the crown of England."

"It is your due." Gifford was emphatic. "How can you come so close, only to run the risk of failure because of your cowardice?"

"I am not a coward!" Mary snapped.

"You must reach out for freedom," Gifford breathed. "Now!"

"What will be, will be."

Throwing caution to the wind, Mary decided to answer the letter. As usual, it would be dictated in French, the language with which she felt more comfortable. Not knowing French, Moira sat staring out the window as the letter was composed. When at last it had been put into code, Nau translated it for her.

"Trusty and well-beloved," she had written.

She expressed her gratitude to Babington and made three separate proposals for the "coup de main," which would get her safely away from Chartley. She might take the air, on horseback, to a moor between Chartley and Stafford, hoping that fifty or sixty well-armed men might meet her there. Or friends might come to Chartley at midnight, set fire to the barns, stables, and outbuildings, and while the fire was being fought, she could escape. Or her rescuers could come with the carters who came to Chartley in the early morning. In disguise, they could pass into the manor; once inside, they could cause havoc and help her to escape during the commotion.

She asked them to advise her of what forces could be raised, what captains they would appoint, and other practical details involved. She advised Babington that he must always have horsemen with them to let her know immediately that the deed had been done—otherwise, as no definite date had yet been fixed, Paulet might somehow receive the news first, and either transport her to another prison or successfully fortify the house against her rescue. She took care to emphasize the terrible consequences should the plot explode prematurely and fail.

"Take special care," she advised Babington, "to be wary of all those surrounding you, for it might be that some who call themselves friends are, in truth, enemies." Mary saw foreign help as absolutely essential. "The Spanish king must be regarded as critical to any actions the English Catholics might plan."

She ended by saying, "God Almighty have you in His protection. Your most assured friend forever. Fail not to burn this quickly."

When she was done listening, Moira looked toward the window again. "Oh, how I wish—"

"That we could get some fresh air?" Mary sighed. "I have that wish too." The Queen brightened, no doubt feeling emboldened by the scheme being hatched. "I'll ask Paulet. Perhaps he would let us go out if we had proper guard." Her laughter was a pleasure to the ears. "If only he knew we have no reason to make an attempt at escape, not now!"

Surprisingly, Paulet agreed, though Moira could not even fathom why. They were accompanied, however, by two bullish men who looked as if they were fearsome men to cross. In a show of good manners, one of the men aided Moira in mounting her horse, a skittish mare that didn't look as though she could travel very far. Of a certainty, she would never make it all the way to London. So much for running away.

Moira savored the feel of the wind in her hair, the feel of the horse's flesh beneath her. It was not total freedom, but would do until Babington and her brothers came, she thought.

"Moira. Moira! Who is that pockmarked man?"

Moira shaded her eyes against the sun, looking in the direction the Queen was pointing. She recognized the man who was beaming at them genially. "Why, that's Thomas Phelippes. Another one of Paulet's delightful servants, I would suppose."

"Or one of the emissaries of our friends come to the neighborhood in order to prepare the way for our liberation." Mary clapped her hands with excitement.

SELBY WAVED at the approaching horseman. Phelippes had come to Chartley in preparation for the momentous letter that Walsingham was awaiting. The fruit of all their labors was soon to be harvested. And he had that missive in hand.

"Take it and pray that we attain her very heart in this letter," Selby said, handing it to Phelippes. Riding to a small outbuilding adjoining Chartley, the two squat, pockmarked men quickly dismounted, took the missive from its envelope, and set to work.

"Generalities. Nothing important. Bloody hell! If I have ridden all the way from London just for idle chatter, I will be—'' Phelippes stopped talking, clutching at his heart. "Damn! Damn!"

"Bad news?" Selby's eyes squinted in disappointment.

"Bad news, no!" Phelippes gave a shout of great delight. "So good, in fact, that my heart nearly stopped beating. We have her. We have her! Listen." He read the letter slowly so that Selby, whom he viewed as having limited intelligence, could understand. "In answer to Babington's remark about dispatching the usurper and the six noble gentlemen prepared to undertake that tragical execution, she is foolhardy in her reply."

"What does she say?" Selby was becoming impatient.

" 'The affairs being thus prepared, and forces ready both without and within the realm, then it shall be time to set the six gentlemen to work, taking order that, upon the accomplishment of their design, I may be suddenly transported out of this place, and that all of your forces be on the field at the same time to meet me in tarrying for the arrival of the foreign aid, which then must be hastened with all diligence.' "

"So?" Selby had a blank expression on his face.

"You idiot! What more do we need? She mentions the six gentlemen. *The six gentlemen!*"

"The dispatchers." Selby guffawed. "Oh—!"

"The letter is damning enough if read by itself; it is fatal when read in conjunction with Babington's missive. She has as good as approved the plan for the murder of Elizabeth. Walsingham's plan has reached fruition. Mary's head is as good as off!" As if they were long-lost friends, Phelippes patted the other man on the back, congratulating him on the success of the mission. Phelippes then wrote to Walsingham, sending his copy of the letter, endorsed with the postmark for utmost speed. On the outside of the letter Phelippes drew the mark of the gallows—a sign of death. "Now you have documents enough."

Chapter Forty-six

THE HEAT WAS ANNOYING. It was much too warm, even for the time of year. What was worse was that there was absolutely no wind for the slightest relief. Ryan Paxton winced, wiping the sweat and dust from his face. With a mumbled curse, he stripped off his doublet, loosened the buttons of his shirt, allowing his chest to show, rolled his sleeves above his elbows, and then set to work unloading the *Red Mermaid* of its cargo. He had just returned from a most profitable journey to France, one which promised to aid his finances. It should have made him deliriously happy, but instead, he was strangely sullen.

"Why the long face, Cap?" one of the sailors asked, taking note of his downcast expression.

"I'm hot and I'm tired. It was a damnable voyage, Winston." Ryan knew that to be a lie. Compared with the winter's journey, it had been pure heaven. No, something else was eating at him, and he knew just what it was—Moira. He recalled the beauty of her face, the grace in her movements, the sound of her laughter. She had been liquid heat beneath him. And yet she had passed him over for loyalty to the Scottish queen. Would he ever understand women? Apparently not. Anyway, she was a damnably stubborn woman.

The docks were seething with early-morning activity. There were ships being loaded, others being stripped of their cargoes. Ryan lent his strength to the task, briefly glimpsing his reflection as they unloaded a mirror, one said to have adorned the wall of the French queen herself. His face was sun-bronzed from the days at sea, making for a startling contrast with his hair. He looked, he supposed, much like the dark-skinned men that frequented the strange lands across the ocean.

Weaving in and out among his sailors, Ryan moved astern to stand upon the poop deck and stare out at the sea. As soon as his crew was rested, he intended to take the ship out again. Only on the ocean could he find any relief from his memories of *her*. London was much too painful for him. Above all, he avoided the Devil's Thumb at any cost. It seemed that there were now two ghosts lurking there—his mother's, and Moira's ever-taunting presence.

"Damn the wench! Damn her, I say," he muttered, putting his hand up to his hair as though he could tear her out of his thoughts.

A discreet cough alerted him that there was someone behind him. He whirled around to see a rotund sailor standing there. "What do you want?" he asked, much too surly, then regretted his foul mood. It wasn't this poor soul's fault his love life was not going the way he wanted it.

"Cap, there's a lad looking for you."

"A lad?" For just a moment, as he remembered all the times Moira had dressed up like a boy, he hoped it was her. She had at last come to her senses, had come to make amends. "By all means bring him here," he instructed. Trying to act nonchalant, he put his hands behind his back and casually strolled the deck. Would he gather her into his arms and welcome her right away, or would he make her suffer a bit, as he had suffered all these weeks? But the matter didn't arise, for instead of Moira, it really was a lad who sought his attention. He recognized the boy as one of Walsingham's pages.

"Sir Francis wishes to see you. You are to come with me at once." The high voice was as commanding as his master's.

"The devil you say!" Ryan's expression hardened for a fleeting instant as he vented his displeasure; he had had his fill of Walsingham. Had it not been for that fool errand, when he'd taken Gifford up the western coast, he might not have been parted from his Scottish miss. Walsingham, ha! Let him find another lap dog.

"Excuse me?" The boy cleared his throat, supposing that Ryan had not heard him clearly. "I said, Sir Francis Walsingham wishes you to give him your attention at once. Follow me, if you please."

"I don't, please." A thoughtful smile tugged at his lips. It was high time that Walsingham was told a thing or two, such as learning not to poke his long nose in other people's business. "Tell your master that I am quit of him. If he wants a ship or a captain, tell him to hire one on his own. Or let Drake or Raleigh do his foolish bidding."

"Tell him what?" The boy was stunned.

"You heard what I said. Tell him to take a flying leap off the Tower of London. It's little that I care." For all Walsingham's promises of how he would use his influence with Elizabeth to further Paxton's cause, it had all come to naught. "Now, leave me alone."

The boy did leave, only to return a half-hour later. "Sir Francis says that you *will* come to him!"

Ryan gave the young page a cold, fixed stare. "I will not. Go back and tell him that if he wants to see me, he can make an appointment and meet me here, on my own ground." Oh, how he hated to be ordered about, and by such a sly, ever-peeping weasel.

"Walsingham said to tell you," the lad said loudly, "that if you refused, he would forever cage your little Scottish sparrow."

Ryan stiffened, his eyes widening as the meaning bored into his soul. "My Scottish— By God!" Moira. There could be no other meaning. Walsingham had her, or at least knew where she was. So the false name that she was using hadn't fooled the great spymaster.

The boy was smug. "Now, you will follow me."

"Not just yet." Grabbing the page by his fancy green doublet, Ryan held him tightly. "Where is she? What is going on? By God, if he has harmed one hair on her head . . ." Just as quickly as he had lost his temper, it swiftly cooled. This was not between him and the boy, but between himself and Walsingham. "Lead me to him," he said. Breaking into a run, he forgot his fatigue, fleeing down the cobbled streets of London to Walsingham's offices. Inside, the smell of books commingled with an odor of ink and smoke.

He found Elizabeth's councilor sitting at his desk, scratching avidly with a pen upon a piece of parchment. Suddenly aware of his heated regard, Walsingham raised his head. "Ah, Captain Paxton. I thought you would see it wise to come.''

"You spoke of a Scottish sparrow," Ryan blurted out. "Tell me what you meant!"

Walsingham's smile was cold. "Precisely what you thought." The look chilled Ryan to the very bone.

"Don't play games with me," he said, dampening his bravado a bit, yet keeping his head held high. Men like Walsingham thrived on fear.

"All right, I'll come to the point." Opening a compartment in his desk, he brought forth a piece of paper. Walsingham spoke in measured tones. "I have here some very damaging evidence. It seems that Mary Stuart is involved in a plot to murder our dear English queen, and a young Scottish lass by the name of Moira MacKinnon is likewise involved."

Though he was trembling at the very thought of what might happen to Moira, Ryan kept his calm. "Not Moira. She would never do such a thing. You have made a serious mistake, Sir Francis." But even as he spoke, he wondered if the spymaster *had* made a mistake. If Moira were involved in such an intrigue, it would explain a great many things—her sudden jaunt up to Chartley, for one, and her change of name to Mowbray, for another.

Walsingham rose abruptly, discreetly lowering his voice. "No, I don't think so. You see, I also have evidence that the girl's two brothers are likewise involved in a plan to free the Scottish bitch from where we have her so well secured. They have been keeping bad company of late. A foolish young man named Babington."

Babington! Ryan had long suspected that one of being up to no good, had seen the young popinjay meeting with his suspicious-looking friends at the Devil's Thumb. "Evidence or hearsay? I would say the latter. They seemed of irreproachable countenance to me." Ryan shrugged his shoulders, as if the matter were absurd. "Foolish gossip, I would suppose, by those who are jealous of the MacKinnon twins' success at court."

"Success? They are all offspring of a half-English traitor, which made me wary right from the first. Roarke MacKinnon turned against Elizabeth to pursue an adulterous Scottish whore. After all the English queen had done for him, he followed the Scottish queen's every whistle. Like father, like sons.'' Walsingham paused in his tirade to clutch at his stomach, then continued. ''I had the boys brought here purposely, and now I will hang them both.''

''No!'' Ryan caught his breath. How could he let such a thing happen? Yet, he was helpless against a man with as much power as Walsingham.

''Just watch me.'' A sneer twisted his face. ''And as for their sister—''

Clenching his teeth, Ryan threw caution to the wind. ''I warn you, Sir Francis, you go too far. The young woman is under my protection. I intend to marry her.''

Walsingham blinked in surprise. ''Oh? I had no idea it had gone so far.'' He stared at the flame of the oil lamp as it flickered. ''Then perhaps we can strike a bargain.'' It was just what he had wanted all along.

''What kind of a bargain?'' Ryan didn't like the sound of that at all.

Walsingham didn't answer for a long time, letting the silence stretch out. The only sound was the tap-tap of his fingers as he drummed them on his desk. At last he spoke, but very softly, as if afraid that someone other than Ryan might hear. ''I'll give you back your smiling Scottish lover and consider lessening her brothers' punishment in exchange for Savage, Ballard, and Babington.''

''In exchange?'' Ryan leaned forward. ''How can I 'exchange' something that is not within my grasp?'' Looking towards the door, he began to wish he had not come here so quickly. Somehow, he sensed that Moira was now in even greater danger.

''Ah, but they are. My, ah, associates tell me that your little tavern is one of their meeting places. Uncautious of you, Captain.''

''My only rules at the Thumb are that the men don't pick fights, that they clean up any messes they make, and pay their bills. I don't dictate to them about matters of politics.'' If looks could kill, Walsingham would have been murderous, Ryan thought. Nevertheless, he went on. ''The Devil's Thumb is open to all.''

''And therefore is the perfect place for a clever man like

yourself to infiltrate a group of miscreants. I want to catch all the rats in the same snare. That is where you come in, Paxton. I believe that when the net begins to tighten, we will see Babington and his friends try to escape. They will seek a ship. You can make a generous suggestion: how convenient if they all come aboard yours.''

"Mine!'' Ryan choked back a refusal. What choice did he have? Such a dirty business, this spying. Was it any wonder he had avoided getting involved too deeply? But was there any way out? He sincerely doubted it.

"Yours. And it is there that I will spring my rat-trap and take them into custody. They'll hang for what they plot.'' Picking up the oil lamp, Walsingham held it up to his face. The light cast strange shadows, making him look like Satan incarnate. "What a perverse irony that by attempting to flee, they seal their own doom.''

There was an even nastier irony in the fact that Ryan would be forced to betray his own conscience as well. Oh, how he hated the very thought of what he was expected to do! Never before had he involved himself in other men's destinies. Now, for the sake of his love, he was bartering away his own honor. He would be leading other men to their death, gruesome endings, to be certain. He knew the penalty for treason—to be hanged, cut down while still alive and disemboweled, or drawn and quartered. Babington was a silly, foppish young man, but Ryan doubted that he deserved such a grisly punishment. As for the others, he didn't know, but didn't want to judge them lest his own sins surface to haunt him.

"Do I have your promise to comply?'' Walsingham held up the letter tauntingly. "If so, if I have assurance that I can trust you, I will burn this incriminating letter.''

"And I have your word that Moira and her brothers will be spared?''

"If you do as I request, I will keep my part of the bargain.''

"Then I have no other choice. I will do as you say.'' Become the devil's right-hand man, Ryan thought sourly, and help send other men to their death. He knew little of Savage and Ballard, but how could they be even half as bad as this monster? "You have my word. On my mother's grave, I so swear.''

"Ahhhh.'' Walsingham sneered triumphantly. "I have al-

ways said that every man has his price. 'Tis enlightening that
your price is love.'' Picking up the lantern, he held the letter
to the wick until it caught, laying it in the dish as the flame
grew. It burned quickly, shriveling into a fragile, skeletal shell
of ash. ''There, you see? I am ever a generous man. Your
lady's name and those of her brothers are forever condemned
to the fire. No one will ever know what might have happened
if not for you.''

''If not for me.'' Such a thought was far from soothing. And
yet he would have done anything to keep Moira from harm—
even selling his very soul. Perhaps, he thought as he walked
away, that was exactly what he had done.

Chapter Forty-seven

THE EVENING AIR was fragrant with the smell of the flowers that bloomed in London gardens, the fresh scent of hay, and the faint, salty mist of the sea. It was a devilishly warm night, so warm that many of the tavern's customers chose tables that Ryan had put out under the shade of the oak and chestnut trees that grew in abundance around the Devil's Thumb. Among those choosing to sit out-of-doors was a party of finely dressed gentlemen whom Ryan recognized right away. Babington and the conspirators! And with them were Donnie and Davie MacKinnon. Trying to make himself as inconspicuous as possible, Ryan watched the proceedings.

"Miss! Miss!" Donnie beckoned the tavern-maid in a gentle, polite manner.

"What will you have, good sirs?" Gwen asked, with a swish of her skirts, eyeing the assembled gentlemen.

"Ale all around, if you please," Davie said, granting the buxom young woman a seductive smile.

"Ale, gents?" Gwen looked hopefully over the shoulder of one patron—less pleasing to the eye—to get a closer look at the handsome, dark-haired young man.

"Wine for me." As usual, Babington's wishes were different from those of the others.

Gwen was gone in a flash, quickly returning with a tray of cups and tankards that she balanced with her usual skillful aplomb. Moving about, she filled and refilled the drinking vessels in her usual flirtatious manner, and might have loitered around the "court gallants," as she called them, had not Ryan given her a few other tasks to do and patrons to look after. He intended to see to this particular group of gentlemen himself, eavesdropping when he could from behind the trunk of a large oak. He had purposely seated Babington's group at this particular table with spying in mind.

"*She* replied to my letter," he heard Babington say, and supposed that "she" was the Scottish queen. Putting the letter to his lips, the young man kissed it. "She is with us." He passed the letter from man to man.

"Then the moment is at hand!" Davie said.

"Precisely! Let us hope that she will not forget what we have done. Let her fly freely, away from her cage." Babington retrieved the letter and secured it within the safety of his doublet, certain that his treasure was a secret.

"The worst-kept secret in the history of England," Ryan thought, looking at the silly young man in disgust.

Fool that he was, Anthony Babington had gathered his conspirators in a tavern that, at the same time, drew Walsingham's spies. The young man thought he was so very clever, yet he was just the opposite; he came closer to being a simpleton. Hardly the kind of man to be at the head of a serious plot, and certainly no match for Walsingham. Conceited in his view of his abilities, Babington had, in a way, brought on his own troubles. Even so, Ryan hated to be party to his downfall, but it couldn't be helped.

Walsingham had detailed the plan to him a few hours ago. Tonight, the first of the conspirators were to be taken. One by one, like apples plucked from a tree, they were to be arrested. The priest, John Ballard, had been targeted as the first sacrifice.

"Ballard! Where is he?" Noticing that one of their large group was missing, Babington voiced his alarm. "Donnie, see if he is perchance inside."

Ryan watched as Donnie MacKinnon complied with the command, though he slammed the door shut behind him as he bolted into the tavern. When he returned, the stiff-lipped priest was with him, dressed not in his usual garb but in the doublet and trunk hose of a layman. It was obvious, even from a distance, that the priest was agitated.

"Something has gone wrong. I feel it," he hissed, as he took a seat beside Babington.

"Nonsense! Things couldn't be better. I have received the reply that I was longing for." Babington took a sip of his wine.

He was so sure of himself, much too sure, Ryan thought.
"Here, read this." Taking the letter he had shown earlier to
the others from his doublet, he passed it to Ballard, who quickly
scanned it.

"Then we must move with utmost care. We must not do
anything to arouse suspicion. This should be our last public
meeting; it is unwise for you to be seen too often in the company
of a Catholic priest." Sensing Ryan's eyes upon him, he
turned, paling as he noted that he was being watched. "Who
is he?"

"His name is Ryan Paxton. He's the captain of the *Red
Mermaid* as well. He can be trusted," Donnie MacKinnon was
quick to say. The innocent faith he put in Ryan pricked the
captain's conscience. But if he was to save Donnie, the others
would have to pay the price.

"He's a—a friend of my sister Moira," Davie added, nodding Ryan's way.

"Nevertheless, it is unwise to trust anyone. I am even wary
of my servants. No man ever expects to be betrayed." Handing
the letter back to Babington, his voice was scolding. "If that
were to fall into the wrong hands, all our gooses would be
cooked. Put it away. Keep it hidden."

"Why, I dare say—" Babington took offense, but did as
he was bidden.

The evening proceeded with drinking and talking. After John
Ballard's warning, the conversation touched on matters that
little interested Ryan. In truth, he was troubled, not liking what
he knew was to follow. At a signal from one of Walsingham's
agents, Ryan was to interrupt the group to tell John Ballard
that one of his servants was awaiting him inside. Then the trap
would be sprung. That time came all too quickly.

"It had better be important!" John Ballard said, rising from
his chair. He bid the others good evening and followed after
Ryan. Once inside, Ryan led him into the taproom, and from
there to a small room abutting the stairs. Once he had stepped
inside, three men cornered him.

"You are John Ballard?" the first man asked.

"I am." Though he looked as if he wanted to flee, the priest
stood his ground.

"Then you are under arrest," a second man answered.

"For what reason?" Ballard held his head high, challenging the man, perhaps expecting a charge of treason.

"For being disguised as a seminary priest." The third man flicked the sleeve of Ballard's doublet.

"For what?" Ballard stared back at the man, amazed, but Ryan knew it was not an unusual reason for being made the Queen's prisoner. Catholic priests daily faced the possibility of arrest on one charge or another.

"Aye," said the first of Walsingham's agents, "you've had as many doublings as a hare. You've given us considerable trouble, but now we have you."

"You are to be committed to the Tower, and thereby the rack." It was a sentence that would have cowered some men, but Ballard just stood his ground without showing any sign of fear. Ryan had to admire the man's courage, even more so when he later learned from Walsingham that although Ballard had been tortured, he had not betrayed any of the others.

"Not that it matters," Walsingham said coldly. "I have all the information that I need." His smile, meant to soothe Ryan, instead had the opposite effect. It only served to make him realize the danger he was in, now that Walsingham's vengeance against the Queen of Scots had begun.

Chapter Forty-eight

THE FLAMES from the wall-sconces flickered, casting eerie shadows against the walls of the hidden tunnel as Davie and Donnie hurried forth. They had been summoned with great urgency by Anthony Babington, and were now answering the call.

"What do you suppose would make him call us out at this hour?" Davie was clearly annoyed.

"It had best be important," Donnie grumbled.

It was, devastatingly so. Babington met them at the secret door. "Ballard's been taken!"

"Ballard?" The cold chill of fear swept up and down the twins' spines. "Then the conspiracy is found out."

"I don't think that is necessarily so." Somehow, despite what had happened, Babington maintained his calm, or at least affected it convincingly. "If we were known to be plotting, why would Ballard be the only one taken?"

With intellectual zeal, the three tried to figure the situation out, concluding at last that Ballard had been taken in because of his religious calling, and nothing more. He was not the only priest to have been so treated.

"But will he betray us?" Donnie and Davie asked the question at the same time.

"No, no. He is one of the bravest, staunchest Catholics that I know. No matter what they put him through, he will keep silent. Even more so than all of us, he wishes to see Mary set again upon a throne. For the good of our faith, yes, he is an inspiration to us all, if we but heed it."

Babington concluded that they must go ahead with their plans, and the twins agreed, standing by as Babington wrote an impassioned letter to Mary entreating her, for the love of God, not to give way to discouragement. "It is an enterprise honorable before God. We have vowed it and will carry it into effect, or it shall cost us our lives."

With vows and oaths, the young men egged each other on. There was one thing that deeply troubled Donnie, however. For all his staunch babbling about bravery and continuing with the Enterprise, Babington let it slip that he was going to apply to Walsingham for a passport to France.

"France, Anthony?"

For a moment a blush stained his cheeks, but he thought quickly. "Ah, yes. You see, I can pursue our ends there. I can pretend to spy on Elizabeth's enemies, but will be in league with Mary and our friends abroad instead. Being a good Catholic, I will have an entry into Catholic strongholds."

"Mm-hmm." Donnie was not at all convinced.

"Do not fash yourself, brother. I can see wisdom in what he says." Davie smiled coyly. "It is a sound plan, even more sound if there be three. We'll accompany him to France." He nudged his brother playfully.

The request was sent to Walsingham, but he did not reply immediately. This was a source of worry to all three men, until one of Walsingham's servants made it a point to make friends with Babington at the Devil's Thumb. He invited him to dine and drink with him. Shortly thereafter, Babington was invited by Walsingham's secretary to a formal supper. Deciding to keep an eye on their fellow conspirator, Donnie and Davie tagged along, keeping themselves at a distance.

Right from the first, there was something that made Davie vaguely suspicious. Too much wine and ale was being passed about, as though the intention was for Babington to loosen his tongue. Though everyone, including the hosts, soon was in his cups, Davie and his brother were careful in what they drank. Then, when it appeared that everyone in the dining room was occupied, the twins saw their chance.

Davie steered his brother around a sharp corner. "Be careful," he cautioned as they fumbled around in the dark. Their destination was a room which Walsingham had seemed to take great interest in. To their disappointment, it was locked, but though Donnie wanted to put an end to the matter, Davie was in a more daring mood. Thinking that they might perhaps find something of interest among Walsingham's papers, they decided to find a way inside. Having had experience with sneaking in and out of windows while residing at James's Court at Holyrood, they made use of their talents, climbing up the wall by means of a tree branch and entering through the window.

"It appears to be the study," Donnie whispered, using his tinderbox to light the smallest candle he could find so as not to draw undue attention. He took the opportunity to explore a scattering of papers on Walsingham's desk. At first it appeared that there was nothing of much interest, but he took a second look. "Davie, come here! Look!"

"Babington's name. Adington's. Howard's. Yours. Mine." Several names were scrawled on a piece of paper, with something written beside them which the twins did not understand.

They might have taken more care to explore further, but the sound of a key turning in the lock startled them. Blowing out the candle, scurrying to the window, they climbed out just in time to escape detection. Peering in, they saw that Walsingham stood in the doorway, his face twisted in its usual frown. At first they feared he might sense that someone had been in the room, but when he did not look around, they decided that they were safe—at least for the moment. Still, they were deeply troubled. Why were their names written down? What interest did Walsingham have in them? Climbing back down to the ground, the twins talked over the matter.

"He knows. Somehow, I think that he knows everything!" Donnie was convinced that the conspiracy was in dire trouble.

Davie was still filled with bravado. "Don't be such a coward. Perhaps it is just a list of Catholics. We're Catholic. Babington is Catholic. Everyone on that list is of the same faith. Perhaps it is nothing more than that."

Upon mentioning the matter to Babington, however, they saw the young man panic. Hastily excusing himself, he left Walsingham's and fled to his own house in Barbican after leaving a message with one of his servants to warn the rest of the conspirators.

Gone was Babington's fortitude. Davie and Donnie witnessed the crumbling courage of their new friend with dismay.

Under stress, Babington revealed his weaknesses. His courage failed, and he ran hither and thither like a hunted rat. Mounting a horse, he rode off into the country, leaving London and the conspirators far behind.

A few days later, the twins received a scribbled note from Babington—"The fiery furnace is made ready in which our faith will be tested." He seemed to be trying to bolster up his own courage.

Whispered gossip drifted about Whitehall like wisps of wind. The brave Anthony Babington had made his way with all good speed to St. John's Wood, a few miles from London. There, he had found a hut and stayed the night. He had changed his complexion by staining it with walnut juice, cut off his hair, exchanged garments with his servant, and sent that unfortunate man back to Barbican.

Moving on to Harrow, he had decided to stay with a Catholic friend until the hunt was over. Babington was a wanted man, and all those who sheltered him were also in dire peril. Davie and Donnie waited anxiously to see if he would escape. They found out in a few weeks that he had not. His capture was not long delayed, despite his cleverness. Babington was taken from Harrow as Walsingham's prisoner and lodged in the Tower. The hunt was over. Or had it, as Davie and Donnie feared, just begun?

Chapter Forty-nine

IT LOOKED to be a perfect August day. Already, the early-morning sun slanted down in golden rays upon the land, touching the greenery with its fiery warmth. In the forests, sunlight streamed through the branches of the trees, playing "peek-a-boo" with the shadows. Brooks and streams meandered through pastureland, glistening with reflected sunbeams. Birds twittered tunefully as they flew from tree to tree, competing with the melodic whisper of the breeze.

Moira crouched on the window-seat of the library, gazing out over Chartley's vast domain, her eyes taking in the splendor. It was much too beautiful a day to be cooped up inside. Oh, what she would not have given for just one hour of freedom, for the liberty of walking barefoot through the meadow, of listening to the gently laughing brooks, or just lying quietly beneath a tree! She had once taken such things for granted. Now they were only a treasured memory of another time and another day, just as Ryan Paxton was.

"Oh, Ryan—"

Lately, her mind had been driven by thoughts of the Englishman, her emotions a restless sea of imagination. She hoarded the precious memories of his love the way Mary hoarded her letters, reliving his ardent caresses, the tenderness of his kiss. Ryan Paxton would return for her, would come to save her from the contemptuous Paulet. He would bear her away to his ship and they would sail away out to sea to live together forever. Oh, how she ached for that day to come.

"Fie!" She was scornful of her own dreams; such things didn't really happen. Hadn't she learned that by now? "He will never return!"

"Never?" From across the room, Mary, at play with her spaniels, looked up. "That is a word one must never say. I thought I would never get out of here, and yet just look at how the future sparkles so with hope. God bless Sir Anthony Babington!"

"Oh, that Ryan Paxton were of the same mettle. If only he knew how I yearned for him, how I needed him."

"I think he does. I feel in my heart that he will come for you. And this time you will go with him!" The very thought made Mary most enthusiastic. Clapping her hands, she made a generous proposal. "I have some finely wrought cloth in one of my trunks that I have saved for a special occasion. It is white with silver thread. I'll give it to you for a wedding present."

"Wedding? I doubt that I will ever marry." How could any other man ever compare with the only man she had given herself to?

"Nonsense, *ma cherie*! If your mother could overcome the obstacle of a cruel husband for the man of her heart, how can you let pride stand in your way?" She tossed a ball across the room, watching as her favorite spaniel trotted after it. "When Babington and his mighty ten come to release us, you must promise to go straight to London, to see to this captain of yours."

"London—" It seemed so very far away. In truth, it was. "How can I even think of going to that fair city when I can't even poke my nose outside?" Resting her chin on her arms, she sighed.

"I tell you, you must not give up hope." Mary was in the highest of spirits, emboldened by the knowledge that there were so many who sought to help her.

"No, I suppose not." Without a measure of trustful longing, life would have very little contentment.

Following after her little dog, Mary picked the animal up in her arms and cradled him tightly. "Something is about to happen, Moira. I feel it! I sense it in my every bone."

Moira hoped the Queen was right.

Surely, it seemed to be a good omen when the dour Paulet came to the Queen's apartment later that day to suggest a ride.

Moira was certain it was the first time she had ever seen him smile with any measure of sincerity.

"Perhaps, Madame, you would like to ride out of Chartley to catch a breath of air." It was exactly what Mary had been begging for over these many weeks. In pleading for more liberty, the Queen had even declared that the weakness of her body made escape impossible. Now she looked to be of robust health at just the mention of a gallop.

"A ride? To where?" Though she welcomed the idea, Mary was still of a mind to be wary. She exchanged a searching look with Moira, as if wondering if she was to be moved to yet another prison. If so, then it might have dire consequences on the matter of the Enterprise.

"Mary and I are quite content here, Sir Amyas," Moira said quickly.

Paulet seemed to sense their thoughts. "No, no, no. I have no intention of moving our household again. Perish the thought." In a mimicry of shooting, he pretended to aim a bow and arrow and let it go. "What I had in mind was that we should ride to Sir Walter Aston's park at Tixall, some nine miles distant, and hunt a stag. Aston has offered up an invitation asking if we would be of a mind to join his party." He clucked his tongue, remembering Mary's constant claim of ill-health. "Or would the ride be too much for you?"

"No! No, indeed!" Seeing the glare the old man was casting the spaniel's way, Mary set the animal down several paces away from Paulet, then approached him. "The warm weather seems to embolden me, take away a bit of my pain. I used to hunt, as you know. I think I can still use my crossbow against a deer and gallop after the hounds."

"Then you would like to go?"

Mary's eyes glittered in anticipation. "Indeed I would!"

"Then I shall send word to Sir Walter."

"As you will." Mary walked a few steps, then looked back at Paulet. "I thank you for your thoughtfulness, Sir Amyas. Such manifestations of goodwill become you."

"Indeed, Madame!" Putting his hand to his mouth, he coughed, then abruptly strode for the door. "I'll give you a few moments to get ready." The door slammed behind him.

"A hunt!" Moira hugged her arms around her body in delight. She had wanted so to get out of doors. It seemed to be an answer to her prayers. Suddenly she sobered. "I can go, can I not?"

In a rare gesture of playfulness, Mary tugged at a strand of her hair. "Of course you may. I wouldn't think to go without you!"

Both Moira and Mary took particular care with their garments. There was every possibility they would be meeting some of the local gentry at the hunt, and wanted to look their best. They chose simple riding clothes of leather and stiffened linen so as not to be encumbered by a farthingale while riding sidesaddle. Mary's choice was light green, Moira's palest yellow; both had a close-fitting ruff that encircled the neck. Always of a generous nature, Mary allowed Moira to wear a pair of her leather riding boots—remnants of the past, when she used to go hunting and hawking with her husband Darnley. Both were certain that they were going to have a very good time.

"Ah, to ride a horse again," the Queen said. The prospect seemed to make her appear young once more. "It has been so long."

"Perhaps Paulet is not as bad as I supposed!" Moira thought it best to give him the benefit of the doubt, based on his recent show of kindliness, not only to the Queen and Moira, but to others on Mary's staff as well. Paulet allowed both of Mary's secretaries, Nau and Curle, to accompany their mistress along with Bourgoing, her personal physician, Andrew Melville, the master of her household, and two ladies-in-waiting.

Though there was a slight breeze blowing, the sun warmed the air. To Moira, the feel of the sun on her face was pure heaven. It was the first time in such a long while that she had felt so free. She loathed the confinement of Chartley, and yet, for just an hour of the forest's beauty, it was worth it. Riding beside Nau, who was smartly arrayed as usual, she gave herself up to the joy of the day, though she did glance mischievously at Nau to ask, "Care to wager on who can fell the largest deer?"

"One of the men, of course," the secretary answered.

"Perhaps not." Moira laughed softly. "I've been hunting since I was no higher than my father's knee. I had to keep up with my brothers, you see." She felt the smooth rhythm of the horse's stride as the procession wound its way across the meadows, coming to the outer trees of the forest.

The entire party was filled with a sense of contentment and rejuvenation. Mary spurred on her horse with a manner that showed her renewed energy. The Queen was cheerful and in a gentle mood. When she noticed that Paulet was lagging behind, she remembered that he had recently been ill, and stopped her horse to let him catch up.

"Everything looks so beautiful, don't you think, Sir Amyas?" Moira heard the Queen say. "A sense of benediction falls upon the soul when viewing God's world on such a day!"

"Indeed." Sir Amyas forced a smile, one that looked as if his body pained him again. Feeling a measure of sympathy, Moira slowed her own horse's pace to join Paulet and the Queen.

The small party trotted through the gates of Tixall Park, but Moira's peaceful mood was suddenly shattered. A party of horsemen was riding towards them. Moira's pulse beat furiously. For one exciting moment, she envisioned the horsemen to be led by Babington, and had come to rescue the Queen. Had the undertaking hinted at in the barrel post been successfully carried out? It was, it must be. Babington had come. Anxiously, she scanned the approaching riders to see if her brothers were among them.

All too soon Moira realized her mistake—no rescuers these. As they approached, the leader of the band rode up solemnly, saluted Mary, and produced an order from the Queen of England. Certainly, in his luxuriously embroidered green serge, he seemed important. He introduced himself as Sir Thomas Gorges, gentleman pensioner of Elizabeth. In bold words, he briefly but unmistakably told Mary that Babington's conspiracy had been discovered, that the proofs of it were in Elizabeth's hands, and that he was charged to arrest Nau and Curle, her two secretaries.

"Madame, my mistress the Queen finds it exceedingly strange that you, contrary to the pact and engagement made between you, should have conspired against her and the State."

Mary was taken off guard. Flustered, she protested her innocence until it was obvious that such a ploy would not work.

Moira thought that Mary undoubtedly remembered the missives she had passed by way of the barrels to Babington. Even so, she insisted that those in her employ were without fault in the matter. Gorges informed her that her servants were to be taken from her nevertheless. Their destination: London.

"No! You cannot do this. Never!" Mary's servants rose to defend her. But what could peaceful gentlemen with crossbows and riding crops do against both Paulet's armed escort and the Queen's men? In the end, there was little choice but to admit defeat.

"And what of me?" Mary's voice, though thoughtfully sub-dued, still trembled with emotion.

"You are to be taken at once to Tixall."

"No!" Mary dismounted and sat on the ground, refusing to go any further, pleading a weakness in her limbs. Paulet sar-castically offered to send for a litter, leaving little doubt that he would use force to get her to her destination.

"By hook or crook, Madame, you will go!"

In the end, Mary relented, realizing that she was powerless to put up a fight. Babington was not going to come after all, Babington who was now housed in the ominous Tower.

"You have won, Paulet. I have no choice but to obey." Rising to her knees, the Queen recited a prayer, asking God to remember David, whom He had delivered from his enemies. She emplored His pity, then stood to accept her fate.

Moira came at once to Mary's side. Shaken and frightened to death about what might have happened to her brothers, she nonetheless held onto some semblance of calm. Hysterics would be of no help now; logic and calm were the only answers. She realized at once the meaning of the invitation to a hunting party. Mary had been lured away from her house so that her rooms might be searched in her absence. It was the only thing that made any sense. And if some of the letters were found, Mary would be in dire trouble. Moira couldn't desert her.

"Then if that is where she is to go, I will go there too."

It was decided. Though they begged and pleaded, Nau and Curle were dragged from Mary's side. Paulet ordered his men to go back and search the Queen of Scots' chambers. "Ransack her room. Tear it apart if you must, but be thorough. We must seize her papers. Notes. Ciphers. Letters of every kind. All her possessions. Even jewelry. We must prevent her from hiding or destroying any proofs against her, and from communicating with her secretaries and confidential servants. It is Walsingham's demand.''

Mary, Moira, and Mary's physician were conducted directly to Tixall. Mary was so unprepared for her fate that she did not have the crucifix she habitually carried—a bad omen.

The fortnight spent in a strange new house jarred Mary's nerves and made Moira jittery. No provision was made for a change of clothes, and Moira thought sadly of how carefully they had dressed, thinking they should impress the people of the shire. Now they were condemned to view their own vanity day after day.

Mary was kept in total ignorance of what was going on, of the proceedings against her. No one came forth to reproach or accuse her. Except for Moira, none of her servants was allowed to visit her. She was not allowed the use of pen or ink, though she begged to be allowed to write a letter to her cousin, Queen Elizabeth.

''I was such a fool, Moira,'' she said over and over again. ''I told you once not to give your trust too lightly. It appears that that is just what I have done. Someone has betrayed me, but I do not know who.'' Feverishly, she went over and over the chances in her favor, tortured herself to remember what papers she had kept and what had been destroyed. In times of her greatest anxiety, she snatched at the fragile hope that the King of Spain would come to rescue her when he learned of the humiliation she had been forced to endure.

When at last they were escorted back to Chartley, Mary saw a number of beggars staring at her as they proceeded along the road. ''I have nothing for you. I am a beggar as well as you. All has been taken from me,'' she said.

Returning to her desolate rooms at Chartley, Mary beheld the evidence that she had been stripped of everything she had once held dear. Tightening her jaw, she said to Sir Amyas, ''Some of you will be sorry for this. Two things cannot be taken from me. My English blood and the Catholic religion, which I will keep until my death.''

Brave words, Moira thought, but it was time to face reality. Walsingham had won. Once but a prisoner, Mary was now an accused criminal, and Moira could not help but wonder just what her own fate would be.

Chapter Fifty

THE CITY OF LONDON RANG with bells pealing Walsingham's triumph. They chimed atop church spires, clamored from the decks of ships, rang from many a window. Bonfires were lit. People made merry in the street, sang psalms, marched about with tabor and pipe, and shouted out the news to any who might not yet have heard it. Their cause for celebration was that a wicked plot to kill their beloved Queen had been squelched, and the conspirators apprehended. A procession was inaugurated to celebrate the rescue of Elizabeth and the imminent destruction of Mary Stuart.

One by one, Walsingham had rounded up the conspirators. He was aided by the tortured chattering of Babington, who had made his confessions on the rack. Confronted with Phelippes' deciphering of his letter to Mary and her impassioned reply, he had admitted the authenticity of both. Moreover, he had babbled about the Enterprise. At last, every detail of the conspiracy was placed in the hands of the great spymaster. More than one man was fatally incriminated.

Walsingham had struck quickly and he had struck hard; even Savage was arrested. Babington and the members of the Enterprise were led back in chains through the streets of London. There was no hope for them. Walsingham was not the kind of man to listen to a denial of guilt; he had worked much too hard to catch them. The verdict could not be anything but guilty.

The trials of Babington and Ballard and their confederates resulted in the terrifying verdict of hanging and quartering, the sentence for treason. All those who had witnessed such an execution knew the procedure well. England had nothing to learn from Spain about cruelty. To deter further plotting, the worst possible death was planned for those found guilty. The populace must see that just vengeance was brought down on traitors.

The condemned would be split open alive, and their hearts and intestines wrenched out. The severity of the sentence depended on whether the victim was cut down alive or allowed to remain hanging until he was dead, so that the butchering was done on naught but a corpse. And now the hour was at hand.

The crowd was assembled in a field at the upper end of Holborn—St. Giles, as it was known. There, a scaffold had been erected, with a pair of gallows of extraordinary height. After being placed on hurdles and drawn through the city, Babington, Ballard, Savage, Chidiock Tichbourne, Henry Donn, Thomas Salisbury, and Robert Barnwell awaited their death.

From their place at the back of the gawking crowd, disguised as a baker and a butcher, Donnie and Davie MacKinnon watched the gruesome proceedings. Ballard was first, and brave to the very end, though he was subjected to unspeakable agonies. Babington was next. He suffered horribly, calling out for mercy again and again. Then, at last, his mutilated body was still. One by one, the others suffered a like fate. The next day, some of the others were executed, but at Elizabeth's command, they were allowed to hang until dead before being cut down.

Rhymes, ballads, and pamphlets followed. It seemed that in the city as well as the country, the ballads were changed so that all of England was acquainted with the terrible conspiracy. London was a ghastly city of unspeakable men, Donnie noted when reading one of the gory verses. He was certain their own end was near; the game was lost. Of all the conspirators, only four had not yet been arrested. Two of those were he and his brother.

"I tell you, we should flee, or we will be likewise doomed," he counseled his brother.

"No. That weasel Walsingham will be expecting us to flee." It was true. The roads were blocked, and the ports were being watched. The brothers were short of money and provisions for any long journey. "We'll stay here until the furor dies down, and then we'll make our move. Besides, there is Moira to think of. Somehow we have to reach her.''

Davie's talk was bold, but the time came when the matter had to be faced squarely. They were hungry. Faced with that and the need to look over their shoulder every time they took a step outside their dingy room in London's east side, Davie and Donnie decided it was imperative that they get as far away from London as possible.

The captain—Paxton. Therein lay their only hope. Not only might he aid them in their own escape, but if the man had any feelings for their sister, and they hoped that he might, he would free her from danger as well. All things considered, Davie and Donnie decided to seek him out. Ducking in and out of the shadows, they made their way to the docks. They were not prepared for what they would find.

''It can't be!'' Davie squinted his eyes against the glare of the sun, thinking that it surely must have been a hallucination.

''But it is,'' Donnie exclaimed.

Dressed in plain leather jerkin, a brightly-hued doublet, and a jaunty hat, Ryan Paxton stood at the railing, deeply engaged in conversation with another man. But it was not the captain that drew the MacKinnons' stares. It was the man at his side, a man swathed from head to toe in black: Walsingham.

''What is he doing with *him?*'' The answer seemed all too obvious. Davie remembered a conversation he had had with Moira on the matter. She had said then that she feared Captain Paxton was involved with Walsingham. But according to a letter she had written, she had changed her mind. Now David knew beyond a doubt that he was thick as a thief with Elizabeth's councilor. A spy, informant, agent—ugly words.

''And I trusted him. Fool that I was, I thought that because of our sister, he would help us escape. And all the while it was he who aided that black-hearted bastard in putting the noose around our necks.'' Davie glowered in utter anger.

''Think of the many times we met in his tavern!''

''He was always so cordial. He must have known then.''

''Aye, and used his smiles to lull us into a false sense of calm.'' At that moment, Davie had never hated another man quite as much. His sorrow for Babington and the others changed to anger, aimed at the English sea-captain. He vowed revenge.

Chapter Fifty-one

THE WATERS OF THE OCEAN were a crystal-clear blue, shimmering as far as the eye could see. From the deck of the *Red Mermaid*, all looked peaceful. London basked tranquilly in the late afternoon sun, or so it seemed. Deceptive and fraudulent, Ryan thought as he stood at the rail. In truth, the city was in a state of turbulence. Throughout the city, as well as the very country, there was a sense of imminent peril. The alarm had been raised that the French had landed in Sussex. A week or so later, a Spanish fleet was reported to have put into a French port. Watch was set to patrol the coasts, and Lords Lieutenants were appointed in each county to muster troops, make ready the beacons, and round up Catholic priests. Gossip abounded that those friendly with Mary of Scots would soon rise up in her defense; the threat from Babington and his plotters was not yet over.

Babington. Even though he had held little respect for the frivolous and foolish young man, Ryan thought back to his execution with abhorrence. He could still hear his screams, his plea of "parce mihi, domine Jesu!" He could empathize with his agony. Abominable tortures had been inflicted upon the unhappy young men who had ventured their lives on behalf of the imprisoned Queen. Babington had suffered. John Savage had actually broken the rope and fell before being mutilated. The torture had been meted out with the full approval of Cecil, Walsingham, and Queen Elizabeth.

That Ryan had had any part in the capture of Savage, Ballard and Babington, small as it was, shamed him to the core. Though it had meant freedom for Davie and Donnie Mac-

Kinnon, he couldn't forgive himself nonetheless. Had any man the right to barter for another's life?

"God's blood, no!" He knew he would be haunted every time he gave himself up to his dreams or came anywhere near a gallows.

Even the London mob, which was not overly squeamish, had witnessed the revolting scene of cruelty in silence. One of the conspirators had made a final noble speech which aroused the pity of the spectators. It was as if the crowd had suddenly had its fill of the horrors, murmuring at the long, drawn-out barbarity of the execution. Perhaps that was why when the others were made to suffer their sentence, they had been shown more mercy, their ordeal shortened. Even so, men had died, and it looked as if there might be other punishments as well. Mary. What was to be done with her?

In gambling houses all over London, bets had been placed on the fate of the Scottish queen. There were those who were certain that she would lose her head. Others argued that Mary was the heir presumptive to the English throne, and that as such Elizabeth could not condemn her to death. Burghley and Walsingham had voiced their stern opinions that as long as Mary lived, there would be those who would conspire to place that crown prematurely on her head, even if it meant the death of Elizabeth. Babington was not the first, nor would he be the last. The threat of assassination was an ever-present danger.

Balancing himself against the rocking and swaying of the deck beneath his feet, Ryan gave vent to his thoughts. How was he ever going to vindicate himself, he who had always been so careful not to implicate himself in such schemes? More importantly, what would Moira think when he told her what had transpired? Would she be grateful to him for saving her brothers and herself, or would she consider him a traitor? Could they put what had happened behind them and think of a future together, or would what had happened always raise its ugly head to spoil their contentment?

As if to give himself at least a measure of hope, he took out the papers safely hidden beneath his doublet and read the words that dotted each page—a pardon of any wrongdoing for Davie and Donnie MacKinnon, a writ to get them safely out of the country. It was their absolution from any part in the Babington scheme, just as Walsingham had promised, but at quite a price: Ryan Paxton's honor. It was a reward placed into his hands by Walsingham himself, who had visited his ship only an hour ago.

"You have done very well, Captain Paxton," he had said. "I could use a man like you in my service."

"Go to the devil!" Ryan had made it perfectly clear that he wanted no part of Walsingham's web. "All I want is to see that David and Donald MacKinnon are allowed to return to their home in Scotland."

"And the girl?" A muscle in Walsingham's jaw ticked convulsively.

"I intend to go to Chartley at once," Ryan blurted out. "You promised that you would not hold her there. You promised, Sir Francis!"

"Ah yes, so I did. I told you that I would open the doors of Chartley to her. It has been done. She is a prisoner at Chartley no longer." Walsingham stared at him for a long moment, his dark eyes slitted against the sun. "What now, Captain Paxton?"

"I am going to make her my wife, if she will have me. I'm going to take her far away from here." So far away that you will never be able to lay your hands on her again, he thought.

With that purpose in mind, Ryan gave the orders to set sail, watching the towers and spires of London gradually recede as the ship moved along. The *Red Mermaid* sailed purposefully down the Thames toward the English Channel. Their destination was to be the western coast of England, whereby he would work his way from Chester to Staffordshire. It was there that his future, his happiness, lay.

RYAN WAS in good spirits as he set out from Chester. Though it was a strangely foggy morning, he didn't let the misty haze bother him. It was a long day's ride to Staffordshire, but his longing to be with Moira gave him stamina. Holding tightly to his horse's reins, he made the journey with but two stops along the way, riding at a furious pace. By the time the towers and walls of Chartley came into view, he was covered from head to foot with the dust of the road. After dismounting from his horse, Ryan assessed his appearance. Hardly fitting company for a lovely young lady—but, under the circumstances, perhaps she would forgive him.

Taking the steps of the rambling stone building two at a time, he found his way blocked by two men-at-arms, their scowls telling him that they thought him a vagabond or other such scoundrel. "I wish to see Moira MacKinnon—Mowbray—at once!" he ordered, ignoring their disdainful looks. To avoid a delay, he showed them the document Walsingham had signed, which allowed him entrance into the manor.

"Moira MacKinnon-Mowbray...?" The guards exchanged questioning glances.

"Mary Stuart's lady's maid. A tall, dark-haired young woman with the face and form of an angel." Passing by a mirror, he brushed off his garments as best he could. "Tell her that I wait below and wish to speak with her." Of a certainty, she would be as surprised today as she had been before. Oh, how he wished this reunion would also be as passionate.

With a feeling of anticipation, he pushed his way through the door and stood in the hall, waiting as the guards strode off. His eyes roamed over his surroundings, taking in the silken hangings drawn back from the latticed windows, the murals, paintings, and tapestries. A fire burned in the great hearth, and he welcomed its warmth. Though it was summer, the nights were still chill.

Strange, Ryan thought—despite the usually hectic time of day, it was relatively silent. He didn't see the usual flock of servants that he had seen before bustling about. There were one or two, but not enough to run a proper household. He looked around him, puzzled by his sudden anxiety. Then, somehow he knew, even before it was told to him. Mary Stuart was no longer in residence here, she had been moved. But to where?

"What is going on?"

He stormed from room to room, up the stairs, down the stairs, interrogating the few servants he encountered. Mary Stuart had been brought back to Chartley after seventeen days spent at Tixall, but Sir Amyas Paulet had immediately enacted changes. A complete list of Mary's household had been drawn up, with suggestions as to how it could be cut from thirty-

eight servants to just nineteen. The Scottish queen's belongings
had been rifled, her cupboards broken open, her personal treasures confiscated.

"Where is Mary Stuart?" The steward announced that she
was gone. The Scottish queen had been taken to another prison.

"And her servants?"

"Gone. Every one of them," the amply-girthed cook revealed.

Slowly, Ryan pieced together the story. The Queen of England's spymaster had made it a point to arrive before Ryan's
ship. With the vilest duplicity of all, Walsingham had made a
pun. It was true that Moira was no longer a prisoner at *Chartley*.
Walsingham had indeed opened the doors of Chartley to her,
just as he had promised, but not to set her free.

"May Walsingham's soul rot in hell!" Ryan hissed. He
paced the long, darkened corridors of Chartley with impatient
strides, waiting as the minutes passed by. He listened and
watched. He had to find out where they had taken her, and if
she was safe. By God, what a cruel trick Walsingham had
played, letting him think he was to be at last reunited with his
lady love. Instead, the spymaster had taken Moira to Fotheringay, where Walsingham intended to use her as a witness
against the Scottish queen.

PART THREE

THE SPIDER
AND THE BUTTERFLIES

Fotheringay

> If I have freedom in my love,
>   And in my soul am free,
> Angels alone, that soar above,
>   Enjoy such liberty.

LOVELACE,
    "To Althea, from Prison"

Chapter Fifty-two

FOTHERINGAY CASTLE, southeast of Staffordshire in Northampton, was a dark, brooding fortress. Built during the time of the Conqueror and rebuilt during the reign of Edward III, it had a stark history. Several years before, Catherine of Aragon, Henry VIII's cast-off wife, had staunchly refused to go there unless bound with ropes and dragged there. It was now used entirely as a prison. Hardly a place to lighten one's mood, Moira thought as she assessed its dimensions. The front of the castle and its enormous gateway faced north, and the mammoth keep rose to the northwest. There was a double-moat system along three sides, with the River Nene winding along the very edge of the castle. The Northamptonshire countryside surrounded the grim towers.

The very sight of the place filled Moira with foreboding. Danger seemed to be lurking behind its walls along with a sense of inevitable doom—real or imagined? She could only wonder. It was the kind of place that seemed to have an aura of gloom about it, even though it was not so very different from other castles. Stone and wood. A large courtyard filled the interior of the building, enclosing a chapel and a great hall. Fotheringay was large, but despite its size, Mary had been incarcerated in comparatively mean apartments. A means of humbling her, Moira thought.

"Fotheringay," she whispered, feeling shivers up and down her back. The journey there had done little to soothe Mary's spirits and much to goad her ill humor. What was more, she had seemed to age rapidly before Moira's very eyes. Was it any wonder? From the suspicious manner in which Paulet was acting, his sense of triumph, and from the many staterooms that had been left empty, Mary suspected that she was awaiting some sort of trial.

"But I am ready to be a martyr if that is what must be," she had said.

Moira remembered very vividly that sinister and frightening moment when they had been taken out of Chartley Hall and to an unknown destination. The men who came to fetch them had arrived with pistols in their belts. Mary's own servants were locked in their rooms and their windows guarded so that they would not be able to witness her departure, or signal their sympathy to her.

Paulet had been tight-lipped on the matter, as mum as a mute. All he had said to Mary on the subject of her new prison was that she was going to be moved. From gossip gleaned from the servants, Mary had in fact believed that she was going to a royal castle about thirty miles from London. Instead, under Elizabeth's direction they had come here.

Whispers from Paulet's servants indicated that, in London, the commissioners appointed to judge the Scottish queen had assembled at Westminster. There, they were read copies of the letters sent by Babington to Mary, her answers, and the evidence of Nau and Curle, who had been frightened by Walsingham into giving their testimony. It had been agreed that Mary should be brought to trial under the Bond of Association, an act passed two years before, and specifically in order to frame Mary. It gave power to prosecute and condemn to death anyone laying claim to the English crown, or who tried to deprive Elizabeth of her queenship by way of conspiracy or foreign invasion.

Elizabeth had written a private message to Mary, addressed merely "to the Scottish," urging her to acknowledge her guilt and throw herself on her cousin's mercy, a gesture Mary met with contemptuous refusal.

"She expects me to beg her for mercy. But I won't, Moira! I will not become a penitent on my knees. I am a queen." The strongest of Mary's instincts was pride, and that seemed to give her strength of will now. "I would rather kneel to lay my head on the block than prostrate myself before that woman, who has ever been my woe. I would rather perish than humble myself."

"Elizabeth will never approve your execution. This I do absolve her of," Moira answered, clutching Mary's hand. "She will not seek your death now any more than she has in the past." In truth, Elizabeth had had ample opportunities, but always refused to kill the Queen. "She seeks to frighten you and nothing more."

"Then I shall demonstrate to her what bravery is." Holding her head up high, Mary tried hard to smile. "But you, Moira. I do not want any of this to do you any harm. I do not want to see you hurt."

"I won't be. I have my mother's strength and my father's resolve. If anything, perhaps I can be of help if I am asked to give any testimony."

Moira did indeed hope that she could counteract the slander by telling the truth about what she had seen. Mary's main intent had always been to end her imprisonment and not steal Elizabeth's crown or to harm her. Always, the tone of the letters had been with that in mind. Surely, as a person unjustly and illegally imprisoned for nineteen years, Mary had a right to free herself by whatever means possible. Moira would make Mary's accusers see that.

Moira was given the opportunity much sooner than she had foreseen. Forty lords and gentlemen, the greatest men in the kingdom, or so it was said, arrived at Fotheringay attended by some two thousand armed horsemen. Cloistered together with Mary in her chamber, Moira scanned the list eagerly, seeking in vain for one friendly or impartial name. Alas, there was none. Walsingham was playing a dangerous card game, and had stacked the deck against the woman he thought to be England's enemy.

"And so the game begins," Mary whispered.

At first, she had protested the decision to bring her to trial, arguing that she was a queen and therefore not under Elizabeth's jurisdiction. She had said that she could not allow herself to be judged by subjects without betraying the prerogative of her son, her descendants, and all princes everywhere. She would not acknowledge herself subject to the laws of a country where she had been kept in prison in defiance of law. Her refusal was noted and forwarded to Elizabeth.

The answer came back that, with or without Mary of Scotland, the Commission would proceed. "But answer fully and you will receive the greater favor from us," Elizabeth had responded.

"No! I will not give in!"

"Your Majesty, think on this. If you refuse to be questioned by the Commission, you might give the world cause to believe that you are guilty." Moira felt the need to voice her sincere opinion.

"Perhaps, perhaps." Mary reasoned the problem out. She knew she had an eloquent tongue, a noble presence. The pathos of her circumstances and her sincerity might at least make a lasting impression on those who heard her speak.

At last, after discussion with those close to her and weighing her choices, Mary abandoned her position and declared her willingness to appear before the commissioners. It was, as Moira said, her chance to exonerate herself before all of England. Certainly, ever since Mary had come into England, she had frequently demanded to be heard by Parliament. Now she would have her chance.

The spectacle of the trial was held in the great chamber at Fotheringay Castle. The large room was a veritable sea of faces. It was bandied about that the provisions of the Bond of Association were so heavily weighted against Mary that she stood absolutely no chance of acquittal. Indeed, Mary was not to be allowed a defender, nor a secretary to help her plead her case. Therefore, she would have to defend herself on her own. Moira could only hope that God, in His wisdom and mercy, would reach out and touch the hearts of those who sat in judgment.

It was a tense moment as all awaited the entrance of the Scottish queen. At one end of the big room a dais with a canopy and a chair of red velvet decorated with a cloth of state had been set up, emblazoned with the arms of England. It was there to represent Elizabeth, who would not be present for the trial. A footstool was placed at one side for the Scottish queen, to emphasize the overlordship of England over Scotland.

Mary entered through the large double doors at the far end of the room, and all heads turned to look upon her. She was dressed in her black robes and flowing long veil, supported on either side by her physician, Bourgoing, and her friend Andrew Melvill, the master of her household.

Contemptuously, she looked around at the assembly. "So many lawyers are here assembled, and not one of them to represent me." Then she made her way to the empty throne, pausing a few steps away from it. She would not let the insult pass without protest.

"I am a queen by birth and have been the wife of the King of France. My place should be there," she said, glancing at the vacant seat beneath the canopy. Her eyes swept the crowd before she sat down, a chilling moment which sent the assemblage into a twitter.

The indictment against her was read, but instead of cowering Mary, it only seemed to bolster her fighting instinct. She repeated her protest that as a queen she could be subject to no tribunal but that of God, that she had consented to come hither to answer to one specific charge.

It was little more than a mime and a mockery of justice, Moira thought angrily; the proceedings continued with Burghley and Walsingham as the two principal actors. She remembered the time that she had gone to the theater with Ryan. Certainly Walsingham's skill in theatrics as he struck out against Mary Stuart equaled anything she had seen on the stage. She was as evil as a viper, he said, a woman who had knowingly and purposefully set out to kill another woman and wear her crown.

Walsingham offered up his evidence against Mary, producing copies of the letters to Babington and others. Mary answered with a flat repudiation and the pertinent demand that the original letters, not copies, be brought as evidence. She espoused the belief that Walsingham was both her enemy and the enemy of her son.

"How can I be certain that you did not forge my cipher to procure my condemnation? Is it not possible that since these are but copies of a supposed original, the decipherer could not have composed my words erroneously, putting down things I did not even say? Indeed, how can anyone here be certain?" she asked aloud for all to hear.

"Madam! How dare you!" Walsingham was curiously agitated for a man arguing that he was blameless in the matter. Rising in a huff, he sought to vindicate himself. "God is my witness that, as a private person, I have done nothing unworthy of an honest man, and as Secretary of State, nothing unbefitting my duty." Trying to compose himself, he clasped his hands together. "Babington acknowledged the authenticity of the correspondence."

"Babington? Indeed. As I recall, he and the others were put to death before these proceedings. Why is that, sir?"

The question went unanswered. Instead, Walsingham spoke of Mary's own secretaries, who had authenticated that the letters were indeed correct copies of what had been exchanged. "Her own secretaries denounce her. I have here signed statements to that fact."

"Signed under much duress, I would imagine." Again Mary was calm. "Why, sir, though my secretaries are still alive— God be thanked—have they not been produced here as witnesses against me?"

Walsingham quickly went on to other topics, concentrating on Savage and his intent to kill the rightful English queen and the confessions of Ballard and Savage, which were produced. Then Burghley took his turn, hobbling before the assemblage, holding the papers with a quivering hand. Burghley dragged forth old and irrelevant matters, such as Mary's adoption of the English arms in the early days of her reign as France's queen. His attitude bristled with hostility.

"You have ever thirsted after the throne of England," he said, his gray brows drawing together in a "v." "You have ever been ambitious, Madam."

"Ambitious?" Mary scoffed. "You and your mistress have robbed me of my youth. I do not seek the throne in the autumn of my years." Mary accused Burghley of being her adversary.

"I am the adversary of the adversaries of Queen Elizabeth," he answered coldly.

Mary's behavior at the trial was emotional, dignified, and full of self-justification. She had written Babington, she admitted, a few letters. But she had not put her hand to any agreement to kill her cousin. She acknowledged the letters to Mendoza, Paget, and Morgan, and admitted that for her own liberty and the comfort of oppressed and persecuted Catholics, she had solicited aid from foreign princes. Where she stood absolutely firm was in her denial of any acknowledgment on the attempt of the life of Elizabeth.

"You lie!" Burghley and Walsingham spoke at the same time.

"You callously and cold-bloodedly planned the assassination of the rightful Queen from the start, drawing young, idealistic men into your web of intrigue," Walsingham continued, leaning towards her until they were practically nose to nose. "You are a murderess of the vilest degree!"

"No!" Moira rose indignantly to her feet, unable to bear any more. It was so obvious to her that Walsingham had planned the entire episode all along. Gifford—how mysteriously and quickly he had arrived upon the scene. And why, when so many others had been severely punished, had he not faced the scaffold? Because he was Walsingham's man all along. The truth was so obvious—she wondered how she had not realized it all before.

"Silence! You have no part in this!" Walsingham thundered.

"I was there and I know." In jumbled, emotionally charged words, she briefly related to the gentlemen in the room how Gifford had sought Mary out with the plan about the barrel post, how it had always been at his suggestion that a new correspondent was initiated. "It was he who first suggested Mary write to Babington. He instigated all." Raising her arm, Moira pointed her finger. "You, Walsingham, you are the guilty one. If anyone here is responsible of deceit, it is you! You planned all of this. Every detail, every move. Just so you could have Mary right where she is now. You want her death! You crave it as some men crave wine. What I cannot understand is why—"

"Close your mouth, woman!" Walsingham trembled with his wrath. Motioning to the guards, he ordered Moira arrested. "Take her from this room immediately."

Moira winced as several hands clutched at her. "Where are you taking me?"

"Out of here! Out of my presence before, so help me God, I strangle you." His cold, black eyes nearly bulged out of his head. "Take her to the dungeons beneath this hall. Lock her up! Throw away the key!" His orders were carried out as soon as he spoke. Though Moira struggled in protest, she was half carried, half dragged from the hall.

Chapter Fifty-three

DESPITE THE FACT that it was autumn, it was uncomfortably warm in the bedchamber. Ryan pushed himself out of bed and padded across the warped wooden floor in his bare feet. Moving to the window, unconcerned with his nakedness, he opened the shutters wide. Noise met his ears, riotous shouting. The people of London were celebrating with wild rejoicing as bells chimed again through the city.

"By God, who has Walsingham had put to death now?" Ryan asked sarcastically of a man down below.

"Not put to death, at least not yet. But he has put the Queen of Scots on trial."

"Mary, Mary, quite contrary, how does your garden grow?" sang a group of girls, their high-pitched voices in perfect unison. "With silver bells and cockle shells and pretty maids all in a row—" It was, Ryan knew, a ditty about Mary, Queen of Scots.

"Put on trial? What? Where? Where is this justice being meted out?" All this time he had been hounding Walsingham, trying to find out where Moira had been taken. Walsingham had been as stubborn as a mule, pretending he didn't know, insisting that he had no jurisdiction over county matters. As though it had not been by his writ that Moira had been removed from Chartley, Ryan thought angrily. The thought struck him now that if he could talk with Mary Stuart, perhaps he could find out.

"Why, Fotheringay Castle. Haven't you heard? The gossip's been bandied all about," the man answered.

Ryan hadn't heard, but now he was interested. "Fotheringay? Where is that?"

"Northampton."

Northampton. It was far closer than Staffordshire. A two days' journey, he calculated. "And how is the trial proceeding?"

"The Commission returned to the Court of Star Chamber here to finish their process. She was guilty, of course. They found the Scottish crow privy to conspiracy and of imagining and compassing her Majesty's death. That's the reason for the celebration. All God-fearing faithful men should be so applauding."

Guilty, Ryan thought. But then, hadn't that been a foregone conclusion? Else Walsingham would not have gone to so much trouble. "And where is Mary now?"

"She is being held at Fotheringay until such time as it is decided what they will do with her. Elizabeth, God bless her, is much too kindhearted to put her cousin to death."

"Ah, yes. She is a veritable boon of compassion," Ryan said dryly. In truth, he imagined Elizabeth was a bit fearful of chopping off a queen's head, lest a few of her detractors get the idea and try to separate her head from her shoulders. It was often unwise to set a precedent. "Elizabeth!" At the moment he wanted to blame his unhappiness on her, though in truth it was his own fault.

Ryan had had a succession of sleepless nights since his return from Chartley empty-handed. To add to his unrest was the fact that although he had done everything he could think of, he had yet to locate the MacKinnon twins. It made him deeply troubled as to their fate. If Walsingham had broken his word so craftily in Moira's case, how then could he trust him on this matter? And yet there had been no public announcement that they had been found, no gruesome punishment dealt. He hoped that to be a good sign that Donald and David were quick enough to have made their own escape, or were clever at hiding.

Shutting the window again, Ryan returned to his bed. Fotheringay. He would get a good night's rest if he could, then proceed there first thing in the morning. He'd take Seamus and the wagon with him. Somehow they would think of a way to get through the gates, even if he had to pretend to be Walsingham himself. Snuggling amidst the pillows and blankets, he chuckled mirthlessly at the thought. But somehow, some way, he would find Moira again. He had to, or lose all hope of ever being truly happy again.

"Moira—" Always, she was in his dreams—pleasant visions of the times they had been together, or darker nightmares where he frantically tried to save her. Every night she haunted him, and every day she hovered in his mind. He had to put an end to this tortured wondering, or be doomed to Bedlam! It was the last thing that flitted through his mind as he closed his eyes to sleep.

The pressure of hands grasping his shoulders awakened him from his slumber, a rude awakening. Through the haze of his awareness, he watched as a somber dark-haired youth reached to pluck away his sword. A duplicate of the young man who held him. The MacKinnons.

"Donald! David!" Seldom in his life had he ever been so glad to see anyone, yet his joy quickly evaporated as he saw that they were armed and their weapons pointed at him. "What? Hold! There is some misunderstanding here."

"A misunderstanding, yes. Yours!" Davie said, his hands surprisingly strong despite his lithe frame. "You vile bastard! How I wish I'd cut your throat the first time I laid eyes on you."

"Strong words." Ryan tried to get up but the two lads held him immobile. "By God, let me go!" In anger, Ryan struggled, only to be subdued when Davie held a dagger to his throat. It seemed the young men were in deadly earnest.

"We saw you with Walsingham. Together, on your ship. Don't tell us you aren't a spy."

"I'm not!" If only they would let him up, he could show them the papers that Walsingham had given him and explain in detail why he had done what he did. God's eternal youth, it was for them!

"You are! Moira told me so, only I just didn't listen hard enough. Now I know." Donnie's grip was not as punishing, yet his eyes glittered with just as much resentment as his brother's. "All the while you were making us feel welcome in your tavern, you were plotting our downfall."

"Not your downfall, your salvation. Damn it, man, if I gave Walsingham any quarter at all, it was to ensure that you wouldn't meet the same fate as your friends." He tried to pull free, but the lads were not taking any chance on his escape. Pulling forth a rope, they brandished it with threatening expressions.

"Should we hang you, Paxton? Make you do the dance of death as Ballard, Babington, and the others were forced to do? Should I take this knife and cut off that which makes you a man, as was done to them?"

Ryan paled at the very idea of such a thing, though he sensed the young men were only bluffing. Violence and cruelty were foreign to their souls. "By God, let me explain."

Donnie laughed sourly. "You expect us to believe anything you have to say?"

"I would tell you the truth! I am saying it when I tell you that I never at any time sought your harm." In a voice that he tried to keep calm, Ryan related the story of Walsingham's bargain, of the pact he had made. He spoke of Gifford and how the priest was in truth Walsingham's man. "In the left sleeve of my red doublet. The proof of what I say is there. Papers given to me by Walsingham. If you had but come to me, you would be well on your way to Scotland by now. That I swear."

"I don't believe you. Why would you care about us?" Davie was scornful.

"Because you are held very dear by the one person on this earth I love the most—your sister. I knew that if anything happened to you, it would deeply grieve her and I didn't want that. Above all, I never want to hurt her."

"He sounds sincere. He might be telling the truth." Donnie was starting to weaken. "At least we can look in his doublet sleeve and see—"

"And give him the chance of breaking free? Donnie, don't be such a fool! Together we are a match for him, but I doubt I could hold him alone. No, we've got to go through with what we vowed."

"And that is?" Ryan asked in a husky voice.

"To kill you as revenge for Babington's and Ballard's death, if not for the others." Davie spoke so convincingly that Ryan flinched. "And then we will go after Walsingham himself."

"And end up meeting an even more dastardly fate than did the others? What brilliant thinking, David MacKinnon. How noble of you. And when you have done this deed, what then do you think will happen to your sister? Indeed, to your family? Is my blood worth it? Is Walsingham's? Think, boy. Think!''

"He's right, Davie. You know how diligently Jamie always tries to stay in Elizabeth's good graces. We will have no quarter there. We would be fugitives forever, here and in Scotland, and our family in disgrace. We can't have that." Donald let Ryan go, flinging out his arms in resignation. "What has happened has happened. We can't change it by killing him. In truth, there's been so much blood already that I'm sick to death of the whole matter. And Moira—"

Without the burden of four hands upon him, Ryan quickly overpowered Davie. "You rash young fool!" Stripping him of his knife, Ryan wielded it, but only as a measure of self-defense.

"And so now you are triumphant," Davie whispered. "Are you going to call your friend Walsingham to take us to the Tower?"

"No!"

"What then?"

Ryan dropped the dagger, watching as it clattered on the floor. "I intend to call a truce between us. There is an important matter afoot. The rescue of your sister." He picked up his hosen, pulled them on, and thrust his feet into his boots. "And just for your information, I am not a spy. I loathe Walsingham as much as you do." Shrugging into his shirt and then his doublet, he held forth the documents the spymaster had given him. "Here, this is my gift to you. Take them and go your own way, or give me your trust. Which is it to be?"

Donnie came at once to Ryan's side. "I, for one, say we should join him. Moira is of our blood, Davie. It is our duty to set her free. I believe him when he says he loves her."

Davie snatched the pieces of parchment from Ryan's hand. Scanning them quickly, he shrugged. "I suppose we can give him a chance to redeem himself. God knows we've made a few mistakes."

"Babington, for one," Donnie whispered. "Whether you want to admit it or not, he was a fool, Davie. A wiser man would never have so easily fallen into an unwise scheme. He was vainglorious. Even when he made his escape, he had little care for what fate held for us. And Gifford. If our anger is for anyone, it should be for him. In truth, he betrayed us worst of all.''

"Yes, he did.'' Davie gave the matter careful thought. At last, he held out his hand. "Then I guess that we will go with you, if you will have us. Tell us what we must do.'' Huddling together in the room, the three men made their plans.

Chapter Fifty-four

IT WAS COLD inside the cell. The stale odor of rotting straw assailed Moira's nostrils as she looked about her. Oh, why hadn't she kept her silence? What had she hoped to accomplish by ranting and raving at Walsingham as she had? Now she was in a great deal of trouble. Walsingham was using her as a means to coerce Mary into admitting that she had plotted Elizabeth's death. He was threatening to send her to the block as a co-conspirator in the Enterprise.

"Naught but a bluff." Or was it? The man had certainly shown himself capable of great cruelty. The very thought made her shiver as she recalled hearing of the fates of Babington, Ballard, and Savage.

Oh, if only I could get out of here, she thought, stretching out her legs in the cramped space. She had not seen Mary since she had been thrown inside the foul environs, but she had heard the men-at-arms talk. Though at first Elizabeth had refused to pass sentence, Burghley, Walsingham, and Leicester, her favorite, were all trying to convince her of the necessity. They were all urging her to agree to an execution. Elizabeth had even sent Lord Burghley to Fotheringay to warn Mary of the verdict the Star Chamber and Houses of Parliament had pronounced against her. But Mary had not even flinched. No repentance, no submission, no acknowledgment of her fault, no craving for pardon could be drawn from her. Instead, she had sat down to make her appeal to the world and her posterity in eloquent and impassioned letters.

There had been a rumor that Elizabeth had sent a letter to Paulet, pleading with him to find a means of shortening the life of the Queen of Scots so that her blood would not be on the Queen of England's hands. But Paulet, as grumbly and troublesome as he could sometimes be, had staunchly refused. "God forbid that I should make so foul a shipwreck of my conscience, or leave so great a blot to my poor posterity as to shed blood without law or warrant," he had allegedly answered.

But what of me?—Moira could not help but be concerned. Walsingham had seemed to want to be rid of his troublesome prisoner, as he called Moira. If he had suggested poisoning, suffocating, or otherwise dispatching the Scottish queen, how could she be certain that he would not do such a thing to her?

Clasping her hands together tightly, she determined to be brave. Whatever was to be, she would try to face it as bravely as Mary. And what of the Queen of Scots? Moira could only hope that Elizabeth would hold staunchly to her vow not to put her signature to the writ of execution. It troubled her that Mary was beginning to act as if she were already a martyr, talking of her death and how she was not afraid to shed her blood for the Catholic cause. It was said that when Paulet entered her room, he found that in the place where her royal emblazonments had hung were now ten pictures of the Passion of her Savior. She had requested that upon her death, her body be carried to France to be buried beside her honored mother.

Death! Dying! Moira was haunted by the prospect. "But I am so young!" She had just barely begun to realize what life was really about. Love, caring deeply for another person. Even in her fear, she thought of Ryan, regretting that their love had never really had a chance. Her fault. Hers! She should never have left him for any reason, even for loyalty to the Scottish queen. If only she had never come to Staffordshire with Seamus. What then? What if she had stayed in London at the Devil's Thumb? What might have happened?

The walls were cold and damp. She clutched her woolen cloak tightly to her body. It was the only possession she had from that time in London. The captain had given it to her, and therefore it was that much dearer to her. Cold, hungry, and miserable, she fought against her tears. What she would have given to have his strong arms enfolding her, keeping her warm with his body.

"Ryan—" She fell asleep calling out his name.

A rattle of keys jarred her from her slumber. Looking up, she saw *his* face through the grille of the wooden door. Raising her head, she blinked her eyes to clear them of the vision. A dream, but so vivid as to almost make her believe that he was really here.

"Moira, I'm going to get you out of this place." *His* voice calling to her. Opening the door, he burst into the small, straw-strewn room. With him was a man she knew all too well: Paulet! Ryan's knife was poised at the old man's throat.

"Ryan! How—?" There was no time for explanations. Staggering to her feet, Moira flew to his side. Behind him was another face she knew as well as her own. "Donnie!" Somehow they had gotten past the guards.

"You will hang for this!" Paulet choked. "It is bad enough that you pretend to be sent from Walsingham, but to threaten violence on a man in the Queen of England's employ will surely bring you to your doom."

"I thought it only of good sense to make use of Walsingham's bribes of me," Ryan said, winking at Moira's brother, as if he would understand. "How fortunate I am, Sir Amyas, that most of your guards can't read. They saw only Walsingham's signature and believed anything I had to say."

"Indeed. And it worked." Even so, Donnie was visibly shaken. "Though we had more than a close call or two."

"And then of course your friend Paulet has been most helpful," Ryan said, nodding towards the man he held captive. "He led me straight to you, love." Ryan carefully explained his plan to Moira. They would tie up Paulet and put him in the cell, then calmly make their way outside. "Pull the hood of your cloak up and gather the folds close to your body. If anyone questions you, lower your voice so that they will think you are one of the lads I entered with. Davie is in the stables procuring another horse for us. We are headed for Scotland, my love, and the sheltering arms of your father. I hope he will have forgiven me enough to give me his protection—as his future son-in-law."

Moira's heart started pounding at a turbulent pace. "I think that he very well might, future husband." She was happy just being with him, seeing his face again, and yet she realized that the worst was not yet over. They had yet to get free of Fotheringay.

It seemed much too easy. They left the cell and walked down the corridor. No one saw them or even tried to stop them. Why? She would have liked to believe that she had been born under a lucky star, but she didn't. Moira sensed a trap.

"Ryan, use special care." Her warning came too late. Like cats waiting for the mice to take the bait, two guards came around the corner, greeting Ryan with drawn swords—a trap. Ryan rose to the challenge. They were good at wielding their swords, but he was much better. Even so, two-to-one were uncomfortable odds.

"Donnie, take your sister to the stables," he said between sword thrusts and parries. "Hurry, and don't look back! Give no thought to me. Ride with all your might towards Scotland!"

"No! Not without you!" Moira was beside herself. She couldn't leave him now, not when they had been reunited.

"Go! By the love I have in my heart for you, you must listen." The sternness in his voice would brook no opposition. Picking up her skirts, her heart close to breaking, Moira followed after her brother. Somehow they had to get away, and somehow they did. Three cloaked and hooded riders galloped through the gates of Fotheringay, heading towards the north, frantically and desperately. Moira was free, but at a terrible price. Had Ryan traded his freedom for her own? If so, then it was much too great a price to pay.

Moira bent close to the churning muscles of her horse, and all the while, the sound of approaching hoofs echoed in her ears. Even so, the English had not reckoned on the horsemanship of the Scottish. She and her brothers had practically been born on horses. From the time she was old enough to walk, she had ridden. With a defiant cry that was echoed by her brothers, she rode wildly onward. They would rouse James to a fury, make him see that he must intervene in his mother's fate. Ryan Paxton would not have sacrificed himself in vain.

It was a long and rough journey over rutted pathways, through forests and glens, through wind and shivering rain, pausing only to catch a bit of sleep. Moira was exhausted and haggard when at last the welcoming stones of her father's castle came into view. Oh, for the warmth of a fire! Following her brothers inside, that was first and foremost on her mind, with the exception of Ryan. Somehow she would think of a way to save him. He had come after her and she would do likewise for him. She would not leave him in Walsingham's clutches, not for the life of her. She would return with an army of her father's retainers if need be.

Wild thoughts ran through her mind as she flew to the fire. Taking off her wet cloak, she basked in its heat, startled to hear a voice behind her. "What took you so long?" Dear God, it couldn't be. But it was.

"Ryan!" She flew to his arms, hugging him so tightly he couldn't breathe. "How did you get free?" In all her life Moira had never felt the swell of love she felt now as she clung to her Captain. Like sweet music the thought that he had escaped, that they were together echoed over and over again in her head. "How did you get here ahead of . . . ?"

"I found a short cut," he answered with a grin, looking down at her.

"A short cut? But how did you get away? How . . . ?"

Ryan's eyes sparkled with love as he buried his face in her hair. "Questions, questions, questions."

"But . . ."

"Me thinks, wench, that you talk too much." His lips took hers in a searing kiss and Moira felt as if her very soul were rising up to meet his, and then there was no more time for words.

Epilogue, Spring 1587

THE DAY DAWNED BRIGHT and clear, without a cloud in the sky. A good omen for a wedding—and what a wedding it was. Roarke MacKinnon had spared no expense to make certain that his only daughter had the best. With a smile, he stood beside his future son-in-law as they both waited for Moira to sweep down the hall of the MacKinnon castle chapel. Walking slowly and regally to the altar, in a dress of pale blue velvet, Moira smiled as she stood beside her groom.

"You are beautiful," he breathed, bending to take her hand. "The most beautiful woman I've ever seen. I thank God that soon you will be mine, my highland bride."

Together they faced the priest, who began his intonation of Latin words in a deep, resonant voice. As the Mass progressed, Moira felt peace and love in her heart, yet a great deal of sadness as well. Though her adventure had a happy ending, the same was not true of the Scottish queen. Feeling that she could hesitate no longer, Elizabeth had signed the death warrant. In a hasty ceremony held in the great hall of Fotheringay Castle in early February, Mary was beheaded. Two masked executioners, asking her forgiveness, had taken her life. Walsingham had had his way. Elizabeth had won the battle between the queens. And yet, perhaps neither had won, for just as she had envisioned, Mary's brave death had made her a martyr.

Moira felt the gold ring touch first one finger and then another, to rest on the third finger of her left hand in an unending symbol of eternity. She would belong to Ryan forever and would make him happy, this she vowed. He had given up so much for her—his country, his property, his ship. Having rescued her from prison, he was now a fugitive, though she hoped that one day James could be persuaded to make a plea on his behalf with the English queen. Already, Davie was using his influence with James, his childhood friend, for the commission of a Scottish ship for Ryan to command. It seemed a likely possibility.

With a deep sigh, Moira sank to her knees to receive the wine from the priest's brimming chalice, wincing as she did so. For as long as she lived, wine would remind her of the blood Mary had shed upon the block. Mary. She couldn't help thinking of her even now. Mary had knelt like this, but before a man of an alien faith. She had not been allowed to confess to her Catholic chaplain, though she had begged to. It was one more blight on Elizabeth's head. Instead, her jailers had offered her an Anglican dean. She had chosen to eloquently whisper her own prayers.

Moira gently touched the golden crucifix around her neck. Mary had worn it on the day of her death, had clutched it before she had died. Then she had laid her head upon the block. It was said that the wig fell from her severed head and revealed her white hair. So much grief and heartache had aged her. In truth, Moira knew the Queen had been but forty-four. She had known a tragic life, but there had been happiness in it too.

"God rest your soul, Mary," she whispered. Strange, but she felt as if Mary was watching this ceremony, and that she approved.

The ceremony was brief, thankfully so, as Ryan had whispered in the impatience of claiming his bride. Before all assembled, he kissed her. Moira slid her arms around her husband's broad shoulders, relishing the ritual kiss, and thrilled with passion to know that this handsome, daring man at last belonged to her.

"Come, my love," he whispered, caressing her in such a heated embrace before her father that she blushed. "It is time we tasted of each other again." Then he kissed her hungrily, enthusiastically, again and again.

The wedding feast was a lively affair, with Seamus's ale served by the barrel, and an array of delicacies. Afterwards there was dancing as a whirling, high-stepping and jubilant Donnie and Davie welcomed a new brother into their clan.

Then, amidst jovial laughter and shouted congratulations, the newly wedded couple were escorted up the stairs to their nuptial bed.

Though several pairs of eyes watched as they took their places in the large feather bed, they barely noticed, nor did they hear the drone of the priest as he gave the blessing. They had eyes only for each other. At last, they were alone.

"My lovely, lovely wife. I love you so very much," Ryan whispered.

"Show me!" Moira's eyes were boldly challenging, in the manner he had come to love.

Ryan's intense gaze clung to her as he beheld her naked beauty. He ran his hand lovingly over the softness of her shoulder, down to the peaks of her full breasts. This was his bride, his mate for ever and ever. She was worth any sacrifice he had made.

With a quick, indrawn breath, he drew her to his chest, molding his mouth to hers in a sweetly scorching kiss. His hands stroked her body, gently igniting the searing flame she always felt at his touch.

A blazing fire consumed them both as their bodies met. With hands and lips and words, they gave full vent to their love. Ryan caught her in his arms and pulled her down, rolling with her until her slender form was beneath his. They were entwined in love, in flesh, in heart, and with their very souls.

"This night, we will conceive a child," Ryan whispered. "A girl. And we will call her Mary."

A namesake. Deep in her heart, Moira knew it would be true, and that it would be the greatest gift of all that they could give the martyred Scottish queen. A legacy of love.

Postscript

THE DETAILS depicted in this book regarding the "barrel post," the "Babington Plot," and Walsingham's role in Mary Stuart's downfall are not fictional, and all the characters apart from the hero, heroine, and her brothers are historical. Walsingham did indeed set about to trap Mary, Queen of Scots, who unfortunately was captured. It has been noted by many scholars on the subject, however, that much of the assassination plot was in fact instigated and fueled by Walsingham's own agents. Certainly Gilbert Gifford played an active role. There are even those who suspect that Walsingham forged the incriminating portion of Mary's reply to Babington.